CRAFTY MOTIVES

CRAFTY MOTIVES

A BEE'S KNEES MYSTERY

JOAN RAYMOND

RED KNOT PRESS

ALSO BY JOAN RAYMOND

For Adults

Bee's Knees Mystery Series

Crafty Alibis (Book One) 2021

Crafty Motives (Book Two) 2022

Crafty Suspects (Book Two) Coming soon!

Women's Fiction

Guardian of the Gifts 2019

For Children

Metamorphosis Series

Fly on the Wall (Book One) 2020

Spaghetti and Meatball (Book Two) Coming soon!

Crafty Motives: A Bee's Knees Mystery

Copyright © 2022 by Joan Raymond

Print ISBN: 978-1-7337915-5-7

Cover Design by Cathy Walker of Cathy's Covers

Red Knot Press
PO Box 41745
Bakersfield, CA 93384

For the parents with Angel Babies. Your loss matters.

DEAR READER

Thank you so much for continuing with the Bee's Knees Mystery Series. I love the quirky townspeople, and of course Ella and Shelby. They are all very special to me. The fact that you're reading this book is a sign you may be enjoying their company as well.

At the end of this book, please keep flipping through the pages as there will be an offer to become a Bee's Knees VIP reader, which is the best way to guarantee you'll know when my next book will be available. You'll also receive a free short story specific to the ending of this book that's not available anywhere else.

Note: If you received the short story at the end of Crafty Alibis, *by reentering your email you will still get this new story, too! Both stories are a gift from me as a way to show my appreciation for your support.*

Thanks for taking the time to read the Bee's Knees next cozy mystery. I hope you enjoy reading it just as much as I enjoyed writing it.

Joan

CHAPTER ONE

S helby Heaton crawled across the thick carpet in search of her errant cat. She paused for a moment in front of the wide picture window as a sunny patch of rug warmed the top of her hand. Continuing her pursuit, Shelby peeked behind the oversized wingback chair. "Mr. Butterfingers? Where are you?" She'd been searching the house for over an hour. Her patience, along with her knees, were wearing out. Shelby waited. She listened, hoping for a sign he might be close by. Nothing.

Shelby's best friend and business partner Ella Denning walked into the front room followed by Oatmeal, her fluffy white Bichon Frise. "You still looking for that cat?" Dressed in light-blue denim jeans and an ivory knit sweater, she held a steaming cup of hazelnut coffee.

"He's been avoiding me all morning." Shelby sat up and leaned against the back of the chair. She picked strands of yellow and white fur from her black leggings and long-sleeved, fuchsia and black striped cardigan. "How did he know I wanted to take him to the vet?"

Ella laughed and nodded to the dog. "We told you not to

use the "V" word. Didn't we, boy?" Oatmeal wagged his tail and settled on the comfy sofa next to what was left of a tattered fabric hedgehog.

"Don't remind me." Brushing a wisp of hair from her eyes, Shelby wiped perspiration from her forehead with the back of her hand. She looked around the room again. *Where was he hiding?*

Seated on the plaid sofa, Ella sipped her coffee. "Better you crawling around than me. I've got a few years on you." She scratched Oatmeal's ears and tried to hide a smile behind her coffee cup.

Shelby snorted. "Seriously? You're only fifty. And, in much better shape."

"You're just sweet-talking me so I'll join your cat-hunt."

Shelby looked at Ella and winked. "Is it working?"

"No. I don't need extra fur on my outfit. I'm meeting with Harold this morning at eight-thirty, remember?"

Shelby stood and nodded. Of course she remembered. Ella was scheduled to meet with long-time friend and venture capitalist, Harold Madrigal. He had helped finance Ella and Doug's first business, The Steamed Bean. The same friend who had lost his investment when Doug was killed by a drunk neighbor and Ella had to close the business. Bearing no hard feelings, Harold wanted to help Ella and Shelby with The Bee's Knees renovation, which included a large area for workshop rooms.

"We'll be the only crafter's outlet with the ability to offer on-site classes in all of Pheasant Valley. Actually, in the entire county." Ella leaned toward Shelby and pointed. "Look over there."

A yellow and orange tail twitched behind the floral fabric curtains. Shelby nodded and walked toward the cat's hiding place. "I think the renovation is a great idea. The vendors can offer classes and teach new skills." Shelby reached down and grasped her bulky cat. "Gotcha." Mr. Butterfingers meowed pitifully and twisted in her hands. "Not so fast. You need your rabies shot and we can't keep putting it off." Shelby pushed the cat into his carrier rump-first and closed the metal door.

Ella stuck her fingers inside and stroked his head. "You poor thing. Going to the v-e-t is no fun." Oatmeal whined and pawed at the carrier.

Shelby plopped on the couch to catch her breath. "El, you riding into town with me or are we taking separate cars?"

Ella finished the last of her coffee. "Let's just take one car. I'd planned to take Oatmeal to the shop so he wouldn't be home by himself all day. Having him ride in the back seat with Mr. Butterfingers might help."

Shelby walked into the cheery, sunlit kitchen. Copper pots hanging in descending order along one wall matched the antique copper sugar, tea, and coffee canisters on the counter. A set of six vintage copper escargot pans with brass handles decorated another wall. Shelby didn't know if Ella even liked escargot, but she thought the palm-sized pans added to the rustic kitchen. She pinched off a thick corner of bacon cooling on a paper towel and popped it into her mouth. Sustenance after chasing the cat. After a few more bites, she rinsed her greasy fingers in the sink, and put the leftover bacon in the refrigerator. Grabbing Oatmeal's leash from the mudroom, Shelby joined Ella by the front door. When Oatmeal saw the nylon leash, the small dog bounded off the couch yipping and dancing. Shelby smiled. "When was the last time he went to the shop with you?"

"Last year, before you returned from Houston and moved in." Ella bent over and attached the leash to his collar. "I'm sure everyone will be happy to see him." Oatmeal barked and placed his paws on her thigh. "Looks like he's ready."

Shelby removed keys from her pocket and picked up the cat carrier with a groan. She looked at Mr. Butterfingers. "You've put on a few pounds. Maybe you should go on more walks like your canine friend." She cinched her sweater and glanced at Ella. "Hopefully, we'll be done quickly so I won't miss much of your meeting with Harold."

Ella locked the front door and let the screen slam. Walking down the wooden stairs and across the driveway, their shoes crunched in the gravel. A row of white-dusted junipers trembled in the wind.

Shelby shivered. "Spring officially begins next week and we still have snow on the ground?"

Ella opened the back door of Shelby's jeep and secured Oatmeal's harness with the seat belt. "It's only mid-March. The snow should be gone by April. Don't you remember these late winters?"

Shelby placed the carrier on the seat next to Oatmeal. She reached for the seatbelt and buckled it over the top of the carrier. "In Houston—"

Ella winked and squeezed Shelby's arm. "—You live in California now."

Climbing in and starting the jeep, Shelby smiled. She knew Ella was right. She didn't miss Houston or Mac, knowing neither city nor past partner missed her. But, for some reason she couldn't shake the guilt for not saying goodbye. Nor the gnawing feeling of her decision to just up and leave. She worried it might bite her in the backside one day. But today wasn't that day. Though she and Ella had expressed feelings for each other, they had stepped back from a close relationship. The last thing they wanted was to ruin their long-time friendship. They each agreed rushing into something without dealing with the past would not be wise.

Shelby needed to stop comparing her old life with her current one. The last four months looked nothing like her past. From a failed relationship with Mac in Houston to a rekindled friendship with Ella in Pheasant Valley. From hopelessness to a life filled with hope. Though frightening memories from her past resurfaced from time to time, Shelby had found acceptance with an old friend. Pulling up to an intersection, Shelby came to a stop, turned, and smiled.

Ella met her gaze. "You're extra quiet this morning. Everything okay?"

When the light turned green, Shelby accelerated then pulled into the empty parking lot at The Bee's Knees. "Yes. Just hoping everything goes okay at the v—appointment." Shelby thought about how life was so much better in Pheasant Valley. The weather, the lack of humidity, and new friends. Everything had been perfect except for Sergeant Dawn Nolan. Dawn had made life miserable for Shelby. Her only solace was knowing the rotten woman had accepted a transfer to another sheriff's department, in another state.

Shelby turned off the ignition and tapped her fingers on the steering wheel. "Have you decided what to wear to the welcome party?"

"You referring to the new deputy sheriff?" asked Ella. "I'm looking forward to meeting her. From what I've heard, she's quite a character when she's off duty."

A crow flew across the sky and caught Shelby's attention. It landed on top of the Pizza Palace across the street. "I'm so relieved Dawn left. After the way she treated us after Buck's death... Hopefully, we'll never see her again."

Ella watched a woman walking along the sidewalk wearing a tall, green knitted hat and momentarily became distracted with how the woman's hat seemed to bounce atop her head with each step. She turned back to Shelby. "I'll always be here for you no matter what."

"That's what friends are for," said Shelby, opening her door.

Shivering, Ella grabbed Oatmeal's leash. "It's getting colder, better get inside."

"No worries. I should be on my way to Dr. Furst's office." As if on cue, a pitiful cry came from the back seat.

A chill swept through the vehicle. "Just a minute, Oatmeal." Her breath appeared then dissipated with the frigid wind. Before Ella closed her door, a late model sedan pulled up and parked next to Shelby's jeep. A tall, well-padded, gray-haired woman emerged with a grunt, grasping a stack of disheveled papers. Unaware of anyone watching, she stood, tightened the belt on her coat, and slammed the door. Scowling, the woman marched across the parking lot toward the entrance of the shop.

Door still ajar, Ella crouched down and watched from the back seat.

"Who was that?" Shelby whispered.

"Agnes Cormack." Ella let out a deep sigh. "Harold's ex-wife."

"What's she doing here?"

"I have no idea. But, whatever the reason, it can't be good."

CHAPTER TWO

After Ella waved goodbye to Shelby, she took Oatmeal out of the vehicle and checked her phone. She had only a few minutes before the meeting with Harold. The sky had clouded over and tiny snowflakes swirled around her face as she led the dog across the parking lot. Agnes stood in front of the door mumbling under her breath. Ella forced a smile. "Good morning."

Agnes glared at Ella. Her lip curled. "What's good about it?"

Ignoring her question, Ella glanced down. Oatmeal looked up and wagged his tail.

"You've got a lot of gall bringing a disgusting animal into a public establishment. I never—"

Ella cleared her throat and moved past Agnes, placing a key in the lock. "We open at nine. Until then you can wait out here or in your car." Ella pushed the door open, then once she and Oatmeal were inside, locked it again. Before Ella headed to the counter, she heard keys tapping on the glass.

Agnes' hulking figure stared inside. Her eyes bulged. Her

face a light shade of crimson. She yelled out. "You can't expect me to stand out here and freeze."

Ella pointed to her wrist and mouthed. "Sorry. Not open until nine." Dropping Oatmeal's leash, she watched him run over and sniff a spot on the carpet. Ella took in the scent of lavender from Laura Vega's calming booth. She stopped for a moment to refocus and let go of Agnes' negativity. A moment later, her phone signaled an incoming call. "Hello? Good morning, Harold... What's that? Yes. It is Agnes standing outside the front door... Back entrance? I don't use it much, but yes... You know Hamm's buildings right behind us? If you park on Juneberry, there's a walkway between their insurance and real estate offices... Oh good, you see it. Our back door is across the alley behind the real estate office. I'll wait for your knock."

Ella shoved the phone in her pocket and glanced back at the door. Agnes stood outside glaring, still tapping her keys on the glass. Ella called to Oatmeal. "Come on, boy. Let's go check the storage room."

The small dog followed Ella into the dark, stuffy storeroom. She flipped on the lights, closed the door behind her, then waited next to the exterior door. Soon, she heard three knocks followed by two knocks. Opening the door, Ella greeted her long-time friend. "Harold, so good to see you again."

Harold gave Ella a quick hug and offered a small treat for Oatmeal, then removed his jacket. Dressed in a dark navy suit and white long-sleeved shirt with no tie, he oozed success. Streaks of light reflected off his gold watch onto the wall behind them. "Boy, that was a close one." Harold's brown eyes twinkled. "What's the queen of doom and gloom doing here?"

Ella shrugged. "No idea. First time I've seen her in quite a while."

"You're lucky. We met up in court a few weeks ago."

"That doesn't sound good." Ella shuddered. No one wanted to come up against Agnes. Especially in court. She didn't blink an eye ruining someone, whether they deserved it or not. Everything was about Agnes, all the time.

"My penance for marrying the witch." Harold chuckled nervously, then pointed toward the shop. "We can still talk about the renovation, but it might be better to stay in here." He looked around. "Is this the area you're talking about?"

Oatmeal yawned and settled near Ella's shoes. "Apparently my dog's not excited about our new business venture. Though Shelby is over the moon."

"Not surprised about the dog." Harold let out a deep chuckle. "Speaking of Shelby. I thought she was going to be here."

Ella shook her head. "When I set up our meeting, I forgot she'd made an appointment to take her cat to the vet."

Harold frowned. "Nothing serious, I hope?"

"Mr. Butterfingers would tell you it was life or death." Ella smiled. "Just annual shots."

"Ah, yes. Unavoidable, but important. Especially for pets living in the hills." He looked around. "Should we postpone until Shelby can join us and my adversary isn't breathing all over your front door glass."

Ella thought for a moment, then snapped her fingers. Oatmeal looked up and settled down again. "Since this is the room in question, how about you look it over? Then we'll meet again, just the three of us."

Harold glanced down and pointed to the face of his gold watch. "It's a quarter to nine. Give me a brief description of what you want done. While you open your shop, I'll assess everything. Then leave through the back door." Anything to avoid the old bat.

Ella smiled. "Works for me." She gestured to the large, dusty room around them. "A lot of our vendors have approached me about teaching classes. You know, like beginning watercolor or knitting. They talked about renting a room at the church or recreation center, but the more I considered it, I remembered we had all this unused space just sitting here. I need about a fourth of it for storage, but that still leaves this large area for workshops. What do you think?"

Harold took out his phone and opened an app. He removed a stylus from the side and began making notes. "It's do-able." He looked down and pushed on the torn carpet with the toe of his shiny black shoe. "Take this out. Replace it with tile." He pointed to the exterior wall. "Replace the sheetrock of the east wall— of course we'll need permits—" He made more notes. "How many people you looking to have back here?"

Ella tapped her fingers on her chin. "No more than thirty and probably not at the same time. We could handle a few classes at once, depending on demand and the crafter's schedules."

Harold pointed to an interior wall and chuckled. "You attached to that?"

"Not really. What did you have in mind?"

Adding to his notes, Harold looked up at Ella. "Let me take measurements and sketch a few ideas, then I'll come up with some estimates. I see a lot of potential here."

Ella touched his arm. "I'm so happy you're willing to take a chance on me again. After last time—"

He held up his hand. "Ella, let's not rehash the past. We

both knew closing the coffee shop was necessary after Doug's death."

"But it wasn't fair to you. You lost a lot of money."

"Every investment carries risk. Sometimes I win— other times—"

"But, you had to file bankruptcy—"

"It's in the past." Harold's deep brown eyes crinkled. "Let's focus on the future."

She bit her lip and nodded.

He glanced at his watch again. "Let me get to this. I'll call you after I have numbers."

"Thanks, Harold. You don't know how much this means to us." Ella left the storage room, locking the door behind her. With Oatmeal at her heels, she started for the front counter. Before she'd gone far, she heard the shop door open. Vivian Conte, her assistant and watercolor vendor, walked in and shook off her coat.

The front door swung open and bounced against the wall with a thud. Wide eyed, Agnes pushed past Vivian and marched up to Ella. She scraped snowflakes off her bulky coat and huffed. "Making a prominent citizen stand out in the cold. You should be ashamed of yourselves." Agnes waved a wad of crumpled papers in Ella's face. "Where is he?"

Ella hesitated. The air seemed to leave the room and she had a tough time thinking. Even though she wasn't the immediate target, there was no denying how much Agnes intimidated her. She hid her trembling hands in her pockets and hoped to delay the woman long enough for Harold to make his escape. He was her friend and she wasn't about to be pushed around by an angry, condescending ex-wife. "He's not in here," said Ella.

Agnes stepped into Ella's personal space and pointed a

thick finger in her face. "You're a liar. Hiding another liar. That con man owes me." She stomped her dirt-caked boots and crossed her arms. "I'm not leaving 'til I find him." Her bloodshot eyes scanned the room. "And when I do, I'll skin that rat alive."

CHAPTER THREE

Agnes clenched her liver-spotted fists and marched up and down each aisle of The Bee's Knees searching for her ex-husband. She glared at Ella and Vivian, then cursed under her breath, turned, and stormed outside.

Vivian grasped the counter. "She forced her way in when I opened the door. I had no idea she'd be in such a mood. You okay?"

"Not the best way to start a Monday morning," said Ella. "A bit stunned, but I'll be fine." She relaxed her shoulders, though deep inside she was concerned. When it came to Agnes' erratic behavior, no one knew what to expect. The vile woman had no regard for anyone but herself.

"Hello, Oatmeal." Vivian reached down and patted the small dog's head. "Haven't seen you for quite a while." Oatmeal offered his paw and yipped. "And such a polite gentleman. What's the special occasion, Ella?"

"Shel had to take her cat in for his physical. Didn't want my boy to be all alone." Ella reached under the counter and brought out the clipboard holding the volunteer schedule.

With over seventy-five vendors, she used the old-school pen and paper method to keep track of the hours when they planned to volunteer each month. They helped run the shop and keep costs down.

"Great minds think alike." Vivian peered over Ella's shoulder and scanned the list. "I was just about to see who else was coming in today." A quiet woman in her late 60s, Vivian created intricate pen and ink and watercolor art. Botanicals, clouds, and mountain life were her favorites to draw and paint, though occasionally she'd compile unmatched objects and turn them into something cohesive and breathtaking.

Ella pointed to the sheet. "Looks like it's you, me and your daughters this morning—" She flipped the page. "—and Laura, Shelby, and Gladys this afternoon."

Vivian went behind the counter and grabbed the duster. "Lilibeth mentioned she and Vickie would be in today. But, for some reason I thought it was later." She wiped down the countertop, then walked over to a corner display booth and continued. "I thought they were supposed to help John with the alpaca this morning…" She smiled. "Almost time for the babies to get here."

Ella opened the register and counted the till while Vivian continued to dust. "I never realized how much work went into running a fiber farm."

After wiping down one of the nearby booths, Vivian turned, holding the feather duster like a conductor waiting to lead the players in a new arrangement. "Couldn't ask for a better son-in-law. John did his momma proud when he took over the family farm after his daddy died."

Ella looked up from her paperwork. "Eleanor told me how John gave up his dream of becoming a veterinarian—"

The front door opened. Laura Vega the lavender vendor

walked in, her gauzy blouse billowing around her like angel's wings. "Good morning, ladies. Thought I'd come in early and stock my booth." She placed a crate of homemade products on the floor next to her booth, then stood still and inhaled. "I sense tension. And… rage." Laura picked through a shelf, then brought over a bundle of dried lavender sprigs. She waved them around Ella and Vivian and inhaled again. "We mustn't let bad karma take our inner joy." Laura walked down each aisle humming an unfamiliar tune while waving the dried flowers. A few minutes later she returned and placed the faded purple flowers on the shelf. "I feel much better. Don't you?"

Ella walked over to Laura and gave her a hug. "Much better. Thank you, neighbor." Not only did Laura live next door to Ella, but she also wrote, edited, and distributed the local newspaper, *The Pheasant Valley Roost*. Laura had been Ella's first vendor, encouraging her during the planning stages of her crafter's outlet concept. Now, three years later, Laura's handmade soaps, candles, and scrubs were some of the most popular items in the shop. Ella watched her for a moment taking in her positive energy. She could brighten any room.

Oatmeal padded up to Laura and yipped. She squatted down to his level and stroked his ears. "And I'm happy to see you too, Oatmeal." Seemingly satisfied, the dog curled up next to an old watering can filled with dried lavender stems and fell asleep.

———

TRUDY DENTON, a silver-haired woman in a tapered denim jacket and bright red pants walked into the veterinarian's office. She cradled a wide-eyed tortoise shell cat wrapped in a fuzzy beige blanket. Waiting for a few minutes at the front desk, Trudy checked the time on a white, gold-plated watch hanging on a thin silver chain around her neck. "I'm thirty minutes early. How did that happen?" Seeing no one at the front desk, she took a seat on a hard, wooden bench with her cat. She murmured something to the cat then noticed a frayed edge on the blanket. She picked at it until it was smooth again.

Always full of energy, Trudy didn't like to wait. Life was too short. And now, a year after becoming an octogenarian, she didn't have the patience for life to happen. Instead, she embraced it fully. A former dance instructor, book and button collector, and long-time poet, she kept herself busy.

A bright-eyed receptionist with blue-streaked hair walked in carrying an armload of paperwork. She nodded to Trudy. "Doctor is still in surgery. I'll be back shortly to get you checked in."

"No worries," said Trudy. She stroked her cat's head and sang a lullaby to help calm the trembling feline. "I guess we'll just have to wait."

VIVIAN TURNED to Ella and whispered, "So what bee was up Agnes' bonnet this morning?"

Ella rolled her eyes. "It's always something with her, isn't it?"

Laura walked over to them, followed by Oatmeal, who'd just woken up from his nap.

"Last I heard, Agnes was spreading rumors about one of the ladies in our button club," said Vivian. "All because the woman was running against her for president. If you ask me, I—"

"Now, Viv," said Ella. "We both know it's not nice to talk about other people. Even those that tend to be more... um...difficult."

"Well, she's a bunch of trouble no matter where she goes." Vivian whispered again, though her voice seemed to carry past the three women. "You know I'm not one to talk about others—"

Laura nudged Ella. "But she's the first one to read the gossip column in the *Roost*."

Ella raised an eyebrow and gave a side glance to Vivian. "Why does that not surprise me?"

Vivian shrugged. "I don't know what you're talking about."

The front door opened and a couple in their mid-eighties walked in. The frail, white-haired woman removed her gloves and shoved them into a jacket pocket. She grabbed the gray-haired man's hand and pointed to one of the shelves.

"Morning," said the gentleman. "Heard a lot about this place. Wife and I had to stop in."

"Welcome to The Bee's Knees," said Ella. "Just let us know if you need help finding something."

The door opened again and Vivian's two daughters, Lilibeth Morgan and Vickie Conte entered talking about the weather. With auburn hair and a big smile, there was no doubt Vickie was Vivian's daughter. She stomped her boots on the welcome mat just inside the shop. "I'm so looking forward to Spring. Enough of this weather, already."

Lilibeth twisted a wisp of dark hair with her long finger. "But, then we'll be at the farm most of the time helping John with the shearing and birthing new lambs and crias."

Vivian came alongside Lilibeth and put her arm around her older daughter. "My favorite time of the year."

Lilibeth rolled her eyes. "You mean the busiest time of the year. Even though we're not doing all the shearing, Vickie and I have almost no time for our needle-felting projects. We're working twice as hard now to build up an inventory."

"I'm sure you'll find time for your cute creations. After all, you are the Wooley Sisters." Vivian gave her daughter a kiss on the cheek and stepped back. "Enough chit-chat, this proud momma needs to get back to dusting."

Vickie nudged her mother's arm. "My house could use a mom's touch—"

Vivian kissed her younger daughter's forehead and laughed. "Nice try, sweetie." She walked away humming while she dusted another row of shelves.

Lilibeth looked at Ella. "So what do you need us to do today?"

Ella thought for a while. "While your mom and I help customers, how about you two work in the storeroom?"

Vickie's eyes lit up. "Does this mean—?"

Lilibeth clapped her hands. "How soon—?"

Ella held up a finger. "I'm only in the process of getting estimates. It's going to be a while before we offer classes."

"But it's going to happen. Right?" asked Vickie.

"Let's just take this one step at a time. First I need to see the costs, then Shelby and I will talk it over."

Lilibeth joined arms with her sister. "You'll tell us as soon as you know something?"

Ella nodded. "Of course. But in the meantime, you two can figure out what classes you might want to teach and your fees—don't forget to include materials—so the students know the totals up front."

"You think by mid-May?" asked Vickie.

"Not sure we can make it happen in two months. It all

depends on what needs to be done." Ella thought back to her conversation with Harold. So many possibilities, but she didn't want to say too much in case the costs were exorbitant. As with most remodels, there were always unknowns. Plus, who knew what might be hidden behind those walls?

"Lilibeth and I don't mind helping out," said Vickie. "We're good at installing sheetrock and painting."

"I appreciate that." Ella pointed toward the back of the shop. "And cleaning out the storeroom will speed things up."

"Fine," said Vickie. "We can take a hint. Lilibeth, let's go see what fun awaits us in the dark, dusty storeroom."

Ella walked the sisters to the storeroom and unlocked the door. Upon opening it, she jumped back. Harold stood behind the door; eyes wide. Ella gasped. She turned to Vickie and Lilibeth. "How 'bout you two go help your mom for a bit. I need to take care of something." After they left, she turned back to Harold and stared at him. "Thought you'd be gone by now."

Harold wiped his forehead with a monogramed handkerchief. "The moment I opened the exterior door, Agnes was waiting for me."

"Why don't you go out the front door? There's quite a few of us here in case you need witnesses."

"Normally, I would chuckle at your attempt at humor, but I need to disappear." Harold grasped Ella's arm and leaned in close. "If only there was a way to make that woman do the same.

CHAPTER FOUR

The veterinarian's waiting room had the distinct odors of disinfectant and stale coffee. Shelby sat on a wooden bench and fidgeted. Mr. Butterfinger's pitiful cries rose from the carrier. She touched her cat's nose through the metal door. "It's okay. We'll be done soon." She listened to a cacophony of whines and meows coming from behind the waiting room door. Pets missing their humans. One of the loneliest sounds in life.

The slender, silver-haired woman sitting across from her caught Shelby's eye and smiled. "They all hate it here, don't they?"

"Yours also looks like it wants to be anywhere else." Shelby stared at the woman trying to place her face. *Was she from Pheasant Valley? Or Houston?* She thought it better the woman introduced herself first, rather than risk an uncomfortable conversation. Once, Shelby had talked to a seemingly familiar woman for twenty minutes before realizing she had no idea who the person was. They finally parted ways, the other woman was none the wiser.

"Mr. Darcy is not fond of his setting at all right now. He'd much rather be home snoozing in the bay window."

"Interesting name for a cat. You must be a fan of Jane Austen."

The vibrant woman laughed and rubbed Mr. Darcy's ears. "A few years back I was reading *Pride and Prejudice* when I found this guy and his sister at the shelter. Her name is Elizabeth. She stayed home today."

A moan came from Shelby's cat carrier. "And my distraught boy is Mr. Butterfingers."

"I'm Trudy Denton. Mr. Darcy and I are pleased to make your acquaintance. And you are?"

"Shelby Heaton. Nice to meet you both." A woman in scrubs came through the door with an overgrown poodle mix. A tall gentleman took the leash and struggled to stay upright as the excited poodle wrapped itself around the man's legs.

Trudy was silent for a moment, then snapped her fingers. "You and the other gal have that crafter's shop near my favorite quilt store. Don't you?"

"Yes." Shelby cocked her head and looked at Trudy. "I knew I'd seen you around town before. You looked so familiar, but I'm terrible with names. And faces."

Trudy brushed a thick curl from her forehead and gestured down at her vest. "I go in the quilt shop all the time —mostly for sewing remnants."

"You made that?" Shelby marveled at the vest's intricate, yet simple, design. Pieced together material in complementary and contrasting hues and textures, it was embellished with metallic blue and gold embroidery.

Trudy nodded. "Sewing is one of my hobbies. Along with button collecting."

Shelby straightened. "Do you know Gladys Purcell? She and Ed own the apple orchard just outside town?"

"Hon, Gladys and I have been close friends for over thirty years—" Trudy paused and listened to the soft clicks the poodle made on the tile floor as he padded past with his owner.

A busty woman wearing a much-too-tight green scrub opened a door and looked at the two women. "Heaton?"

Shelby smiled at Trudy then picked up Mr. Butterfingers. The assistant's tag was decorated with little stamped paw prints and the name Beni.

"We just need to weigh Mr. Butterfingers." Beni pointed to a silver platform. "Please place the carrier there. I'll get his weight."

Shelby took the carrier over to the platform. She and Beni watched until the digital readout stopped and beeped.

"Twenty-two pounds. Please take Mr. Butterfingers and have a seat again. I'll call you back in a bit. Doctor had an emergency surgery. I apologize for the delay." Beni checked the schedule and called Trudy up to the scale with her cat. After some cajoling Trudy got Mr. Darcy to stay on it long enough to register his weight.

Shelby sat on the bench and waited for Trudy to get settled. "So you and Gladys collect buttons? I remember seeing her collection a few months ago. Jars and jars full of them."

"Yes, we're both members of the Blue Ridge Button Society. Along with the joy of collecting and swapping buttons, the club helped me trace my genealogy."

Shelby frowned. "How do buttons help you find your relatives?"

"My dear, buttons open up an entire world of historical significance. When grandad passed, my granny had a lot of his clothes from the war between the states—you know, the Civil War." Trudy waited for a response.

Shelby nodded.

"When Mama passed, I inherited them, along with some extraordinarily rare buttons on Grandad's frock coat. I started nosing around and realized they could be traced to a specific region and time period. In other words, I traced some of my family history just by the buttons on their clothes."

Mr. Butterfingers meowed and Shelby stuck her fingers in the carrier and rubbed his nose. "That's really interesting. Maybe someday you could show me some of your buttons. I mean, if you don't mind."

Trudy's eyes lit up. "I love sharing my collection with younger gals like you. Us old ladies need someone to keep our clubs going after we're gone. Not many young folks take an interest in buttons, but let me tell you—" She leaned closer and lowered her voice. "Some of them can be worth a pretty penny."

"Oh yeah? Like a few hundred dollars?"

Trudy's eyes twinkled. "Once saw one valued at over one hundred thousand dollars."

"You're kidding."

A Latina woman in neon blue scrubs walked into the waiting area and held the door open to an exam room. "I'm Alicia. We're ready for Mr. Butterfingers."

Holding her hand up to stop Shelby, Trudy grabbed a card from her pocket. "Here's my Button Society card with my contact information. Call me. I'd love to show you my collection."

"Thanks so much, Trudy. I will." Shelby picked up the carrier and shoved the card in her pocket. "Be sure to stop and say "Hi" next time you're at the quilt shop."

Trudy nodded and waved as Shelby followed Alicia into the small exam room.

―――――――

HAROLD PACED a tight circle in the storeroom of The Bee's Knees. Knocking a cobweb out of his way, he stopped and glared at Ella. "That woman makes my blood boil." He picked bits of the sticky web from his coat sleeve and continued to pace again.

"I agree she tends to bring out the worst in everyone around her," said Ella. "But you can't let her get to you."

He stopped in front of Ella. "You've got that right. She better not get anywhere near me or I'll—" Harold thought for a moment, choosing his words with care. "I won't be able to control my actions." He stopped when he heard heavy pounding on the back door followed by muffed cursing.

Ella reached out to Harold. "Don't you think you should deal with her sooner than later? She's disrupting your life."

He pulled away from Ella and shook his fist at the door. "I'll disrupt her life."

"Harold, I don't think I've ever heard you talk like this. Or seen you so angry. I'm genuinely concerned about you."

Kicking a box out of his path, he stared at Ella. "My big mistake was marrying the old bat. From the day we said, 'I do,' we haven't agreed on anything."

"You must have been in love at one point."

"If we were, I don't even remember. It was too many fights ago—" He thought back to the days before the wedding. Harold had never loved Agnes. But she knew his secret. One that he had buried so deep inside it seemed more imagined now than reality. On a blustery, winter day in front of a grumpy justice of the peace and two of Agnes' friends as witnesses, Harold agreed to marry her. That decision still haunted him to this day.

SHELBY FOLLOWED Alicia into the exam room at the veterinarian's office. Alicia pointed to the carrier. "Place it up here so the doctor can have a look at Mr. Butterfingers."

Hoisting it up onto the cold, metal table, Shelby opened the door. She peered in. Mr. Butterfingers was pressed up against the back end. When she reached in to get him, he hissed. Shelby jerked her hand back and sighed. *Poor thing.* She didn't blame him for being so afraid. Shelby shuddered thinking about her own fears. Of doctors. Of shots. And of small, windowless exam rooms.

"Just open the door and stand back." Alicia smiled. "Curiosity will draw him out."

Shelby gazed around the room as they waited. Posters on one wall featured cute kittens and puppies. A bulletin board full of thank-you notes and pictures of patients with their animals hung on another wall. A few pictures included a man in his mid-forties wearing scrubs and a stethoscope, holding an animal. *Most likely the doctor.*

Moments later whiskers followed by a nose appeared at the opening of the carrier. Soon, the rest of the large cat slinked out onto the metal table.

Alicia took hold of Mr. Butterfingers, lifted his tail, and insulted his dignity by taking his temperature. Pitiful meows followed a futile attempt to escape on the slippery surface. After Alicia removed the thermometer, a broad-shouldered man walked in. Shelby noticed gray strands in his dark-brown hair and a hint of gray in his neatly trimmed beard.

He extended his warm hand and took hers in a firm handshake. "Steven Furst. And this must be the famous Mr. Butterfingers."

Shelby shook the doctor's hand then stroked her cat's back "Nice to meet you. Though I can't say I speak for both of us."

Dr. Furst chuckled. "That's okay. Most of my patients tend to feel the same way." After a thorough exam he gave the necessary set of shots (much to Mr. Butterfingers' dismay). Then, he rubbed the cat's ears until he purred. "So sorry, big guy. But you'll thank me for it later."

"Thank you, Doctor. So, everything looks okay?"

Dr. Furst opened the carrier door. After Mr. Butterfingers hurried back inside, he closed it. "I'm not anticipating any problems, but since he's due for a full check-up, okay if we keep him until this afternoon? We still need to collect blood and urine samples"

"Yes, I suppose that would work." Shelby looked through the carrier's wire opening. "You be a good boy for everyone."

Dr. Furst handed the carrier to Alicia who took him out of the room.

"Unless you have questions, I've gotta run. Surgery put me behind and I hate to keep my patients, and their owners, waiting."

"No questions I can think of. Thank you." After the doctor left the exam room Shelby walked into the waiting room. Trudy and her cat were gone. *Probably in the next room.* Shelby nodded to the receptionist and walked out into the brisk wind.

Before Shelby headed back to the shop she checked her phone and sighed. "Nine forty-five. Probably missed the entire meeting with Ella and Harold."

Pulling onto First Street, she headed east toward The Bee's Knees. With no other traffic in front of her, the six-block trip didn't take much time. Waiting to turn left onto Pinecone, she glanced toward the shop. Her heart rate increased and she gasped. Why was a police car parked out front?

CHAPTER FIVE

S helby parked in the lot behind The Bee's Knees and turned off the engine. *Now what?* With trembling hands she removed her cell from her pocket. "Hey El, everything okay? I see a police car... You're kidding...? Guess I missed everything. Is it safe to come in? ... Great."

Mindful of ice patches, Shelby eased out of her jeep then hurried up to the shop's entrance. Sergeant Alton Nolan, stood on the sidewalk next to his patrol car. Just over six foot tall, with muscular arms, buzzed brown hair and dark eyes, he was one of a half-dozen Pheasant Valley police officers. While Shelby tried not to stare, she caught the outline of someone in the back seat of his unit.

Shelby opened the shop door and inhaled the thick scent of lavender. Just what she needed to calm down. Glancing around, she noticed Ella and Vivian walking toward her. "What happened? Were we robbed?"

Ella took Shelby's hand. "Everything's fine."

Vivian cleared her throat. "Well. It is now."

Ella leaned in closer to Shelby. "Remember how Agnes stomped past us this morning? Apparently she was after

Harold. Poor man couldn't leave here without being accosted."

"Ella finally called Alton to come restrain her," added Vivian. "And let me tell you— Agnes was not happy at all."

Shelby's eyes widened. "Glad you had Alton come and deal with it. Did you find out why Agnes was so upset?"

Vivian started to talk, but Ella held up her hand. "Ladies, this gossip is none of our business."

"What about Harold?" Shelby asked. "Is he okay?"

Ella pointed at the front door. "Once Alton showed up, he persuaded Agnes to sit in his car. That's when Harold took off."

"And you should have heard Agnes," said Vivian. "Words like that coming from a refined woman."

"Refined?" Ella turned to Shelby and winked. "Yes, she was a bit upset—"

Oatmeal pawed at Shelby's leg and barked.

She looked down at him then at Ella. "I'm relieved everyone's okay. Must have been frightening."

Vivian clicked her tongue. "After hearing her spew threats at everyone within earshot, I'm steering clear of that woman." She glanced up at the antique clock on the wall. "Oh my, quarter past ten already. I better get back to my dusting." She leaned in next to Shelby and whispered, "If you want the skinny, just let me know." Then she turned and walked down an aisle dusting and humming.

Ella rolled her eyes. "For a quiet woman, she sure enjoyed today's excitement."

"Well," said Shelby "Probably better than all those old shows she watches." Her eyes caught Ella's. "You sure you're okay?"

"I'm fine. But I'm concerned about Harold."

"Why do you say that?"

Ella hesitated. "Agnes really rattled him. Don't think I've seen him so frightened before."

"You don't think she's really capable of hurting him, do you?"

Ella raised an eyebrow. "You weren't here. If they were to meet up alone. I don't think it would end well." She thought back to past encounters with Agnes and shuddered. The woman never took "no" for an answer and bullied her way into every situation.

THE SNOW HAD TURNED into a driving rain, smacking against the patrol car windows. Inside, Agnes Cormack muttered under her visible breath. "Well. I never."

Alton wiped raindrops from his forehead, then opened the back door of his police unit. "I'll walk you to your car, Agnes." He grabbed an umbrella from the front seat, though it didn't help much.

Grunting as she climbed out, Agnes stood, now eye to eye with the sergeant. Rain rolled down her bulky coat. She thrust her shoulders back and glared at him. "You big goon. What nerve you have. Treating me like a criminal."

Alton held the umbrella over Agnes with one hand, while he used his other hand to grasp Agnes' elbow, steering her away from a slippery puddle in the middle of the parking lot. "Just go home before you catch a cold."

She yanked her arm from his grip and stopped. "Got bursitis in that elbow. I should sue you and your department for inflicting pain on a poor, defenseless woman."

Alton motioned ahead. "Look, Agnes. I'm just doing you a favor."

"You should have arrested him," she said through gritted teeth.

As they arrived at Agnes' car, Alton crossed the drenched sleeves of his beefy arms. "On what grounds, Agnes?"

She faced him and scowled. "For stealing my money." Agnes unbuttoned her coat and yanked it off in such a rush, one of the big gold buttons popped off and rolled under the car. She turned to Alton. "I'm charging your department for that lost button. It was a treasured family heirloom."

Alton pulled his collar over his neck, then bent down on one knee and reached under the muddy sedan. He found the wayward treasure and pressed the button into Agnes' hand. "Go home."

Agnes tossed the coat, her purse, and the wad of papers on the front seat, got in, and slammed the door. Glaring at her reflection in the rearview mirror, she pushed a stray gray hair back in place, then watched Alton walk back to the shop's entrance. "If Harold thinks he can avoid me, he's got another thing coming."

She twisted the key in the ignition and shoved the shifter into reverse. Gravel flew around the tires as she skidded to a stop, shoved it into drive, and left the parking lot. Not looking left or right, Agnes turned onto the street, making her own lane. She glared at the driver next to her and gave him the one-finger salute. "You idiot. That's what you get for crowding in too close."

When Agnes came to the intersection, the light was red. She fumbled in her purse for her cell. The light changed before Agnes was ready. When the car behind her honked, she slapped the steering wheel. "You can wait." She swiped the contacts icon and located her attorney's number. After initiating the call, she held the phone to her ear and accelerated across the street. "Come on, Stu. Pick up the phone. Why am I paying you by the hour if you're not...?

"Hello, Stuart. It's Agnes. Do you think I care if you were on another call? No... he wouldn't talk to me. In fact that shop owner called the cops and they made me leave. No, I didn't make a scene... Why would you think that? Look, we both know he owes me a tidy sum. Well, that's your problem now isn't it? Civil court didn't seem to make a difference... It's time for you to file for a de facto something, or indictment... Oh heck, I don't know what it's called. You know what I'm trying to say—freeze his assets. Then he'll have to pay attention to me... Hold on..."

As she pulled into her own driveway, Agnes pushed 'speaker' and tossed the phone on the seat. She gathered her purse and grunted when she picked up the crumpled papers. "Look Stu, you were hired for one reason and if you can't do your job there are plenty of other money-hungry lawyers who would jump at the chance to help me."

Stuart cleared his throat. "Agnes, you have to understand there's due process. I can't just take matters into my own hands. You'll have to be patient—"

Agnes laughed, then grabbed the cell off the shiny leather seat and held it within inches of her face so she wouldn't be misunderstood. "If you won't take matters into your hands then I'll have to resort to my own methods."

OATMEAL WHINED, snapping Ella out of her memories of past encounters with Agnes. She bent down and patted her dog's silky head. "Missing your friend?" Ella looked up at Shelby. "When do you pick up Mr. Butterfingers?"

"After four. I figured we could go by after we close up."

"Sounds good," said Ella.

Shelby looked around the quiet shop. "Just you and Vivian?"

Ella pointed toward the storage room. "Lilibeth and Vickie are helping clean up. Laura's around somewhere. Before she leaves to work on this week's newspaper, she wanted to cleanse the shop with her lavender after Agnes' bad karma."

"Laura is really amazing, isn't she?"

"And multi-talented—" said Ella.

Before she could continue the front door opened and Alton walked in, bringing a rush of frigid air with him. He unzipped his dark blue jacket, cracked his neck, then walked up to them. He acknowledged Shelby with a quick nod.

"Heard there was some excitement," said Shelby. "Though, can't say I'm sorry I missed it."

Alton paused. He leaned his head to the side, listened to the mic on his collar, then faced the two women. "Just one of those things, I suppose."

"Everything okay outside?" asked Ella.

Alton nodded. "Got Agnes calmed down, which wasn't easy. Then escorted her to her vehicle, told her to go home, and waited for her drive away."

"Guess that's the best you can do for now," said Ella.

Alton nodded. "Harold might want to look into a restraining order."

"Will that really help?" asked Shelby.

"Might make Agnes think twice next time." He shrugged. "But who knows."

Ella reached out to shake Alton's hand. "Thanks for coming. I just didn't want to see anyone get hurt."

After releasing Ella's hand he hooked his thumb through a loop on his pants. "When tempers run high people say things they later regret. It's better you called than tried to deal with it on your own."

"Thanks again," said Ella. She and Shelby watched Alton zip his jacket and head back into the rainy morning.

Shelby turned to Ella. "Was it really that bad?"

Ella's eye caught hers. "Honestly— I'm afraid Harold's in real danger."

CHAPTER SIX

S taring out the large storefront windows above the polished front doors of The Bees Knee's, Ella watched as dark thunderclouds hung low in the sky. They were the type to burst open at any second and drench everything and everyone in their path. She shivered and reached for the granola bar she'd stashed in her purse, hoping the sugar boost would help her concentrate on the end-of-day closing duties.

The shop door opened, bringing in a rush of wind. In walked a ruddy-faced man with a large handlebar mustache and even bigger grin. He waved to Ella and called out in a deep baritone voice. "Howdy, ma'am. Still open?"

"Welcome to our shop." Ella pointed up at the clock. "Until five. Baskets are at the end of each aisle. In case you need one."

"Hope an hour gives me 'nough time." The man gave a deep laugh and picked up two wicker baskets lined with red-checked cloth, pivoted on his boot heel, and stopped at a booth with beaded jewelry.

Shelby walked up to Ella, phone at her ear. "Sounds good. We'll be there before six to pick him up."

"Mr. Butterfingers ready to go home?" asked Ella.

Shelby tucked the phone into her back pocket. "I'm sure he's more than ready."

Oatmeal, who had been sleeping on a wool blanket behind the counter, raised his head and barked. "Yes," Ella said to him. "You heard us mention your friend, didn't you? Poor thing."

Shelby cocked her head. "Who are you referring to? My cat or your dog?"

Ella laughed. "Both, I suppose." She turned as the front door opened again. A young woman held it with her hip while she struggled with an oversized pink stroller.

"Hold on," Shelby called, rushing over to grab the door while the woman came in.

"Thanks so much." Pointing to a chubby-cheeked toddler asleep inside, she smiled. "Was hoping not to wake her so I could look around." She navigated around a corner and stopped at a booth filled with colorful knitted scarves.

Shelby walked back to the counter and stood next to Ella. "Seems to get busy right before closing time..." Watching the woman with the stroller, Shelby massaged her barren womb. She remembered the elation of being pregnant. Plans for decorating the nursery. Picking out colors...

Ella slid her arm around Shelby's waist, but didn't say anything. Ella had never been able to have children, and though she'd not lost babies to miscarriage like Shelby, she felt her friend's pain.

Shelby blinked back tears and cleared her throat. She turned and stared out the window, not focusing on anything.

"Crazy day, huh? I never even had a chance to ask about your meeting with Harold."

Gladys stacked the last jar of apple butter on a shelf in her booth. She straightened and walked over. "Are you talking about our workshop room?"

Ella raised an eyebrow. "How did you hear us from way over there?"

Gladys wiped her hands on a hand-embroidered dishtowel and laughed. "Hon, though I'm coming up on the back side of eighty-one, not everything is going south. Especially not my hearing." She pushed a silver bracelet up toward her elbow. "Actually, it's improved quite a bit since Ed and I started indulging in a hot toddy each night. Can't beat the healing powers of lemon and honey."

Ella laughed. "And bourbon…"

"No, really," said Gladys. "Ed says it's the natural ingredients. But, I say whatever makes us happy. With him and those noisy police radios, I almost wish my hearing was less sharp. But we just celebrated sixty-four years this past Valentine's Day, so I suppose we're doing something right."

Shelby pointed to Gladys' booth. "You've got the best apple farm and apple butters this side of the Mississippi. We never had anything like that in Houston."

Gladys turned to Ella and winked. "And we all thought she came back 'cause she missed us."

Shelby shifted and glanced down at her bright, pink tennis shoes. "Well, even though I missed the apple butter, I missed y'all, more."

The mustached man came up to the counter with two overflowing baskets. He set them down and grinned. "Figured I'd only buy as much as I could carry— though I really wanted one of those game boards. Just couldn't find a way to fit 'er in."

"I don't blame you," said Ella. "They're very popular."

His voice boomed out. "And quite the variety—checkers, parchisi, and some others I haven't seen since I was knee-high to a jackrabbit." He smoothed his mustache and pulled a leather wallet out of his wool-lined jacket.

Ella picked up a business card and wrote on it. "Here's the number of Susan Rivas. She designs and makes those game boards. Does custom designs, too."

The man added the card to his wallet. "Much obliged." While Ella rang up each item, Shelby wrapped and bagged them.

A while after he left, the woman with the stroller came up and paid for two purple and white scarves and a wooden toy car. Before Ella rang up her purchase, she turned to Shelby. "I've got this. Why don't you find Gladys and Eleanor and let them know we're just about ready to close up."

Shelby nodded, then glanced down at the sleeping child. She wanted to reach down and touch her rosy cheek, but stopped herself. Running her hand along the handle, Shelby thought back to her own pregnancy. In her heart she felt it was a girl, though she lost the baby too soon to know for sure. Secretly naming the baby Charisma because it was a miracle pregnancy, Shelby hadn't told anyone about the name. Not Mac. Not even Ella. Sometimes, miracles weren't meant to be… Shelby turned and walked to the back of the store, hoping no one had noticed the tears rolling down her face.

After covering the child with a pink blanket, the mother navigated the stroller outside. Ella glanced up at the clock. Four forty-five. She locked the door early to avoid last-minute customers. Normally, she'd wait, but they had one lonely, and most-likely, irritated cat to pick up at the vet.

As Ella sorted the day's receipts, Eleanor, the shop's crochet and knitting expert, followed Gladys behind the counter. After signing out, they grabbed coats, hats, and oversized purses and continued talking as they made their way over to the front door. They spoke in hushed tones, though Gladys stopped long enough to give Ella a brief wave before they walked out. "Nite ladies," she said, but she didn't think they'd heard her. When Ella turned back around Shelby stood behind her, wide-eyed.

Ella reached for her hand. "I didn't know what to say earlier. I'm sorry you're still hurting."

Shelby's eyes glistened. "Thank you."

"You know you can talk to me anytime. About anything—"

Shelby nodded. "I'd like that. But, right now, there's something more important to discuss—"

Ella frowned. "Everything okay?"

"I'm not sure." Shelby caught Ella's eye. "You'll never believe what I just overheard."

CHAPTER SEVEN

Ella reached out to Shelby. "What happened?"

"I didn't mean to eavesdrop." Shelby leaned on the counter. "I came up behind Gladys and Eleanor stacking baskets. As I got closer, I heard them—"

Ella straightened her shoulders and arranged a stack of spring sale flyers on the counter. "This isn't more gossip, is it? You know how I feel about idle chit chat in our shop."

"No. At least I don't think so. I mean, it's not gossip if you're talking about yourself, right?"

"Now, you've got me curious." Ella smoothed the corner of a bent flyer. "Might as well tell me what you heard."

"While I don't know everything that happened this morning with Harold and Agnes, I have a pretty good idea... Apparently, they said Agnes will do whatever it takes."

"Wait. I thought this had to do with Eleanor or Gladys."

"I'm getting to that," said Shelby. "From what they were saying, Agnes knows about some scandal involving Harold. Eleanor is friends with Harold and is upset because Agnes threatened to ruin Harold's reputation if he won't deal with her—"

Ella cocked her head. "Deal with Eleanor?"

"No, no. Deal with Agnes," said Shelby. "Agnes threatened Harold about this thing. I don't know if it was an emotional or physical threat, but either way, it wouldn't be good."

Ella nodded. "It only brings out the worst in a person."

Shelby thought back to last year, when Sargent Dawn Nolan hurt her emotionally after she returned to Pheasant Valley. Everyone involved ended up getting wounded.

"And what was this 'thing' you heard them talk about?" asked Ella.

"I don't know, El. But it's huge. And those were Eleanor's words. Something that would devastate everyone involved."

Ella tapped her fingers on the counter. "I've known Harold for years, and Eleanor, too. I think Agnes is just grasping at straws to get her way." Ella tried to call to mind a rumor she'd heard many years ago. Though she'd ignored it, now it nagged at her. Could it be the same thing Gladys and Eleanor had discussed? As much as she hated gossip, part of her wished she could recall the conversation. Dismissing her doubts, Ella picked up Oatmeal's leash and attached it to his collar. "So what else did they say? You seem mighty upset over a few rumors."

Shelby cinched her sweater and stared at Ella. "Eleanor's tone. She said, and I quote, 'I can't let Agnes do this to him. I've got to stop her, no matter what.' It was unnerving."

Ella's eyes widened. "That doesn't sound like Eleanor. She's one of the gentlest people I know. Granted, she loves to talk—a lot. But she's always kind to everyone."

Shelby followed Ella and Oatmeal out the front door. "If only you'd heard the way she said it. This was a different side of Eleanor. Like someone who'd been backed into a corner."

Outside, the incoming storm bent newly budding branches of nearby trees. Dark clouds threatening rain hid the last slivers of the setting sun. Ella stopped to pick up Oatmeal. "Better carry you, dog. It's freezing out here."

Shelby got into the jeep and buckled in. She turned to Ella. "Eleanor sounded dead serious."

Ella rubbed her hands in front of the heater vent. "After what Alton said this morning, it sounds like Agnes has made quite a few enemies. I just hope nobody does anything stupid."

AFTER A RESTLESS NIGHT, Ella got up early and made coffee. Sitting on the couch, she watched the sun rise from behind the mountains into a clear, cerulean sky. With time to herself to think over the previous day's revelations, she tried to relax. Eleanor's strange display of anger had kept her awake. And though she'd tried to remember the forgotten rumors, she only ended up with a throbbing headache and no further along than the previous day. The coffee helped, but the lack of sleep made her head foggy.

After a quick breakfast, she got up from the table, avoiding the glaring sunlight streaming through the kitchen window. She placed her dishes in the dishwasher and closed the lid, only to find Oatmeal staring up at her, tail wagging. "No. You can't go to work with me again today. You need to stay home and monitor Mr. Butterfingers." Patting her dog's head, she glanced at the cat sprawled out on the back of the couch. "And you, Mr. B. No more shredded toilet paper." Mr. Butterfingers opened one eye and yawned as if to say, "Yeah, right."

Ella checked her phone again and walked to the end of the short hallway between the kitchen and her bedroom. She had heard Shelby pacing upstairs in the wee hours of the morning and figured her friend also had a restless night. *Better to let her sleep.* One overly tired person was enough, let alone two. Someone had to be awake enough to run the shop. After another hour, Ella went to the bottom stair and called up. "Better hurry, Shel. Almost eight-thirty."

A few moments later, Shelby bounded down the stairs, carrying a large notebook. She rushed past Ella and into the kitchen. "Sorry. Just checking my inventory. I wanted to jot down bolt numbers so I can place an order from that fabric warehouse in Bakersfield." She grabbed a travel mug, filled it with coffee, and bid goodbye to their pets.

Ella locked the front door, taking in the crisp, clean air. "Your scarves sold well this past winter, Shel. Any idea for what you'll create for spring and summer?"

"I was thinking—" Shelby stopped and pointed. "Look. A SOLD sign in front of Hope's old house."

Ella turned. "After years and years of hoarding, it took a while to get it listing-ready."

"Kent mentioned his crew hauled away several overflowing dumpsters of trash," said Shelby. "From what Laura and I had seen of the inside, that place was a disaster."

"It sold quickly," said Ella. "Wonder who our new neighbor will be?"

Shelby shrugged, then let out a squeal. "Look. A deer."

The women stood near the porch and watched a young doe nibbling on new grass near the fence. Ella smiled. "I can always tell spring is close when they come down from the hills. Soon, we might see fawns."

"That's so cool." Shelby pulled out her phone to take a picture, but as Ella's phone buzzed with an incoming call, the doe raised her head. She turned, leapt across the yard, and darted behind their property.

"Sorry about that," said Ella, swiping the phone to take the call. "Hello? Yes, Harold. Good to hear from you." She motioned toward Shelby's jeep and they walked across the gravel driveway. "Hold on a sec while I get buckled in—" Ella put the phone in her lap for a moment, then resumed the call, "—Just headed into the shop. Yes, Shelby is driving while I'm talking—Tonight?" She turned to Shelby to confirm.

Shelby nodded, then pulled out into the cul-de-sac.

"Seven? Yes, looking forward to it—Bye, now." Ella ended the call and sighed.

"Everything okay?" They waited at the corner for another car to pass, then Shelby turned east and headed toward town.

"Harold's coming by after dinner with the information we need about the remodel."

"You don't sound thrilled about it."

"Maybe all that talk about Agnes and Eleanor. I just have this uneasy feeling."

Waiting at the four-way stop, Shelby turned. "I'm not sure I follow you."

Ella stared out the window, focusing on the tall pines in the distance. "Don't know how to explain it. Harold seemed to be holding something back." She drew a question mark on the cold window with a gloved finger and said nothing else.

ELLA'S MOOD lightened when they arrived at the shop. Eleanor stood outside, waiting by the front door. As Ella and Shelby exited the jeep, Eleanor rushed up to them. Crafting bag slung over one shoulder; strands of thick blue yarn trailed after her in the breeze. Her teeth chattered, "S-s-s-o happy to s-s-s-ee you both." She pulled at the ends of her beige, oversized cashmere sweater.

Shelby rolled her eyes and laughed. "Again?"

Eleanor nodded and followed them inside, rubbing her hands on her denim pants. "Yes. Locked my keys *and* my cell phone in the car. Again."

"Oh, Eleanor," said Ella. "How many times this month?"

Her cheeks turned crimson, although it might have been from standing out in the cold. "Three. Maybe four."

Shelby pointed to her crafting bag. "You need to knit yourself a key chain and attach it to a belt loop on your pants. That way, you can't leave the car without them."

Eleanor stifled a laugh. "You mind if I use one of your phones to call the auto club?"

Shelby nodded, then motioned to the shop phone under the counter. "We should put their number on speed dial for you."

As Eleanor made the call, Shelby stood at the register readying the store for customers while Ella went to the back of the shop and made hazelnut coffee, everyone's favorite. A few minutes later, she placed a steaming mug on a small table between two chairs in their makeshift sitting area, then went to the front and motioned to Eleanor. "Come with me and warm up with a fresh cup of coffee."

Eleanor, still on the phone, nodded. "Be right over. Thanks."

Ella went back and poured herself a cup of coffee. Holding it close, she took in the thick scent, and looked around her shop. With most of the booths rented, customers already loved the vendors' handcrafted products. But she wanted to offer them more. After Eleanor came back for her coffee, Ella finished hers, then joined Shelby behind the counter. "Won't it be nice when we can finally have an actual area for our customers to sit and chat?"

Shelby wrote something on the schedule, then leaned closer to Ella. "This place has so much potential."

Ella nodded. "Let's just hope it won't cost too much to make it happen."

"Guess we'll have to wait until tonight to find out," said Shelby.

CHAPTER EIGHT

Ella pushed her chair back from the table. "How about I start on the dinner dishes before Harold gets here?"

"You barely ate." Shelby pointed to Ella's plate. "Are you really that stressed?"

"Thought I was hiding it better."

Shelby shook her head.

Ella turned. "This is really important to me. To us. And the future of our shop." Making all the decisions after Doug was killed wasn't easy on Ella. Though she never explained all her concerns, their new renovation plans were well out of her comfort zone. Repaying Harold, getting in debt over their heads, the possibility of failing. Every fear formed a bigger lump in her throat and a larger knot in her stomach.

"It will be okay, El."

"It wasn't last time," said Ella. She placed her dishes in the sink, then turned.

"Is there something you're not telling me?"

"You know Harold helped Doug and me with *The Steamed Bean*—"

"Yes," said Shelby. "The coffee house downtown."

"And after Doug's death, I had to close—"

"It was such a terrible time for everyone. But this time—"

"I never told you that Harold lost just about everything."

Shelby's eyes grew wide. "I don't understand. You said he recovered financially."

Ella shook her head and leaned against the counter. "It almost ruined our friendship. I vowed never to borrow money from a friend, even a real estate investor friend."

Shelby took her dishes to the sink, then squeezed Ella's shoulder. "Harold came to you. I'm sure he trusts you or he wouldn't have offered."

"I—" Ella wiped a tear from her cheek. "I can't let him down again."

"Something tells me he doesn't see this renovation as a bad risk."

Ella sighed. "I don't want to get my hopes up."

"Hope is all we have right now. Otherwise, our brains will head down that dark hole of fear and who knows what else. El, I know you're expecting the worst. I totally understand. I struggle with negative thoughts, as well. This is huge. But we're in this together, right?"

Nodding, Ella turned and loaded the dishes into the dishwasher. "It's just…"

"Believe the best—We have to believe the best, together."

Ella closed the dishwasher, dried her hands, and glanced at Shelby. "Fine. But it's always been my nature to prepare for the worst."

———

BRINGING his late model Jaguar to a slow stop, Harold parked in front of Ella's home. Lights from the front room cast a warm glow through the windows. Though the temperatures outside hovered below freezing, he wiped perspiration from his forehead. With Agnes' relentless badgering, his health had declined more rapidly than expected. He unwrapped a black, cherry-flavored cough drop and popped it into his mouth. Anything to quiet the cough he so desperately wanted to hide.

———

OATMEAL RAN from the kitchen and into the front room, barking. A sharp knock at the front door sent Mr. Butterfingers skittering under the table.

Ella took a deep breath, then opened the front door with her dog right on her heels. "It's okay, Oatmeal. He's an old friend."

Harold walked inside and let out a hearty laugh. "Not that old." He offered Ella his gloved hand.

She pushed his hand away and embraced him in a tight hug. "How are you doing, my not-so-old friend?"

"Still kickin', as my granddad used to say." He chuckled and removed his dark gray overcoat and gloves. "Where should I put these?"

Ella pointed. "Coat rack behind the door."

"Been a while since I've been here."

Motioning to her friend, Ella smiled. "You remember Shelby, don't you?"

Harold extended his hand. "Nice to see you again, hon."

"You too, Harold. Can I get you something to drink? Coffee? Tea, perhaps?"

"Nothing for me, thanks." He unbuttoned his gray suit jacket and pointed to the couch. "Here or at the table?"

Ella shrugged. "Either is fine, Harold."

"Table might be better." He spread his arms and bowed. "Lead the way."

While he was amicable, Ella noted he wasn't his normal chatty self, but more business-social. To be expected, she figured, since they were talking money, though it didn't help the growing knot in her stomach. She tried to remember Shelby's advice to believe the best.

Harold stood and waited for the women to be seated, then he reached into his jacket pocket and pulled out a bulky white, business-sized envelope. Easing into his chair, he placed the envelope on the table. "Everything you need is in there—" His phone buzzed. He raised a finger, took it out, and stared at it for a moment. Grimacing, Harold mumbled something under his breath, dismissed the call, and shoved it into his jacket. He looked up and drummed his fingers on the table.

Ella reached for his hand. "Harold, is everything okay?"

"Fine, hon. A lot on my plate. Don't mean to sound blunt, but I'm dealing with a situation that has me on edge—"

"I'm sorry."

He sighed. "Not as sorry as I am."

"Anything we can do to help?" asked Ella.

Harold rubbed thin fingers across his five o'clock shadow. The kitchen lighting stressed dark circles under his eyes and worry lines across his forehead. He massaged his temples, closed his eyes, and sighed again. When he opened them, he pointed to the envelope. "The expansion is very do-able. In the neighborhood of ten grand…"

Shelby began to say something, but he stopped her. "Let

me finish." After clearing his throat, he continued. "That's just permits and materials—sheetrock, paint, flooring, plus basic furniture. Not labor. That will run you twice as much, depending on who you hire."

Ella gasped and looked at Shelby. "Much more than I expected."

Shelby nodded, but said nothing.

Harold reached down into his suit pocket and pulled out a set of keys. Then, sliding one under the flap of the envelope, he opened it and laid the paperwork on the table. "Way I see it," he pointed to the top page and continued, "there are required expenses—those that keep the city happy and ensure the walls don't cave in. But—" he rapped his hairy knuckles on the next page, "—if you could find some experienced volunteers for the labor, you could save a small fortune."

Ella arched a brow. "Cutting costs is always a good thing."

Harold stared at the papers for what seemed to be forever, then cracked his neck. "Now, about my involvement—"

Ella's heart sank. This was the worst-case scenario she'd feared. "Harold, I know you're leery about investing in me again. Especially after what happened."

He pushed back from the table and stood. Grasping the back of the chair, he caught Ella's eye. "That was in the past. If it were up to me, I'd write you a check for the entire expansion right now. But, unfortunately, my hands are tied."

"I don't understand," said Ella.

Harold clenched his fist. "It's—" He caught himself and paused for a moment. "It's this dad-gummed thing with Agnes. She's got me in an awkward position. Found a hot shot, pimply faced attorney who's threatening to freeze all my assets." He paced behind them. "As far as I know, I could wake up tomorrow dead broke." Harold stopped. He pulled his phone from his jacket and willed it to ring so he would have an excuse to leave. When it didn't, he stifled a cough and spoke in a hushed tone. "I'd help you if I could, but until this blows over. I'm sorry, Ella. I didn't even want to come tonight, but we've been friends for too long. I owed you an explanation in person." He shoved the phone in his jacket and headed into the front room.

Shelby and Ella looked at each other, then got up and followed.

By the time they caught up to him, Harold had already buttoned his overcoat and slipped on his gloves. Grabbing the knob, he rested his forehead on the door. "I'm truly sorry."

Ella reached for his arm. "It's okay. I understand…"

Opening the front door, the rush of frigid air matched the coldness in Harold's voice. "I've got to make her leave me alone. She ruined my life once. I won't let it happen again." He walked out, slamming the door behind him.

CHAPTER NINE

After Harold left Ella's house, Shelby stared at her friend. "El, did he just threaten to do something to Agnes?"

Wide-eyed, Ella shrugged. "Maybe he meant he'd take care of the court thing and pay her off. Then she'd leave him alone."

"It sounded much more serious than that." Mr. Butterfingers padded back into the front room and jumped on the couch, purring. Shelby brushed the soft fur along his back. "Nice for you to join us again." He licked one of his paws, then settled on his spot and closed his eyes. Plopping down on the couch, Shelby rested her head on the cushion behind her. "Now what?"

Ella sat, but said nothing. Oatmeal hopped up and settled between them. Rubbing his ears, she thought back to what Harold had said. She'd known him a long time. He never minced words. Nor was he one to back down.

"He offered suggestions for the labor," said Shelby.

"Without materials or a contractor, all the volunteers in town won't do us any good."

Shelby picked at a hangnail, then chewed it off. "What about Kent? He knows about construction. Not only did his company completely remodel Hope's house, but Susan told us how he renovated her kitchen last year."

"And what good will that do?" asked Ella.

"El, the vendors want this expansion as much as we do, right?"

Ella nodded.

"How about we call an emergency meeting?" asked Shelby. "Present the facts, including the cost of materials, labor, and everything. Explain what we need. We have a lot of enthusiastic crafters with vast resources. After all, this will benefit them, too. It'll mean much more if they all have a stake in it."

Ella sat up and stared at Shelby. "You mean like a co-op or something?"

"It's like sweat-equity. Like for families who want a house and are part of the building process. We'll just find a way for everyone to contribute something."

"Actually Shel, that could work."

"And we won't have to go into debt to make it happen."

Ella smiled. "What would I do without you?"

"You'd always think the worst."

"So, what's our next step?" asked Ella.

"We set up a meeting."

Ella pulled out her phone and scrolled to a calendar app. She held it up for Shelby to see the screen. "How about this Thursday night? I mean, it's short notice, but the sooner the better."

"Should be fine for a preliminary meeting," said Shelby. "You should invite vendors' spouses and their partners. It'll increase our chances of finding materials and volunteers."

"Good idea," said Ella. "I'll set it up for seven p.m. and message everyone tonight."

"Mention we'll serve cookies and coffee." Shelby laughed. "Treats will bump up the attendance."

Ella looked up from her phone. "Okay, an expansion meeting with cookies for anyone interested. Anything else?"

Shelby thought for a moment. "I'll make some half-sheet flyers for the shop, in case anyone missed the email."

"Like Gladys, who claims she never checks hers."

Shelby stretched her toes under the coffee table. "I told you this would work."

"There are a lot of details to deal with."

"El, we're a lot closer than we were twenty minutes ago."

As MUCH AS the night before had been tough for Harold, the next morning wasn't going any better. He checked his watch. Once. Twice. A third time. Only five minutes had passed, but it seemed like an eternity. Easing himself off the exam table, he walked over to a Food Pyramid poster hanging on the wall. The cartoon-like drawings showed the recommended basic food groups and how many servings of each should be eaten each day. Rolling his eyes, Harold let out a long sigh. His favorite treats were missing. Maybe a few wouldn't hurt. Not now, at least.

He turned to another poster behind him. It touted, "Dream Big," with a runner on a beach, back-lit with a golden, setting sun. Harold's shoulders slumped and he climbed back onto the exam table. He turned his wrist to check the time again when several knocks came from the other side. The door opened.

"Morning, Harold. So sorry to keep you waiting." Dr. Minke, a short, balding man wearing a blue shirt, black trousers, and a blue and white polka-dotted bow tie, walked in. He shook Harold's hand. "How are you doing today?"

Harold pointed at the food chart and let out a weak chuckle. "I'd be much better if they'd add chocolate chip cookies."

"Ah, yes." Dr. Minke smiled. "I'm sure an occasional cookie wouldn't hurt." He stared down at the shiny linoleum floor and cleared his throat.

"Did you get the results?"

Dr. Minke nodded and pulled Harold's patient folder from under his arm.

"How about we do the Good News, Bad News thing? Eh, Doc?"

Bringing his eyes up to meet Harold's, Dr. Minke spoke in a hushed tone. "I'm sorry, Harold. This time I don't have good news—"

THURSDAY AFTER WORK, Shelby stayed at The Bee's Knees prepping for the meeting while Ella made a quick trip home to take care of the pets and bring back dinner. Shelby wondered how many people would actually show up since the shop had only a dozen folding chairs, and half were wobbly and in disrepair. *It would have to do for now.* Shelby rubbed her growling tummy and paced near the front door. She stopped for a moment and glanced out the window. Ominous clouds previously stalled over the mountains had shifted and were hovering above the small town.

Shelby noticed Ella rushing across the parking lot, her short hair disheveled by the gusts. She grabbed the handle and held the door open for her friend, then locked up to keep it from blowing open.

Ella carried two grease-stained bags to the counter and set them down. She unbuttoned her sweater and looked around. "Can you get me the screwdriver? The wind just dislodged our sign out front."

Shelby shivered as splatters of rain smacked up against the glass doors. "I think Kent used it a couple of days ago to fix a shelf. I'll have to look around for it."

Ella pulled out a wad of paper towels and separated the food order. "You think we should postpone the meeting? I don't want everyone out if this storm worsens."

A flash of lightning streaked across the sky, illuminating the shop. A roar of thunder followed a few moments later. Shelby pointed at the ceiling. "Sounds like it's already on us."

"Maybe it will be over soon." Ella squinted at the wall clock. "Still an hour before we start."

"You know how they say March roars in like a lion and out like a lamb. Maybe it won't be so bad." Shelby tore open two catsup packets and squeezed them over the fries. She popped a thick-cut fry in her mouth and gave a thumbs up. "Sorry, just couldn't wait any longer."

Ella laughed. "Don't worry about it. I'm just going to check the weather on my phone, then find that screwdriver. I don't want the sign to come loose and bonk someone on the head."

Shelby carried her food to the chair area and sat. Resting a paper towel on a knee, she devoured her burger. By the time Ella joined her, she'd finished more than half of the fries. "So what did you find out, Ms. Weather Lady?"

"Sounds like the lion will roar for quite a while. Winds are supposed to gust over seventy miles per hour between now and midnight bringing torrential rains…" She glanced at her phone again and scrolled. "… with possible hail and lightning strikes. They're warning everyone to stay inside because of the dangerous conditions."

Shelby swallowed. "That's not good."

Ella fingered a fry, then dropped it back in the bag. "I'm going to message everyone and cancel before——" Several whacks at the door interrupted her.

"Might be too late." Shelby jumped up, scattering the last of her fries on the carpet.

They dashed over to the door.

Laura and Gladys, along with Vivian and her two daughters, Lilibeth and Vickie, stood under the eave, drenched. Shelby unlocked the door and held it with both hands as Ella ushered them all inside.

"My goodness," said Gladys. "That wind just sucked my winter hat right off my head."

"Are you okay, hon?" Laura rubbed Gladys' shoulders and turned to Shelby with wide eyes. "Earth Mother is very unhappy tonight."

"You're not kidding," said Lilibeth. She looked at Ella. "Don't think John is going to make the meeting. Said he needed to stay home and tend to the ewes getting ready to lamb. Storms like this are a nightmare to us."

Ella glanced around at the rain-soaked women. "I can't believe all of you braved the weather. I was just about to message you."

Vivian brushed raindrops off her jacket. "It came up so fast. There was only a slight breeze when I picked up the girls."

More pounding came from the door. Shelby hurried over and let in another shivering, windswept group that included Kent, Susan, and Eleanor, who shielded her yarn bag from the downpour.

"Haven't seen the sky open up like that in a while," said Kent. "You have coffee made? If not, I'll make it." He stopped and turned. "By the way, your sign outside is loose. I can take care of that after I start the coffee." He pointed to his back pocket. "Took the screwdriver home with me the other night, but just remembered and brought it back."

Ella waved to Kent. "Yes, thanks. I didn't want anyone to get hurt."

He walked away as Laura glided past them, waving sage and lavender. "Coffee sounds wonderful. I'll take a cup once I finish making peace with the Earth."

Susan followed Kent to the coffee pot as the others settled in. Gladys' chair wobbled as she sat. "Might get seasick if I stay on this one." She stood. "Anyone want to trade?"

Vickie raised her hand. "Take mine, Gladys. It seems stable."

Eleanor sat down, wiggled her butt, then, with a satisfied look, pulled out a half-knitted scarf. Soon, her knitting needles danced and clicked.

Shelby looked over at Ella. "Is everyone here?"

Checking her phone again, Ella pointed to a message. "Got a few responses saying they couldn't make it. And though about twenty vendors RSVP'd, I'm sure the storm changed their plans. Let me count. Only nine counting us. I was really hoping Paige and Harold would show, too."

Shelby glanced at the clock. "It's only six-forty-five."

Ella grabbed a bottled water and unscrewed the lid. "I doubt anyone else will brave this weather—" A blinding flash of lightning lit up the windows. Ear-splitting thunder followed.

"Let's hope not," murmured Gladys. She turned and looked out the window. "I hope my Ed is okay."

Vivian patted her hand. "He's probably tuned to his radios."

Gladys nodded and took a cup of steaming coffee offered by Kent. "Thanks so much, hon."

He eyed the rest of the small group. "Anyone else?" Several hands shot up. He handed out mugs as Susan poured coffee from the pot.

"There are cookies, too," said Shelby, motioning toward the front counter. "I'll go get them." As she approached the front of the shop, she saw several figures huddled by the front entrance. Shelby ran over and opened the door.

Paige ducked in, waving her red, glittery nails. "Thanks, Sweetie. I brought pie from the Café." She swayed her hips as she pranced over to the others and set the pastry box on the counter. After opening it, she looked at Ella. "Where's your knife so I can slice it up?"

Ella got up and rummaged through one of the cabinet drawers. Scissors. Forks. *Chopsticks?* She held up a long, skinny knife. "Paige, will this do?"

"Perfect." She took the knife from Ella, cut a few wedges, then left it next to the pie.

Ella came back to the group with a tray of cookies and served them while Shelby opened the door again. Harold slipped in, brushed rain off his high-end raincoat, then eased down in an empty seat. One last arrival, wearing a soggy black knitted scarf, pushed her way inside.

"About time you let us in," she said. "Thought I'd drown out there."

Shelby grabbed a chocolate chip cookie and sat next to Harold. He turned and groaned. Leaning close to Shelby, he whispered, "Melt is more like it."

Shelby's eyes widened.

A well-padded woman trudged across the carpet and plopped down in a chair across from them. She unwrapped her rain-spattered scarf, looked Harold in the eye, and scowled.

CHAPTER TEN

E lla looked around the small group. Her eyes stopped on one person. "Agnes, what are you doing here?"

"Sticking her nose where it doesn't belong," said Harold. He got up, cut himself an ample slice of pie, picked out a few cookies, then took a seat next to Shelby.

"I most certainly belong," huffed Agnes. "Your flyer said it was a public meeting for anyone who was interested."

"You can stay, if you're civil." Ella took in a deep breath. *This promises to be an interesting evening.*

Agnes glared at Ella. "I'm always civil." She craned her neck and snapped her fingers at Susan. "Where's my coffee?"

Kent cleared his throat. "Making more. Should be ready soon." A flash of lightning followed by a long, low rumble silenced the conversation.

"My goodness," said Gladys. "Hope I remembered to bring my inhaler."

Shelby turned. "Are you okay?"

Gladys stopped twisting the scarf in her hands and dug through a red and white cloth bag stamped 'Purcell's

Orchards.' Soon, she held up a small plastic container. "I'm good."

Harold leaned close to Shelby, though his voice carried around the small circle. "Better than I can say about some people."

Ella caught his eye and wagged her finger. "Behave or I'll ask you to leave, too."

He muttered something to himself and went back to eating.

Ella motioned for quiet. "Alright, let's take our seats and get started. Shel and I appreciate you coming out tonight, though I'm sorry the weather turned so quickly..." The lights flickered, then dimmed.

Gladys gasped.

Laura, who sat next to Gladys, patted her knee. "You okay, hon?"

She nodded and waved at Ella. "I'm fine. Please continue."

"The primary reason we are here is about the expansion..."

Vivian clapped. "This is so exciting."

Lilibeth put a finger to her lips. "Mom, shush."

"I know everyone's excited, and I wanted to give an update..." said Ella. The group collectively leaned forward. "I've got good news. And bad news..."

Paige popped a big pink bubble, then sucked it back into her mouth with a whooshing sound. "Might as well tell us the other news. Ain't fair makin' us wait."

Shelby gave a toothy grin, though Ella wasn't sure if she was encouraging her to continue or glad she didn't have to say anything. "The renovation won't be as costly as we expected..." said Ella. The lights flickered again.

Harold swallowed a bite of pie and looked around. "Have any flashlights? You know, to be prepared."

Shelby stood. "Behind the counter. I'll get them."

"If you're going that way, here's the screwdriver." Kent removed it from his pocket and handed it to her. "Don't want to take it home again."

"Thanks," said Shelby. "I'll leave it on the counter in case we need it later."

"While Shelby checks on the flashlights, let's focus on why we're here." Ella paused for a moment, then continued. "We need materials... lumber, sheet rock, paint, flooring, plus all that goes with it."

Agnes snarled. "Sounds pricy to me."

Ella clenched her jaw, then forced a smile. "As I was saying—"

Something pelted the windows and then the roof. Like thousands of rocks dropping from the sky. Everyone looked up and cowered. As Shelby came back with a flashlight in each hand, she pointed to the windows. "Look. Ginormous hail. Like we used to get in Houston."

Vivian and Vickie dashed to the front door. "It's covering the entire street," said Vivian.

"Like it just snowed," gasped Vickie.

Susan and Kent rushed over to them, followed by Lilibeth and Paige.

Ella rolled her eyes. "Might as well go watch the historic hailstorm. I can't keep talking if no one's paying attention."

Laura went to her booth and grabbed a handful of lavender and sage, then circled around the chairs, waving the herbs.

Agnes snorted. "What the heck are you doing?"

Laura slowed and stood behind Agnes. "Protecting us

from negative karma. The tension is heavy on my soul. I'm making peace on behalf of everyone."

Agnes shrugged her off. "Well, I never."

Between the brief attention spans, Gladys' wheezing, the ongoing feud between Harold and Agnes, and the anxiety caused by the weather, Ella sunk into her chair. *I've lost control of the meeting.* She tried to compose her thoughts as hail continued to bombard the roof and windows.

Shelby clapped her hands. "How about we get back to what we were discussing so everyone can go home?"

Agnes pointed a thick finger at the door. "You can't possibly expect me to go out in that mess?"

"She didn't mean right away, Agnes," said Ella.

One by one, the others returned. "There're still goodies," said Ella. "Grab some pie or a cookie and we'll get started... again." She took a deep breath and continued. "The bottom line is that we need materials and labor..."

Agnes opened her mouth, but Shelby pointed at her. "Don't interrupt."

Ella's heart swelled. She flashed Shelby a thumbs-up.

"While we don't have a lot of capital, Shelby and I would like everyone to pool their resources. Then we can all share in the ownership of the extra space."

The lights flickered again as a flash of lightning lit up the sky. Sparks shot out from a nearby transformer. "That was close," said Vivian. "Maybe we should leave."

"It's too dangerous right now." Ella stood. "Since we're stuck here for the time being, let's put our heads together and brainstorm ideas."

Kent raised his hand.

Ella smiled. "Yes."

"So you're thinking about making this a co-op type

project? Like whoever helps with materials or labor has a mutual interest in the shop?"

"Not the entire shop, just the classroom area," said Ella. "Whoever puts in sweat equity would share in a percentage of the profits."

Agnes glared at everyone. "I'm not lifting a finger."

"Then why are you here?" Ella took a breath and counted to five.

Agnes flicked an invisible speck off her wool coat. "I'm nosy."

Harold elbowed Shelby. "At least she admits it."

Agnes stood. "Better than what you won't admit."

Ella put her hands up. "Enough, you two."

"What about you, dear?" Agnes glared at Eleanor and sneered. "Do you think Harold is truthful?"

Eleanor looked up from casting off a row and turned crimson. "I'm not sure what you mean."

Ella took out her cell and pointed it at Agnes. "I'm calling Pheasant Valley PD. Someone will escort you home." She pushed nine-one-one and held the phone to her ear. Nothing. Ella ended the call and tried again. After several seconds, it connected. "Yes, this is Ella Denning at The Bee's Knees. We have a domestic dispute. Can you send over a patrol car?"

Agnes jumped up and pulled her coat together. "Well, that's unnecessary."

Gladys tried to speak, but it turned into a coughing fit. Paige popped her gum in rapid succession. Harold typed something into his phone.

Shelby looked at Ella. "It's too dangerous to let anyone leave." The lights flickered. Lightning flashed. Then everything went dark, inside and outside.

"Well, that's a fine kettle of fish," said Gladys after she stopped coughing.

Ella suppressed a laugh. It was that or cry. What a disastrous night. "Okay, nobody move. I don't want you to trip over something. Or each other."

Shelby flipped on a flashlight. The beam lit up a small circle on the floor. Lightning flashed again, silhouetting several figures headed toward the door.

"Who's leaving?" Ella called, but a crash of thunder muffled her voice. The door whooshed open. It hit against the wall and banged several times.

"I'll go deal with that." Shelby handed Ella another flashlight. "You stay here."

Ella flipped it on and noticed several seats were empty, including those previously occupied by Agnes, Harold, Vivian, and Eleanor. Even Eleanor's knitting bag was gone.

Shelby came back and stood near Ella as the others talked amongst themselves.

"Now what?" Ella asked. "It's pointless to continue."

Laura came up behind them. "I don't have a good feeling about this."

Pounding at the front door caused Ella to jump. "Oh my, now what?" She grabbed Laura's arm and handed her a flashlight. "Please stay with Gladys while Shelby and I go see who's out there."

"I'm coming too," said Kent.

"Don't leave me behind," said Susan.

The small group held onto each other as Ella used a flashlight to navigate across the windblown room. As they neared the open front door, she aimed the beam of light at a hooded figure standing in the doorway.

CHAPTER ELEVEN

The flashlight's beam lit up the face of the person standing outside The Bee's Knees. Ella relaxed her shoulders. "It's Alton," she said, opening the door.

Pushing back the hood on his jacket, the sergeant entered the shop. "Power's out all over town. Cars stuck. Escaped livestock, though the sheriff's handling that. Both departments had to call in full crews. At least the storm seems to be moving on." He aimed his flashlight at the store. "You called in about a domestic disturbance, Ella?"

"Harold and Agnes, again."

Alton stepped further into the shop. "Where are they now?" He inclined his head close to his shoulder mic and listened to a dispatcher's chatter.

Shelby shrugged. "We don't know. They were arguing. After the power went out, several people left."

Alton ran his thick fingers through his short, brown hair. "After hours get-together?"

"Vendor meeting," said Shelby. "Ella discussed the expansion and tried to keep the group calm, but when the transformer blew…"

"Everyone okay?" he asked.

Ella pointed behind them. "We think so, though Gladys was having health challenges."

"Gladys Purcell? Where is she now?"

Ella and Shelby led Alton to the chairs. "Laura, how's Gladys?"

Gladys cleared her throat. "I can speak for myself, dear. I'm not a goner yet."

"Sounds like you are just as feisty as ever, Gladys." Alton laughed. "What seems to be the trouble?"

As he crouched down and questioned Gladys, Shelby went to Ella. "What happened to the happy couple?"

"I do not know."

The lights flickered for a moment, came on, then went out again.

"Darn," said Gladys.

Alton looked up. "She seems to be fine, but to be on the safe side, I'd like to call the paramedics."

Gladys poked him in the arm. "There's no need for that. If someone can give me a lift home, I'll be okay. It was just a cookie crumb that went down the wrong pipe."

"Are you sure, hon?" Laura rubbed her arm. "I don't mind going with you."

Gladys jumped up and did a half-dozen jumping jacks. "Does this look like someone ready to keel over?"

Alton raised his hands and backed away. "You don't have to prove anything to me. I'm just trying to avoid the wrath of your husband."

Gladys sniffed the air and turned to Laura. "I'd prefer you just take me home."

Laura smiled. "The woman has spoken."

Ella shook her head. "To be that energetic when I'm in my... um, 60s?"

"Eighty-one years young and proud of it," said Gladys.

They paused for a moment as the lights flickered again and stayed on. Laura mumbled a thanks to the universe and Gladys clapped. Paige walked up to Alton and popped her gum. "Lookin' good as ever, big guy. Next time you come into the Café, slice of pie's on me." She winked at him, then as everyone watched, she turned and left the shop, swinging her hips.

Alton's cheeks flushed. He stared at his muddy shoes.

"Interesting way of wording that offer." Ella chuckled.

Kent stifled a laugh. "Want me to stack the chairs in the back room for you, Shelby?"

"That would be great. Thanks." She joined Ella, who was talking with Lilibeth and Vickie.

"So you don't have any idea why your mom left?" asked Ella.

"No," said Vickie. "We came in the same car. I called her, but I couldn't get through."

"Most of the cell towers are out," said Alton. "Service will be spotty until morning." He cracked his neck, then turned to Ella. "Not much more I can do here, so I'll be taking off. If you need me, best to use a landline."

Kent helped Susan put on her jacket. They waved goodbye, then followed Alton out the door.

A few minutes later, Vivian walked in. Vickie rushed up to her. "Mom, where were you?"

Her hands trembling, Vivian attempted to unbutton her jacket. She gave up and gripped the back of a rickety chair. "Outside, trying to keep the peace. Harold and Agnes started arguing, then Eleanor got involved."

"Should we let Alton know?" asked Ella.

Vivian shook her head. "They took off around the

corner before the power came on." She rubbed Vickie's arm. "Didn't mean to frighten you, sweetie."

Vickie turned to Ella. "You need us to stick around?"

"No. Kent took care of the chairs. Shel and I'll make sure everything is secure and go home. I suggest you all do the same."

Shelby held out the bakery box. "Why don't you ladies take this home? Lilibeth, offer some to your dear hubby for weathering the storm on his own."

Following Vivian and her daughters to the front, Ella locked the door after they left. She turned to Shelby. "Probably should check the alley, just to make sure there're no wires or branches down."

After reaching the store room, Shelby flipped the light switch. "Even with the lights on, this room creeps me out." Cobwebs hanging from the ceiling caught her sweater as they walked through.

Ella pointed. "I'll be glad when that wall is down."

Shivering, Shelby unlocked the back door to the alley. She pushed on it to check the area, but nothing happened. She turned and looked at Ella.

"What's wrong?"

"Something must have blown down during the storm," said Shelby. "Can't get it open."

Ella walked over and pressed her body against the door. "It's not going anywhere."

"Now what?"

"We'll access it from the other side. If we can't move it, I'll call Alton on my ancient landline."

"Fine. Rub it in." The women each took a flashlight and walked out the front door into the chilly air making their way through the melting puddles of hail. Shelby grabbed

Ella's arm as they rounded the building. "I don't like it back here," she whispered.

"Shine your light up ahead," said Ella.

Something skittered across their path. Shelby jumped.

Ella froze. "Don't do that."

Shelby clenched her flashlight. "Couldn't help it."

Ella shuddered and squeezed Shelby's trembling hand. "You know we're going to be okay, right?"

Shelby took in a ragged breath and nodded.

They turned the corner into the alley. Ella aimed the beam of light across their path while Shelby aimed a trembling beam further ahead.

Shelby gasped. "What's that?"

"Something is blocking the door," said Ella. "Though, I can't tell what it is."

"How about I wait for you to check it out first?"

Ella reached for Shelby's hand. "How about we go together?"

She hesitated and took another step, stopping about ten feet from the door. A rat scrambled away, its feet skittering across a nearby trash can.

Ella let loose of Shelby's hand and straightened her shoulders. "Wait here."

"Not arguing." Shelby aimed the beam of the flashlight in front of Ella's steps.

"Oh no." Ella's voice changed in pitch. "Don't come any closer."

"Why?"

"We need to call Alton."

Shelby leaned against the brick building. "What's wrong?"

Ella rushed back to Shelby. "It's… it's a body."

Shelby struggled to catch her breath.

"Shel, listen to me. You're going to be okay."

"Finding someone in the cemetery last year..." said Shelby. "Now this..." She swallowed and leaned on Ella. "Did you recognize who it is?"

"It's Agnes."

CHAPTER TWELVE

After their frightening discovery, Ella and Shelby rushed back inside The Bee's Knees.

Shelby paced. "You sure it was Agnes?"

Ella nodded.

"And she's dead?"

"She wasn't moving." Picking up the corded phone, Ella punched in a number. She drummed her fingers on the counter. "It's taking them forever to… No, I can't hold. This is Ella Denning at The Bee's Knees. There's a dead body in the alley behind my shop… Fine. I'll hold…"

"How are you not hyperventilating like me?"

Holding the phone away from her ear, Ella massaged her forehead. "I'm sure I'll fall apart once we get home. I just hope the police get here soon." Stretching the cord to its fullest reach, she paced near the shop's front door as the antique wall clock ticked off the seconds.

Memories of the last dead body they'd found flooded back to Shelby. Back then, Ella was the primary suspect. This time, they both had strong alibis. *Thank goodness.* Sirens in the distance grew louder. Red and blue flashing lights reflected on nearby buildings and in the puddles outside. Shelby opened the front door as Ella hung up the phone.

A lanky police officer stepped inside, raising his voice over another wailing siren. "Can you show us where you found the body?"

Ella rushed to him. "Come with me. I think she had a heart attack."

The officer and two paramedics followed Ella past a fire truck parked near the alley. She pointed to a lifeless lump laying near the shop's back door.

"Please wait here," said the officer.

Ella stopped and leaned in to catch their conversation.

The paramedics checked Agnes' body, then stepped back. As they walked away, the police officer talked into his lapel microphone. Ella only made out a few words. "Sergeant... Forensics... Coroner..."

A second Pheasant Valley unit pulled into the alley, its lights flashing red and blue. Muffled radio chatter increased when Alton stepped out. He motioned to the officer. "Jackson, secure the area. We have an active crime scene. That box is evidence, too."

Ella stood near the brick wall, staring at an oversized cardboard box close to Agnes' body.

Alton leaned into his lapel mic and mumbled numbers Ella didn't understand. She thought of Gladys' husband Ed and his police scanners. He could translate the ten-codes and shed some light on what was unfolding.

Ella turned when she heard more footsteps coming closer. A short, stocky police officer carrying what looked like a fishing tackle box walked up to Alton. After a quick chat, he walked to the body as Alton headed over to Ella.

"Williams, I'll be inside if you need me." He turned to Ella. "How about we go inside where it's warmer?"

"What happened?" she asked. "I thought she had a heart attack."

"More like an attack of the heart," said Alton.

"What are you talking about?"

Alton led and Ella followed him into the shop. "I need to ask both of you some questions."

Shelby stared at Ella. "Why do I have a bad feeling about this?"

Unzipping his jacket, Alton leaned against the counter and removed a notebook and pen. He opened to a new page, but looked up when the first responding officer walked in. "Excuse me, ladies," said Alton. A few minutes later, the officer walked outside again.

Alton turned his attention to the women. "I think we'd all be much more comfortable sitting."

Ella nodded and led them over to the coffee area, then pulled out a few folding chairs. After setting them up, she eased down next to Shelby and stared at Alton. "What did you mean by an attack of the heart?"

"I shouldn't have said anything…"

"But you did," said Ella. "Are you saying someone murdered Agnes?"

He let out a long sigh. "Tell me what you saw when you found her."

Ella looked at Shelby, then spoke first. "When we couldn't open the back door, we checked the alley. As we got closer, I recognized Agnes and called the police."

"Do you have anything to add, Shelby?"

"Not really. I didn't see much waiting by the wall."

"Did either of you touch the body or move the box?"

Ella shook her head. "We didn't touch anything."

"That's good," said Alton. "Shelby, do you remember who went outside with Agnes?"

She thought for a moment. "Vivian. Harold... And Eleanor."

"Anyone else?" he asked.

"Don't think so. The power was out. We only had flashlights."

Alton turned to Ella. "Do you remember if anyone else left with Agnes?"

"Just the four of them, I think. But Shelby's right. Anyone could have slipped out. I was distracted when Gladys started coughing."

He flipped the page and tapped his pen on the notebook. "I'll need a list of everyone who attended tonight's meeting. Please note those who left and returned."

Ella looked at Shelby, then back to Alton. "I'll do my best. I just can't believe..."

Alton clicked his pen, stuck it and the notebook in his shirt pocket, and stood. "I'll be outside if you think of anything else."

Shelby raised her hand. "Can we go home? Our animals must be starving..."

"You've had a stressful evening," said Alton. "I have everything I need for tonight. Except for the list of names. First, last, and any contact information." He zipped his jacket, then regarded Ella. "Make the list, then go home and have a glass of wine. I'll be in touch tomorrow." He turned and walked out the shop's front door.

"Already past ten," said Ella. "Tonight's been something else."

Shelby frowned. "When this news gets out, tomorrow won't be much better."

CHAPTER THIRTEEN

S helby sat at the kitchen table stirring sugar into a second cup of morning coffee. Mr. Butterfingers twisted around her legs and meowed. She looked down at the persistent feline. "Sorry, no more eggs for you." Glancing up at the clock, she rubbed her eyes. Not even eight o'clock and Ella had already taken a half-dozen phone calls.

"Yes, Viv. We'll be in…" Ella walked into the kitchen, holding her cell between her chin and shoulder. "About an hour. I need to eat something, then we'll…" She looked at Shelby and rolled her eyes. "Let's talk when I get there… Okay, goodbye…" Swiping the phone, she laid it on the table and let out a groan.

"Did you just hang up on Vivian?"

"Couldn't get in a word edge-wise. She kept asking questions about Agnes' death."

"El, why don't you sit? I'll make you breakfast. Eggs? Coffee? What sounds good?"

"Going back to bed and forgetting last night ever

happened." She stretched her neck. "Just coffee for now, I guess."

Shelby poured a cup of steaming coffee, added hazelnut creamer, and set it on the table along with a plate of warmed eggs and bacon saved in the oven. Shelby knew Ella wouldn't want her to make anything. She also knew she wouldn't refuse something already made.

Ella gazed up and smiled. "You know me all too well."

Shelby nodded. "I know you were talking to Vivian. But who else called? Your phone hasn't stopped ringing."

Ella ate a forkful of eggs, then sipped her coffee. "Harold called first. Then Alton. He had a few more questions. Then Gladys, Laura, Alton again. And, finally, Vivian."

Shelby carried her dishes to the sink, rinsed them, and stacked them in the dishwasher. "All about last night's gruesome discovery?"

"Harold seemed concerned they might blame him for Agnes' death. Laura needed information for the newspaper. Gladys and Viv… curious."

"Did Alton mention how she died?"

"He had the coroner's preliminary report, but didn't reveal the cause of death. During both calls this morning, he seemed extra interested in Harold and Eleanor's whereabouts. He also said he needed to talk to us again and asked if we'd rather meet at the house or shop."

Shelby shivered. "What did you tell him?"

"Said if he could make it before eight-thirty, here was fine. The shop, if after." She looked up at the clock. "Guess it will be at the shop, since it's nearly eight-thirty."

"I still can't believe it," said Shelby. "While Agnes was a pain in the rear, why would someone kill her?"

Ella sipped her coffee and finished the eggs, pushing a

tiny portion to the side of her plate for the animals. She popped the last of the bacon in her mouth. "… in the middle of a thunderstorm."

"… in that alley," said Shelby.

Ella got up and scraped part of the eggs into Oatmeal's bowl and the other onto Mr. Butterfingers' plate. "What do you make about that box they found near Agnes' body last night?"

Shelby rubbed her chin. "I'm sure the wind blew it there after we left."

Ella nodded. "Probably no big deal." Her phone buzzed on the table. She glanced at it, then at Shelby. "Should I take it or ignore it?"

"Check who's calling before you decide."

"It's Harold." Ella sunk into a chair. "Letting it go to voicemail."

"Sounds good to me. I need to get my shoes and a sweater. Be right back." Shelby went into the front room and saw one sparkly pink sneaker by the couch, though the other one was nowhere to be found. She peeked under a blanket. Behind the curtain. Next to the wingback chair. Nothing. She loved those shoes. Shelby shouted toward the kitchen. "El, you see my other shoe?"

"Not from here."

Shelby laughed. "Yeah, sorry." She glanced around and spotted the end of the sparkly sneaker in Oatmeal's bed. "What the…?" She looked down at the dog, wagging his tail. "Playing hide and seek with my shoes, eh?"

Ella rushed into the front room, holding her phone. "Harold's message…"

"What's wrong?" Shelby finished tying her shoelaces and stood.

Ella's voice tensed. "Alton just questioned him about

Agnes' murder." She leaned against the couch while Shelby listened to the message. Oatmeal nudged her leg and whined. "Alton alluded to murder last night, but he gave no details."

"You're the one who saw the body. Did it look like…?"

"I only saw her face," said Ella.

"You don't think Alton suspects one of us. Do you?"

Ella went over to the front window and stared outside. Tiny buds appeared on the branches of small trees. Soon the front yard would be a wash of green again. She turned and shook her head. "We were in the room with everyone else…"

"Not everyone," said Shelby. "When Agnes left, so did Harold, Eleanor, and Vivian."

"I can't imagine any of them… I don't even want to think about it." Ella turned and gazed outside again.

"El, right now we're just speculating on what might have happened. While I don't look forward to talking to Alton, it might be prudent to wait until we know more before jumping to conclusions."

Glancing down at her phone, Ella nodded. "We need to leave if we're going to meet him before customers show up." She sighed. "Not how I wanted to start the day."

After the women bid goodbye to the pets, they left the house and headed into town. Ella asked Shelby to drive so she could reply to emails on her phone. Not only had she received several calls, but her inbox was also full. Crafters apologized for not making last night's meeting. Others asked about the expansion. Kent followed up with suggestions for obtaining low-to-no-cost supplies. Ella looked up from her phone as Shelby parked. "That was a quick trip."

"Same as always, you were just pre-occupied." She

pointed to a police car parked at the far end of the lot. "Yellow tape is still up. There's Alton."

Ella groaned. "Would you rather chat with him first or make coffee?"

Shelby laughed. "Coffee."

"Thanks," said Ella, slamming the car door. They walked across the lot and met Alton at the front entrance.

He nodded. "Morning. Sorry, I didn't make it out to the house. Needed to come back and go over the crime scene again."

Ella unlocked the shop door, then looked up at him. "You get any sleep last night?"

He shook his head and covered a yawn. "After the coroner found marks on the body, Officer Williams and I spent hours searching for a murder weapon."

"Marks? What marks?" Shelby asked as they walked inside the shop.

Alton raised an eyebrow. "You know, I rarely give out this much information. But you two seem to have a knack for—"

Shelby put her hands on her hips. "One time. And that was pure luck."

Alton shook his head. "Solving that murder last year was more than luck. You had a way of talking to people and finding out more than I could in that short amount of time."

"Maybe, but who knows?" Shelby took off her sweater and tucked it behind the counter. "If y'all don't need me right this minute, I'll go make coffee. Be right back."

"So, what happened last night?" asked Ella. "And how can we help again?"

Alton leaned on the counter. "Think back to last night. Did anyone have a sharp object?"

Ella frowned. "Sharp object?"

He cleared his throat. "When the coroner examined the body, she noted puncture marks on the victim's side."

Ella gasped.

Shelby walked up, drying her hands with a paper towel. "Coffee's brewing. Did I hear you mention puncture marks?"

Alton pulled a small, ragged notebook from his shirt pocket. He flipped through and stopped. "Victim stabbed twice through the ribs directly into the heart…"

"With what?" asked Ella.

"We're not sure." He looked at Ella, then Shelby. "Whatever was used, the murderer removed it and Agnes bled to death."

Ella put a hand to her face. "Oh no."

"Do either of you remember sharp objects from last night?" asked Alton.

"The sign," said Shelby.

Ella turned. "That's not a sharp object."

"Not the sign. Kent used the long screwdriver to fix the broken sign."

Ella nodded. "Didn't he give it back to you?"

Shelby walked behind the counter and pointed to a spot near the cash register. "I left it here in case we needed it again. Now it's gone." She pulled out drawers and looked inside the cash register. Shelby looked at Ella and Alton. "I can't find it."

"Paige brought a pie with a knife," said Ella.

Alton flipped back a page in his notebook. "Coroner's report said a thin object… Long and rounded, not flat. Close your eyes and try to remember who was in the room and what they held in their hands."

Except for the sound of coffee brewing and Alton's raspy breathing, it was quiet. Ella closed her eyes and pictured the room. Gladys and her cloth bag. Susan, though Ella didn't think she'd brought anything. She squeezed her eyes tighter… then opened them. "Harold was using one of his fancy silver monogrammed pens."

Alton made notes. "Anything else?"

Shelby paced and mumbled to herself. A moment later, she stopped and stared at them. "I just remembered something. But, she couldn't have done it…"

Ella went over to Shelby and touched her arm. "Who are you talking about?"

"Eleanor. She brought her knitting bag and was working on some project."

Ella stared at Alton.

He flipped back a page. "Eleanor Morgan? Didn't she leave with Agnes and the others?"

Shelby nodded.

"Do you remember what happened to her knitting bag?" he asked.

Ella looked at Shelby, then back to Alton. "It was missing after she left."

CHAPTER FOURTEEN

After Alton seemed satisfied with Ella and Shelby's answers, he put on his jacket and showed himself out of The Bee's Knees. Following his departure, Ella opened the shop for several customers waiting outside.

Shelby nodded to a young couple and two women as they passed by, then leaned in close to Ella. "El, you don't think Eleanor could have…?"

Ella shrugged. "It's all too bizarre."

The front door swung open. Vivian hurried in, tossed a canvas bag behind the counter, and rushed over to the women. "Ella," she said, catching her breath. "I need to talk —"

"Viv, can it wait?" Ella motioned to two older women perusing Laura's lavender butters.

Shelby walked over to Laura's booth and pointed to a jar. "Guaranteed to bring calm."

A white-haired woman wearing a lime-green pantsuit lifted her glasses and scrutinized the label. "You've used it?"

"I wouldn't be without it," said Shelby.

Ella left Vivian at the counter and joined Shelby. "That stuff works wonders."

The other woman looked at her friend. "Do you think we should try it, Claire?"

Claire regarded Shelby. "What about for headaches? Mavis gets the worst migraines…"

"I haven't had one since I started using it," said Shelby.

The women eyed each another and grabbed two jars each. Claire elbowed her friend. "Mavis, better stock up since we won't be back this way for a while." Heading to the counter, they discussed liniments and potting soil. A moment later, Mavis rushed back and tucked two more jars under her arm. "Just in case." She gave Shelby a wide grin and joined her friend. Ella rang up and bagged their purchases and the women left the shop chatting about their newfound migraine cure.

Shelby traced a circle on the floor with the toe of her sneaker and watched Vivian pace. "El, go chat with her. Something has her riled up."

"I just can't listen to any more gossip," said Ella. "I love Vivian, but sometimes she gets caught up in what's going on. It's hard for her to separate reality from rumors."

"But she might just need to talk. You know, she was outside last night when everyone left. Maybe she knows something."

"I suppose you're right."

As Ella walked around the counter, Shelby reached out to her. "Wait. I just thought of something that might be important."

Ella stopped. "What's that?"

"Remember a few days ago when I overheard Eleanor and Gladys talking?"

"Too much has happened. Remind me."

"Eleanor said she couldn't let Agnes do something to Harold because of something. She vowed to stop Agnes, no matter what it took."

Ella leaned closer. "Think we should have mentioned that to Alton?"

"Mention what? I only heard part of their conversation and didn't know what thing they were talking about. I'd hate to say something that might——"

"——make her look like a suspect?"

"El, we were all there last night. That puts us in an awkward position. During the meeting, four people left. Later, one was murdered."

"If we have information, we should share it with Alton. Unless... Are you protecting Eleanor?"

"I think we should talk to her first——" Shelby paused when footsteps approached.

Vivian stood a few feet back and motioned to her phone. "Pardon the interruption Ella thought you'd want to know we'll be a little short on volunteers this afternoon."

Ella picked up the volunteer sheet and scanned it. "Who canceled?"

Vivian shifted her feet. "Most everyone."

"What are you talking about?" asked Ella. "We had Eleanor, Gladys, Vickie, and Lilibeth scheduled."

"Gladys called. She'll either be late or won't be in at all. While I was talking to her, I got a voice message from Eleanor. She's sick."

"What about Vickie?"

"She tried to call in sick too, but I told her to show up because we were short-handed. Mom's prerogative to guilt her daughter into coming in."

Shelby raised an eyebrow.

Ella glanced up at the antique wall clock. "Hopefully, we'll be okay with just Vickie if Gladys doesn't make it."

Vivian waved her phone at Ella. "I can stay."

"Great," said Ella. "You up to staying this afternoon, Shel?"

She nodded. "Just need to grab some lunch. What do you ladies want?"

"I brought a cucumber sandwich from home." Vivian smiled. "Don't want to be a bother."

Shelby touched Vivian's arm. "It's my treat. Save the sandwich for later." She gestured at the Pizza Palace across the street. "Let me know what toppings y'all want. I'll call it in and pick it up."

After they settled on a few mouthwatering choices, Shelby left the shop, hoping it would give Ella and Vivian a chance to talk. It also gave her a chance to check an earlier voicemail. She swiped the icon and listened. But before the message played out, she punched delete and shoved the phone in her pocket.

Walking north on Pinecone, Shelby rubbed her hands together since she'd left her gloves at the shop. On the corner, waiting for the light, she glanced up at the pewter clouds shifting across the sky. After the light changed, she made her way across the street alongside a short, squat woman walking a snuffling boxer-type dog. At the corner, the woman kept walking and Shelby turned left and headed south.

As Shelby grabbed the cold metal handle outside the Pizza Palace, a car's backfire caught her attention. She stepped back into the shadow of the doorway and observed the parking area of Act One Theatre across the street. The door of a late-model gray sedan opened. Two women wearing oversized hats and dark-colored scarves rushed across the parking lot. They looked around, slipped into a side door, then disappeared. While their faces were almost covered, Shelby felt a twinge. It was two of the missing crafters—Eleanor and Gladys.

CHAPTER FIFTEEN

Outside the Pizza Palace, a deep voice brought Shelby out of her thoughts. "Going in or staying out?"

She glanced up at a thin gentleman wearing a tweed cap holding the door. "I'm so sorry," said Shelby. "Going in."

The man walked out and tipped his hat. "Have a lovely day."

"Thanks." Shelby peered out of one of the leaded windows and scanned the parking lot north of the Pizza Palace. What were Gladys and Eleanor doing at the Theatre? She glanced down at her phone, silencing another call. The pizza would take about fifteen minutes, giving her a chance to watch for the wayward women.

Shelby inquired about the status of her order, used the restroom, and rushed back to the window. *What the…?* It had only been a few minutes. She hurried to another window, hoping to get a better view, but no matter where she stood, the gray car was already gone.

Shelby cracked her knuckles and plopped down on an antique oak bench. The tempting aromas of pepperoni, pineapple, and yeasty dough enveloped her.

"Hon, is that you?"

Looking up, Shelby scrutinized the vaguely familiar face of a silver-haired woman wearing a tapered denim jacket and bright jade-green pants. "I know I've seen you recently. But I'm terrible with names…"

"I'm Trudy Denton," said the woman. "We met at Dr. Furst's office. I was waiting to see the vet with my cat. If I remember, yours wasn't too happy."

Shelby jumped up. "Trudy. Of course. With the cats named after the *Pride and Prejudice* characters."

Trudy chuckled. "I thought you were bad with names."

"People, I forget," said Shelby. "Book characters and animals, those stay with me. By the way, how is he doing?"

"According to the vet, Mr. Darcy is fit as a fiddle." The women sat on the bench. "And your boy?" asked Trudy.

"Much happier at home." Shelby pointed to a to-go bag on Trudy's lap. "I see you've already eaten."

"Best calzone in town. One will last me a few meals." She leaned close to Shelby. "It's my monthly indulgence."

"Shelby?" A twenty-something, red-haired woman with dangly silver earrings placed a square white box on the counter. "Large combo, double pepperoni, extra pineapple, to go."

"That's my order." Shelby went and picked up the box, then walked back to the wooden bench. "If you're not busy, Trudy, you should come by the shop."

She scrutinized a small silver watch pinned to her jacket. "I have time before my quilt club meeting. Perfect opportunity since I've been meaning to drop in."

"Great. It's just across the street. We can walk together."

Passing the register, the cashier held out a small paper bag. "Don't forget your napkins, peppers, and parmesan cheese." Shelby thanked her, then walked outside with

Trudy. She took one last peek at the Theatre parking lot, but still no sign of the car. Waiting for the light, she turned to her new friend. "So tell me about your quilt club."

"There's about six of us regulars working on a sampler quilt for an upcoming charity auction."

As the light changed, they stepped off the curb and proceeded across the street. "A sampler quilt?" asked Shelby.

As the women walked, Trudy used her hands to imitate a large square. "Each of us makes quilted blocks about this big, pieced together with different fabrics. We come up with our own block patterns, then sew them together to form one quilt." When they arrived at The Bee's Knee's door, Trudy held the door open for Shelby.

Ella and Vivian met them at the counter. Shelby placed the box on top and motioned to the women. "Ladies, this is Trudy Denton. We met at the vet's office last week."

Ella offered her a hand. "Nice to meet you, I'm Ella. Did I hear you talking about quilting?"

"Yes, you did," said Trudy. "Are you a quilter?"

"Not anymore." Ella opened the lid. Steam escaped, along with the sweet and tangy odors of freshly baked pizza. "My grandma. She used old scraps and leftovers from sewing projects. Grams taught me several patterns... Will you join us for lunch?"

Trudy held up her bag. "Thank you, but I'd just finished lunch when I saw Shelby."

Vivian grabbed a thick slice and laid it on a paper towel. She eyed Trudy. "You attend the button meetings, don't you?"

Trudy glanced at Viv's name tag and snapped her fingers. "Vivian. I remember seeing you there a few months ago. Guess I've missed several meetings since then." She winked at Shelby. "See, I forget names, too."

Shelby smiled. "Glad I'm not the only one." The front door opened. She turned to see Laura had entered, then nodded to Ella. "Didn't see her name on the roster for today."

Laura breezed up to the women, her linen blouse flowing behind her. "Just dropping off the weekly newspaper. Oh, yummy. Pizza looks scrumptious."

"Stay and have a slice," said Shelby. "There's plenty."

Laura paused for a moment, then shook her head. "Maybe next time." She placed the newspapers on the counter. "Sorry to be the bearer of sad news. Isn't it just a shame about Agnes?"

Trudy stiffened. "What are you talking about?"

Shelby touched Trudy's arm. "Oh no. You knew Agnes? I'm so sorry for you to find out about her death this way."

Laura looked at the women, wide-eyed. "It's in today's edition."

Trudy picked up a copy of the newspaper. Flipping through it, she tucked it under her arm then gave everyone a wry smile. "I'm not one to speak ill of the dead. But after what Gladys told me, I'm not surprised."

CHAPTER SIXTEEN

E lla picked up a copy of the local newspaper from the stack on the counter of The Bee's Knees. Pondering Trudy's off-the-wall comments about Agnes' death, she browsed through *The Pheasant Valley Roost*... Guitar sale at Poisy's Noise. Buy one, get one pie free at the Corner Café. Auditions for *Arsenic and Old Lace* at Act 1 Theatre... A few pages later, she came across the article on Agnes but dropped the paper on the counter. Reading it would rile her up again, and she didn't need that. She grabbed a piece of pizza and joined Shelby in the sitting area, leaving Vivian and Trudy to chat.

Easing into the upholstered folding chair, she bit into the gooey slice.

"You and Vivian have time to talk?" asked Shelby.

Ella nodded and swallowed. "Viv said Alton stopped by her house this morning. Since she was one of the last people to see Agnes before her death, he had a lot of questions." Ella took a sip of water and wiped her chin. "He asked her about Eleanor, too, since he hasn't been able to reach her."

Shelby straightened. "That reminds me… You wouldn't believe who I saw when I picked up lunch."

"Mind if we join you two?" Trudy stood next to Shelby's chair as Vivian took the seat next to Ella. Vivian balanced a plate on her knees and ate.

Trudy glanced around, her eyes taking in the different crafters' booths. "Can't believe I've never been in here, Ella. You have the most charming place."

"Thank you." Ella stood and motioned to her empty chair. "Would you like to sit? I need to help customers."

"Thanks, but I'll browse a bit." She turned, then stopped and looked back at Ella. "I hope you don't mind an inquiring question. Gladys mentioned you might expand the store soon."

"Yes, that's true." Ella smiled. "Why do you ask?"

"The gals and I make quilts, plus I host a poetry group, and a once-a-month book club…"

Tossing her plate in the trash, Ella followed alongside Trudy as she walked up an aisle. "My goodness," said Ella. "You're a busy lady."

Trudy laughed. "That doesn't include my button club, volunteering at the library, or choreography coordinator at the theatre. I try to stay busy. Keeps my mind sharp."

"Trudy was asking about the expansion," said Ella as Shelby joined the women.

Trudy nodded. "I'd like to rent a space for our book club to meet."

"Never even thought about hosting community events," said Ella.

"Me either," said Shelby. "Though we should consider it if scheduling isn't going to be a problem."

Trudy checked a silver watch on her jacket. "Oh my. Look at the time. The quilting gals will wonder what happened to me." She waved to the women. "It was a pleasure meeting you, Ella. Vivian, see you at the next button meeting."

Shelby watched Trudy leave while Ella helped a middle-aged man with bushy eyebrows find Kent's woodworking booth.

When Trudy walked outside, she waited for someone walking up the sidewalk wearing a wide-brimmed hat. Shelby realized it was Gladys and watched them from inside the shop. They hugged, then chatted. Both were engaged in an animated conversation and pointed across the street several times.

Shelby walked up to Ella and motioned to the women. "Lively conversation."

"No kidding," said Ella. "Maybe they're discussing last night's events."

Shelby turned and looked around. "Speaking of last night's events, where's Viv?"

"Little girl's room," said Ella. "Why, what's up?"

Shelby lowered her voice. "I overheard you mention no one had seen Eleanor since last night."

Ella nodded. "She called in sick today."

"Yes, but if you recall, Vivian said Eleanor called in when Gladys was on the phone. She supposedly left a voice message. I wonder if Vivian really talked to her."

"And this is important, because?"

Shelby glanced around again. "When I picked up lunch, I thought I saw Gladys and Eleanor sneak into the theatre across the street."

"Are you sure?"

"One woman was wearing the same hat Gladys has on right now. And the other, well, let's just say she resembled Eleanor. Same height. Same build."

The front door opened again and Gladys came in, rubbing her hands together. "Cold outside." She marched behind the counter, placed her floppy hat under the shelf, and picked up the volunteer sheet. "Such a treat seeing Trudy."

"Yes," said Ella. "Nice woman." She thought back to what Shelby had just told her. "I thought you told Viv you'd be in late today."

Gladys looked up at the clock and then wrote her time on the sheet. "My errands didn't take as long as expected." She continued to stare at the sheet and run her finger over the list of names. Her finger hovered over Eleanor's name, then continued.

Ella caught Gladys' eye as she looked up. "Viv mentioned Eleanor wouldn't make it in. Something about a terrible cold?"

"Really?" said Gladys. "That's too bad. Haven't talked to her since last night. She was out in that storm, you know. Hope she didn't catch pneumonia."

Shelby stepped closer. "Gladys, have you seen her today?"

Gladys cleared her throat and straightened. "I meant to check up on her..." She turned to Ella. "I should quit my gabbing. What do you need me to do?"

Ella looked at Shelby, then back at Gladys. "Only a few customers right now. We have time to chat."

Vivian came back from the restroom, wiping her hands on a paper towel. "You talking about Eleanor? No one's heard from her... except when she left that message."

Gladys' eyes darted from Ella to Shelby, then to Vivian. "She said she was sick. I'll check on her later if it will make all of you feel better." She paused, then focused on the newspaper, still open to the page about Agnes. "Oh my goodness. No."

"I'm so sorry…" Ella placed her hand on Gladys' trembling arm and closed the paper. "Are you okay?"

Jerking her arm away, Gladys stepped back. "I need to go." She grabbed the newspaper from the counter and rushed out the door.

CHAPTER SEVENTEEN

Shelby and Ella watched Gladys rush out of The Bee's Knees. "I've never seen her act like that," said Ella.

Vivian went behind the counter and held up Gladys' hat. "I've never seen her go anywhere without this."

"Maybe one of us should make sure she's okay," said Ella.

Vivian nodded. "I can take it to her later if you—"

"—Shelby had plans to go see Ed and Gladys."

"I did?" *What was Ella talking about?*

Ella turned and stared at Shelby with wide eyes.

"Oh… yes," said Shelby. "Now, I remember. I had plans to go see her… um, button collection?"

The front door opened and Lilibeth came in. "Hi everyone." She bent down and brushed something off pants.

Vivian walked up to her daughter. "I thought you were sick, hon."

Lilibeth shrugged off her thick sweater and held it close to her chest. "I was exhausted. When I got home last night, John wasn't home. I couldn't reach his cell and didn't know if the ewes were lambing or what was going on."

"Oh, no," said Shelby. "Was everything okay?"

Signing in on the volunteer sheet, she looked at everyone, then nodded. "Turns out the neighbor tried to install a dishwasher, but a hose came loose. They had water everywhere and called John for help. Walking home, John heard coyotes, and checked on the animals to make sure everything was okay."

Vivian touched Lilibeth's arm. "And then what happened?"

"John stayed outside until everything calmed down. By the time he came in, it was well after one in the morning. He tossed his wet, muddy clothes in the washing machine and took a shower before coming to bed. Of course, I couldn't fall asleep until I knew everything was okay." Vickie picked a strand of hay from her sweater. "I was also late because I helped him feed the animals this morning."

Vivian picked a few more strands off the sweater, then grinned at her daughter. "Sure you two weren't rolling in the hay?"

"Seriously, Mom?" Lilibeth shoved her sweater behind the counter and laughed. "Sometimes we get more hay on us than in their feed troughs." She turned to Ella. "What do you need done? I don't mind working in the storeroom again."

"You've been busy in there lately," said Ella. "How many more boxes do we need to go through?" They walked toward the back of the store, leaving Shelby with Vivian.

Vivian pointed to an article in the paper. "Bag of books for two dollars at the Comet Book Store."

Not in the mood for small talk, Shelby took up where Ella left off. "You mentioned you took the call from Eleanor this morning."

Vivian nodded, but said nothing.

"Eleanor never misses a shift. So she must be quite sick."

"I suppose. Didn't really pay attention to how she sounded since I was talking to Gladys when the call came in."

Something struck Shelby as odd. Vivian had told them Eleanor left a message, and she listened after finishing her call with Gladys.

"Did you save the voice message?"

Vivian took off her glasses, pulled a tissue from her sweater sleeve, and wiped each lens. "I didn't… save it… I mean, I didn't think it was necessary…" Her eyes became watery, and her nose turned red. "I'm so forgetful…"

"Vivian, it's okay. I was just concerned."

She wiped her eyes with the same tissue she'd used to clean her glasses. "This whole Agnes thing has got me going in circles."

Shelby patted her arm. "I didn't mean to upset you…" *Now what?*

"Between Alton's visit this morning," she sniffed. "And Eleanor's dis… I mean, sickness… I'm just not thinking." Vivian opened her mouth to say something else, then stopped.

Shelby grabbed a bottle of water and handed it to her. "Why don't you go sit and relax for a bit? You've had a stressful morning."

Vivian accepted the water, mumbled something to herself, and wandered back to the sitting area as Ella came back from the storeroom.

While Shelby was trying to figure out another way to question her, the bushy eye-browed man came up to the counter, lugging two heaping baskets. He groaned, lifting them onto the counter. "Too many choices. Couldn't pass them up." Smiling, he took out his wallet.

"We have a lot of talented crafters." Shelby rang up each item, then wrapped and bagged them.

He tapped his finger on the paper laying on the counter. "Hometown newspaper?"

"Yes."

"I'd love to read it. How much for an out-of-towner who's considering a move up to your lovely mountain community?"

"Free," said Shelby. "Especially for a new neighbor."

"That's mighty nice of you. Name's Hank, by the way."

"Shelby. Nice to meet you, Hank."

Hank paid for his purchases, then tucked the paper under his arm. He grabbed the bulging bags and staggered toward the front door.

Ella hurried to hold it open for him, then came back over to where Shelby was standing. "Where's Viv?"

She pointed to Vivian who was now pacing. "As we talked about Eleanor's message, she became flustered."

Ella glanced at Vivian, then at Shelby. "You know she's incapable of lying, right?"

Shelby leaned against the counter and tapped her chin. "What do you suppose she and Gladys are hiding?"

CHAPTER EIGHTEEN

S helby acted on Ella's not-so-subtle suggestion to follow up on Gladys. Grabbing the woman's hat from under The Bee's Knees' counter, she left the shop.

A few minutes later, Shelby pulled up to a four-way stop and turned south on Maple. The drive out to the Purcell's home was a pleasant change of scenery. Snow-capped mountains rose above a foggy haze. Crows skimmed the tops of pine trees, calling to each other along the way. Rows upon rows of apple trees displaying tiny pink buds greeted her as she turned off the main road onto their vast property. Last time she'd been out there with Ella, the dark, foreboding trees scared her. During the day, it was much more inviting.

Shelby drove up the dirt-covered side road until she reached a mailbox with PURCELL on it. Parking her jeep, she grabbed Gladys' hat and walked up the gravel path. A fluffy shepherd mix pup bounded near, gave a playful growl, then raced after a fast-moving critter behind a group of parked cars.

Taking in a deep breath, Shelby noticed how the smoke

from the chimney left a woodsy scent in the air. Empty flowerpots lined the exterior wall of the front porch. No doubt Gladys was waiting until the last freeze before planting.

Shelby knocked on the door and waited.

No response.

She knocked again.

Still nothing.

Scanning the wall above the flowerpots, Shelby spotted a vintage door knocker—solid brass with an ornate pull chain attached to a rustic bell. *Such a unique piece.* She pulled the chain and waited.

Moments later, Ed opened the door. He peered through a dusty screen door. "Can I help you?"

"Mr. Purcell, I mean, Ed… It's Shelby. I was here last year with Ella…"

"You must be here for the meeting." He pushed open the door. "Better hurry, they've already started." Walking through his converted den with all the police scanners, also known as his shack, Ed pointed to another adjoining room.

Shelby didn't know what meeting Ed was talking about, but figured she'd go along with it out of curiosity. Approaching an open space with large windows overlooking the property, she heard women's voices.

"Here ya go," Ed whispered, then turned and walked away.

Six women sitting in a half-circle focused on a stout silver-haired woman wearing a white pantsuit and a bright red scarf. "And these…" she opened a wooden box. "Are French Cloisonné." She picked several objects out of the box and placed them on a felt-lined tray. "Notice the delicate hand-painted details."

Though Shelby tried to be quiet, Gladys' hat caught on

a low table. She stumbled, hitting her shin. Yelping in pain, the women turned and stared at her.

"Oh, Shelby." Gladys jumped up. "So, um, good to see you. I didn't realize you'd be coming today."

Shelby held up the hat with one hand while massaging her aching shin with the other. "You left this at the shop."

"You didn't have to go to all that trouble to bring it back." Gladys regarded the other women. "But as long as you're here, might as well join us."

Shelby scanned the room and smiled. Except for Gladys, none of the women looked familiar, which was odd. Being in Pheasant Valley the last four months, she thought she'd met just about everyone when they'd come into the shop or while she was running errands.

Gladys cleared her throat. "Oh, where are my manners? Meet the members of my button club. That's Ruby in the red scarf. And Jeannie, Dee and her twin sister, Betty, and… Clara."

Shelby nodded. "Nice to meet y'all."

Ruby motioned to Shelby. "Nice to see you young gals interested in buttons. Come sit over here." The women scooted around to accommodate another chair and, though she felt welcome, Gladys' fidgeting made her uneasy.

Jeannie smiled and waved a frail hand as Dee and Betty took turns acknowledging Shelby. With matching white hair and round, silver-framed glasses, it was hard to tell the twins apart. She glanced at Clara, but the woman didn't bother to acknowledge her, focusing on a notebook instead. *Maybe she was shy around strangers.*

Gladys patted Shelby's shoulder. "Tea? Coffee? Or maybe a glass of wine?" She held up a half-empty glass and giggled. "We like to indulge… a bit."

"Tea sounds good. Thank you."

When Gladys headed to the kitchen, Clara dropped her notebook and followed while Ruby continued to talk about the painted vintage buttons. "Although mine appraised at a lot less, individual buttons like these in mint condition can be worth over five thousand dollars…"

Shelby blinked. When the other women didn't seem surprised, she tried to hide her shock. Five thousand dollars for a button? She'd never been close to anything so small worth so much money in her life. The women passed around the buttons, making comments on clarity and other terms she didn't understand.

When Dee (or was it Betty?) handed the tray to Shelby, she wasn't sure what to do and just stared at it.

"Won't bite you," laughed the woman.

Shelby looked at her and gave a half-smile. "I don't want to damage it if it's worth so much."

Ruby waved her hand. "They're old. And been through a lot of wear and tear. You can't hurt them, dear."

Shelby took the tray from the white-haired woman and set it on her lap. After studying the buttons, she picked one up. "Such delicate features. I can't believe it's lasted so long." As she admired it, Gladys and Clara came back into the room talking in hushed tones. Shelby placed the button back on the tray and handed it to the woman next to her. Turning her head, she hoped to listen in.

"No," whispered Gladys. "Stay. It will be fine…"

Clara's voice tensed. "But what if she figures it out?"

CHAPTER NINETEEN

"Viv, would you watch the counter for a bit? I need to take this trash out to the alley." Ella buttoned her thick sweater, slipped on her gloves, and walked to the front door of The Bee's Knees.

"No problem," said Vivian. "Oh, those are cute. Are they new?"

Ella glanced down at her blue leather sneakers. "Shelby gave them to me. Glittery stars and all."

"They're darling."

"Hate to admit, they wouldn't have been my first choice shopping for myself." She turned her foot and laughed. "But they're super comfortable and I really like the glitter."

Once outside, Ella walked around the corner of her building and into the alley. She avoided the taped-off area where they'd found Agnes. Shivering, she tossed the trash into the dumpster and turned around. As she walked, her sneaker landed on something. It rolled, almost causing her to stumble. When she regained her balance, Ella squatted to see what she'd stepped on. "Oh my," she said out loud. "A knitting needle."

Reaching out to touch it, Ella jerked back her hand. *Is this what Alton had been searching for when they'd mentioned Eleanor's missing knitting bag?* She took her phone out, removed her glove, swiped the screen, and called Alton.

Only getting his voice mail, she left a message. "Alton, this is Ella. I found something in the alley that might interest you regarding Agnes' death. Please call or come to the shop. I'll be here until five." She ended the call and put on her glove.

Now what? It was too cold to wait outside, yet she didn't want to walk away and leave the item out in the open. As Ella paced the width of the alley, her thoughts went back to what Alton had said—a long, sharp object might be the murder weapon. She gazed down. *Could it be?* And, if it was, did she just get DNA evidence on the bottom of her new shoe?

Ella's phone buzzed. Off with the glove again. She made a mental note to buy gloves she could use with her phone. "Alton, yes I called. I found something that might be import... half an hour... or more? Well, it's a knitting needle... I stepped on it... No, I didn't touch it, just my shoe... It's outside the taped-off area..." Her phone signaled an incoming call. She held it away from her ear and glanced at the screen. *Shelby.* She listened to Alton again. "What was that? Okay. Thanks. I'll wait..."

Her fingers were so stiff from the cold, Ella struggled to swipe the screen and end the call. Unable to leave, she returned Shelby's call. Her teeth chattered, waiting for Shelby to answer. "Sorry, Shel. Was on the phone with... You're on your way back, but stopping to let Oatmeal out and give them treats... Twenty minutes. Okay, see you soon." She put on her glove and dropped the phone in her pocket again. She hugged herself, wishing she'd worn a coat.

As Ella contemplated ways to stay warm without disturbing potential evidence, a Pheasant Valley patrol car pulled into the alley. Expecting Alton, it surprised her to see Officer Williams exit the vehicle. He stood, stretched his legs, then reaching back inside, he grabbed his forensic toolbox and shut the door. "Ma'am. Sargent Nolan said you might have found something of interest."

Ella pointed to the knitting needle. "Not sure, but I thought someone should know."

"You touch it?" he asked in his high-pitched voice.

"Only with my shoe."

"Ma'am?"

"I stepped on it by mistake."

After taking several pictures with his phone, he put on a pair of protective gloves. He crouched down, picked up the knitting needle, and dropped it in a plastic bag. Williams looked up at Ella. "Going to need your shoe."

"You're kidding, right?"

"No, ma'am."

"But these were a gift. First time I've even worn them…"

"Ma'am, we need to send it to the lab. Might contain trace evidence…"

Ella gritted her teeth. "When will I get it back?"

"After the case is closed." He opened another, larger bag and held out his gloved hand. "I'll give you a receipt."

"That's not the point." Ella balanced on her other foot and removed the tainted sneaker. Frozen raindrops dotted the alley and Williams's jacket. Ella pulled her sweater tighter, though the icy rain still pummeled her exposed face. "I need that shoe back sooner than later…"

The forensics officer dropped Ella's shoe into a plastic

bag, then closed it. "You'll have to talk to the Sargent. I'm only here to collect evidence."

Realizing she wasn't getting anywhere; Ella shook her head and sighed. "Do I need to stay here or can I go back inside? It's cold and raining. And now I only have one shoe…"

"No problem, ma'am. If I have questions, I have your contact information." He wiped rain from his forehead with the corner of his sleeve and handed her a receipt. "Thank you."

Ella hopped out of the alley. Once on the sidewalk, she walked back to the shop on the icy walkway, trying to keep as dry as possible. It was a lost cause. By the time she got inside, she was soaked.

Vivian pointed to Ella's wet, dirty sock. "You lose something?"

"Would appear that way, wouldn't it?" She limped behind the counter and blotted her ice-spattered sweater with a paper towel. Before Vivian could ask another question, Ella's phone signaled an incoming call. She held up a finger and checked the screen. Harold. Not the best timing. She let it go to voicemail.

Lilibeth strolled to the front of the store. After wiping her hands on her dusty jeans, she gave her mom a hug.

Vivian smiled and kissed her daughter on the cheek.

Ella stayed behind the counter, hoping to avoid further questions about her missing footwear. The front door opened. Shelby walked in, followed by Alton.

He unbuttoned his jacket. "Afternoon, ladies. Ella, you and Shelby have a moment to chat?"

Ella glanced down at her soiled sock. "Viv, Lilibeth, would you excuse us for a few moments?"

Mother and daughter walked to the sitting area as Shelby and Alton waited. "Everything okay?" asked Shelby.

Ella rolled her eyes. "Never a dull moment."

Alton took a notebook from his front pocket and leaned against the counter. "According to Williams, you might have found our murder weapon."

Shelby gasped. "What did I miss?"

"Sharp object in the alley," said Ella. "Promise I'll fill you in later." She patted Shelby's hand and glanced at Alton. "Did my discovery help your investigation?"

He flipped through his notebook and nodded. "Yes, for the investigation. But not looking good for Eleanor."

Ella straightened. "What do you mean?"

He cracked his neck. "She hasn't returned any of my calls. No one knows where she is. And until I can interview her, she's looking more like our prime suspect."

CHAPTER TWENTY

S helby waved to an older couple leaving The Bee's Knees. "Hope to see you again." A few minutes to five, she locked the door and changed the sign to "CLOSED."

Vivian walked up, wiping her hands on a cotton towel. "Coffee pot's cleaned and ready for tomorrow morning's volunteers."

Ella looked up from her paperwork and smiled. "Thanks for staying all day, Viv." Then, she turned to Lilibeth, who was putting on a jacket. "How's the storeroom coming along?"

"Almost done. Though I'm not sure what to do with those unlabeled boxes."

"Remind me when you come in again and we'll tackle them together," said Ella.

Vivian noted her and her daughter's hours on the volunteer sheet, then donned a powder-blue jacket with a matching knitted scarf. "We'd better be on our way before the rain gets any worse."

After letting the women out, Shelby waited for Ella to

join her at the front door. "You've been extra quiet this afternoon," said Shelby.

"Between finding that knitting needle in the alley and giving up my brand new shoe..." Ella balanced on one foot as she locked up the shop. "Glad you parked at the curb, so I don't have to hop across the parking lot."

Inside the frigid jeep, Shelby rubbed her hands together. While waiting for the heater to kick in, she nudged Ella with her elbow. "Something else going on?"

Ella leaned her head against the back of the seat. "Too many things don't add up."

Shelby shifted into drive and pulled away from the curb. "Such as?"

"I'm still wondering why Eleanor would call in sick, yet not contact Alton?"

"Good question." Shelby stopped at the intersection and waited for the light.

"Then, Harold called. Twice."

"And…"

"Both times he left the same message, but it was hard to understand."

Shelby looked at her friend, then sped up. "What did he say?"

Ella removed the cell from her pocket and swiped the screen. She turned up the volume and played the messages. "I need your help—you and Shelby's. The apple doesn't fall far from the tree." The second message was the same, but with more desperation in his voice.

"What do you think it means?" asked Shelby.

"I was hoping you might know. By the way, did you notice that odd noise in the background? I can't make it out."

"Too much road noise. Let's listen again once we get

home." Shelby concentrated on the road as the pattering of rain and swish swash of wiper blades filled the void of conversation until they pulled into the driveway. "You need me to run in for your slipper or something? It's pouring."

"If you can help me up to the porch, that would be great."

Shelby offered her arm, and Ella hopped to the steps. By the time they reached the bottom one, Oatmeal's whines and scratches intensified from the other side of the front door. Shelby helped Ella up the stairs. When she opened the door, Oatmeal ran around their legs, barking.

Ella leaned down and petted the fluffy, quivering dog. "Yes, I missed you, too."

Mr. Butterfingers sat on the edge of the couch swishing his tail. Shelby scratched his ears, then went into the kitchen to reheat the previous night's chunky beef and vegetable soup.

Ella pulled off her damp sock and tossed it in the laundry room. She came back from her bedroom wearing fuzzy slippers. After letting Oatmeal out, she fed the animals while Shelby set the table.

"Feeling better?"

"Much," said Ella. "Though I'm just sick about having to give up my shoe."

"El, it's okay. You'll get it back soon enough." Ladling the steaming goodness into two bowls, Shelby placed them on the table. Almost ready to sit, she rushed back to the counter and grabbed a half-loaf of French bread. "Can't forget the best part."

Ella sliced a piece of bread. "Perfect meal for a cold, rainy night."

Shelby slurped the broth and focused on her food, as thoughts of the day swirled around in her head. She replayed the night of Agnes's death in her mind. The four people who had left. The three who might have known what happened in the alley.

"What's on your mind?" asked Ella.

Shelby looked up. "I don't understand how they missed the knitting needle after scouring the entire alley."

"Maybe someone tried to hide it. Then the rainy weather brought it back into plain sight."

"I suppose that's plausible." Shelby placed her spoon in the almost-empty bowl and tore off another hunk of French bread. "Maybe we should listen to that message from Harold again."

Ella turned her phone over and opened the voice mail icon. They leaned forward, listening.

"Once more." Shelby turned her head and cupped her ear. After it ended, she stared at Ella. "Kinda sounded like a crying baby."

Ella laughed. "Didn't think about that until now. Maybe there were people nearby."

Shelby finished her broth, then ate the leftover chunks of beef, carrots, and potatoes—in that order.

"Harold likes to multi-task." Ella pushed a carrot to the side, cut it up and fed the pieces to Oatmeal. "But it doesn't explain the message."

"True. But I'm too tired to decipher it tonight."

"Do you have the energy to tell me about your exciting trip to see Gladys?"

"That's part of the reason I'm so drained." Shelby rubbed her eyes. "Going out there was weird."

"How so?" Ella dipped a wedge of bread in her remaining broth.

"Gladys was hosting a button club meeting. The agenda on her coffee table noted it was a meeting of the Golden

Mountain Button Club. I thought Vivian and Trudy were members of that group. But they weren't there—just a bunch of women I'd never met before."

"Viv never mentioned missing her club meeting to be at the shop today. Could there be more than one club?"

Shelby frowned. "Trudy told the name of hers…" She looked up and squinted. "What was it called? Blue Ridge Button Collectors, or something similar."

"I don't recall."

"Along with the unfamiliar faces, Gladys seemed ill at ease. Like I'd barged in on a secret meeting. Do you remember when Trudy first came into the shop? She mentioned gossip about Agnes, though I don't recall the details."

"I don't either. But I'm sure you could find more info on local clubs online, which might answer some questions. And help with our sleuthing."

"Sleuthing? You think Agnes' death and the button clubs are connected?"

"Who knows?" Ella took her bowl to the sink and rinsed it out, then came back and sat. "With all this secrecy, should we get involved again?"

Shelby placed her hand on Ella's and smiled. "First, you've known Harold for a long time. He's done a lot for you, no questions asked. Second, Eleanor is our friend. How can we not?"

CHAPTER TWENTY-ONE

As the sun rose higher in the sky, Ella traced circles on the kitchen table with the tip of her finger. She refocused and looked up at her friend. "You up to a bit of investigating before we go into the shop this morning?"

Shelby sipped her coffee and nodded. "My brain kept me awake half the night, so we might as well tackle the unanswered questions. What do you have in mind?"

"Do you remember if Alton mentioned anything else about Eleanor?"

"Like what?" asked Shelby.

"How about we go sit on the couch?" Ella stood and stretched. "These wooden chairs are not good for my backside."

Shelby nodded. "Let me get my laptop. Be right back."

The animals ran ahead of the women, settling in their favorite places. Mr. Butterfingers sprawled on the back of the couch. Oatmeal sat on the middle cushion, wagging his tail. Ella laughed. "Either you two are used to our routine or understand what we're saying." After she got comfortable, Oatmeal rested his head on her lap and fell asleep.

Shelby came in and pointed to an empty cushion. "Thanks for leaving room for me." As she sat, Mr. Butterfingers' purr grew louder. He kneaded a blanket on the couch and when Shelby turned toward him, he sniffed her nose, licked it, then stretched out and closed his eyes.

"Aww. A good morning kiss," said Ella.

"Maybe his way of saying we should forget the sleuthing for now," said Shelby.

Ella looked up at the mantle clock. "It's barely seven. That gives us a few hours before we need to leave."

Shelby entered her password and waited. After the machine whirred to life, she searched for local button clubs. "I found the Blue Ridge Button Society," she said, pointing at the screen. "Says they meet on the second and fourth Thursdays… four o'clock pm…"

"Where was the meeting?"

"At… the quilt shop behind The Bee's Knees."

"Seriously?" said Ella, taking a sip from her coffee cup. "That means they met Thursday before our vendor meeting."

"Yikes. That's right. I wonder who attended that meeting, then came to ours?"

"Good question." Ella inched closer to get a better look. "What else does that site show… contact info, for example?"

Shelby clicked on 'Contact Us,' and scrolled down. "It lists Agnes Cormack as president, Trudy as vice president, and Gladys as secretary."

"With Agnes gone, would that make Trudy the new president?"

Shelby glanced at Ella and shrugged. "I suppose the bylaws would explain the chain of command, or whatever it's called."

"Doesn't look like they've updated anything. Though it's only been a few days since Agnes…"

Shelby straightened. "Look at this. Minutes from last month's meeting regarding the recent election. It says Eleanor and Agnes ran for president, but they disqualified Eleanor, leaving Agnes unchallenged. Without anyone running against her, she won."

"Disqualified? Why?"

She scanned the document. "It mentions an order of business, but then the meeting went into executive session." Shelby stared at Ella. "What does that mean?"

"Executive session is when they decide to discuss a matter off the record."

"But wouldn't it reflect in the minutes?"

Ella shook her head. "Just the decision. In fact, once they call executive decision, no one may talk about what they discussed outside the meeting. Does it say anything else?"

Shelby scrolled through the document. "Only that they disqualified Eleanor from becoming president. That stinks."

"Print that out and let's keep looking. Did you find any other button clubs in the area?"

Sending the document to the printer, Shelby continued to search. "Closest one is over two hours away. And it doesn't seem like they've met in a while. The last event was over a year ago."

Ella placed Oatmeal on the floor, then retrieved the paper from the printer. "Try the name of that other club. What did you say it was? Something Mountain?"

Shelby held up her finger. "Golden Mountain…" Pausing, she read through more information. "Nothing here… but hold on. Apple Mountain. No, they're up in NorCal… Golden River, that's east of us, almost in Nevada.

Ella put her hands on her hips. "Try Mountain Button Club."

"Okay," Shelby said, typing. "Hold on... Here's a link to a Guilded Mountain Button Club. Just formed in the last month."

Ella sat again. "Where's it located?" After patting the couch cushion, Oatmeal jumped up and settled next to her.

"It lists a post office box. The zip is local, here in Pheasant Valley."

The women looked at each other.

"Does it mention when or where they meet?" asked Ella.

"Introductory lunch meeting... third Friday this month."

Ella snapped her fingers. "That was yesterday."

Shelby scanned the laptop screen. "No location listed, just a phone number to call for details."

Ella grabbed her phone. "Read me the number..."

"Are you going to call now?"

"Why not?" Ella winked. "Might answer some questions."

Shelby read the number aloud and Ella entered it into her phone. As it rang, she put it on speaker. One ring. Two rings. Three. Voice mail. "Thank you for calling the Guilded Mountain Button Club. We're sorry we missed your call. Please leave your name and number and we'll get back to you as soon as possible." Ella ended the call.

"Oh no." Shelby gestured to the phone. "Did you recognize that voice?"

"No, why?"

Her eyes widened. "El, if I didn't know better, that sounded like Eleanor. Call and play it again. At full volume."

Ella swiped her phone, pushed redial, and turned it up

to the highest setting. They listened as the message played a second time.

Shelby pointed to the screen. "Did you hear that?"

Ella ended the call. "Crying babies? Wasn't that the same sound we heard in Harold's call for help?"

CHAPTER TWENTY-TWO

S helby stood up from the living room couch and stretched. "Before we go further, another cup of coffee is calling my name. Want anything, El?"

"Sounds good to me as well."

"Okay. Be back soon. In the meantime, you mind getting a notepad and pen? Might come in handy." As Shelby poured the coffee, Oatmeal came in and sat in the middle of the kitchen floor. She looked down at him. "And what are you waiting for?"

He padded up to her and barked.

"Fine. I'll give you half a biscuit. Just don't tell…"

Mr. Butterfingers walked in and sniffed the air.

Shelby laughed. "You, too?" She placed a handful of treats on the floor for the cat, then grabbed the two steaming mugs and walked back into the front room.

Ella was on her phone. She nodded to Shelby and continued to talk. "Sorry I didn't call you back, Harold… Is everything okay?" She looked up at the clock. "In fifteen minutes? It's almost eight… No, don't worry about it. See you then…"

Shelby handed Ella a mug and sat. "Don't tell me Harold's coming over this early."

Ella blew into her coffee mug, wondering what could be so important that it warranted an early-morning visit.

"Well…?" asked Shelby.

Ella smiled. "You just told me not to tell you."

Shelby rolled her eyes. "So what's going on?"

"Said he needed to talk." Oatmeal placed his paws on Ella's leg, but she nudged him down. "Coffee is not for doggies."

Shelby pointed to the dog with her spoon. "Don't let him fool you. They got treats in the kitchen."

Ella wagged a finger at Oatmeal and stood. "Someone ratted you out. I'll start a fresh pot, then bring in the carafe and another mug. I'm sure Harold will appreciate it." She went into the kitchen and opened the sealed bag of ground coffee. Looking down at her trembling hands, she rubbed them together. Should they tell Harold they'd help him? Or would it be better to keep it to themselves for now? She was concerned about her friend, now more than ever.

As Shelby cleared the coffee table, the aroma of hazelnut coffee drifted into the front room. She took in a deep breath and closed her eyes, savoring the calming scent. She wondered about Harold's sudden visit. The mysterious message. The odd noises in the background. Should they ask him more about it?

A few minutes later, Oatmeal jumped up and trotted to the entry. He barked as several sharp knocks sounded. Noticing the laptop screen's last search was still visible, Shelby closed the lid, then went over and opened the door for their guest.

Harold stood on the porch brushing rain off his coat.

"Thank you for letting me come by so early..." He walked in, took off his hat and coat, then hung them in the entry.

"You made it sound urgent." Ella came from the kitchen and offered a hug. "Come in and sit while I get you some coffee."

"Thank you." Dressed in dark blue slacks and a black cashmere sweater, he pushed up one sleeve and glanced at his gold watch. "Promise to be out of here in thirty..."

Ella came back holding a tray with a new mug, the coffee carafe, and a plate of jam-filled butter cookies. She placed it on the coffee table and sat next to Shelby as Oatmeal jumped up and settled down between them.

Harold sat on the edge of the couch. He covered a deep cough with his hand, then tapping his foot, he checked his phone several times.

Ella patted his arm. "Is everything okay?"

"Yes. Why? I mean... No, not really." He let out a ragged breath and sat back, but a moment later, sat up, staring at his phone again. He looked at Ella. "Waiting for a call..."

Ella poured coffee and handed him a cup. She cradled her own and took a sip. "Harold, your call earlier. What were you trying to tell me? Something about the apple..."

"Oh, sorry. This whole Agnes mess has me rattled. Just delete that message. It's not important."

Ella turned and glanced at Shelby, then back to him. "I've known you for a very long time and from what I remember, Harold Madrigal never gets rattled."

He looked at her, then put his cup on the table and stood. "After the argument with Agnes... Now Eleanor's missing. If they find her, they'll charge her with..." He turned away, then back again. "It's my fault. I need to talk to them and make things right."

Ella straightened. "I'm not sure I follow you. What's your fault? And who do you need to talk to?"

He walked over to the wingback chair and lowered himself into it. "Everything's my fault. After we argued and left the meeting, Eleanor and Vivian followed. Why? I do not know. The power went out. It was dark. Eleanor called to us..." He paused and glanced at his phone. "She was only trying to protect me, but I yelled at her. Told her to stay out of our business... Agnes grabbed me. Eleanor only tried to help. She swung... It was dark. The rain... Lightning. Then thunder..."

Ella leaned closer to him and placed her hand on his arm. "What happened, Harold?"

He closed his eyes. "I don't know. They had words. Angry, mean words. Agnes threatened to tell... Eleanor chased her further into the alley." He opened his eyes. "Everything happened so fast. I ran after them, but when I reached the middle of the alley, it was quiet. When the lightning flashed, I saw someone lying on the ground." He tried to suppress a cough, but it turned into a coughing fit.

Ella picked up Harold's cup from the coffee table and handed it to him. She motioned to take a drink. He sipped the coffee, then unwrapped a cough drop and sucked on it until the coughing subsided. After he recovered, he took out a monogrammed handkerchief and wiped his watery eyes. "I didn't know who was on the ground. Not knowing what to do, I rushed off."

Ella cleared her throat. "Are you saying Eleanor stabbed Agnes?"

"I don't know." He blew his nose. "I loved her and now she's gone."

Shelby sat up and whispered. "You still loved Agnes?"

He shook his head. "No. Eleanor."

CHAPTER TWENTY-THREE

E lla gasped. The front room clock ticked off the seconds as Harold's words sunk in. "I'm confused," she said. "You married Agnes? But, loved Eleanor?"

He looked at the women and nodded.

"You've mentioned nothing about this before."

"Ella, there's a lot about me you don't know." He stared at his phone again, then looked up. "I need to find Eleanor and talk to her."

"Harold, we can't help if you keep talking in circles." Ella rubbed the base of her neck, hoping to relieve the building tension.

Oatmeal jumped off the couch and placed his chin on Harold's thigh, prompting their anxious guest to scratch the dog's ears. Focusing on Oatmeal, Harold laid his cell on the table and sat back in the chair. He stared at the wall and smiled. "It was a long time ago. Eleanor was in her last year of high school. I was a freshman in college. We were in love… But her parents prevented us from seeing each other. They didn't want me to ruin her life any further…"

"I'm so sorry, Harold," said Ella.

He glared. "After fruitless attempts to convince her parents otherwise, I gave up and moved away to pursue my real estate career. Many years later, after her parents passed, I moved back, hoping we would reconnect. By then, Eleanor had been married to Richard for several years and John was in his early teens. It was too late."

Ella tucked her legs under her body. "I remember Viv saying something about John's father passing away when he was in his early twenties. That's when he dropped out of veterinary school. Viv's daughter, Lilibeth, married John a few years after that."

Harold let out a long sigh. "I wanted to be more than just friends with Eleanor, but I was engaged. When that didn't work out, I met Agnes on the rebound and we married soon after. After our divorce, I hoped Eleanor and I could start over, but close to forty years had passed…"

Harold sat up and took a cookie from the plate. "Though Eleanor never seemed interested in rekindling our relationship, we still had a connection. Like when she tried to protect me from Agnes…"

Shelby cleared her throat. "Maybe she's afraid to call."

Harold's eyes widened. "I need to know she's okay."

"You know she's sick," said Shelby.

His head jerked up. "You talked to her?"

"Not exactly. She was supposed to come into the shop yesterday, but left a message with Vivian that she wouldn't be in."

Pounding his hand on the arm of the chair, he tensed. "I feel so helpless. She's been through so much, and now this."

Ella wondered what he was referring to, but decided not to pry.

Harold checked his watch and stood. "I promised thirty minutes and don't want to overstay my welcome."

Reaching for Ella's hand, he smiled. "Thank you for listening."

She stood and nodded.

Letting loose of Ella's hand, Harold picked up his phone. He walked to the door, then slipped on his coat and hat. "If you hear anything... please let me know."

"Of course. You take care now." Closing the door, Ella went back to the couch and sat. "Unrequited love. So sad."

Shelby rubbed her chin. "You've known Harold for quite some time. Yet, he's never mentioned this to you before now?"

Ella refreshed her coffee and dipped a cookie into it. "Not that I remember. Why?"

"Do you find it odd that he's just now telling the story about Eleanor?"

"Not really. Who talks about a lost love? The man was distraught and rambling."

"El, he also reiterated the entire sequence of events surrounding Agnes' death. Then, to prove Eleanor was protecting him, he confessed the forbidden love story."

"Do you think he's trying to protect Eleanor?" asked Ella.

Shelby picked up the pad of paper and pen and made notes. "Something doesn't feel right."

Ella sipped her coffee. "What's bothering you?"

"Would someone so distraught be so exact? I mean, who remembers so many details, unless they're crafting someone's motive?"

Ella blinked. "Are you saying Harold's the killer, but trying to make it look like Eleanor?"

Shelby tapped the pad of paper. "That's one scenario."

"You have more?"

"Yes," said Shelby. "Let me run these by you. They're in

no particular order…" She made notes while she talked. "Think about it. Big argument. Harold and Agnes leave. Vivian and Eleanor bail on the meeting. Someone killed Agnes. Harold and Eleanor run their separate ways while Vivian comes back, all nervous. Then yesterday, Vivian takes the call from Gladys—who had errands, and a voice mail from Eleanor—who supposedly is sick. Honestly, I don't think Viv even talked to Eleanor."

Ella stared at Shelby. "What makes you think that?"

"It was how she reacted when I asked about it."

Ella opened her mouth to say something, but Shelby held up a finger. "Hold that thought."

Ella nodded and stroked Oatmeal's ear.

Shelby cleared her throat. "Remember when I went to get pizza and saw the two women head into the Theatre? They bore a striking resemblance to Gladys and Eleanor. I might have been mistaken, but then when I asked Gladys about it, she freaked out and left the shop."

Ella nodded. "Have to admit, I've never seen Gladys act like that before."

"And then, when I went to her home to return the hat, a bunch of women, who I'd never seen before, were having a button club meeting, which wasn't odd because maybe that's where they planned on meeting—"

"What about Harold's cryptic message? You know the one about 'the apple not falling far from the tree'? He said it was a mistake, but that's not like him at all, either."

"El, I think they all know something."

"But Gladys never went outside. She had a coughing attack, remember?"

Shelby nodded. "Did you ever consider she might have faked it to keep us from going after the others?"

Ella massaged her forehead. "You really think they are hiding something?"

Shelby eyed her friend. "Or, hiding someone."

"Should we tell Alton?" asked Ella.

"What would we say?" Shelby shook her head. "I think we should keep pressing each of them for information. Eventually, somebody will talk."

CHAPTER TWENTY-FOUR

Shelby opened an eye and checked her phone. She wasn't fond of Mondays, especially when wild gusts had pounded her bedroom wall most of the night, allowing for little sleep. Sitting up, she watched fat raindrops splatter against the windows. She pulled a thick sweater over her pajamas and went downstairs. After letting Oatmeal out, she fed the animals and made a fresh pot of coffee.

As it sputtered to life, liquid caffeine dripped into the glass pot. Shelby watched the rain hit and run down the window over the sink until a shrill beep startled her. She strolled over to the machine, filled a mug, and added two spoonfuls of sugar and a splash of milk. Just what she needed to wake up on the cold, bleak morning.

After downing her first cup, she walked down the hall and knocked on Ella's half-open door. Oatmeal followed close behind, then scampered inside, leaving the door wide open.

"Hey," said Shelby. "You gonna sleep all day? It's almost eight."

Ella rolled over. "Don't feel so good."

"Oh, no." Shelby went and sat on the edge of Ella's bed. "Can I bring you something?"

Pulling the covers away from her neck, Ella whispered, "I ache all over. Maybe some pain relievers, so I can get up and go into the shop.

Shelby held up her hand. "You need to stay home and rest." She went into Ella's bathroom, found the requested bottle, and brought it back. Placing her hand on her friend's forehead, she frowned. "I'm so sorry."

Ella eased herself up and took two pills. "My throat was scratchy last night, but I thought I was just tired."

Shelby sat on the bed. "Between stressing over the expansion and Agnes' death, you've been under a lot of pressure. I'm sure being outside in the rain last week without your shoe didn't help." She tucked the blankets close to Ella's chin. "You rest. I'll handle the store. I'm sure Oatmeal and Mr. Butterfingers will enjoy keeping you company."

Reaching for her phone, Ella winced. "Hands are so achy." She leaned back and closed her eyes.

"Just take it easy. I'll bring crackers and juice before I head out. How about some Corner Café's chicken soup for lunch?"

Ella nodded and gave a half-smile.

"Plus, it will give me a chance to check on you and let Oatmeal out. It's pretty nasty, so I don't want you going outside. Promise?"

She nodded again, then turned over and snuggled in her blankets. "Thanks."

Shelby went back into the kitchen, washed her hands, and made herself some peanut butter toast. Not enough time for a shower, she changed into her powder-blue jeans, cherry-pink sweater, thick pink socks, and sparkly sneakers.

After giving the animals their treats and taking juice and crackers to Ella, she headed out the front door.

Though the rain had stopped, the wind gusted at full force, pushing her back against the house. She gripped the porch rail, made her way down the steps, and rushed to her jeep. Pulling out of the driveway, Shelby noticed Ella's sweater in the passenger seat. She smiled, thinking about her life since she'd come back and settled in Pheasant Valley. She and Ella had spent their time together with no stress or drama. Their friendship was easy, never tiring of each other's company. Such a refreshing change from being with Mac. Though they had been together for a couple of years, Mac and Shelby always had to work hard to maintain good standing in their relationship. Shelby was proud of herself for leaving Mac and Houston behind—a past she was ready to forget.

While stopped at the four-way intersection, her phone beeped with an incoming text. Shelby glanced down. Her breath caught. She swiped DELETE without even opening it. Shelby accelerated and focused on the road, though her mind wandered until the ping of more messages startled her. She clenched her teeth and pulled into The Bee's Knees parking lot, unaware of the path she'd taken to get there.

Fat raindrops fell as Shelby opened the shop door. She switched the CLOSED sign to OPEN and turned on the lights. Though dreary-dark outside, the cheery colors of the crafters' items and the calming scent of Laura's lavender products brightened her mood. She pulled out the clipboard with the crafters' volunteer hours, but before she could check her phone's calendar, it rang. She stared at the caller ID and swiped DECLINE. An icy chill traveled down her spine. Maybe it was just a fluke.

The door opened and Paige waltzed in. "What's shakin', Shelby?"

She turned from her preoccupied thoughts and forced a smile. "Not much. You?"

"Just all the wiggly parts." Paige snorted and looked around. "Where's Ella?"

Shelby stepped behind the counter. "Not feeling well."

"Bummer." Paige pushed a button on the side of a large, round watch, then wrote her time in the slot after her name. "Hope she gets to feelin' better. Eleanor gots the p-numonia."

Shelby stared at Paige. "Did you actually talk to her?"

Paige opened her small red purse and dug through it, pulling out a stick of mint-scented gum. She unwrapped the paper, folded the gum in half, and pushed it into her mouth. "Naw, didn't talk to Eleanor. Just repeatin' what Viv told me at the Café last night. She didn't sound good either, like she was getting' sick, too."

"Hope it's not going around," said Shelby. "Probably best they all stay home and get better." She scanned the volunteer list and noted Kent and Susan were also scheduled for the morning. Gladys and Laura in the afternoon. A moment later, Kent walked in. He was wearing a faded pair of jeans, a long-sleeved dark blue t-shirt, and a charcoal-gray knitted beanie, a gift from Eleanor. When he mentioned working outside in his wood shop was difficult in the colder weather, she surprised him with an oversized cap. The way it slouched reminded Shelby of a giant chocolate kiss stuck on his head.

"Good morning, ladies," he said, smiling. "Ella around? I have some exciting news about the renovation project."

Paige smacked her gum. "Out sick." Then she turned and walked down an aisle.

Shelby stepped closer to Kent. "I can pass along your message or you can call her later."

Kent handed Shelby an envelope. "Names of all the local contractors willing to donate labor. Plus, suggestions for cheap or free materials."

"Kent, this is amazing." Shelby wanted to hug him, but held back since she didn't know him well enough. "Thanks so much. Ella will be thrilled."

He pushed up his sleeves and blushed. "No prob. Just trying to help you two out." He turned as Susan walked in, then went over to greet her.

Shelby thought they might be a couple, though they showed no affection around the shop. But just the way they talked to each other, the things they had in common, and how they always worked the same shifts made her smile. They made a cute pair, both shy and introverted. What could she say? People in love always made her happy.

An African American woman came in and gave everyone a friendly smile. Wearing a purple leopard-print dress and leggings, her hair caught Shelby's attention. It was the same purple hue as the woman's dress. She picked up a shopping basket and browsed Laura's lavender booth. After her, a steady stream of younger and older customers followed, making the morning pass by quickly. So much so that by the time she had a break it was almost noon.

She took her phone from her pocket and swiped the CALL icon. "Hey, Ella. How are you feeling? Okay, glad you got some rest... I'm headed out to pick up the soup and will be home as soon as possible." Ending the call, she glanced around to find the volunteers. Paige stood at the register, helping an older gentleman with his purchases. After checking down several aisles, Shelby spotted Kent holding a shelf and chatting with Susan. She hurried up to them. "Kent, I need to take Ella lunch and check on the animals. You guys going to be okay for a bit?"

He nodded. "Paige's shelf came loose again. You know where the screwdriver might be? I looked in the drawer, but it wasn't there."

"If you're talking about the one you used at the meeting last Thursday, it's still missing."

He looked at Shelby. "After I fixed the sign outside, I know I put it back on the counter. Right next to the apple pie box."

"I'll look into it." Shelby turned and walked back up front to get her things, remembering Alton had also been looking for the knife since the night of Agnes' murder. So odd. Screwdrivers and knives just didn't get up and disappear by themselves.

CHAPTER TWENTY-FIVE

S helby arrived home with containers of hot chicken soup and fresh-baked bread. The animals padded up to her after the front door closed. "Miss me?" She looked down at them, then went into the kitchen. A pale Ella sat at the table, sipping tea.

"I probably don't need to ask, but how do you feel?"

"About as good as I look."

Shelby smiled. "That bad, huh?"

Ella nodded. She raised her head and sniffed the air. "Something smells amazing."

Shelby left the food on the table along with the envelope from Kent. She brought over bowls and spoons, then ladled the hearty soup for each of them. Tearing a chunk off the bread she dipped it in her bowl.

"Just what I needed." Ella inhaled the steam drifting up and took a bite of crusty bread. "I'm sure I'll be feeling better by tomorrow."

"Don't rush it," said Shelby. "From what Paige told me, Eleanor has pneumonia and Viv has come down with something, too."

"When did Paige talk to Eleanor?"

"She didn't really say. I'd planned on pressing her for more information but got distracted by helping customers. Never asked. Sorry." She ate a few more spoonfuls, then looked up. "Oh, before I forget. Kent gave this to me to give to you." Shelby pushed the envelope to Ella.

"What's this?"

Shelby smiled. "Open it and see."

Ella tore it open, read it, then grinned. "This is wonderful. Looks like we'll have more than enough volunteers to help with the remodel. And look..." She laid the paper in front of them and pointed. "Discount lumber, donated supplies... I can't believe it."

Shelby patted Ella's hand. "You know everyone loves you, El. They are more than willing to help see the shop expand. It's not only going to help our crafters, but also the entire community."

Ella looked at Shelby, teary-eyed. She grabbed a tissue and wiped her cheek. "It's just so overwhelming and humbling." She sniffed. "I'm sure I'm emotional because I don't feel well."

Shelby's phone pinged with another message. She grimaced and turned it over. Fortunately for her, Ella was feeding Oatmeal bits of chicken and didn't notice. She didn't want to explain what had been happening over the last few days. Or had it been weeks? She'd tried hard to ignore it and didn't want to say anything. Not until she knew more.

Finishing her soup, Shelby glanced at her phone. "Looks like I need to head back soon. You want anything else before I go?"

Ella shook her head. "Tummy's full. Pain meds are in

the bedroom. The animals are keeping me company...
though it's not the same without you here."

Shelby smiled. "You need your rest. We'll chat when I
get home." She got up and walked to the back door. "Come
on, dog. Let's take you out again before I leave." After a few
minutes, they came back inside. Shelby gave the animals
their treats and elbow-bumped Ella. "See you a bit later."

Shelby left and walked out to her jeep. After getting in,
she stared at her phone. Shaking her head, she swiped
DELETE on three new text messages and two voice mails,
as if that would make it all disappear. Shelby knew better.
Once she wanted to find Shelby, nothing would stand in her
way until she made contact.

———

SHELBY ARRIVED BACK at The Bee's Knees just before one
o'clock. Kent and Susan walked up to her. Kent smiled.
"Hope Ella's feeling better."

Shelby nodded. "I think so. Anything exciting happen
while I was gone?"

Kent tapped his whiskered chin and thought. "Paige had
to leave for work, but otherwise it's been slow since you left.
Gladys called to say she'd be about an hour late." He
turned, then stopped. "Oh, we met the new deputy sheriff.
She's a hoot."

"Oh no. Wish I'd been able to meet her."

"Actually, she was here before you left," said Kent.

Shelby furrowed her brow. "Really? What did she look
like?"

Kent smiled. "Remember the woman wearing purple,
with the purple hair..."

"You're kidding," said Shelby. "Why didn't she introduce herself?"

Susan let out a chuckle. "She just wanted to blend in like a regular customer."

"Well, she sure stood out with that awesome hair," said Shelby.

"Apparently, out of uniform, she loves to match her hair and clothing styles," said Kent. "And what a sense of humor... LaTonya... I mean Deputy Lewis... Wonder how she and Alton will get along. I mean, they are polar opposites."

"LaTonya Lewis... When did she get into town?" asked Shelby.

Kent and Susan looked at each other. "Don't think she said," said Kent.

"Although," said Susan, "She mentioned something about staying at the motel until her furniture arrived... which should be tomorrow."

"She bring up where she moved from... or where she'd be living?" asked Shelby.

Kent shrugged. "No. Just that she just got into town, ate at the Café, and was browsing a few local stores to get a taste of the community."

"Eating at the Café is a terrific way to taste the community." Shelby laughed. "Wish I'd met her. She sounds like a lot of fun."

An older woman walked up to the front counter with full hands and Shelby went over to help. As she stepped behind the cash register, a long, thin envelope with a green sticker and bar code caught Shelby's eye. "Hey, Kent. What's this?"

"Oh, sorry. Almost forgot to tell you." He went behind the counter and handed it to her. "This came while you were gone. Hope you don't mind. I signed for it as I figured it was important."

Shelby's eyes widened when she noticed a Houston return address. Why would Lone State Title send her a certified letter?

CHAPTER TWENTY-SIX

S helby stared at the certified letter from Houston and thought back to the ignored voice mails. Maybe it would have been prudent to listen to them. Wishing she'd read the now deleted texts, her heart rate increased. While Shelby didn't know what the letter contained, it couldn't be good. Nothing from that part of her past ever was.

"Excuse me. Ma'am?" The woman tapped the counter at The Bee's Knees with her credit card. "My total?"

Shelby pushed the fearful thoughts away and turned her attention to the woman. "I'm so sorry." Though her head felt fuzzy, she did her best to focus on the register total. "That'll be twenty-nine, ninety-five. Cash or—"

"Put it on *this* card." The woman pushed the plastic at Shelby and crossed her arms.

"How about a free sample of Laura's lavender butter? Guaranteed to calm frazzled nerves..." Shelby grabbed a container and added it to the woman's cloth bag. She handed the card back and forced a smile.

The woman picked up the jar, opened the lid, and

sniffed. "If you insist." Dropping it back into her bag, she huffed out of the shop.

"Didn't know we gave away free samples," said Susan.

Shelby rolled her eyes. "We don't. But anything to keep the customer happy."

"Hope she uses it," said Kent. "The woman was gruff to me and Susan from the moment she walked in."

Shelby nodded.

Susan came up to Shelby. "We can stay longer if you'd rather go home and take care of Ella."

"She just needs rest," said Shelby. "You two go. I'm sure you have other plans." The last thing Shelby wanted to do was leave. Then she'd have no choice but to read the letter and deal with it. Staying meant she could keep busy and stave off a massive panic attack. She wished she could hide behind her comfort pillows and feel safer.

The shop's front door opened and everyone turned as Laura walked in, her long skirt flowing behind her. As she came closer, she stopped, set her bag on the carpet, and rushed to Shelby. "You okay, hon? I sense trouble deep inside."

"Just a crazy day." Shelby smiled. "Thanks for asking."

Laura placed her hands in front of Shelby, then over her head, moving them along the sides without touching her. "Your aura says differently." She picked up several springs of dried lavender and handed them to Shelby. After a quick hug, she picked up her bag, then stepped behind the counter and signed in. Making eye contact with her distraught friend, she said, "If you need to talk, hon, I'll be here all afternoon."

Shelby smiled. "Thanks." She folded the envelope in thirds, then shoved it in her back pocket. She hoped out of sight, out of mind, would help, though the folded edges against her backside reminded her of the thing she could no longer ignore.

OATMEAL SAT UP AND BARKED. He jumped off Ella's bed and ran into the other room. She turned over and glanced at her phone. It had only been a few hours since Shelby had left. *Was she already returning home? Who or what might be at the door?* Maybe they'd leave thinking no one was home. She tried to ignore Oatmeal's insistent barking and whining, but couldn't relax.

Ella rolled out of bed and steadied herself while pulling a thick sweater over her cotton pajamas. She made her way down the short hall, through the kitchen, and into the front room. She stopped, holding on to the back of the couch until a dizzy spell passed.

"Oatmeal, hush."

He trotted over to her and then back to the front door, scratching and whining.

Ella looked through the peephole but saw no one. "What are you barking at? There's nobody out there." She reached down to pet her fluffy, white dog, but he pulled away and went back to the door and growled. "Okay, fine. Let's see what's outside that has you so riled up."

She unlocked the deadbolt, pulled the door open a few inches, and scanned the front porch. Verifying the screen door was locked, she opened the door wider and peered out. She stared at her dog, then pointed outside. "Just Laura's cat visiting our porch again."

Oatmeal pushed his way through her legs, nosed the screen, and sniffed. He looked up at Ella, then let out a long, deep growl.

"What has you so upset?" Meows came from behind them. Ella turned. "And I suppose you need to check everything out, too. Huh, cat?"

Mr. Butterfingers padded over to the screen but didn't seem impressed with Oatmeal's display of protection. He walked away and jumped up on the couch.

Satisfied there was no imminent threat, Ella pushed on the door. Before it closed, Oatmeal growled, then barked. Mr. Butterfingers meowed and skittered into the kitchen.

Ella bristled when someone stomped up the front porch stairs.

"Don't close the door." A deep voice came from beyond her line of sight. "I've been looking for you."

———

ELEANOR MADE her way around the small kitchen. She turned on the faucet and cut up a large yellow onion. She kept the water running to avoid the stinging burn of onion-tears, a painful phenomenon caused by the vegetable's chemical irritant. Since Agnes' death five days earlier, Eleanor had done more than enough crying.

A few days after they'd found Agnes, her son John, hid her away in an out-building, a one-room cabin on the fiber farm's expansive property. Usually reserved for seasonal help, he told his mother it would be the best place to stay until everything calmed down. No one else knew she was there. Not his wife, Lilibeth. And especially not Harold. Gladys had tried to persuade Eleanor to stay with her and Ed, but John talked her out of it. Though she and Gladys talked by phone daily, Eleanor had never revealed where she'd been staying.

She turned off the faucet and tossed the last few chunks

of onion into a large crock pot. Six hours later, it would become a savory stew, complete with beef, carrots, peas, potatoes, and of course, onions. Eleanor gave the mixture one last stir, then added a pinch of thyme, a dash of coriander, and one more sprinkle of salt. Dropping in two bay leaves, she covered it, then wiped her hands on a dishtowel. Heading to the living area, Eleanor stood by an armchair. The only actual piece of furniture, except for a twin bed in another corner of the room. John would be there soon, as he did each afternoon, to check on her and bring groceries or other needed items.

After a set of familiar knocks at the door, she opened it. "Good to see you, John. Come in."

"Something smells good. Whatcha making?" He shrugged off his denim jacket and tossed it on the back of the chair.

"Stew. Enough to last me a few days." She gave him a quick hug, then stepped back. "Did you find everything on my list?"

John handed her a canvas tote. "I rarely shop for yarn, so I hope it will do."

Eleanor opened the bag and looked inside. "Thank you." She placed it on the chair. "Something to keep my hands busy. I don't know how much longer I can stay cooped up in here. Not able to open the curtains or talk to my friends, well, except Gladys."

"Mom, you know if you leave, Alton will take you in for questioning,"

"But I didn't… I couldn't have killed her. She was alive when I left the alley."

John looked at her. "As much as I believe you, the bigger question is, will Alton? And since you know what really happened, how long will it be until he uncovers the truth?"

"I need to call Harold." Eleanor wiped a tear running down her cheek. "He deserves an explanation."

John's eyes flashed. "He deserves nothing." He balled up his fists and pounded the back of the chair. "Stay away from him."

"John, you don't understand."

"I don't need to. I'm warning you. Harold is out to take advantage of your naïveté."

"It's not like that at all, John…"

Her son's phone signaled a received text. He pulled it out of his back pocket and checked. "Ewe's lambing. Seems in distress…" He picked up his jacket and put it on, then kissed his mom on the cheek. "Do *not* call Harold." John left, slamming the door behind him.

Eleanor locked the deadbolt and made sure the curtains were drawn. She picked up the knitting supplies and settled in the lumpy wing-back chair. She tried to get comfortable, but gave up. Fingering the long, thin, cool aluminum knitting needles, Eleanor chose a skein of thick cream-colored yarn, leaving two navy blue ones for another project.

Draping the tail of the yarn over her thumb, she attempted to cast on the first row of stitches, but her trembling hands made it impossible. After several failed attempts, she shoved the needles into the skein, then put everything back into the tote.

Eleanor got up and paced. Near the kitchen area, past the chair, and next to the bed. She knew what she wanted, more like needed, to do, but was fearful of John's wrath. But who was he to control her? Who was the parent and who was the child? Since last week, John had been acting like the parent. Eleanor was tired of it.

Enough was enough. She picked her phone off the table,

searched through her favorites, and swiped CALL. With each ring, her heart pounded faster. Her breath caught when the call was answered. She held back sobs and barely got the words out. "I'm sorry I've been avoiding your calls. We need to talk…"

CHAPTER TWENTY-SEVEN

S helby tried to keep busy at The Bee's Knees, but still checked her phone and the wall clock every few minutes. Five o'clock seemed like days away. She longed to close the shop and read the letter in her back pocket, but the thought of it triggered more anxiety and anger. Not only toward the sender, but toward herself. All attempts at positive talk escaped her. Her mind continued to focus on worst-case scenarios.

While Laura helped with the occasional afternoon customer, Shelby wandered the store. If she were into counting steps, she would have not only met, but exceeded the recommended daily goal. But she didn't wear a step counter, nor did she care to start. Too many painful memories of being shamed for her body weight. Walking by a display of wood-framed full-length mirrors, Shelby stopped. She stood back and admired her plus-sized figure, finally content with who she was and what she looked like. Now, she rejected anything and anyone who might guilt her into losing weight or keeping fit.

Gladys walked up holding a feather duster. "Hon, you're so distant today."

Shelby forced a smile. "Just sorting a few things out."

Gladys patted her arm. "By the look on your face, I'd say it was more than a few things. I don't mind listening if you need to talk."

"Thanks, Gladys." Shelby gave her a hug, then stepped back. "I'm fine. Really." She knew Gladys meant well, but to avoid a full interrogation, the subject needed to change. "By the way, have you heard from Eleanor? Is she feeling any better?"

Gladys propped the duster against a display. She took a tissue from her bra and wiped her nose, then pushed the tissue back inside. "She texted and said she was on the mend, but needed a few days to regain her strength."

"That's good. Let her know we miss her and hope to see her soon." It still seemed odd that Gladys was the only one in contact with the missing woman. No one else had heard from or seen her in days. As Gladys picked up the duster, Shelby stopped her. "Any news on when the next button meeting might be? I really enjoyed the last one. In fact, when I was going through my sewing stash, I found a jar of old buttons my auntie gave me. I was hoping someone could help me—"

"With Eleanor ill, and…" Gladys worked a splayed feather into place. "We, um, didn't set another meeting. Not yet…" She fidgeted and checked her phone. "Incoming call… but I'll let you know." She answered it, then rushed down an aisle, and out the front door.

Shelby frowned. She didn't hear the phone ring. *Why was Gladys avoiding the question? What was she hiding?* Shelby's hand brushed against the folded envelope in her back pocket. She straightened. What was her letter hiding? It seemed they both had secrets.

ELEANOR SWIPED END and dropped her phone in the tote. She drew in a long breath and let it out. After turning the crock pot to OFF, she washed the paring knife and large spoon, laying them on a towel to dry.

She went into the bathroom and splashed water on her face, though it did nothing to reduce the puffiness in her red, swollen eyes. She ran her fingers through her short, grey hair, then stared at her reflection in the distorted mirror. "You know, this is probably another one of your worst decisions..." She pointed to herself. "But you can't ignore it forever."

Eleanor opened a grocery bag hidden under the sink and pulled out an ashy-blond wig, oversized hat, and a dark-colored scarf. Thank goodness Gladys had a set of the keys to the theatre. Finding the wig had given Eleanor some freedom to be in public, even pretending to be Clara at Gladys' button meeting. She thought Shelby would recognize her, but apparently not. No one asked who the new woman was. No one cared until John found out and demanded she go into hiding. She tugged the wig into place, smoothing the fake hair down on her forehead.

Dropping her medicines in the yarn bag along with a toothbrush and a change of underclothes, Eleanor pulled on the hat and draped the scarf around her neck. She looked around the small cabin one last time, then closed her eyes in silent prayer. Leaving the small structure, she stepped out onto the damp dirt and closed the door behind her.

She stopped and looked up at the sky for a moment. The

sun pushed through a fluffy cloud and warmed her face. Eleanor took it as a positive sign from the Almighty. She hurried through a thin grove of trees and made her way out to the country road leading into town.

A car passed. Then another. She scanned the road, hoping John wouldn't see her. Eleanor's heart pounded as another car passed. She waved and watched it slow down and back up. Rushing up to the idling vehicle, she opened the door, got in, and leaned her head against the head rest. The driver nodded to her, then made a U-turn. Moments later, they headed toward the freeway, away from Pheasant Valley.

AT EXACTLY FIVE minutes to five o'clock, Shelby helped the last customer. They walked to the front door of The Bee's Knees together, then Shelby locked up and turned the sign to CLOSED.

She thought about how Gladys never came back after her supposed phone call. That made several times within the week for such an abrupt exit. Abnormal for a woman who prided herself on being on time and staying late. Though nothing about the last week had been normal. With Laura's help, they finished the closing tasks quickly.

"Hope Ella continues to feel better," said Laura.

"Thanks." Shelby locked the door and nodded. "I'll give her your best."

Laura took Shelby's hand in hers. "I hope your heart heals."

"It will…" Their eyes locked, and she knew Laura's gift of empathy had revealed her inner feelings. Shelby smiled. "… Eventually." After a hug, Laura walked away, leaving

Shelby alone. Heading to her jeep, Shelby pulled the envelope from her pocket. After getting in, she locked the door and unfolded the letter from Lone Star Title. A knot grew in her stomach.

Tearing open the outside, Shelby held it against the steering wheel to keep the paper from shaking. She scanned it and gasped. "She did what? Without telling me. And now she expects me to—"

Shelby crumpled the paper and tossed it in the seat next to her. She clenched her jaw until it ached. Willing herself not to cry, she shoved the key into the ignition. She needed to tell Ella, but first she needed to talk to an attorney.

CHAPTER TWENTY-EIGHT

After pulling up into the driveway of their home, Shelby parked the jeep, got out, and slammed the door. She trudged through the gravel, stomped up the steps, and jabbed the key in the deadbolt. She turned it. Nothing. Yanking it out, she forced it in again. It wouldn't budge. Oatmeal's whines came from the other side. During a third attempt, it opened.

Ella stood inside, leaning against the threshhold, smiling. "Challenges?"

Shelby grumbled and walked in, ignoring Oatmeal's yips for attention and Mr. Butterfinger's outstretched paw. "Stupid lock wouldn't open." She tossed the keys on the coffee table and marched into the kitchen.

Ella picked them up and called out. "Maybe because you were using the shop key instead of the house key?"

Shelby trudged back into the front room and frowned. "Stupid me." She took them from Ella, shoved them in her pocket, and turned toward the kitchen again.

"Bad day?" asked Ella.

Shelby whirled around. "You think?"

Ella put up her hands. "Just concerned. Do you want to talk—?"

"Need to cool down. Don't want to say something I'll regret." She pulled out her phone and scrolled through her contacts. "I also need to call an attorney."

"Wait. What?"

Shelby closed her eyes and counted to ten. She opened them, drew in a deep breath, and stared at Ella. "I need the name of a real estate attorney."

"Why not just call Harold? He's well-versed in real estate law."

Shelby rubbed her temples. Her shoulders relaxed. "I guess that'll work. Hold on." Searching through her phone's contacts, she swiped the CALL icon, and walked into the kitchen.

Ella sat and patted the couch. Oatmeal jumped up and settled in her lap. "Guess we need to be patient."

A few minutes later, Shelby came back. "Had to leave a voice message." She plopped down in the wingback chair and kicked off her sparkly sneakers. Leaning her head back, she closed her eyes.

Ella stroked Oatmeal's fluffy ears. She wasn't sure what to do or say. Maybe not saying anything would be best, though she needed to tell Shelby about the strange visitor.

A knock at the door caused Mr. Butterfingers to skitter into the kitchen. Oatmeal darted to the door and barked. Ella stood, then leaned against the couch for support.

Shelby looked up. "Hold on, let me get that." She jumped up and walked over to the door. Opening it a crack, she peered outside.

"Just me, hon." Laura stood on the porch holding something.

Shelby opened the door wider. "Do you want to come in?"

"No, no. Not here for a visit. Just dropping off dinner."

Shelby opened the screen. "You didn't have to do that."

Laura handed her a large bag, with a smaller one balanced on top. "Monday's my treat day. I special order chicken pot pies from the café."

"What's so special about them?" asked Shelby.

"No onions," said Laura. "I'm allergic, and the café is the only place I've ever found that takes special orders—and gets them right." She stepped back. "And since they're onion-free, you can share with the fur babies. With your busy day and Ella not feeling well, I thought I'd bring over something nourishing." She winked and pointed to a white paper bag on top. "And decadent."

"I don't know what to say, Laura," said Shelby. "You're so thoughtful."

"Just watching out for my best friends." She turned and walked down the steps.

Shelby closed the door, mouth agape, and stared at Ella.

"She never ceases to amaze me," said Ella.

Taking the bags into the kitchen, Shelby set them on the table, then came back and stood in the doorway. "You want to eat on the couch or in here at the table?"

"Let's splurge and sit in the front room. I'm okay if I'm not moving around too much."

Shelby slapped her forehead. "I'm so sorry. With everything on my mind, I never asked how you were doing."

"Better." Ella smiled. "How about we eat, then talk? I'm excited about trying the chicken pies. It's been ages since I've had one."

Shelby gave a toothy grin. "I'm excited about the decadent bag."

"Well, no one ever said we have to eat dinner first. Let's live dangerously and go with dessert."

Shelby laughed. "Thought I was supposed to be the goofball."

"I've been in bed most of the day and am ready to shake things up."

"Speaking of shaking things up," said Shelby. "We need to talk."

"I figured as much. Someone came to the door looking for you."

"That doesn't surprise me," said Shelby.

ELEANOR WALKED into the motel room and sat her bag on one of the full-sized beds. She crinkled her nose as she detected the faint odor of cigarette smoke even though the sign posted said "NO SMOKING." Sitting on one of the hard back chairs, she stared up at Harold. "Thank you for rescuing me."

He eased into a chair across from her and nodded. "It was you who rescued me last week."

"When Agnes went at you with my knitting needles, I don't know what happened. My mind just went crazy."

"You have one mean right hook, lady." Harold smiled. "Remind me not to get your dander up."

"You don't really think I killed her?" Eleanor looked at him with tired eyes. "Do you?"

"Once she went down, I hightailed it out of there." He rested his warm hand on hers. "Honestly, cold-cocking her in the jaw shouldn't have."

"But what if she hit her head on something? I'd still be guilty of…"

"Eleanor, don't even think that way." Harold covered his mouth and coughed. "From what I heard…" He began coughing again and waved his hand. "Water…?"

She got up and filled a plastic cup, then handed it to him. "That cough doesn't sound good. Maybe you should see a doctor."

Sipping the water, Harold shook his head. "No more doctors. What do they know, anyway?"

She put her hand to her lips. "Is there something… wrong?"

Harold squeezed her hand. "Nothing you need to worry about now. We're here to deal with your problems, not mine."

"Harold? What's going on?"

His phone signaled an incoming call. He checked the caller ID, then let it go to voice mail. "Shelby. Probably about the shop renovation. I'll call her later."

"You didn't answer my question," said Eleanor.

"I'm hungry. Aren't you hungry? Let's order something."

"Harold, what are you not telling me?"

He caught her gaze. "This is the first time we've talked in a very long time. Can't we just enjoy tonight?"

Eleanor forced a smile. "Promise we'll talk about it tomorrow?"

"Yes."

SHELBY FORKED the last piece of flaky crust into her mouth. "Probably the best chicken pot pie I've had."

Giving tiny bites to the dog, then the cat, Ella nodded.

"And this pecan praline brownie thingie was amazing."

Shelby licked the back of her spoon and wiped her chin. "So good, I dribbled."

Ella laughed. "Do I need to get you a bib?"

"Probably the next time I eat another chicken pie. How many did she bring?"

"Six total. There are four left," said Ella.

"And brownies?"

"Only four," said Ella. "Though another one is calling to me."

Shelby chuckled. "You must be feeling better."

"Yes…" Ella caught Shelby's gaze. "Not to change the subject, but…"

Shelby jumped up from the couch. "Let me toss these tins in the garbage, then we can talk." She walked into the kitchen, wondering how Ella would take the news. Would she understand? Or…? Shelby didn't dare go there. She had to tell Ella her deepest secret. One she'd held in her heart far too long.

Shelby walked back into the front room and sat on the couch. Tucking a leg under her, she turned to Ella. "I need to tell you something. Promise you'll listen before you judge me?"

Ella grasped Shelby's hand in hers. "Hon, you know you can tell me anything without judgement."

Shelby looked up at the ceiling and hesitated. She'd come this far, only to be taken back to the past. Hopefully, Ella would understand. If not, she didn't know what she'd do.

CHAPTER TWENTY-NINE

Alton Nolan finished the last of what seemed like never-ending paperwork at the Pheasant Valley Police Department. The town had little crime, except for a few stolen chickens and the occasional speeder, but the murder of Agnes Cormack stumped him. He tapped his thinking pen on the page of a small notebook. Going over his notes, he tried to decipher clues by re-reading each interview. Four people, Agnes, Harold, Vivian, and Eleanor, left the shop during the thunderstorm. Hours after Harold and Eleanor rushed out of the alley and Vivian went back inside The Bee's Knees, Ella and Shelby found Agnes dead. The victim of a stabbing from two carefully placed knitting needles. The primary suspect, Eleanor, was still missing.

Another officer walked up to Alton's desk and waited. "Excuse me, Sergeant," the woman whispered. "We received a call you might be interested in."

Alton looked up at the department's newest rookie. Since completing field training a few weeks ago, she was hungry to learn as much as possible. "What is it, Cooper?"

Andrea Cooper cleared her throat. "Sir, dispatch

received a call from John Morgan about a kidnapping." The twenty-something woman, barely five feet tall, straightened her shoulders and stood on her tiptoes.

Alton dropped his pen, then picked it up. "Say again?"

"John Morgan called in to say someone kidnapped his mother, Eleanor."

Alton stood and pulled on his jacket. "Eleanor's been missing for days. How would John know someone had kidnapped her?"

"Not sure, sir." Cooper held up a piece of paper. "He called a few minutes ago. Sir, he requested you be the one to come investigate."

"I was just getting ready to head home," said Alton. He glanced at his watch and sighed. "Looks like a long night ahead."

"Yes, sir." Cooper rocked back and forth on her toes.

"Would you like to come with me?"

"For reals?" She blushed, then cleared her throat again. "Yes, sir. Whatever I can do to help, sir."

"Get your jacket and duty bag." Alton smiled. "And the location of the alleged crime."

As Cooper hurried away, Alton rifled back through his notebook. He'd interviewed John the day after Agnes' murder. He flipped through the pages and chewed on his bottom lip. "No mention of knowing his mother's whereabouts…"

"You say something, sir?" Cooper stood in front of the sergeant, staring at him. Her blue eyes sparkled, one hand resting on her leather belt.

"Just thinking out loud…" They headed out the police department door and into the chilly night to their units.

"So you're not surprised someone came looking for you?" asked Ella. "The guy was pretty adamant that I was *the* Shelby Heaton he was looking for and said I needed to deal with some urgent business."

"What did you tell him?"

"I asked for his ID. He appeared to be a process server. But before he came to the door, he'd been in our backyard without permission, so I told him to get off my property or I'd call the sheriff."

Shelby's eyes widened. "Did you?"

"No. He smirked and dared me, which really made my blood boil. Instead, I shut the door in his face. Probably didn't make things any better, but I was feeling light-headed and didn't want to deal with him…. Are you in some kind of trouble?"

Shelby shifted. "I need to explain."

Ella's heart pounded. What had Shelby been keeping from her? Something so terrible she was afraid to share. Thinking their friendship held no secrets, she mentally prepared herself for the worst.

Turning to Ella, Shelby opened her mouth, but nothing came out. She tried again, only to break down into tears. "I'm so sorry." She sat forward and pulled the certified letter from her pocket and handed it to Ella. "She can't do this to me…"

Ella pulled out the letter and unfolded it with trembling hands. She scanned it, then frowned at Shelby. "I don't understand. This letter says Mac's selling the house and needs you to sign the final escrow papers. Shouldn't this make you happy?"

Shelby shook her head and sobbed harder. "I'll never be able to go back and visit her."

"Mac?" asked Ella.

Shelby shook her head again. "Charisma."

Ella gasped. *Was Shelby hiding a secret relationship?* Waiting for her to explain, she listened to the clock's second hand. Tick. Tick. Tick. Each one seemed louder and louder, filling the room with a countdown of sorts. But to what?

Shelby wiped her eyes and blew her nose. "If Mac sells the house, I'll never... be able to spend time with Karisma again..."

Ella closed her eyes and took a deep breath. She needed to be present to her friend's needs.

"You must hate me," said Shelby, grabbing a handful of tissues.

"I don't hate you. But I am confused." Ella cleared her throat. "You never mentioned Karisma before."

"That's because I told no one about her. Mac knew I lost her, but she never knew I named her..."

"Named her?" Ella straightened. "Shel, who are you talking about?"

Shelby looked at Ella as tears ran down her cheeks. "My baby. The second miscarriage. Mac was at work. I started bleeding, then cramping. It got so bad... Then something came out and I knew I wasn't pregnant anymore.... I held what used to be inside me in my hand. In my heart, she was a girl, but who knows? I didn't go to the doctor because the first time, they took 'it' away and put 'it' in a specimen jar so they could run tests." Shelby used finger quotes to show her disdain. "This time, I didn't bother. I knew what had happened. This time I wouldn't let them take my baby." She shifted on the couch and wiped her eyes with a wadded up tissue.

"We'd been redoing the backyard preparing to plant a bunch of bare-root roses. The holes were already there... so I wrapped her up in one of my grandma's embroidered hankies, and buried her. Then planted a yellow rose on top. It gave me closure, which I never got with my first loss. I named her Karisma. It means gift. She was supposed to be my gift...." Shelby leaned into Ella and sobbed.

Ella held her grieving friend and cried with her.

After some time, Shelby sat back and stared at Ella. "That's why I stayed so long with Mac. Not because we were happy. But because I couldn't leave my baby daughter behind. But finally, I had to. For my mental health. But now, I'll... I'm going to lose her again. This time forever."

"I'm so very sorry, Shel." Ella drew in a deep breath. Unable to bear children, she felt Shelby's pain. Ella held her friend until the sobs subsided, then pulled back.

"Both of our names are on that house. Mac never even asked before she put it on the market," said Shelby. "Now, it's sold and I have to sign the papers by the end of next week." Wiping her eyes with the back of her hand, she swallowed the hard lump in her throat. "According to the letter, escrow's closing next Friday..." She buried her face in Ella's shoulder and burst into tears again.

Ella pulled out her phone. "We need to contact Harold."

CHAPTER THIRTY

C ooper followed Sergeant Nolan's unit along the dirt road leading to John and Lilibeth Morgan's home. Soon, a two-story ranch-style house nestled on the Morgan Fibre Farm's expansive property came into view. It stood out among the lush grazing meadows dotted with sheep and alpaca.

Grabbing his jacket, Alton exited his unit and waited for Cooper. He glanced up and watched the moon and twinkling stars disappear behind low, billowy clouds. Echoes of ki-yipping coyotes came from the hills behind them. He sniffed the air as Pheasant Valley's newest officer came up to him. "Not bad…"

She raised an eyebrow. "Pardon?"

"Sheep farm. I was expecting more of an… earthy odor if you know what I mean."

"You might be thinking about pigs or goats," said Cooper. "Normally, sheep and alpacas don't smell bad, sir." She zipped up her jacket and smiled.

"Sounds like you know farm animals." Alton motioned toward the house.

"Four-H. I raised a few pigs and goats back in high school. My friend had sheep, which didn't offend the senses as much." As they walked to the porch, Cooper stopped. She looked up at the house, then at Alton.

"Just take notes," he said. "Something's just not right." Followed by Cooper, Alton walked up the wooden steps and knocked on the front door.

A moment later, John opened it. He came outside onto the wooden porch, his boots making a clunk-tap with each step. He motioned to several wicker chairs placed together on the long porch. "Let's sit out here. Lilibeth is watching her shows and I don't want to disturb her."

Alton nodded and pointed to the other officer. "John, this is Officer Cooper. She's helping with the case."

"Thanks for coming so quickly."

Alton waited for John to sit, then positioned himself facing the man. He moved the other chair to the side of John, then motioned to Cooper to take it, effectively blocking the stairs in case his questions might cause John to bolt.

Pulling out a notebook and pen, Alton stared at the fidgeting rancher. "John, tell me what happened. Starting with when you called, and work your way backward to when you think your mother was kid—"

John balled up his fists. "I don't *think* he kidnapped Mom. I *know*."

Alton waited, but said nothing. He focused his gaze, keeping steady eye contact.

John clenched his jaw. "That murderer took her."

Cooper held back a gasp as she scribbled in her notebook.

Alton stared at John. "You're saying you know who allegedly abducted your mother?"

"Isn't it obvious?" The sides of John's chair crunched as his grip tightened. "It was that Madrigal guy. Been stalking my mother for years. First, he murdered his ex, Agnes, then he took Mom." John didn't blink, nor did he look away. "You know, he has a history of abusing women. Even murdered another one, saying it was self-defense…"

The low baaing and bleating of ewes and their lambs sounded in the distance while an icy breeze tousled Cooper's shoulder-length copper hair. A coyote called out and others yipped in response. Straightening, Alton broke eye contact and wrote in his notebook. He looked up again. "John, when we spoke a few days ago, you said you didn't know where your mother was. Are you changing that?"

John cleared his throat and looked at Cooper, then Alton. "Didn't know where she was when we spoke. I just found out. Told her to call you." He folded his arms across his chest. "Look, while you're asking these stupid questions, my mother could be in grave danger."

"Where was Eleanor when she was allegedly taken?" Alton held his pen over the notebook, waiting.

"She must have snuck into one of our cabins. I didn't know she was out there."

"Then how do you know she's missing?" asked Alton.

"Because. I… I saw a light. When I opened the door, I found Mom cooking. We need to get to the cabin… I'm sure you'll want to dust for prints or whatever cops do when someone's been kidnapped."

Alton raised a brow. "So you said you didn't know she was there? But now you're saying you knew she was there? Which is it?"

John stood and crossed his arms. "Why am I being questioned like I did something wrong?"

Alton stood and matched John's stance. "Did you do something wrong?"

John's eyes widened. "No. But you're making me sound guilty." He moved toward the stairs, then backed up when Cooper stood.

Alton pointed to the chair. "John, please sit. I'm just trying to get everything clear in my mind. No one's accusing you of anything." Alton noted John's behavior and backed off, hoping the man would calm down.

Cooper sat after John did, though she remained alert.

"You said your mother was in a cabin. Correct?"

John stood again and pointed away from the house. "Why won't you go investigate?"

"We're waiting for forensics. Please… take a seat." Alton smiled, then took a deep breath. "I know this must be hard. But there are protocols I must follow so we don't tamper with evidence. Did you touch anything inside the cabin?"

John shook his head. "After I opened the door and didn't see her, I closed it again."

"That's good. Do you know if Harold was on the property?"

"He must have been."

"Did you see signs of a struggle?" asked Alton.

John's face twisted. "What do you mean?"

"Any type of disorder?" Alton sat forward. "Furniture tipped over. Clothes askew. Did you see anything like that?"

John closed his eyes. For it to be a crime scene, it would have to look like one. The one detail he hadn't thought about. With forensics coming any minute, he had to think fast. He couldn't involve Lilibeth. Or could he?

"STILL NO ANSWER?" asked Shelby.

Ella shook her head. "Harold hasn't been well lately. Maybe he turned off his phone and went to bed." She covered a yawn. "I hate to leave you alone right now, but I need to get some rest."

Shelby smiled. "Thanks for listening. I was so afraid you'd be upset once I told you about my secret in Houston."

"How many times do I need to tell you I'm here for you no matter what?"

Shelby leaned her head back and closed her eyes. "It's hard for me to trust anyone."

Ella sat forward and squeezed Shelby's hand. "I know a lot of people who said they loved you have hurt you. But I'm not your father. Or your ex-partner." She caught Shelby's eye. "I hope you know you can trust me. Now. And forever."

"My heart tells me I'm safe," said Shelby. "But my brain forgets. It goes back into that dark place, and I..." She brushed a tear from her cheek. "Just keep reminding me, okay?"

Ella nodded. "Not that I want to stop talking, but I really need to go back to bed. You headed upstairs?"

Shelby shrugged. "Soon. Until we can contact Harold, I'm going to do some research online. Maybe I can find something to give me peace of mind."

"I don't know real estate law, but I don't think she can sell the house without your signature," said Ella. "You might have more control over this than you think."

"Let's hope so. Goodnight."

After Ella and Oatmeal left the room, Shelby opened her laptop. Her fingers paused over the keyboard. Which keywords she should try? Texas real estate law brought up too many search categories. She closed her eyes, but opened them when Mr. Butterfingers settled in her lap. She stroked his ears and relaxed when he purred. "You're lucky to be a cat. Not having to worry about anything except sleeping, eating, and who's going to scratch your ears—" Shelby's phone signaled an incoming text. She picked it up, her heart racing. She stared at the screen.

GOT YOUR MESSAGE. NEED MORE INFO. WILL CALL TOM.—H

Shelby removed the scrunchie from her hair and scratched her head. Tomorrow was forever away. Walking into the kitchen, she uncovered the last three brownies. She wanted to eat them all. Mr. Butterfingers meowed. "Yes, I know the chocolate will keep me awake." He meowed again. "Okay, I'll wait until tomorrow." After giving the cat a few treats, she ate a banana. Trudging upstairs to her bedroom, Shelby hoped for some much-needed sleep.

JOHN STOOD and stretched his back. With Alton and Cooper watching him, he couldn't just leave. His mind raced. To prove Harold had kidnapped his mother, he'd have to act fast. Forensics was minutes away. He'd only have one chance to get this right. "Hey," he said, clearing his throat. "You mind if I go in and use the can? Since I won't be able to touch anything in the cabin, it might be better…"

Alton stood. "That's fine." He glanced at Cooper. "We'll wait here."

After John jumped up and rushed into the house, Alton motioned to the officer. "Head around the back of the house. I don't want him taking off."

She nodded. Pulling out her high-powered flashlight, she hurried off the porch and disappeared into the dark night.

Alton pushed the button on his two-way mic and spoke into it. A few minutes later, he received confirmation the forensics unit was en route. Less than five minutes ETA. He stood alert, watching, waiting for John to return. Two minutes passed. Three. Then four. *Did the guy use the one upstairs?* A quick zip and go shouldn't take that long. Just as he was about to pound on the front door, John came out, followed by his wife, Lilibeth.

Alton approached them. "What's going on?"

"Just a got a call from a neighbor—coyotes are on the prowl," said John. "Since I have to deal with my mother's kidnapping…" He looked at Alton, then to Cooper as she came around the side of the house. "How about a little help, Nolan?"

"Forensics will be here any minute," said Alton. "Officer Cooper has a lot of experience with farm animals. I'm sure she'll be more than helpful." He watched the silent interaction between John and Lilibeth as they reacted to his suggestion.

As Cooper rushed back to her unit to get her rifle, Lilibeth went back into the house, returning with a shotgun.

John cussed quietly under his breath, and motioned to his wife. "Ewes are probably in the far back pasture. Head out there and do what needs to be done."

Lilibeth nodded. "This way, Officer." Holding a flashlight under the stock with her left hand, she motioned toward a worn path away from the house and the women headed southeast into the dark pasture.

Tires on the dirt road, then a flash of headlights behind them caused Alton to turn. "Finally." He looked back at John. "Now we can get out to that cabin and examine it for evidence."

Alton moved the wicker chairs, then he and John went

out to the arriving unit. Williams, the short, stocky police officer, walked up to the sergeant. They spoke briefly, then Alton turned to John. "Take us to the cabin."

As they started down a path in the opposite direction from the one Lilibeth and Cooper had taken, John stopped. "I need to go back and get my flashlight."

Alton and Williams held up theirs. "No need," said Alton.

They started walking again. John paused. "The key. I forgot the key in the... upstairs head."

"Moments ago you were pushing us to get out to that cabin." Alton glared at John. "Why are you stalling?"

John fished around in his pockets and held up a key ring. "Sorry, had it with me all the time."

"No more excuses." Alton pointed ahead. "Take us there now." He noticed they passed the same stretch of fence at least twice. Were they walking in circles? The hair on his neck bristled when coyote yips seemed closer. He wanted to believe there was a danger to the Morgan's flocks, but was it too much of a coincidence?

The three men made their way past the woven wire fencing on the interior of the fibre farm a third time. "This way," said John. He pointed to a distant area away from them. "And make sure you watch out for that exterior fence. It's electric. Supposed to keep the predators away."

"Must not be working if you're so concerned about those coyotes," said Alton.

"Guys were working on it earlier today. Issue with the grounding. They were supposed to get it fixed and back on. Just warning you in case—"

Rifle fire followed by a shotgun blast echoed across the canyon. Alton tapped his lapel mic, shouting into it.

"Cooper? Do you copy?" He unholstered his gun and shouted again. "Cooper. Do you read me?"

Except for baas and bleats of ewes and lambs and distant barks and yips of coyotes, there was no response.

CHAPTER THIRTY-ONE

Alton aimed his flashlight in the distance. "Cooper. Do you copy?"

Newly budded leaves rustled on nearby bushes. Tall grass swayed in the breeze.

"Cooper, what's your 10-20?" The sergeant aimed his flashlight in all directions, then tried his radio again. "Cooper, your location?"

Faint crackling came through the mic, then Cooper's voice. "10-12, standby."

Alton pressed his mic button. "What's going on? We heard shots."

"… Coyotes, Sir. Big ones. Lilibeth… (garbled)… shot."

"My wife's been shot?" John rushed up to Alton. "What happened?"

"10-9. Cooper, repeat." Alton held up his hand to block John's advance. "10-78. Repeat. 10-78. Do you require medical assistance?"

"… (garbled communication)… 10-69. Message received. 10-23. Stand by."

John paced and cursed under his breath.

Alton holstered his gun and tapped his foot.

Williams stood by, holding the forensics box.

Cooper's voice came through the mic. "… Situation under control," she said. "Repeat. Situation under control."

John stopped pacing and pointed at Alton and the forensics officer. "If we lost stock—"

Alton straightened. "Before you jump to conclusions, cool down and wait until they get back and explain."

John folded his arms across his chest and glared.

"Where's the cabin?" asked Alton.

He pointed to an area less than fifty yards away. "There."

Alton raised an eyebrow, then spoke into his mic. "Cooper, meet us at the cabin. About fifty yards from…" He looked around. "Two big rocks and the exterior fence. Southwest corner of the property. Copy?"

"Copy that, sir." Cooper's voice came through clearly. "On our way."

Alton's shoulders relaxed as he and Williams followed John. They made their way along a dirt path up to a small, dark cabin. When John reached out to unlock the door, Alton put out his hand. "Give me the key."

"I'm coming in with you. To show you… um, around."

Alton turned. "You'll wait with me while Williams gathers evidence."

"It's my property." John raised his voice and puffed out his chest. "Don't you need a search warrant or something?"

"You gave verbal consent when you told us to find your mother," said Alton. "Now, if you want me to wake up a district attorney and explain why I need a warrant, who will then wake up a judge to sign it, I don't mind. It'll delay our investigation by an hour. Maybe more…" He grabbed his cell, scrolling for the district attorney's number.

John stomped his boot on the dirt. "When this is over, I'm contacting your superiors."

Alton put his cell back in his jacket. Then he turned, rolled his eyes, and unlocked the door. The three men stood near the doorway and stared inside. Alton turned to John. "Stay outside. This place is in shambles."

OFFICER WILLIAMS WALKED through the door, then closed it behind him. He pulled on a pair of gloves and began the tedious process of photographing each area of the cabin, first with a wide-angle lens, then switching to a micro-lens to better capture the alleged crime scene. He noted the lamp askew. A kitchen chair turned on its side. The crock pot's hearty aroma. Several dishes drying on the counter. Various pieces of scattered clothing. After taking images of the living and kitchen areas, he proceeded to the bathroom. He dumped out the contents of the trash and meticulously photographed each item, as they all could be evidence. More images. An open medicine chest. Toilet lid up. Toothbrush missing.

Next he dusted surfaces with a fine grey powder. He used adhesive tape to lift them, knowing many would be useless. Latent prints could stay on surfaces for up to forty years, meaning some might belong to anyone who had access to the small cabin, not just recent visitors. He made notes while he walked around, making sure he didn't miss any detail, small or large. Sometimes the most minute thing would mean the difference between conviction and acquittal.

HEARING FOOTSTEPS BEHIND THEM, John and Alton turned. John walked up to his wife. "What happened?"

"Large pack of coyotes," said Lilibeth. "It's good we both went."

Cooper came up to Alton. "Sorry for the confusion, sir."

"You had us concerned," said the Sergeant.

"Lilibeth's flashlight caught the yellow eyes of a dozen coyotes," said Cooper. "We both fired. Don't think we hit anything, but it scared them off."

"Just make sure you file an incident report."

"Yes, sir." She looked around. "What do you need me to do?"

Though Alton monitored the couple, he led Cooper away from them and lowered his voice. "I'll stay here while you go in and look around. Williams's in there now. After you note everything, we'll switch places."

"Still have that gut feeling something's not right?" asked Cooper.

Alton nodded. "And I'm not leaving them alone until we're done here."

Cooper headed up to the cabin, then opened the door and stepped inside.

Marching over to Alton, John stopped a few feet from the sergeant. "How much longer? My wife's been through a lot tonight."

Alton looked at his watch. "Shouldn't be too much. While we're waiting, do either of you have anything to add?"

The couple looked at each other.

"Like what?" asked Lilibeth, shifting on her feet.

"Anything out of the ordinar—."

"Like my mother being taken by a murderer?" asked John. "If you'd been better at your job, you'd have found her days ago." He straightened. "If anything happens to her, it's on you, Nolan."

Alton stepped forward, forcing John to back up. He took another step, then a third. Each time, John moved back. "I understand you're upset. But, if you——"

Cooper opened the cabin door and called out. "Sir, you need to see this."

John maneuvered away from Alton and started up the dirt path. Williams stood at the door, blocking the entrance. "I'm sorry, Mr. Morgan. This is still a crime scene."

Alton arrived at the doorway. "Everything okay?"

Williams glanced at John, then leaned into Alton. "Sir, you need to see what Cooper uncovered."

ALTON MADE his way into the small cabin. He found Officer Cooper standing next to the counter. "What is it?" he asked.

"Actually, a few things. For one, this crock pot."

Alton lifted the lid and sniffed. "Stew?"

"Apparently, sir. But do you notice something odd about it?" Cooper waited.

Alton looked at the appliance, then the officer. "Why don't you tell me so we can get out of here?"

Cooper nodded. "The crock pot was in the 'off' position. Everything inside is cold."

Alton furrowed his brow. "What do you make of this?"

"If someone took Eleanor against her will," said Cooper. "Would she have taken the time to turn this off?"

"Anything else?"

"Yes." Cooper motioned for Alton to follow her into the bathroom. She picked up several crumpled receipts laying on the floor, then smoothed them. "Williams already photographed and dusted for prints, so we can handle them. Look at the dates. From Saturday through today, groceries, knitting supplies…"

Alton tapped his finger on his chin. "Seems Mom's been here for a while." He took the receipts, bagged them, and placed them in his jacket pocket. "John's story seems to be unraveling. Lilibeth appears oblivious. At this point, I'm not sure who to believe."

"Should we question them again, sir?"

"I have a better idea." Alton walked back into the kitchen area. "Let's call it a night. Not say anything when we go outside. Let them stew a bit." He smiled, then laughed at himself. "Pun intended. While they might not be willing to talk to us, it's time to ask our friends for help."

CHAPTER THIRTY-TWO

Alton turned the corner and drove up the street of an older, quiet neighborhood in town. He pulled up and parked in front of a beige Mediterranean-style house with a tile roof. A chill hung in the air, though the sun had just risen over the mountains, promising a warmer day. He exited his unit, shivered, and suppressed a yawn. Walking up to the house, he noticed a rolled up newspaper askew on the porch next to a potted fern. He knocked once. Then twice. No response.

"You looking for Harold Madrigal?"

Alton turned and noticed a stout, balding gentleman in a lime-green bathrobe waving from the driveway next door. He stepped off the front porch and approached the man. "Yes, I am. Do you know if he's home?"

"Left yesterday. Haven't seen him since."

Alton came closer and extended his hand. "I'm Sergeant Nolan. And your name?"

The man grabbed Alton's hand and pumped it. "Eduardo Gonzales. Need me to spell it? E-D-U—"

"No, I think I have it." Alton took out his notebook and

pen. "Mr. Gonzales, would you know when Mr. Madrigal left yester—?"

"Got it all right here." The man dug through the oversized pockets in his bathrobe and brought out his own notebook and pen. He flipped through a few pages, then cleared his throat. "Three oh-two in the p.m." He held it out for Alton to see, then squinted at the page. Pulling a pair of reading glasses out of another pocket, he scrutinized it again. "Left the house, didn't return."

"Do you normally keep track of the comings and goings of Mr. Madrigal?"

Gonzales held his belly as he laughed. "Keep notes on everyone in the neighborhood. I am the designated captain of our Block Watch Team. For example, Mrs. Harrison across the street in 4313... Her son likes to play the drums all day. Stops precisely at nine-fifty-nine each evening, so I've not had to make a report."

"I'm not sure how that applies to Mr. Madri—"

"And Mr. Grant there in 4312, he walks his dog every morning at seven-fifteen and every evening at seven-fifteen sharp. And while he carries a poo-bag, he'll toss it in anyone's trash." Gonzales stepped closer to Alton and stared up at him. "When I called your department to see if that was an infraction in the city code, no one—I mean no one ever got back to me to let me know if I should report it or not."

"I'm sorry about that, Mr. Gonzales. But—"

He flipped to another page in his notebook. "And did you know, Mrs. Hayward over there..." He pointed at another house and clicked his tongue. "She likes to take gentleman callers at all hours. Even—"

"Sir, I'm sorry to cut you off. But I'm in the middle of

an investigation. Can we get back to Mr. Madrigal?" Alton tapped his pen on his notebook page.

Gonzales cleared his throat again. "Just trying to do a thorough job of protecting my street." He flipped back a page or two, then squinted at his writing. He lifted his glasses, then adjusted them. "Madrigal's quiet. Gets his mail each night. Newspaper each morning. Takes his trash out—"

Alton raised his hand. "I appreciate the information. Can I get your contact information in case we need to—"

Gonzales dug into his pocket again and pulled out a card. "Here's my Block Watch Team card. All my pertinent information is on there."

Alton looked at it, then put it in his shirt pocket. "I'll be in touch." He extended his hand and shook Gonzales' outstretched one.

Before releasing it, Gonzales looked up at Alton. "What about Mr. Grant?"

Alton stepped back. "Mr. Grant?"

"The poo-bag in others' trash guy?"

"How about you call and ask for Officer Cooper? She should be able to help you." Alton suppressed a smile. "Just don't tell her I said anything. You know, let's keep this between ourselves."

Gonzales scribbled in his notebook. "Mighty grateful for that tip. Have a good one, Officer."

Alton started walking up Harold's driveway toward the garage when he heard footsteps behind him. He turned and saw Gonzales at his heels. "May I help you?"

"Just tagging along if that's okay. I've never worked with an actual police officer…"

Alton smiled at Gonzales, then his eye caught someone walking across the street. "While I'd love for you to help, I see your neighbor is out with his dog. Since I've got this covered, why don't you note his behavior instead?"

Gonzales whirled around, then turned to Alton. "I'm on it, sir." He gave Alton a weak salute, then rushed down the driveway, his bathrobe flapping behind him.

SHELBY ROLLED over and checked her phone. No messages. She sighed. It was Tuesday. The house should close the next Friday. Her chest tightened. Mr. Butterfingers stretched a paw toward her and meowed.

"Give me a sec, then I'll feed you." She pulled on a sweatshirt, dashed into the bathroom, and headed downstairs, followed by her cat.

Shelby nudged Ella's bedroom door open. "How are you feeling this morning?"

"Better. Not one hundred percent, but getting there."

Shelby rested her hand on Ella's forehead. "No temp. That's promising. Let me feed the fur babies, then I'll make breakfast."

Ella stretched. After putting on her robe, she made her way into the kitchen. She poured water into the coffee maker, then spooned dark grounds into the filter. Once she closed the lid, the sounds of boiling water and the aroma of fresh-brewed hazelnut coffee filled the room.

Shelby walked back in. "Weather's gorgeous today. Sunny, thin clouds, slight breeze."

"And after that fine weather report, let's turn it back to sports…"

"Okay, that did sound canned." Shelby laughed. "Tomorrow is the first day of Spring and I'm thrilled you're feeling better."

Ella nodded. She filled their cups and placed them on the table. "Think I'll take one more day... That is, if you don't mind."

Shelby rubbed Ella's shoulders. "That's fine. Staying busy at the shop will help keep my mind off Harold's call."

"Speaking of..."

Shelby came around and faced Ella. "You heard from Harold?"

"No, hon. But I received an interesting text from Alton."

Shelby straightened. "Interesting in a good or bad way?"

"Not sure. Said he needed our help and would be in touch."

Shelby exhaled. "Okay. That's vague." She fed their pets, then made breakfast while Ella checked her emails.

FINISHING the last of her eggs, Shelby's phone signaled an incoming call. She dropped her fork and swiped the icon on her phone. "Harold, thanks for calling... No, just finished breakfast..." She stood and paced.

Ella waved at her, pointing at her ear.

Shelby placed the phone on the table and pushed the speakerphone icon, then continued to pace. "FYI. I've got Ella on speaker. Yes, well... here's the problem, and it's confidential...

"... of course," said Harold.

"Mac and I bought a house a few years ago. Now, she's sold it and I have to sign the escrow papers..."

"And..."

"She never even told me. Now, I'm getting registered mail and being harassed by process servers to sign the papers by next Friday, or else..."

"How did they list your names on the title?"

"I don't remember," said Shelby. "First, middle, last? What difference does it make?"

"Not the order," said Harold. "I mean, was it joint tenants or tenants in common?"

"Who knows?" Shelby pulled out a chair and sat. "It was years ago. How can I find out?"

"Do you have a copy of the title deed?"

Shelby looked at Ella and shook her head. "I left all that stuff behind in Houston."

"You should be able to contact the county recorder's office…"

Ella pushed a pen and pad of paper to her friend.

Shelby turned to Ella. "Thanks," then back to her phone. "Can I get that online?"

"Unfortunately, I'm not familiar with Texas real estate laws. I suggest calling…" He coughed. "Hold… on…." The phone silenced, but still showed connected.

Ella and Shelby looked at each other but said nothing. A minute passed, then another. Shelby pointed to her phone and held up three fingers. Ella nodded, then shrugged.

"Hope he's okay," whispered Shelby.

A moment later, Harold's hoarse voice came through. "Sorry… about that."

"Are you okay, Harold?" asked Shelby.

"Nothing to worry… about." The sound of running water came from the background and the phone went silent again. A few moments later, Harold spoke. "Call the recorder's office in that county…." He cleared his throat. "Whatever you do… sign nothing… until you get the information. Hopefully… you'll get what you need, if not…" The phone silenced again.

"If not, what?" Shelby stood. "Harold, if not… I didn't hear the rest."

Harold's raspy voice struggled for breaths between words. "You'll have… to… go… to Houston…"

ELEANOR BROUGHT another cup of water from the bathroom and offered it to Harold. His breathing was more labored, his face pale.

"Here, try to sip this," she said. Sitting next to him on the bed, her fingers trembled. His condition had worsened since the night before. Should she call an ambulance?

Harold handed back the cup and managed a smile. "Time for us to talk?"

"Can you?"

He nodded. "It's too bad… we've lost so much time…"

She took his frail hand in hers. "It never seemed to be the right time. You left town. I got married…"

"And now…" He looked at her with tired eyes. "When we could have years…" He shook his head, then lowered it. "We might only have weeks…"

She gasped. "No, Harold. What are you saying?"

He drew in a ragged breath. "Stage four… lung cancer."

"There must be something somebody can do."

"Inoperable." Harold shook his head. "And it's only going to get worse. Worser."

Tears rolled down Eleanor's cheeks. Her shoulders trembled.

Harold moved closer and stroked her cheek, wiping away the tears. "I never stopped loving you…" He closed his eyes, then opened them. "If only I'd stayed."

"My parents refused to let me see you."

"In their eyes, I ruined your future."

"But you didn't." Eleanor reached up and held Harold's hand. "I loved you."

He gazed into her swollen eyes. "And now?"

Eleanor looked away, then back. "I... Yes... But so much has happened... Does anyone else know?"

"Just me and the doc."

Eleanor gasped. "This is a lot for me to process..."

"Hon, I have very little time. Will you stay with me... until...?"

She buried her head in her hands and sobbed. "You can't leave before..."

"Before what?" asked Harold.

"Before we tell him the truth."

CHAPTER THIRTY-THREE

Ella entered the kitchen, drying her hair with a thick, blue towel. "Find out anything?"

"Spoke to a pleasant woman at the Harris County Clerk's Office," said Shelby. "After being transferred a few times, another woman helped me sort things out. Apparently, I can order a non-certified copy of the title deed via email for just a few dollars."

"That's great news, Shel." Ella sat next to her. "How long will it take?"

"Could be a just a few days, or longer. She said end of the week, or maybe next week, if they needed to do more research."

"Hopefully, it's sooner, than later," said Ella.

Shelby nodded. "I've already printed out the paperwork. Just need to fill it out, scan it, then email it back."

"Anything I can do to help?" asked Ella.

"Remind me not to panic if I don't have it by Friday."

Ella squeezed Shelby's hand. "At least you don't have to go to Houston."

Shelby looked at Ella with tired eyes. "Not yet."

SHELBY PULLED into the parking lot of The Bee's Knees. Walking up to the entrance, the warm sunshine brightened her mood. She unlocked the front door, but as she turned to start the pre-opening duties, Alton's police car pulled up. Shelby watched him exit his unit. He checked his teeth in the side mirror, slicked back a stray hair, then straightened his shoulders. Turning, he walked up the sidewalk to the shop.

She opened the door for him. "Morning."

Alton entered and unzipped his jacket. "Sorry to stop by without calling, but I needed to chat with you before everyone started coming in."

Shelby raised an eyebrow. "Ella mentioned something, but I thought you wanted to talk to both of us."

"Not knowing when Ella will come back to work, I'm hoping you can get things rolling."

Shelby motioned to a side counter. "Can it wait until I make coffee?"

Alton laughed. "Sure. Though don't make it on my account."

"It's for me." She glanced up at him. "It's been quite a morning."

Alton nodded. "I hear you."

Shelby started the coffee, then turned back to Alton. "What's going on?"

"Since you've been helpful in the past…" he said. "Do you mind chatting with Lilibeth Morgan?"

Shelby shrugged her shoulders. "I guess not."

Alton smiled. "You know when she'll be in?"

"Let me check." Shelby wiped her hands on a paper towel, then went behind the front counter. She pulled out the schedule. Running her finger along the days and times, she stopped and pointed to the clipboard. "Looks like she and Vickie will be in… this afternoon. And first thing tomorrow morning."

Alton tapped the counter. "Good."

"Am I supposed to talk about anything in particular?"

Alton stroked his smooth-shaven chin. "Ask about the ewes' lambing. Predators. How they keep them out…"

Shelby looked at him and frowned. "Excuse me?"

"Look, I can't say much. But something's going on and I need to know…" He turned and looked around him. "Are we alone?"

"I hope so. If not, I'd be calling you about a break in."

"Fair enough." Alton smiled. "I think Lilibeth and John are hiding something. They won't talk to me, but I know you and Ella have a way to—"

"Uncover things?"

Alton nodded. "You know how people say things when their guard is down?"

"This sounds serious," said Shelby.

"Very serious," said Alton.

As Alton and Shelby finished up their conversation, Gladys rushed into The Bee's Knees. She stopped when she saw the sergeant. "Morning, Alton. Everything okay in our fair city?"

"Gladys. Yes, of course. The sun is out…"

She clicked her tongue and placed her hat and oversized purse behind the counter. Giving Alton a sideways glance, she sniffed. "I wasn't referring to the weather."

He smiled, then nodded. "You gals have a wonderful day." Whistling an unfamiliar tune, he made his way out of the shop.

Gladys slapped her hands on the counter. "Did he tell you what happened last night?"

"No," said Shelby. "What happened?" She turned as Paige strutted in, chomping a wad of gum.

Gladys elbowed Shelby. "We'll talk when it's clear."

Shelby frowned at Gladys. *What did that mean?* Sometimes Gladys watched too much TV and couldn't separate fiction from reality.

"Mornin' ladies." Paige blew out a large purple bubble, then sucked it back in. She carried a cardboard box to her booth and set it down, then walked back to the front of the shop. Running her pink sparkly nail over the sign-in sheet, she glanced at the women. "Was that Alton leaving? No trouble, I hope."

"Everything's fine," said Shelby. "Just stopped by to, um, shop…"

Gladys smirked, then leaned in to Shelby. "Good cover."

Shelby rolled her eyes. "So how's life, Paige?"

"Good. Stockin' more of my Teddy bears. Seems they've been sellin' like hotcakes." She stuffed her purse on a shelf under the register and snorted. "And the hotcakes have really been sellin'."

Gladys drummed her fingers on the counter.

"We should let you get back to restocking, Paige." Waiting until she walked away, Shelby turned to Gladys. "What is going on?"

Gladys leaned in and lowered her voice. "You know how Ed has all those radios and police scanners, right?"

Paige walked back up to them. "Coffee ready? Mine's busted and I'm needin' somethin' to get through this mornin'."

Gladys rushed over to the steaming pot. She poured a

cup, added two spoonfuls of sugar, and stirred it. "Here you go, hon. I'll carry it to your booth for you."

Before Paige could say anything, Gladys had hurried off, coffee in hand. Paige shrugged, then followed. A moment later, Gladys rushed back, slightly out of breath. "Okay, I think it's safe to continue."

Shelby eyed the spry octogenarian, then looked around them to appease the woman. "Okay, the coast is clear. Lay it on me."

"As I was saying. Ed's radios... Well, he was listening to them last night while I was watching one of my courtroom shows. You know those things have to be rigged when the defendant—"

"Gladys, we might not have time for the plot line. Just tell me what upset you."

She cleared her throat. "Yes. Yes, of course." Brushing a stray gray hair off her forehead, Gladys leaned in again. "Call came through dispatch to investigate a kidnapping."

Shelby straightened. "Say what?"

Gladys looked around her, then continued. "That's just what I said when Ed came and got me. But it's true. A real-life kidnapping."

"Where? When?" asked Shelby.

"John Morgan's property. Apparently, somebody made off with his momma."

ALTON LEANED back in his squeaky swivel chair at the police station. The acrid odor of bitter coffee wafted past him. Phones rang and were answered. The low hum of conversations paused, then continued in waves. Tapping his thinking pen on a notebook, he stared at the ceiling. Water stains. Half-dozen or more. Not good. Need to have someone check the roof now that the weather was warming.

Someone cleared their throat and brought him out of his thoughts. He nodded to the petite officer standing in front of his desk. "Cooper. Anything new to report?" While waiting, he picked up his cold coffee and took a sip.

"No, Sir. Though I received an odd tip from…" She glanced at a piece of paper. "A Mr. Gonzales."

Alton coughed and spat out the coffee, covering several folders and his notebook. "So sorry, went down the wrong way." He grabbed a used paper towel and blotted his desk. "You were saying."

Cooper wiped the front of her uniform, then glanced at the sergeant. "Something about a poo-bag in the wrong trash… Sir, would you know anything about this?"

Alton held his cup up to his lips and suppressed a smile. "Not that I recall."

Cooper pointed to the paper. "Did you find out anything about Harold Madrigal's whereabouts?"

"Not yet." Alton dug through his mountain of paperwork, flipping open files, then setting them back down again. He looked up. "Did you?"

Cooper rubbed her nose, then crossed her arms. "I know I'm the new one here. But really? A poo-bag caper, sir?"

"Would you rather patrol the waste water treatment plant outside the city? I've heard it gets quite ripe in the evening…"

Cooper cleared her throat. "No, sir. Sorry to even bring it up. I'll get back to Mr. Gonzales. Thank you." She backed away, mumbling something under her breath.

Alton turned, then chuckled. "Poo-bag caper." He leaned back in his chair again and stared at the ceiling. A few moments later, shouts erupted from the front desk area. He stood and rushed over.

John Morgan towered over a flustered clerk. His face was red, his fists clenched. "I demand to see Alton Nolan."

Alton walked up. "What's going on?"

John turned; his eyes fixed on the sergeant. "I demand you find my mother and bring her back."

Alton reached for the man's shoulder. "John, how about we go over to my desk—"

John pulled back, then shoved a chair, causing it to topple and crash on the floor. "My mother is missing and you're here drinking coffee and eating donuts. You're not doing squat." He poked Alton's chest with his thick finger. "I pay your salary." Poke. "You need to get off your—"

Other officers had gathered around the two men. Cooper stood next to them, her hand on her leather belt. Alton took a step forward into John's space. "I'd suggest backing down, Mr. Morgan. Unless you want to be arrested for assaulting a police officer." He stared at John, not breaking eye contact.

John stared back. Not blinking. Not flinching.

Alton took another step, forcing John against the wall. "Did you hear me, Mr. Morgan?"

John lowered his hand. He inched away from Alton, then glared at the officers. Looking directly at the sergeant, he jutted out his chin. "This isn't over." Then he turned and stomped out of the station.

CHAPTER THIRTY-FOUR

Oatmeal pawed at Ella's leg and barked.

"You need to go out?"

He yipped and ran into the kitchen. Ella eased herself up, then followed. In the mudroom she put on a light jacket and slipped on tennis shoes, and went outside with her furry companion. Oatmeal sniffed around and did his business on the lawn. Heading back to the porch, the beep beep beep of a truck backing up caught their attention. Ella crouched behind a four-foot hedge, watching with her dog. A large yellow truck had stopped in the driveway next door.

She looked at Oatmeal. "Looks like our new neighbor is moving in." Attempting to stay out of sight, Ella tried to glimpse at the new family. Her plan would have worked until Oatmeal welcomed the new arrivals by letting out a series of high-pitched yips, followed by a growl and barking.

"Shush, dog. I don't want them to think I'm spying—"

A woman's voice called out to her. "Hey there, neighbor."

Ella peeked over the top of the hedge and waved. "Welcome to the neighborhood."

A plus-sized African American woman with purple streaked-hair dashed across her property. She extended her hand over the hedge. "LaTonya Lewis."

"Nice to meet you, LaTonya. I'm Ella. Ella Denning."

"Don't you co-own that cute crafter's place downtown?"

Ella nodded.

"I met your business partner the other day. Shelby, right?"

"Yes…"

"Well, I just had to drop in and see what's buzzing in town. You have a great staff and the handmade things… I coulda spent a month's pay in there easily."

"What brings you to our community, LaTonya?"

She hooked her thumbs in imaginary suspenders and rocked back and forth on her heels. "I'm the new deputy sheriff in town."

"You're Sergeant Lewis?"

"In the flesh. And honey," she wiggled her hips and chuckled. "I've got a lot of that."

Ella laughed. "Shelby said you were a character."

"Ah yes, word gets around fast in these small towns."

Someone from LaTonya's front yard yelled for her. She waved to the moving crew. "Be right there." She turned to Ella. "Guess I'm needed. Don't want the kitchen dishes to end up in the bedroom. Look forward to chatting more after I get settled. Later taters." With that, she gave a backhanded wave and jogged back to her house.

SHELBY STOOD at The Bee's Knee's front counter watching Gladys unpack a box of apple butter. The spry woman turned each container facing the aisle so potential customers would see the cheerful labels touting each homemade product.

After she was happy with their placement, Gladys meticulously staged the jars with sprigs of cinnamon, bringing a full sensory experience to anyone passing by the welcoming booth. She stood back, admiring her work, then moved one jar a bit to the left. Placing her hands on her hips, she nodded. "Looking good, if I say so myself." She picked up the empty box and headed over to Shelby.

On her way, Paige called out. "Gladys, come look at my bears. Somethin' seems off, but I can put my finger on it…"

Shelby watched the camaraderie of the vendors and smiled. Each willing to help one another, offering comments on displays and product placement. A win-win for them and customers. She walked behind the counter to check the schedule again when her cell signaled an incoming call. "Hello, Lilibeth. How are—Oh, not coming in today. I'm sorry to hear… Need to stay at the ranch… Vickie, too… Trade with someone else…? I guess I can… Oh, thanks for the—" The call ended abruptly without explanation of why either woman wouldn't be able to work their volunteer hours. *Did it have something to do with Gladys' kidnapping story? Or Alton's visit?* Something wasn't right, but there wasn't much she could do at the moment. Unless…

Shelby looked down at her phone, found a number, and swiped CALL. "Vivian. Yes, it's Shelby at the shop. How are you…? That's good to hear. I was wondering… A few volunteers cancelled this afternoon… You would? That's great Viv… After lunch is fine, say one o'clock? Thanks so much. See you then. Bye."

As Shelby erased Vickie and Lilibeth's names in the afternoon time slot and penciled in Viv's name, Gladys came up to the counter. She stared at the schedule. "Hmmm. Mighty suspicious, don't you think?"

Shelby raised an eyebrow. "How so, Gladys?"

Gladys looked around, then moved closer. "Kidnapping at the Morgan's. Girls don't come in…"

"Probably just a coincidence." Though Shelby didn't voice her opinion, her sleuthing brain agreed with the woman's assumption.

Gladys peered over her shoulder, then placed her hand on Shelby's arm. "Look, I wasn't supposed to tell anyone this… but Eleanor was never sick. She was…" She looked around again. "You can keep a secret, right?"

Shelby nodded.

"Eleanor was hiding out at the Morgan farm. In one of those little cabins. We were in communication every day… well until yesterday. No matter how many times I call, she won't answer. If you ask me, that son of hers is up to no good. And now he's pulled the girls into it…"

"Gladys, why would you even say that?" asked Shelby.

"Say what?" Paige walked up, her jaw working on a large wad of gum. "Sounds like some juicy gossip. Tell me. Tell me."

Gladys cleared her throat and picked an invisible fuzz from her sweater. "Just talking about, er… a TV show I was watching last night."

Paige looked over at Shelby and sniffed. "I wasn't born yesterday. How 'bout I share my gossip if you share yours?"

Shelby straightened. "What are you talking about, Paige?"

Paige smoothed her hands on her skin-tight, hot pink capris, then smiled at the two women. "Let's just say waitressing those tables and standing at the register, one hears a lot of talk at the Corner Café. And yours truly heard plenty last night."

⸺

ELEANOR EASED onto the unmade bed in the dingy motel room. Although it was mid-morning, the olive-green drapes were drawn to keep anyone from looking into their first-floor window and to buffer out the bright sunlight so Harold could rest. Sleep hadn't come easy for either, but Eleanor was relieved he was finally resting. Ever since he revealed his terminal illness the night before, he seemed to deteriorate by the hour.

She brushed her trembling fingers through Harold's unruly hair, stroking a damp curl on his forehead. Except for the gray, he still had the same boyish charm that had caught her eye when he was nineteen and she was almost eighteen...

An incoming call from John jarred her from her thoughts. He'd called and texted over a half-dozen times since yesterday. Eleanor had refused to answer. Nor would she listen to the voice mails, adamant to not let him get to her. Moments after her phone ceased ringing, Harold's phone vibrated. She got up and stared at the display. According to the screen there had been several missed calls and messages from Alton, Gladys, Shelby, and another number with no caller ID. While she was staring at the phone, Harold stirred, then coughed.

Eleanor went to him and sat on the bed. She leaned in and whispered. "Are you hungry? Thirsty?"

He sat up and shook his head. "Maybe some water..."

Eleanor reached for a cup and held it to Harold's pale lips. He sipped the water, then pushed it away.

"How about some crackers? Or…"

Harold shook his head. "Not hungry. Just… want… to… rest." He coughed deeply, lay back down, then closed his eyes.

When Eleanor's husband Richard was in the end stages of his cancer battle, he'd preferred rest over food. She tried to remind herself how Harold had enjoyed dinner the night before, so she needn't worry. But her heart knew better. Deep down, she knew Harold had come back. To be with her. And die.

———

SHELBY HELPED a customer with his purchases while Gladys dusted nearby shelves and Paige filed her nails. As soon as the man left, the three women gathered in the middle of the display floor and stared at each other. Shelby cleared her throat. "So what did you hear, Paige?"

She tapped a sparkly pink nail on her chin. "Well, rumor has it…" She looked around. "Harold and some woman left town last night… headed west on the 58 toward Bakersfield."

Shelby cocked her head. "Who told you this?"

Gladys straightened and stared at Paige.

Paige's eyes widened. "You know Harold's so friendly and never forgets his manners. But when he pulled up next to Joleen at the fillin' station, she waved and yelled 'howdy', but Harold never turned to acknowledge Jo, even though they've been neighbors for years… And there was some woman sittin' in the front seat who wouldn't even look Jo's way when she tapped on the window. Don't ya think that's odd?"

"Harold ignored Joleen?" Gladys nodded. "She's one of the friendliest people in town."

Paige pointed a finger at Gladys. "Jo, um, my source, said them two looked to be in a hurry and as soon as the tank filled, they took off like a bat outta... well, you know. Squealed the tires and everything like one of them race car drivers."

Shelby suppressed a smile at Paige's description of Harold's actions. Did Harold really kidnap Eleanor? It was too bizarre to think about.

Popping her gum, Paige leaned in close to Gladys. "I spilled, now it's your turn. What did you hear?"

Gladys fidgeted. She pulled a tissue from her bra, wiped her nose, then pushed it back inside. "I'm not supposed to tell anyone..."

"Yeah, whatever," said Paige. "We had a deal."

Gladys rolled her eyes. "Fine. Ed alerted me last night when there was a report of a kidnapping out at the Morgan ranch. Apparently, John called in to say someone had abducted Eleanor. But..." She took in a deep breath and let it out. "I know for a fact that Eleanor was staying out there, even though John said he didn't know where she was."

Paige listened saying nothing. She didn't even chew her gum.

"So, could he have taken Eleanor against her will?" asked Shelby.

Gladys shook her head. "No way. Those two were..." She clasped her hand over her mouth.

"They were what?" asked Shelby.

Paige put her hands on her hips and smiled. "They was in love, wasn't they?"

Gladys coughed. "I've said too much. Need to get back to my dusting.

Before she could take a step, the women blocked her path. "Spill it, Gladys," said Paige. "We need to know."

Gladys backed down. "Fine. But this goes no further." She pointed her finger at Paige and Shelby. "Promise you won't breathe a word of this anywhere…"

They nodded.

Gladys wrung her hands and licked her lips. "Years ago, Harold and Eleanor were a thing. But something happened and they broke up. They've always been in love. But the timing was off. When ol' Agnes came into the picture, she knew something about their shared past. She hinted around at it, trying to get a rise out of Eleanor, but it never came to anything. Even got her kicked out of the button club by starting more rumors. All that fighting… had nothing to do with Harold and Agnes' divorce. It was all about some dirt Agnes had on them. Guess the old bat went too far, and well, someone made sure she would never tell."

"Are you saying Harold or Eleanor killed Agnes?" asked Shelby. "And now they're running away?"

Gladys eyed Shelby, then Paige. "I'm not saying anything. But if you put two and two together, things add up."

"Okay, so they ran off together," said Shelby. "I get that. But why would John accuse Harold of kidnapping his mother? It makes no sense."

Paige raised her hand like she was in school. "I know. I know."

"Paige, do you have something to share?" asked Shelby.

"John's had it in for Harold since, well, forever. Can't stand the man. Makes sense that he's protectin' his momma by callin' in a fake snatching. Harold gets arrested for kidnapping and murder and never bothers Eleanor again. John's happy. End of story."

"Harold couldn't kill anyone, right Gladys?" asked Shelby.

Gladys paused, then brushed a stray hair from her forehead. "Well… about twenty years ago, before either of you came to Pheasant Valley…"

"Wait. What?" asked Shelby.

"The way I remember it, Harold was married," said Gladys. "Her name was… Lydia, I think. Their marriage was good for a good while, then things turned ugly. A divorce was pending. Soon after, they found her shot dead in their front room."

Shelby opened her mouth, but said nothing.

"Harold said he thought someone had broken in. He called out a warning, then aimed and fired. Turns out the soon-to-be ex used a spare key to help herself to some heirlooms. He maintained he was protecting himself. But, who knows…" She paused, then continued. "After a thorough investigation, they ruled self-defense and Harold wasn't charged."

Paige popped another bubble and stared at Shelby. "Didn't see that comin'."

"Well, that wasn't all…" said Gladys. "Supposedly, Eleanor and Harold had a thing going on before her husband Richard's death. Both married to other people, yet tending each other's gardens, if you know what I mean."

"You think that's why John hates him?" asked Shelby.

"I'd bet my priceless button collection on it," said Gladys. She picked up a feather duster. "Enough gossip for one day. Those shelves are calling to me."

Gladys turned and walked down an aisle, followed by Paige. Shelby went behind the counter, pondering Gladys' story. While it answered some questions, now even more were swirling around in her mind.

CHAPTER THIRTY-FIVE

S helby pulled into the driveway of Ella's home and parked. After exiting her jeep, she paused and watched the cloud-filled sky transform into brilliant shades of yellow, orange, and red as the sun dropped behind the Pheasant Valley mountains. Listening to the coyotes yelping in the distance and the owls' mournful hoots echoing from a nearby pine tree, she smiled. Coming home was the best part of her day.

As Shelby walked through the front door, Oatmeal yipped and danced. Mr. Butterfingers opened an eye, then stretched out along the back of the couch and resumed his nap. The scent of roasted chicken and something sweet tickled her senses. She closed her eyes and took in a deep breath, savoring the moment.

Ella approached from the kitchen, wiping her hands on a dishtowel. She greeted Shelby with a hug. "How was your day?"

"Better now that I'm home." Shelby removed her sweater and dropped her keys on the coffee table. "Something smells wonderful."

"I was feeling better and made a special dinner for us. Chicken and all the fixings." Ella pointed to the animals. "Along with some pet-friendly pumpkin biscuits."

Shelby plopped onto the couch and slipped off her pink tennis shoes. "If it's all the same to you, I'll stick with the brownies from last night."

Ella laughed. "Long day?"

"More like a weird one."

Ella sat next to her. "In what way?"

Rubbing her eyes, Shelby told Ella about the day's events. "But when Gladys told us all about Harold's past—"

"Harold's past?" asked Ella.

Shelby shared Gladys' story. "Hard to believe, isn't it?"

Ella nodded. "He had alluded to something before helping Doug and me buy the coffee shop, but never went into details. I'm at a loss for words."

"Well… I called Viv to take her daughters' place, hoping she might offer insight on the kidnapping—"

"A kidnapping?"

Shelby recapped the conversation and brought Ella up to speed.

"Still at a loss for words," said Ella. "I can't believe…. Did Viv offer any insight?"

Rubbing Oatmeal behind his ears, Shelby shook her head. "When I pressed, Viv got all flustered and was a bundle of nerves for the rest of the afternoon. Guess I shouldn't have said anything."

A timer dinged, and Ella stood. "Well, a most interesting day for sure. Seems we have a lot to untangle during dinner."

"If you don't mind, I'd rather talk about something else." Shelby pushed herself off the couch and followed Ella. "What about your day? Anything happen?"

"Actually, yes. But not nearly as exciting." Ella opened the oven, took out a deep iron skillet, and placed it on a burner. "Chicken in one pot."

"I like it," said Shelby, setting the table.

After the women had served themselves, they sat, flanked by their pets. Ella smiled and turned to Oatmeal. "Promise there will be plenty, so no begging." She speared a piece of chicken and held it up, allowing the steam to rise. "I met our new neighbor today."

Shelby looked up from her plate. "Oh really? And…"

"Turns out you already know her. LaTonya Lewis, our new deputy sheriff."

"Seriously?" asked Shelby. "That's awesome."

"I'm looking forward to getting—" Ella's phone signaled an incoming call. She looked at the display and gasped. "It's Harold…"

LILIBETH MORGAN CURLED up near the crackling fireplace in her front room. John had stayed in his office for most of the evening, even during dinner. Hearing footsteps, she looked up from a book she was reading and watched her husband pull his jacket from a peg on the wall, then shove a set of keys in his pocket. "Headed somewhere?" she asked.

He stared at his wife. "Got business to do."

Lilibeth folded back a page corner, closed her book, and stood. "Need any help?"

John shook his head and rested his hand on the doorknob. "This doesn't concern you."

"John…"

"Don't wait up." He left, slamming the door behind him.

Vickie had been coming down the stairs, but paused while the couple exchanged words. After the door closed, she stepped off the last stair wearing a well-worn pair of flannel pajamas. "Everything okay, Sis?"

Lilibeth sat again. "Don't know. Something's up with John. Have you noticed how fidgety he's been?"

"Seems angrier to me." Vickie joined her sister on the couch. "If that's even possible."

"I'm worried, Vic. He's preoccupied with something. Usually he tells me everything, but now... he's gone a lot, making weird requests—"

"You mean like last night?" asked Vickie.

Lilibeth nodded. "John said Alton needed help training that new cop. Cooper, I think, was her name."

"I enjoyed making that old cabin look like a tornado hit it," said Vicki. "Hopefully, it helped."

Lilibeth shrugged her shoulders. "I never asked. After he came home, he seemed more upset than ever."

"You think it's because I've been staying here?" asked Vickie.

"No, you come every spring during lambing season," said Lilibeth. "He's never complained in the past. In fact, he always enjoyed your company."

Facing her sister, Vickie rubbed Lilibeth's hand. "You don't think he's seeing another wo—"

Lilibeth straightened. "Not John. Why would you even think that?"

Vickie frowned. "Sneaking out at night. Not letting you go with him... Lying. All the signs are there, Sis. You need to open your eyes."

EDUARDO GONZALES OPENED the blinds in his front room window just enough to get a view of the neighborhood. With notebook and pen in hand, he began his nightly report, using military time to make it look more official:

19:05—Harrison (resident at 4313) drum noise from garage.

19:15—Grant (from 4312) walks dog.

19:19—Grant tosses full poo bag in resident 4313 trash can.

"Ha," he said aloud. "Caught him red-handed again. Need to contact Officer Cooper and update—" He watched a vehicle slow down, then park.

19:20—Unidentified truck in front of Ricardo residence (4309). Red Chevy. Extended cab. Dent in left rear quarter panel, trailing blue smoke, possible blown gasket.

Eduardo forced the blinds wider and squinted. "If only I could make out the license plate…" He turned his head to the side. "Tree trunk in the way. Unfortunate. Can't make out who's inside either…" Eduardo wondered if he should alert the police. After thinking about his obligations to the neighborhood, he knew what he had to do.

ELLA KEPT her phone on the table while answering the call from Harold. After swiping the icon, she quickly put it on speaker. "Harold, so good to hear from you."

"Ella, this is Eleanor… I'm calling from Harold's phone."

Ella suppressed a gasp. "Eleanor? Why are you on Harold's phone… Is he okay?"

Shelby stared at Ella. "Eleanor?"

Ella nodded.

"I'm sorry to bother you." Eleanor was silent for a moment, then spoke. "I didn't know who else to—"

"Hon, what's going on?" Ella pulled the phone closer to her. "Where's Harold?"

"He's here with me… He's not, um, feeling well. I hate to ask you this, but he needs his medicine and left it at home…"

"Where is he?" asked Ella. "Where are you?"

"Look, I shouldn't even be calling… But Harold and I… We had to go… Ella, I need your help… I can explain everything when you…"

"When I what? Eleanor… what do you need me to do?"

Shelby grabbed a pen and piece of paper. She slid it to Ella and waited.

Eleanor continued. "I need you to go to Harold's house. Get his medicine and bring it to us." As they heard violent coughing in the background, the phone muted.

Waiting, the women stared at each other.

"Sorry about that," said Eleanor. "Can you please help us, Ella? I can't leave and Harold can't…"

"Of course, Eleanor," said Ella. "Just tell me how to get into Harold's house and what I'm looking for. Then, you'll need to tell me where you are…"

An audible sigh of relief came from the phone. "Thank you. And one more thing," said Eleanor. "As much as I care about Shelby, I need you to come alone. We can't risk anyone else knowing where we are… (coughing in the background)… I've said too much. Please call me at this number when you get to his house. I'll walk you through getting inside. Then we'll go from there…. Is that okay?"

"Of course, Eleanor. Anything for you and Har—"

The call ended. Ella glanced at Shelby. "What do you think that was all about?"

"Who knows?" said Shelby. "But this is huge, El. Do you realize that you'll finally be able to talk to Eleanor and Harold and find out where she's been and why she's been hid—"

Ella raised her hand. "Hold on. Something's not right. I'm concerned about both of them, but the last thing I'm going to do is walk in and interrogate them. That's Alton's job."

Shelby gave Ella a side-glance. "You going to tell Alton?"

Ella rubbed her forehead. "Not until it's absolutely necessary."

"And when will that be?" asked Shelby.

"Guess I'll know when I get there."

CHAPTER THIRTY-SIX

Officer Cooper walked past Sargeant Nolan carrying a stack of file folders. She nodded to him as she proceeded to her desk.

Alton glanced up at the clock on the station wall. He'd been sitting far too long and his backside wasn't happy. He stood and stretched. "Burning the night oil, Cooper?"

"Just finishing up some case work, sir." She followed Alton's gaze to the clock. "Hope to be out of here before nine."

He picked up his coffee cup and went for a refill. After pouring, he spooned powdered creamer into it and stirred, though his mind was elsewhere.

"Sir..."

Alton looked down, but it was too late. He'd splashed coffee out of the cup and onto his uniform. "Well, that didn't go as planned."

Cooper brought him a stack of paper towels, then hurried back to her desk so the sergeant wouldn't notice the smile on her face. For a man so meticulous about his looks, she found the situation humorous.

After flipping through files on her desk, she observed Sergeant Nolan frantically wiping his shirt and talking to himself. She was so caught up in trying to hear his muttering, she failed to notice the clerk standing next to her.

A red-haired woman cleared her throat. "Excuse me, Officer Cooper. You have a message from a Mr. Gonzales—"

Cooper rolled her eyes, then took the piece of paper. After reading it, she stood and thanked the clerk. The officer went over to Alton's desk, where he was still wiping and mumbling. "Sir, you might be interested in reading this…"

Alton studied the message, then looked at the young officer. "What do you think, Cooper?"

She took a step back. "You're asking me, sir?"

Alton looked around, then back to her. "Who else would I be talking to?"

"I'm sorry. I didn't mean to be disrespectful." She straightened. "Mr. Gonzales seems to enjoy watching his neighbors. As for this unidentified truck, it could be anything or nothing at all."

"Agreed," said Alton. "Though heading over might be prudent. How about you take an unmarked car, drive through the neighborhood, and observe for yourself?"

Cooper looked at the files stacked precariously on her desk. "Guess the paperwork can wait."

"Only until you get back from your patrol. I need those reports before you clock out for the night."

Cooper's shoulders sagged. "Yes, sir. On it." She pulled on her jacket and headed toward the front of the station. Everything inside of her knew it was a waste of time, but orders were orders. Maybe some fresh air would do her good.

ELLA LEFT HOME, then headed south on Lupine Road to Harold's house. He lived in the gated community near Dr Parke's old home. Thinking back to last year's tragic end to Parke's life, she tried to bring back fond memories of the deceased dentist, though it was difficult under the circumstances of his death.

She pulled up to the gate and stopped. Without someone to let her in, she wondered how she would gain access. Taking out her phone, Ella's heart-rate increased as she searched for Harold's number to call Eleanor for the gate code. Before long, another car drove up, and the gate opened. Ella dropped her phone on the seat and followed the other vehicle. Crisis averted.

Once inside the gates, she marveled at the older neighborhood's charm. Overgrown eucalyptus trees framed the streets. Every house had neatly kept lawns welcoming visitors. Some had decorative lights leading up the sidewalk to the front entrance while others sported well-manicured shrubs dotting the properties.

Although it had been years since Ella had been a guest in his home, everything became familiar again as she turned left, then right, on her way to Silver Ridge Lane. When Ella and Doug owned the Steamed Bean, they'd been to Harold's many times for quarterly Chamber of Commerce meetings. Back in those days, all the downtown merchants met to discuss how to reach new customers by cross promoting their businesses. A win-win for everyone.

Ella turned onto Silver Ridge and stopped in front of Harold's home. She got out of her car and took in the minty, camphor scent of eucalyptus. It reminded her of the forest and helped clear her head. Feeling comfortable, Ella marched up the sidewalk to the front door, completely unaware of who was watching her every movement.

Ella stood under the porch next to a potted plant she couldn't identify. She called Harold's phone and waited for it to connect. "I'm here," she said. "Now what?"

Eleanor's voice remained calm as she walked Ella through getting into the house and finding the pain medicines. After intense coughing came from the background, Eleanor promised to call Ella back and ended the call.

Finished with the first part of her 'mission,' Ella went back to her car and buckled in. She used the light from her phone to read the prescriptions. "Two types of opioids for pain management… extended release pills and a spray for immediate relief…. Oh, Harold…"

Her phone signaled a call from Harold's phone. After answering, she put it on speaker to enable her to drive and talk. "Eleanor…"

"We can chat when you get here."

"And where's here?"

"About forty-five minutes west of Pheasant Valley, at a motel on the outskirts of Bakersfield. Just before you get into the city limits."

Ella blinked. According to information shared by Paige, Shelby thought they had headed toward the sprawling city. While it had been years since she'd lived in the large town, it wasn't unfamiliar. "Okay, give me time to get on the 58 and head your way."

"Call me when you get close to town and I'll give you the address. And Ella, please make sure no one follows you…"

Ella swallowed, knowing she was about to face the two people wanted in the murder of Agnes Cormack. The two

214

people who had been the topic of conversation and rumors over the last few days. The same two people Alton had asked for her and Shelby's help in locating.

Raindrops dotted the windshield and her heart pounded as she made her way out of the gated neighborhood, turning left on Lupine Road. Remembering Eleanor's warning, she checked her rearview mirror. A truck emitting a blue haze and another car had followed her out, but Ella dismissed it as an overactive imagination. Her breathing calmed as she merged onto westbound highway 58 and headed down the hill. Telling her Bluetooth to call Harold, she waited for Eleanor to answer. "Hey, I'm on my way... No, I didn't see anyone following me."

CHAPTER THIRTY-SEVEN

After Ella left to help Eleanor, Shelby tried to stay busy. As she paced, the animals followed until Mr. Butterfingers seemed to get bored. He retired to the top of the couch and yawned, then fell asleep. Oatmeal settled next to Shelby once she sunk into the wingback chair. She stared up at the ticking clock, wondering what was going on. The awaited call and update had not happened. Shelby noticed her leg bouncing and stood. Oatmeal looked up at her.

"Sorry, dog. Just can't sit and wait any longer." She went upstairs to her room and turned on the overhead light. Searching for her sketchbook, she noticed movement in the house next door. Shelby stood near the open blinds and looked out the rain-streaked window for just a moment. LaTonya Lewis was unpacking and… dancing. She laughed. Only LaTonya could elevate unboxing to a joyful event.

Shelby closed the blinds and went to her workspace. Glancing at the floor, she let out a long sigh. She still hadn't unpacked the last two lopsided boxes she'd brought with her when she moved in with Ella last November. Opening one, she pulled out a stack of old design journals. Shelby pushed aside winter clothes and fabric piled on the floor with her socked foot and sat in the middle of the surrounding chaos. Flipping through the first journal, she smiled. Maybe it was time to get back to designing.

Oatmeal yipped and licked Shelby's face. She scratched the small, white dog behind his ears. "So you think I should start designing again, too?"

Another yip, followed by tail wagging.

"I don't know why I've waited. Guess I never thought I was good enough." She looked at Oatmeal and he responded by cocking his head. "Thanks for listening, dog." Twisting a drawing pencil into her messy bun, Shelby took the notebook and went downstairs.

Back on the couch, she stared at the blank page. As much as she tried to draw something, even a small doodle, her mind went back to Ella. As the rain pinged on the front awning, the wind chimes tinkled a multi-toned melody. Shelby looked at Oatmeal. "Should I call her? Just to make sure she's okay. I mean, it is raining?"

Oatmeal yipped.

"Awesome-sauce. I'm taking that as a yes." Shelby swiped her phone, put it on speaker, and waited for Ella to answer.

"Hello, Shelby?"

"I'm so sorry to call El... but——"

"Hold on a sec, let me adjust the volume... The sound of a semi-truck passing muffled your last words. Okay, that's better... I'm so glad you called..."

"Do I dare ask where you are or where you're headed?"

Ella nodded, even though Shelby couldn't see her. "Down the hill. Supposed to meet them at the edge of town at some motel..."

"I didn't catch that last word, but it sounded like you're going to Bakersfield?"

"Yes."

"Are you okay?" asked Shelby.

"Well, I'm heading somewhere in the rain to meet up with someone in an undisclosed location to deliver medicine and then…"

"And then, what?"

"Hopefully, I can convince them to come back to Pheasant Valley and talk to Alton. But…"

Shelby scratched Oatmeal's ear and waited. But when Ella didn't finish, she tapped her foot. "If that doesn't happen, then what?"

"Don't know. Guess I'll have to see what happens."

"How's the rain?"

"Not bad, just trying to avoid the over-spray from the semis in front of me…. Hey, the traffic is slowing. I need to concentrate on the road."

"El… take care, okay?" As the call ended, Shelby looked at Oatmeal. "Gotta keep me company, boy. Tonight's gonna be a long one for all of us."

As Ella passed over Towerline Road, she told her Bluetooth to call Harold. She waited. And waited. And waited… Voicemail. "Oh no," whispered Ella. "Now what?"

A moment later, her phone signaled an incoming call from Harold's cell. She answered, her heart pounding. "Eleanor?"

"Yes, I'm here," said Eleanor, catching her breath. "So sorry, had to visit the ladies' room."

Ella smiled and unclenched the steering wheel. "Okay, I'm getting closer…"

"You're going to exit at the 178, then head north, past Edison Highway…"

"The exit for the 178 is… hold on, sign coming up… five miles."

"Good. Almost there. You'll be looking for Breckenridge Road. Turn right and the motel will be on the right side. End of the Road motel."

"The motel is at the end of the road?" asked Ella.

"No, that's the name," said Eleanor.

Sounded grim to Ella, but she said nothing. "Okay, I think I've got it. If I get stuck, I'll call again."

"I'll be watching for you," said Eleanor.

"Wait… What room are you in?" But the call had already ended. "Guess I'll have to call again when I get there," she said out loud. Checking her rearview mirror, she exited the highway. A few cars followed, but she paid little attention since it the first big exit with restaurants, gas stations, motels, and hotels. The windshield wipers kept up a steady swoosh, swoosh, lulling her back into a relaxed state. She passed Edison Highway, then turned right on Breckenridge Road. Driving slower, she squinted ahead through the misty rain. Bright headlights, mixed with neon, created a weird glow around the different signs.

After Ella passed a small white food truck on the side of the road, a broken, half-lite neon sign blinked, "E-d of t-- -oad Mote-." Shuddering, she pulled into the small parking lot. Ella glanced around and spotted Harold's car parked at the far end of the L-shaped building. With trembling hands, she swiped her phone and made the call. "I'm here."

"Lucky room number 13," said Eleanor, then she ended the call.

"Let's hope so," Ella whispered as she exited her car. Zipping her jacket, hoping to avert the cold, driving rain, she made her way to their room.

CHAPTER THIRTY-EIGHT

Watching fat raindrops bounce off the sidewalk outside the motel room, Eleanor waited. She opened the door for Ella, then feigned a smile. "Thank you so much for coming." After closing it, Eleanor secured the lock, then slid the safety latch closed.

Ella gave Eleanor a hug, then stepped back. "So sorry, I'm covered in rain." She brushed off her clothes, then looked around, her eyes stopping on the bed. She gasped. "Harold?"

Eleanor grabbed Ella's hand. "He… he's not responding to me anymore. Maybe…"

Ella rushed over and sat. Rain dripped from her hair, spotting the dingy blanket covering her pallid friend. She grabbed Harold's frail hand, and held it, then looked up at Eleanor. "What happened? We just talked a few days ago…"

She walked over to Ella and sighed. "He didn't want anyone to know. Stage four lung cancer—"

A car door slammed outside. Voices became louder as someone walked past their room. Eleanor closed her eyes and waited. A few moments later, she looked at Ella. "Sorry. I'm just so afraid…"

Harold stirred, then coughed.

Ella pulled the medicine from her pocket and gave it to Eleanor, then stared at Harold. "I just… I don't know what to say."

Eleanor spoke softly to Harold, then sprayed the medicine in his mouth. His eyes fluttered, but then he appeared to go back to sleep.

"Have you eaten lately?" asked Ella.

Pointing to the stacks of takeout food containers, Eleanor nodded. "I have, but not Harold… nothing since yesterday."

"Not even water?"

Eleanor shook her head and brushed a tear rolling down her cheek.

"I'm so, so sorry," said Ella. "I wish there was something I could do. Or say. But…"

"It's okay. I'm just glad you're here." Eleanor glanced away. She wanted to explain what had happened. She needed to explain. But everything about the night Agnes was killed seemed like ages ago. Now, nothing mattered but keeping Harold comfortable until…

Ella patted the bed. "Eleanor, come sit. You look… well, you look exhausted."

"The last few days have been tough," she said, sitting next to Ella. "I wanted to call… But I was… afraid. No one knows we're here. Except you."

"I'm glad you trusted me enough to call."

Eleanor nodded. "Between Agnes' death and Harold… It's just too much." She covered her face with trembling hands and wept.

Ella held Eleanor and rubbed her back. She wanted to

say something, but decided no words would compare to the comforting touch of a friend. Feeling her eyes prickle, she allowed her tears to flow. In empathy with Eleanor and in grief for the imminent loss of her good friend, Harold.

The women rocked and held each other until Eleanor pulled back. "Thank you for... everything." She wiped her eyes and blew her nose in a tissue. "You... don't have to rush back home... do you?"

Ella's voice softened. "I can stay."

Eleanor smiled, then got up. She pulled a chair next to the bed and eased into it. "I'm just so... so tired. Of hiding... of—"

Harold coughed violently, then was quiet again. His breathing became labored.

Ella held one of Harold's hands while Eleanor held the other. "We were supposed to have a long life together. It was supposed to be our time... But I was afraid Alton would..."

"I'm so sorry," said Ella. "You know, he only wanted to ask you a few questions."

Eleanor's head snapped up. "I didn't kill her, you know. It was an accident. I was only protecting Harold."

Ella stiffened. "What are you talking about? What was an accident?"

"Her death. I mean, she died because I hit her."

Frowning, Ella made eye contact with her friend. "Do you know how she died?"

Eleanor shook her head.

"Someone stabbed her in the side of her heart with a pair of knitting needles," said Ella. "It was in the newspaper. John didn't tell you?"

Eleanor's face reddened. "He told me it was my fault. That I knocked Agnes out and killed her. That's why..." She clamped her free hand over her mouth.

"Why what, Eleanor? Please tell me."

"John said they knew I did it." Her eyes widened. "He told me I had to hide in one of his outbuildings until we could sort things out."

"How would John know what happened?"

"I told him… that I knocked Agnes out when she tried to stab Harold. They were fighting in the alley. It was…" She covered her face. "And I hit her. She fell backwards and hit the pavement with an awful thud. After she didn't move, I ran." Eleanor looked up. "I ran and didn't look back. I didn't know where anyone else was, but I just wanted to get out of there…"

PARKED across the street from the End of the Road Motel, a man in a truck sat and watched. Drumming his thick fingers on the steering wheel, he decided he'd waited long enough. He'd observed Ella go into a room, though he wasn't sure which one. Opening the glove box, the man grabbed something, then got out. Zipping his jacket, he pulled up the collar and made his way across the dark, empty road. Rain pelted his face, but it didn't matter. He was used to the cold mountain wind and snow. He walked up to each door and put his ear to them, listening for familiar voices.

"I KNOW YOU WERE SCARED, but I wish you'd told Alton," said Ella. "I'm sure he would have listened and not arrested you."

Eleanor stared up at the ceiling. "I'm so stupid for not trusting anyone. But John… he told me I couldn't."

"I wish you'd trusted me." Ella smiled. "Or Gladys... We believe in you."

She looked at Ella and blinked several times. "You said someone stabbed Agnes with one of my needles?"

"That's what it seems. Why?"

"Sounds like someone would have gotten lucky or known what they were doing."

Ella frowned. "I'm not sure I follow you."

"Years ago, I had heart surgery. I remember the surgeon saying that they needed to separate the ribs to get at the heart. So, if someone were to stab a person..."

"They'd have to know where to stick the needle for the most impact."

Eleanor nodded. "Agnes was wearing a heavy coat. The power was out, and that alley was dark. If I'd tried, I wouldn't have had any idea where to stab her."

"What about strength?" asked Ella. "Didn't they have to use a saw or something to open your ribs?"

"Yes."

"We need to tell Alton..."

Harold took in a deep breath, then muttered something.

"No." Eleanor stood. "I mean, not tonight at least. Tomorrow?"

Ella nodded. "I suppose we can—"

Loud banging came from the other side of the door. "Harold, I know you have Mom in there. I have a gun. Open the door or I'll break it down."

Eleanor's eyes went wild. "John? How did...?"

"Don't move." Ella stood and took her phone from her pocket. "I'm calling nine-one—"

Another voice, a female's, was heard. "Drop the gun." Then scuffling and footfalls on the pavement.

Eleanor and Ella stared at each other. After it quieted

down outside, Ella walked to the window, held the curtain back a bit, and peered out. She motioned for Eleanor to stand next to her.

Looking outside, they saw several police units, their lights reflecting off the wet pavement. Officers stood around a man, now cuffed. As the women watched, Eleanor gasped. "They've arrested John."

One officer put him in the back of a local police unit. There seemed to be more conversation between the officers, then a female officer in a Pheasant Valley Police uniform broke off from the others. She walked toward motel room number thirteen, her hand resting on her leather belt.

"She knows I'm here." Eleanor stepped back from the window. "Ella, please don't let them arrest me."

CHAPTER THIRTY-NINE

S harp knocking, then a woman's voice called out.
"Pheasant Valley police. Please open the door."

Eleanor looked around the small motel room and gasped. "I can't... leave him."

"We have to talk to her," said Ella.

"What if...?" asked Eleanor.

"I'm not going anywhere. We'll talk to her together." Ella straightened her shoulders and walked over to the door. Then she opened it. "Officer."

Andrea Cooper stood outside. "Is everyone okay?"

Ella nodded and looked at Eleanor. "Yes, just shook up. Would you like to come in?"

"Thank you," said Cooper. She entered the room. "I'm Officer Cooper. Pheasant Valley PD. We had a report of a kidnapping..."

Ella stepped forward, extending her hand. "Ella Denning." She nodded to Eleanor and introduced her, then Harold.

"Does the gentleman need medical attention?" she asked.

Eleanor shook her head. "No."

Cooper took a small notebook and pen from her jacket pocket. "Ma'am, I need to ask you a few questions. Can we step outside?"

Eleanor hesitated. "Officer Cooper, if it's all the same, I'd rather stay in here. My friend Harold is... well, he's dying and I have nothing to hide from Ella."

Cooper relaxed her shoulders and nodded. "Let's sit at the table."

Ella sat on the bed and held Harold's hand while the women talked.

Eleanor gave her account of the night of Agnes' death as Cooper sat quietly and took notes. "... and after John told me to stay in the cabin, I didn't dare talk to Alton, I mean Sergeant Nolan."

Cooper frowned. "I don't understand."

"John said I was the prime suspect and would be arrested. I was afraid."

"Ma'am, did you know your son owned a gun?"

Eleanor muffled a chuckle. "He has to keep the herds and flocks safe from the coyotes. I think just about everyone in our mountain community owns a gun, at least a shotgun."

Cooper caught Eleanor's eye. "Do you own a gun?"

Eleanor sat back. "No. I don't."

"Ma'am, he just threatened to break the door down and said he had a gun," said Cooper. "He wasn't here to scare off coyotes."

Ella cleared her throat, causing the women to turn. "Sorry... I have a question if you don't mind."

Cooper turned. "What is it?"

"How did you know John was here?" asked Ella. "I

mean, there was quite a police presence just after he pounded on our door."

Cooper smiled. "Thanks to an anonymous tip, we knew John had gone to Mr. Madrigal's house. I was there when you came out the front door. I followed both of you into town. After observing Mr. Morgan in his truck, I called Bakersfield PD, just in case."

Ella stared at Eleanor. "I'm sorry, I did not know anyone had followed me..."

Eleanor sighed. "It's okay. It all worked out for the best." She faced Cooper. "So now what happens?"

"Sergeant Nolan wants me to bring you back to Pheasant Valley to interview you."

Harold stirred, then was silent again.

Eleanor's eyes teared up. "I can't leave. Just not yet..."

"Officer Cooper, can this wait?" asked Ella. "Just for a day or two?"

Cooper shifted. "I can't make that decision."

Ella picked up her phone and searched through the contacts. "If I call Alton and explain..."

Cooper looked at Ella, then back to Eleanor, and nodded. "But whatever he says, I'll have to abide by. You understand, right?"

Ella stood, went into the bathroom, and closed the door.

Cooper looked at Harold. "This doesn't appear to be a kidnapping to me..."

Eleanor managed a smile. "It never was. I do not know why John would even say that. Harold and I... We loved each other... And still do..." Tears rolled down her flushed cheeks. "I can't bear to think about not having him in my life..."

Cooper laid her hand over Eleanor's and squeezed it. "I'm very sorry."

As Ella emerged from the bathroom, Cooper's phone signaled an incoming call. She stood and answered it. "Yes, sir. I understand. Thank you." She looked at Eleanor and smiled. "Looks like Ella worked it all out."

Eleanor turned to Ella, then back to the officer. "Worked what out?"

Cooper smiled. "Ella will be responsible for you until you're able to come back to Pheasant Valley. She'll bring you to the station to meet with Sergeant Nolan."

Eleanor nodded, and managed a weak "Thank you."

Cooper put away her notebook and pen, then stood. "Is there something I can do before I go?"

The women looked at each other, then at the officer. "I think we've got this," said Ella.

Cooper walked over to the bed, looked down at Harold, then turned to Eleanor. "Again, I'm so very sorry." She opened the door and walked out into the cold, rainy night.

"Not coming home tonight?" asked Shelby. "What's going on?"

Ella sighed as she paced the small bathroom, talking to Shelby on speaker mode. "Long story, but here's the condensed version." She filled her in on the details of John showing up, Cooper's questioning, and Alton's arrangement. "I really don't expect to be here too long…" She stopped to compose herself. "Harold looks terrible. I'd be surprised if he lasted another twenty-four hours…"

"Oh, Ella, I'm so sorry. Are you sure Eleanor can't hear you?"

"She's watching TV." Ella wiped her eyes. "I feel terrible for her… I just…"

"What, El?"

"I hope Harold goes quick. He's in so much pain... I can't stand seeing him like this."

"Virtual hugs," said Shelby.

"Thanks. I need a lot of those right now." She sat on the toilet lid, inhaled, then exhaled. "How are you holding up? This hasn't been the best week for you either, waiting on that title information. I'm sorry I've been distracted with being sick and now this..."

"It's okay. You're there for Eleanor and Harold, and that's all that matters right now. I'll take care of the shop..."

"Thanks, hon. Well, I should go. I'm sure it's going to be a long night."

"Love you," said Shelby.

"Love you, too." Ella ended her call, then walked back into the small, dingy room. Eleanor sat on the bed, holding Harold's hand. When Ella entered, Eleanor muted the TV. Except for rain hitting the roof, the only other sound was Harold's occasional gasps for breath. Each time, Ella wondered if it would be his last. She counted to herself. Thirty seconds, then a minute before she saw his chest rise and fall. After sitting with her dying grandmother, she knew Harold's end was near. She brushed tears from her eyes and sat at the table.

"Thanks for being here," said Eleanor. "It means more than you know."

Ella smiled. "I just wish I could do more."

"Do you believe in prayer?"

Ella turned. "Yes, I do."

Eleanor closed her eyes. "Only a miracle will save him now."

CHAPTER FORTY

S helby woke just after sunrise on Thursday morning. She checked her phone for messages. Nothing. Maybe no news was good news, though the way Ella had sounded when they talked, no good news could be expected.

After letting Oatmeal out and feeding both animals, she forced herself to eat a bowl of hot oatmeal with a dash of cinnamon and maple syrup. Nothing too sweet. Her tummy wasn't accustomed to being up so early. Besides being concerned for Ella, the anticipation of receiving the title information from Houston gnawed at her.

She washed her bowl and cleaned up the kitchen, then headed up to her room to change. Not being able to wait any longer, Shelby texted Ella.

How r u? Any news...

No change. How are you?

Ok... Keep me updated...

Will do. (Hugs)

(hugs)

Shelby tossed her phone on the bed and shrugged off her pajamas. Hoping something colorful would cheer her up, she put on jeans, a sparkly pink shirt, striped socks, and her favorite sparkly tennis shoes. At least her friends at the shop would help keep her mind occupied.

ELLA STOOD AND STRETCHED. Fortunately, the motel had sent them a roll-away bed for her to sleep on. Unfortunately, the mattress was thin, so she got little sleep. She looked over and saw Eleanor still lying next to Harold, holding his hand. They both seemed to be asleep, so she tip-toed into the bathroom. When she came out, Eleanor was sitting up.

"Everything okay?" asked Ella.

Eleanor sighed. "Thought we'd lost him a few hours ago... but he's still hanging in there."

Massaging her own back, Ella sat on a chair. "I'm getting hungry. What do you want to eat?"

"I don't think I can—"

"You need to eat something," said Ella. "Harold needs you to be strong. If you don't eat—" An incoming text interrupted her. Checking her phone, she noticed it was from Alton.

Ordered breakfast. Should be there soon.

Thanks so much.

"What's going on?" asked Eleanor.

"Apparently, breakfast is on its way," said Ella. "Complements of Alton."

Eleanor looked down at her hands. "I can't believe he's being so nice."

"He's a good guy." Ella got up and placed a hand on her friend's shoulder. "He cares about everyone in town."

A few minutes later, someone knocked on their door. Ella looked out the window. A meal delivery driver waved to her. Opening the door, a bearded, lanky young man handed her two bags from a nearby 24-hour restaurant chain.

Ella took them. "Hold on, I need to give you something."

The man stepped back and put up his hands. "My instructions were to deliver your food, but not accept anything in return. It's been paid for, plus a generous tip was already added." He smiled, then turned, and left before she could even offer a thank you.

Closing the door, Ella placed the bags on the table and opened them. She set out several white Styrofoam boxes and popped each one open. Thick smoky bacon, toasted hash browns, scrambled eggs, and blueberry pancakes topped with butter and maple syrup. She motioned to Eleanor. "Looks like quite a variety. Come eat before it gets cold."

Eleanor hesitated, then went into the bathroom and washed her hands. After joining Ella at the table, she bowed her head and offered a quick prayer of thanks for the food and for Ella and Harold. She looked up, then smiled. "Thanks again for being here. I couldn't do this without you."

WHEN SHELBY ARRIVED at The Bee's Knees, the lights were already on. Looking through the glass, she saw Vivian vacuuming the rug. Not wanting to startle her, Shelby opened the door, then walked around in front of her and waved.

Vivian jumped and put her hand to her chest. "My goodness. 'Bout gave me a heart attack."

"I'm so sorry," said Shelby, reaching for Vivian's arm. "You okay?"

"Yes, but earlier things were kinda weird…"

Shelby stared at her. "Viv, what are you talking about?"

"Couldn't sleep last night, so I came in a bit early for my shift. Thought I'd stay busy by tidying up a bit… you know, vacuuming, dusting, all the things to keep me busy… Oh, I digress. So when I opened up, I had this feeling…"

Shelby raised an eyebrow.

"Like I was being watched."

"Did you call the police?" asked Shelby.

Viv shook her head. "I looked around but didn't see anyone. It was a weird feeling. Don't even know how to explain it."

AFTER BREAKFAST, Ella and Eleanor took turns sitting with Harold. By nine o'clock, his breathing fluctuated from rapid breaths to nothing for longer periods at a time. Not more than an hour later, he was unresponsive to sound or touch. His hands became colder. His skin, blotchier. Whoever wasn't sitting with him paced. Both in deep thought, neither woman spoke, grieving in silence. They only offered comforting words to Harold, knowing his end was near.

A few minutes after ten o'clock, Shelby jumped when the shop door opened. Kent walked in arm in arm with Susan. They were laughing about something. Shelby smiled when they came up to the counter. More people around just in case... but in case of what? Too many things on her mind and none of them were in her control.

"Morning," said Shelby, forcing herself to appear cheerful.

Kent handed the sign-in sheet and pen to Susan and waited. "I've got more good news on the renovation."

With everything going on, Shelby hadn't even thought about the project in days. "Oh cool. What's the news?"

Kent signed in, then looked up at Shelby. "Not only did I get more donated materials, but I also found a few more people willing to volunteer. I think you can do the entire project for less than ten grand."

Shelby blinked. "That's awesome."

Kent smiled. "I also have a few crowd funding ideas. We could make this happen. I mean if you and Ella are okay with it."

Shelby nodded. "I promise I'll talk to her as soon as possible."

"She still sick?" asked Susan.

"No," said Shelby. "She's with a friend who needed her."

Susan took Kent's hand in hers. "Friends are important."

Smiling, Shelby wanted to congratulate them, but since there'd been no formal relationship announcement, she waited. "Yes, and Ella's a friend to just about everyone in town."

The front door opened again. A thin blond woman walked in. Short-cropped hair, no jewelry, torn jeans, and a leather jacket. She had a presence that couldn't be ignored. She walked down an aisle, then turned to observe the three people chatting at the counter.

"That's why we love our Ella," said Susan.

Shelby nodded and smiled. "Yes, we do——" Something caught her eye. Looking away from the couple, her smile faded when she recognized the person standing twenty feet away watching her.

"Are you okay?" asked Kent.

Shelby didn't move or respond.

He put his hand on her arm and turned toward her focus. "Shelby?"

She stared at the woman making her way to the counter, then turned to Kent. "Please don't leave me alone."

"Do we need to call the police or something?" asked Susan.

Shelby shook her head. "Not yet."

The tall woman came closer, her eyes focused on Shelby. She stopped a few feet from the group, then forced a smile. "Shelby. Good to see you."

Shelby's heart pounded. Her body trembled. She gritted her teeth, then took a deep breath before she responded. "Mac. What are you doing here?"

"I might ask you the same thing."

Shelby went behind the counter. "I live here."

"What a coincidence. I also live in the area."

Gripping the counter until her fingers turned white, Shelby's mouth went dry. "Is that why you're selling the house?"

"*Sold* the house, dear." Mac smiled. "It's a done deal..."

"Except that you still need my signature."

Mac glared at Kent and Susan. "You both catching all

of this domestic dispute stuff?" She turned to Shelby. "How about we go someplace to discuss this in private?"

Shelby swallowed the lump in her throat. "I have nothing to say to you."

"Oh, but you owe me some answers. Like why you left. Why you're back here..." Mac glanced around the room. "Oh wait, all your friends are here..."

Shelby's entire body trembled. "These people care about me."

"And I didn't?" asked Mac. "I thought we had something special."

The front door opened and two women walked in, chatting about the weather. "And you just have to try this apple butter," said one. They walked down an aisle toward Gladys' booth, away from the tense conversation.

The door opened again and Laura breezed in, the tails of her blouse floating behind her. She stopped, then rushed behind the counter to Shelby and took her hands. "Are you okay, hon? I sense tension." She slowly turned and stared at Mac. "Lots of tension."

Unfazed, Mac smiled at the others. "Don't be rude, Shel. Introduce me to your friends. This is why you came back, isn't it?"

Laura patted Shelby's hand. "I'll take care of this." She offered her hand. "I'm Laura. This is Kent and Susan. And the woman dusting over there is Vivian. And you're... Mackenzie, aren't you? Shelby has told us *so* much about you."

"All good, I hope." Mac smiled at Shelby, revealing a deep dimple in her right cheek. "And you can call me Mac."

Shelby winced. "I need to get back to work."

Mac stepped forward with her hands on her hips. "Not until we talk..."

CHAPTER FORTY-ONE

Eleanor gasped. "Ella…"

Ella stopped pacing and sat on the motel bed next to her friend. "Is everything okay?"

"Harold hasn't breathed in several minutes. I think…" Just then he took several quick breaths, then coughed. "Oh man," said Eleanor. "I thought…"

"It's going to be okay." Ella sighed. "I mean, it doesn't feel okay to us. But it is going to be okay."

"That's not very comforting," said Eleanor. "Do you know how hard this is? To watch someone die. Someone you love so deeply that it hurts."

"I do. I was with my grandmother when she passed…" said Ella. "And I wish I could say something to help. But I can't. I know it's painful and nothing I do or say will make it better."

"I have so many regrets. And no time to make them right." Eleanor looked up at Ella. "Why didn't I go to him sooner? Why was I so stubborn?"

Placing her hand over Eleanor's, Ella nodded. "I'll always regret having Doug go into town that Halloween night. We didn't need to do our banking deposit, but I insisted. End of the month stuff. And if I'd only had him wait until morning… he'd still be alive today."

"Ella, you can't change the past. You just need to move for—" Eleanor smiled. "Ah, clever."

"We all beat ourselves up but what good does it do?" asked Ella. "You've got good memories. Hold on to those with all your strength."

Eleanor laid her hand on Harold's chest. "I don't feel anything." She looked up at Ella with wide eyes. "Do you?"

Ella gently rested her hand on Harold and leaned closer. "Maybe… I think so."

The women waited. Nothing.

Ella touched his skin. "So very cold."

Eleanor used the corner of the sheet to wipe her eyes. She stared at Harold, hoping, praying for some sign of life.

His chest rose slowly as he took a breath, then sank.

Eleanor closed her eyes.

Ella watched Harold's face turn pale white, then within a brief time, grey. Eleanor's eyes were still closed, though she was holding Harold's hand. Surely she must have known he had passed. Ella didn't say anything, other than a silent prayer for Eleanor.

TAPPING her fingers on the counter at The Bee's Knees, Laura stared at Mac. "Shelby, why don't you two chat in the sitting area? Shel, if you need anything, we're all right here…"

Shelby picked up her sweater from behind the counter and held it in front of her. She walked to the chairs near the coffee pot and eased into one of them.

Mac followed, choosing a chair next to Shelby. "Look," she said. "Nothing I'd planned to say has come out right." She sighed deeply. "I'm sorry."

Shelby wrapped her arms around the sweater and stared at her ex-partner. "Excuse me?"

"I said, I'm sorry. For taking that job. For moving us half-way across the country. For... everything."

"This is a first," said Shelby.

Mac stared at her hands. "After you left, I took a long hard look at myself. I realized I hated my job. It turned me into someone even I didn't know." She leaned in and whispered. "I started therapy which helped me see how I took out my frustrations and anger on you."

Shelby's shoulders relaxed. "I'm glad you've been able to talk to someone."

"It's only been four months, but I've learned a lot. I quit my job and transferred back to Kern County. Still in the oil industry, but a less demanding position. I couldn't stay in our house. There were too many painful memories..."

Shelby nodded.

"I should have never blamed you for losing our babies. All it did was drive a wedge between us. I shamed you for something that was never your fault."

"Thank you." Shelby wiped at the tears running down her cheeks. "That means a lot."

"I've been back for a couple of months, but waited to contact you. I needed to figure out some stuff before seeing you and apologizing. And..."

"And, what?" asked Shelby.

Mac straightened. "Ask for a second chance. I know we have a lot to work out, but—"

Shelby raised her hand. "I should stop you right there."

"I get it. It's too soon. Maybe we can go to couple's therapy, work things out. Then…"

Shaking her head, Shelby sighed. "I'm happy now. And while I appreciate your change of heart, I can't."

"I sold the house so I'd have no strings tying me to Houston." Mac's breathing increased. "I'm here for good. Doesn't that mean anything to you? That I gave up my dream job, so I could make up with you?"

Shelby sat back, her arms hugging her sweater. "Why didn't you tell me about the house? Why did I only hear about it when someone came looking for me so I could sign those papers?"

"Excuse me?" said Mac. "I called and texted umpteen times. What was I supposed to do when you didn't respond?"

Shrugging her shoulders, Shelby averted Mac's gaze. "I didn't want to talk to you."

"Well, sweetie. Now we have to talk. The house has been sold. All that's holding it up are those papers… The new buyers have already started on the landscaping. First to go were those stupid dead rose bushes…"

Shelby gasped. "What? Why?"

"Hon, those were gone soon after you left. I didn't do anything with them and all but one died from neglect…"

"Gone?" Shelby couldn't hold back the tears. She sobbed, her shoulders shaking. "I. Can't. Believe. You…"

"They were just a bunch of stupid stems with hardly any blooms," said Mac. "Dead. Just like our relationship."

"But my rose… I…" Shelby sobbed. "I needed that one rose bush."

"Yeah, you always seemed obsessed with those stupid thorny sticks." Mac looked at her phone, then cracked her knuckles. "Look, we aren't getting anywhere. I should go."

She stood, then looked down at Shelby. "If you'd bother to read the escrow papers, you would have noticed I made sure you got half of the equity in the house…"

"I don't want anything from you. Especially after you destroyed her. I mean my roses."

"Calm down. They were dying. Nobody wanted them. Like I said, once you sign those papers, you should get a check for just over twelve thousand dollars. You can buy all the roses you want and have enough for that design business dream…"

Shelby sat rocking on the chair.

"Oh, when I was moving out, I found some of your stuff. It's in my jeep… Where do you want it?"

"I'm staying with Ella." Shelby looked up with red, puffy eyes. "Leave it at her house. Then leave me alone."

"I should have known you'd be staying there. Your little shelter in the storm."

Shelby pounded her fist on the chair arm. "She's a much better friend than you'd ever hope to be…"

Mac raised an eyebrow. "Excuse me?"

"You need to leave now," said Shelby through clenched teeth.

"Like how you left me—" sneered Mac.

Shelby turned as Kent walked up to them. "It's time for you to leave, Mackenzie," he said as Laura and Susan stood behind Shelby rubbing her shoulders.

Mac stepped back. "Nice way to welcome someone to your place of business."

"Thank you for visiting our establishment." Kent stepped forward. "Now, go."

Looking down at Shelby, Mac huffed. "I'll be in touch." Then she marched away and out the front door.

Laura crouched down next to Shelby. "You okay, hon?

We couldn't help but notice it was getting loud. I hope you don't mind…"

Shelby shook her head. "Thank you. All of you." She wiped her eyes. "I need to go home and be alone for a while. I must look like a mess."

"You're beautiful inside and out, hon." Laura brushed a stray hair from Shelby's forehead. "Don't let anyone define your worth. Especially someone who's heart has turned cold."

"Thank you, Laura…" Shelby stood and gave her a hug. "And, hon…"

Shelby pulled back and looked at Laura's sparkling eyes.

"The one thing you think is gone… it's not." She touched Shelby's chest. "It's in your heart forever."

As ALTON HAD REQUESTED the night before, Ella called to let him know of Harold's passing. He offered to contact Doctor Minke, Harold's physician and Pheasant Valley's coroner. The doctor agreed to ride with the mortuary attendents down to the motel to declare Harold deceased, then start the necessary paperwork and process of moving the body back to the funeral home in their town. He would also drive Harold's car back to their town.

An hour later, Dr. Minke arrived to find Eleanor still sitting next to Harold's body. He asked both women questions, including the time of death, if there were any known living relatives, and who would be responsible for the body (and subsequent financial obligations).

"Current spouse? Sisters, brothers, children…?" asked Dr. Minke.

Eleanor remained stoic while Ella answered. "Harold

never spoke about any living relatives. And both ex-wives are deceased," she said. "If it's okay, I'll take responsibility."

The doctor nodded. "Weeks ago knowing the end was near, he mentioned asking you, Ella, to be in charge. He had pre-paid funeral arrangements, even budgeted for any unknown expenses and a celebration of life so there shouldn't be too much out of pocket. But we can discuss the details later."

"Harold was always a planner... even to the end." With tears in her eyes, Ella turned, then she looked back at Dr. Minke. "I'm sorry... we've been friends for years. I'm still trying to process everything."

The doctor put his hands over Ella's. "Take your time. Harold was not only my patient, but a loyal friend. He was like an uncle to my kids..." He wiped his eyes, then cleared his throat. "Eleanor, how are you holding up?"

She looked in the doctor's kind eyes. "I've had better days. Better weeks in fact. I just need a lot of sleep."

"I can give you a prescription if you need it..."

Eleanor shook her head. "I'll be okay. But thanks."

Dr. Minke looked down at Harold's body, then up at the women. "When you're ready, I've got transport waiting outside."

"I'm ready." Eleanor stood. "You can take him home now."

"Doctor, should we wait outside?" asked Ella.

"No, no," said Dr. Minke. "You can stay." He opened the motel room door and motioned to someone outside. A few moments later, two men walked in, pushing a stretcher. As Eleanor and Ella stood back, the men carefully wrapped Harold's body in several layers of what looked like white sheets. After they moved him to the stretcher, they changed the bedding, then made up the bed. Before leaving, one of the men laid a red silk rose on the pillow. "We're very sorry for your loss, Ma'am." Then, as Ella and Eleanor gripped hands, they watched them load Harold's body into the transport vehicle and drive away.

Dr. Minke offered a hug to each woman. "I'm very sorry. Harold was an amazing person. Everyone will miss him. He'll be in our hearts forever." Then he turned and walked out, leaving the women alone in the motel room.

CHAPTER FORTY-TWO

At The Bees Knees, Laura went to her booth and grabbed several sprigs of dried lavender, pressing them into Shelby's hand. "Hon, are you sure you'll be okay?"

"I need to process what just happened between me and Mac." Shelby held the purple flowers under her nose and breathed deeply. "I can't believe she just showed up…"

"My heart aches for you," said Laura. She pulled Shelby in for a tight hug and whispered, "I'm here if you need to talk."

"Thank you." Shelby stepped back, then turned to Kent, Susan, and Vivian, who were close by. "Thank you for your friendship and love. You have no idea…" Shelby wiped her eyes and left the store.

"I hope she finds some peace," said Susan.

"She will." Laura smiled. "And soon."

AFTER DR. MINKE left in Harold's car, Ella and Eleanor checked out of the dingy motel room and headed back to Pheasant Valley. The blue sky brightened their spirits, though neither woman did much talking as they left Bakersfield. Eleanor stared out the window while Ella focused on the road keeping a safe distance from the long-haul truckers. The big rigs would vie for positions in the two right lanes before the steep grade would slow their ascent.

"Nothing from Shelby?" asked Eleanor as they continued up the hill.

"No," said Ella. "Probably busy with customers at the shop. I'll call her once we get to the house."

SHELBY DROVE HOME IN A DAZE. How could Mac destroy Charisma's rose bush? The only connection she had to her lost child. She fought back tears, though anger welled up inside her like a pressurized can. The more she thought about it, the more her hurt intensified. She didn't remember if she'd stopped at red lights or waited for other cars at the four-way crossing. She drove blindly, unaware of anything or anyone around her.

A horn honked. She looked up in time to see a car swerve out of her way. Shelby pulled over and pounded the steering wheel. "My little girl has been taken away from me again. What did I do to deserve this?" Her fists ached, but she kept pounding. "Nothing matters now. Nothing." Though she felt a searing pain in one wrist, Shelby didn't care. She just wanted to go home and hide. Hide in the shame of trusting. Of being vulnerable. Of believing she was worth anything to anyone. After all, her parents made it clear she wasn't wanted. She wasn't 'normal' because she liked girls. Mac made it clear she wasn't loved. She couldn't even carry a baby to term. Her design business was still a dream in her own mind... A total failure to everyone, even herself. Shelby knew she was spiraling, but couldn't come out of it. Not here. Alone on the side of the road.

She tried controlled breathing, but it only made her dizzy. A happy place? What happy place? In her mind, it didn't exist. A sound outside caused her to glance at the passenger seat. Noticing a bright pink envelope, she picked it up and opened it. The card inside was from Ella. It contained three simple words. "I love you." Underneath the words, she'd drawn two hearts tied with a pink bow. A sparkly bow. Shelby smiled. Her body relaxed as she stared at the card and read the words repeatedly. Shelby turned the key, shifted, and pulled away from the side of the road. A few blocks later, she parked in the driveway of Ella's home.

As she neared the porch, she noticed several boxes stacked on the top step. She rolled her eyes. Her old stuff from Mac's house. She stomped up the stairs and pushed them aside. As she pulled out her key to open the door, Shelby spotted a familiar ceramic planter sitting on the patio table. Inside, planted in rich soil, was a short stem with one yellow bud, ready to bloom. She spotted a scribbled note on yellow legal paper tucked underneath:

Shelby. I'm not good at in-person confrontations. I know I messed things up even more by coming to the shop, so please read this. I was wrong to say those things to you today. And I'm truly sorry for all the pain I caused you. All the roses died, except one. This one. When the landscapers were removing them, they pointed this one out to me because it was different. It had a small pink ribbon attached to the bottom. Attached was a metal charm with the word Charisma. I had them save

*the rose and replant it. For the first time since we lost our baby,
I realized your hurt was more than physical pain. It was
personal pain. I'm sorry I wasn't there for you. I'm sorry I
blamed you for our loss, like it was unimportant. It wasn't. I
never grieved with you. Or let you grieve. I acted like a jerk.
I'm glad you're finally happy. You deserve the best. Mac.*

SHELBY RAN her fingers along the thorny stem and held the small ribbon with the charm and her baby's name on it. She sat in a wicker chair, picked up the planter, and held it while she rocked.

———

ELLA MERGED into the far left lane to pass a slow-moving semi-truck. With three more semis ahead, she didn't want to get stuck behind them. "The mountains are finally looking like spring."

Eleanor nodded. "All the wildflowers are so pretty. Every year I promised myself to take that walking tour… This year Harold, and I had planned…"

Ella patted her friend's hand. "I'm so sorry, Eleanor."

"Not the way I'd plan to celebrate the first days of spring…"

"That makes two of us," said Ella.

"Thanks for calling Alton and explaining everything," said Eleanor. "I'm feeling better knowing I'll be talking to him at your house."

"He'll be over after dinner, giving you time to eat and get some well-deserved sleep," said Ella.

Eleanor covered a yawn and stared out the window. "I'm

tired, but my mind is ping-ponging all over the place. I doubt I'll be able to sleep." After a few minutes, she faced forward again. "It's interesting."

"What?" asked Ella, merging into the middle lane.

"How much John hated Harold."

Ella turned to look at her friend for a moment, then she focused on the road again. "Do you know why?"

"No. But he loathed the man."

"They have an argument?" asked Ella.

"As far as I know, they never even talked…"

Ella tapped her fingers on the steering wheel. "Maybe you should ask John."

"I'm… concerned," said Eleanor. "I don't know how to explain it, but over the last six months, his personality has completely changed."

"Like how?"

"It's hard to put into words…" said Eleanor. "And now, the way he acts around me. Suspicious… Angry… Like I've done something wrong."

Ella signaled and merged into the right lane, taking the offramp leading to Pheasant Valley Boulevard. "You said over the last six months or so?"

"Yes." Eleanor sighed. As they passed by the airport just outside of town, she pointed to a construction site nearby. "Didn't see that on my way out. You know what it is?"

Ella glanced over. "I've heard rumors about a new ice arena. They hope to have it ready for skating and hockey leagues by the Winter Festival."

"Looks like an extensive project," said Eleanor. "I'm sure it will be a big draw for our folks, especially when the snow closes the roads to Bakersfield."

"From what I hear," said Ella, "Several business owners and a few venture capitalists got the project off the ground.

Some big money went into making it happen." She pulled up to an intersection and waited for the light to change. "Thinking back to what you said about John... Maybe it has nothing to do with you or Harold. Maybe it's the farm... or..."

Eleanor turned to Ella. "Or what?"

"I don't know. It could be several things."

"We used to talk more..." said Eleanor. "Then, one day, when I mentioned something about revisiting my relationship with Harold, John became livid. He stormed out of my house and we barely talked until after Agnes' death."

Ella turned west and headed home. "I think the only way you're really going to know is by asking John. With Harold gone, maybe he'll be more willing to talk to you."

Wiping a tear running down her cheek, Eleanor turned and stared out the window again. "I can't believe Harold is really gone."

"I can't either."

ACROSS TOWN in her American-Colonial style living room, Trudy Denton sat on her custom-designed toile fabric couch with its intricately carved hickory wood legs, organizing her vast button collections. One of her cats, Mr. Darcy, was curled up next to her, purring. She sorted through a wooden box and picked up a display board covered with over twenty rare 18th century buttons. From jewel encased bone to a much sought-after matched decoupaged set, this one collection was worth well over fifty thousand dollars. Running her fingers over the buttons, she thought back to how long it had taken her to find each piece. And what she had gone through to gain them.

She held the board at an angle so the tiny lights from the handcrafted brass chandelier reflected in the much-coveted buttons. Sipping her perfectly made cup of mint tea, Trudy nodded to her other cat, Elizabeth, sprawled under the table, tail twitching. Standing, Trudy laid the board in the box, closed the lid, then carried it to a rustic armoire. She pulled on the polished brass knobs, placed the box on the top shelf, then closed the doors.

Checking the time on her white gold-plated watch hanging on a thin, silver chain around her neck, Trudy went back and sat on the edge of the couch. She picked up her phone, located a contact, and swiped to start a call. "Voice mail? How dare you ignore my call?" She tapped her thin fingers on her leg and waited for the proverbial beep. "It's me. You're late. Now, it's doubled." After ending the call, she refilled her teacup, then scratched Mr. Darcy's ears. "Looks like your mama will acquire some new buttons soon..."

CHAPTER FORTY-THREE

Ella pulled up in front of her house and parked. "Looks like Shelby's home. Probably to let the dog out."

Eleanor grabbed a small overnight bag and got out of the car. "I'm not much in the mood for conversation. Hope that's okay."

Rubbing her friend's shoulders, Ella smiled. "I'm sure Shelby will understand."

After Ella opened the front door, Oatmeal greeted them. He ran around Ella's legs, yipping and whining. "Oh, you poor lonely doggie. Though I'm sure Shelby's spoiled you like crazy."

Eleanor held out her hand while Oatmeal and Mr. Butterfingers sniffed it. Once Oatmeal licked it, she reached down and rubbed his ears. "Nice to see you again, Oatmeal."

"Where's Shelby, boy?" asked Ella. She turned to Eleanor. "Just set your things down in here and come into the kitchen. I need to use the bathroom."

"I'm next," said Eleanor. "Something about a car ride always does it to me."

"You and me both." Ella laughed. "You want to use the one down here? I can go upstairs."

Eleanor thought for a moment. "That might be best."

"Right through the kitchen and down the hall," said Ella. "Can't miss it. I'll meet you back in the kitchen.

As Eleanor went one way, Ella headed upstairs, followed by Oatmeal. Arriving at the top of the landing, she noticed the door to Shelby's room was closed. She approached the door, lightly knocked, then opened it, finding Shelby asleep on the bed. Several half-opened boxes lay on the floor around the bed. Near the boxes, her eye caught a small planter with a single rose stem. Next to it was what looked like a letter. Though Ella was curious, she didn't want to invade Shelby's privacy. Watching her sleep, Ella wondered what had happened while she was away. While her own heart broke over the loss of her friend Harold, a new brokenness crept over her. Wanting to give Shelby space, she left, closing the door behind her. It seemed both of them would have a lot to talk about.

Back downstairs, Ella found Eleanor in the kitchen. "I see you're getting to know Mr. Butterfingers."

"I used to have cats," said Eleanor, looking up. "But Richard was so allergic, I had to give them away after we married."

"I've always had a cat or dog, or several of each," said Ella. "A house doesn't seem like a home without some sort of fur baby." She opened the fridge and peered inside. "How about a sandwich? I've got turkey and roast beef."

"Whatever you're having." Eleanor continued to rub Mr. Butterfinger's ears. "I'm not hungry."

Ella made lunch while Eleanor focused on the cat. She remembered how much getting Oatmeal had helped her when Doug was killed. Ella knew she wouldn't have survived those first few months alone. "Maybe you should think about getting a pet…" said Ella. "I mean once you're back home and up to it."

Eleanor shrugged. "I can't think that far ahead right now."

Ella set the sandwiches on the table, along with some condiments, and a bag of ruffled chips. "Water okay, or do you prefer juice… or coffee?"

Eleanor picked up a chip and bit off a corner. "No on the coffee. Just water. After this, I want to shower and try to sleep."

Mr. Butterfingers settled under the table, while Oatmeal went back and forth between the women, looking up at them while putting a paw on a leg now and then.

"And what do we have here?" asked Eleanor. "Is it okay if I give him something?"

Ella laughed. "Just a tiny piece of meat—" Her phone signaled an incoming call. "Excuse me." She laid her sandwich on her plate and left the room. A few minutes later, she returned. "That was the funeral home. They need us to come down and…"

Eleanor's eyes teared up. "I don't know if I can deal with this all. Not right now. I mean, with Alton tonight…"

"It's okay," said Ella. "I'll go with you. We can go tomorrow…"

Eleanor wiped her eyes. "I wish I could fall asleep and wake up next week when this is all over with."

"We'll get through this."

Eleanor looked up at Ella. "Promise?"

Ella nodded. "Yes."

HEARING footsteps and talking in the hall, Shelby stirred. Glancing at her phone, she realized hours had passed since coming home. Shelby sat up and rubbed her eyes, recognizing Ella's voice and someone else's... Eleanor. Then it hit her. They were home because... A new grief washed over her. She wanted to go out and comfort Ella, but wasn't ready to explain why she was home in the middle of the day when she should have been at the shop. Shelby rubbed her neck. Crying left her eyes stinging. Hitting the steering wheel left her hand purple and throbbing. Her entire body ached like she was coming down with something. She looked around and her eyes focused on the small rose bush. It hadn't been a dream. It was real. As she got out of bed, she heard a light knock. "Come in," she whispered.

Ella opened the door just a crack. "You okay?"

"I should ask you the same thing," said Shelby. "I'm so, so sorry for..." She went to Ella and embraced her.

"I'll be okay," said Ella. "I'm more concerned for Eleanor."

"Will she be staying with us?" asked Shelby. "She shouldn't be alone."

"I'm hoping she will. After everything she's gone through." Ella stepped back. "How about you? Are you up to talking?"

Shelby sat on the bed. "Mac came by the shop. We had a big fight. Then I came home and found... that." She pointed to the rose planter. "She left me a note and apologized for everything."

Ella gasped. "Your hand, it's... did you actually hit her?"

Shelby shook her head. "No. I took my anger out on my jeep's steering wheel."

"Looks like the wheel won," said Ella. As she reached out to touch it, Shelby winced.

"I'd have the doctor look at it," said Ella.

"It's just sensitive. I'll be okay." Shelby motioned to the note on the rug. "You can read it."

"I don't need to."

She looked up at Ella. "I don't have any secrets from you."

Ella got up and picked the note off the rug. She sat next to Shelby again and read it. Afterwards, wiping her eyes, she laid the paper on the bed and put her arms around Shelby. "I'm so sorry you had to deal with this without me."

"Actually," said Shelby. "It was your note that helped me deal with it."

Ella turned. "My note?"

"The pink envelope you left in my jeep."

"I put that in there last month for Valentine's Day. You just found it?"

Shelby nodded. She watched Mr. Butterfingers come inside the room and nose around the half opened boxes. He peered in one and jumped in. "Something tells me I wasn't supposed to see it until today."

"I'm sure Laura would agree with you," said Ella. "Speaking of… who's watching the shop?"

"Laura, Kent, and Susan… by the way, did you know they are a couple?"

Ella smiled. "They finally say something?"

"They didn't have to," said Shelby. She scooted back and leaned against a stack of pillows. "So, what's going on with Eleanor? Do you have to take her to Alton?"

"Actually, he's coming here after dinner," said Ella. "Trying to make things as easy as possible."

"You ever find out more about John and all that went on?"

"Not yet," said Ella. "I'm hoping to nudge Alton into giving more information tonight."

"Do you think he might offer more info on Agnes' death?" Mr. Butterfingers peeked out of the box, jumped out, then hopped up on the bed, purring. He padded over to Shelby and plopped down next to her.

"I hope you'll come and eat with us. Then you'll be downstairs when Alton comes by. You know, to listen in. Maybe some new ideas will come to you about this whole mess."

Shelby rubbed her cat's ears. "I'm sure Alton would see through our thinly laid plan."

"He always said people talk easier around us than him," said Ella. "I'm sure he'll welcome our company."

Shelby rolled her eyes. "Tell you what. I'll come down for dinner. But no promises on sticking around for Alton's questioning."

Ella chuckled. "You know you want to be there."

"What can I say?" Shelby looked down at her cat. "I'm curious, like this guy."

"We could learn some much-needed clues," said Ella.

"Or..." said Shelby. "Some terrible truths."

CHAPTER FORTY-FOUR

After pulling his truck into the circle driveway of the house, John slammed the door and looked up at the cloudy sky. The sun had set. The low bleating of ewes drifted past him as a barn owl screeched and a coyote's high-pitched yips pierced the cool air. He grumbled and stomped up the steps. Jerking open the front door, he slammed it shut and tossed his keys on the table.

Lilibeth and Vickie sat on the couch watching a TV game show. A half-empty bottle of red wine was on the coffee table, along with two full glasses. "Nice of you to show up after… twenty-four hours," said Lilibeth.

"Not now," snarled John, trudging across the room.

She stood, wineglass in hand. "You owe me an explanation."

John turned. "I owe you nothing."

"Who is she?" asked Lilibeth.

John flushed. "Who's who?"

"The woman you've been seeing." Lilibeth pointed at her husband. "Something's going on and we need to talk about…"

"You're crazy." He turned and ascended the stairs.

She watched her husband until he was out of sight. Swirling her stemmed glass, she gulped the sweet liquid. "Probably handled that all wrong."

"You had every right to ask where he's been." Vickie picked up a prescription bottle and shook it. "I need a refill or my migraines will come back." She stood. "You want to come? Shouldn't take too long."

"I'm in no condition to go anywhere," said Lilibeth.

Vickie grabbed a set of keys on the table. "Be back soon."

Lilibeth paced the front room. "I just don't understand what's happening." She stopped and refilled her glass, then downed part of it. Plopping down on the couch, she stared at the TV.

As ELLA CLEARED the last of the dinner dishes off the table, Oatmeal's ears perked up. He ran into the front room, barking. Eleanor looked at Ella with wide eyes. "I'm not ready for this..."

Shelby went to answer the door while Ella held Eleanor's hand. "It'll be okay."

Eleanor's face paled when Alton walked into the kitchen. "Ella, Eleanor... my sincerest condolences."

"Thank you," said Ella. "Please have a seat. Some coffee?"

Alton removed his jacket and hung it over the back of a chair. "Yes, thank you." He sat, then pulled out a notebook and pen and laid them on the table.

Shelby leaned against the doorframe and waited. Part of her hoped they didn't need her, while the other part was curious and wanted to stay. Her hand throbbed. The pain had intensified since dinner. Maybe a visit to the doctor was needed.

Alton nodded when Ella set a steaming cup in front of him. "Thank you." He cleared his throat and looked at Eleanor. "How are you doing?"

She moved her trembling hands to her lap. "I'm exhausted. And terrified. And…"

"I understand exhausted." Alton's eyes softened. "But why terrified?"

"I'm afraid you're going to… arrest me." Big tears rolled down her cheeks. She wiped them away with a shaky hand.

"Eleanor, I'm only here to ask you questions. What makes you think I'm going to arrest you?"

Her voice shook. "Because John said… it was my fault."

Alton closed his eyes and sighed, then opened them. "I don't know what John has told you, but I'm only here to get clarification."

"Sorry I never came forward," said Eleanor. "I just…"

Alton took a sip of coffee and smiled. "Would it help if your friends stayed while we chat? If they promise to just listen."

"Thank you." Eleanor's shoulders relaxed. "That would be great."

Ella looked at Shelby. "You joining us?"

"I'll just stay here, if it's okay with everyone."

Nodding, Ella brought two more steaming cups to the table. She placed one in front of Eleanor and the other in front of herself. She sat and waited.

Alton opened his notebook and asked Eleanor about the events of the night of Agnes' death. From the time she arrived at the shop to the argument in the alley.

"Everything you're saying matches the other

statements," said Alton. He sipped his coffee and then tapped his pen on the notebook. "Are you sure no one else saw what happened after you left Agnes?"

Eleanor hesitated. "It was dark. I only remember Agnes' body hitting the ground and then hearing footsteps. Running in several directions. Probably Harold's and Viv's."

"From the others' statements, there was a gap in time before Vivian returned to the meeting," said Alton. "Do you have any idea where she might have been?"

Eleanor looked at Alton. "Once I left, I don't know who stuck around. Even if there was someone, I doubt they'd seen anything. That alley was pitch black. I almost tripped over a downed tree branch. If it weren't for a flash of lightning, I would have fallen and probably broken a hip or something."

Alton flipped back through his notes. "Forensics found three clean sets of fingerprints on the knitting needle. Yours, Harold's, Agnes.' Then another one, but it was smudged. We're still trying to get a match."

Ella gasped.

Eleanor looked directly at Alton. "During the argument, Agnes grabbed them from my bag and threatened Harold. Of course, he grabbed them from her to protect himself. I can't help you with that last set."

Alton scribbled notes in his book, then looked up. "What happened after Harold had them?"

Eleanor let out a ragged breath. "That's when I hit Agnes in the jaw and she fell. Harold ran one way down the alley, I ran the other."

"Did Harold take the needles with him?" asked Alton.

"I don't remember," said Eleanor, dabbing beads of sweat from her forehead.

The wall clock ticked away the minutes while Alton

jotted more notes. He turned to a previous page. "Let's go back to Vivian. You said she didn't return right away because the dark made her disoriented. What about you? Did you lose your sense of direction?"

"I ran away from the street at first. Then during a huge lightning flash, I realized I was headed toward the quilt shop. That's when I turned around."

Alton read over his notes, then flipped to another page and read. He looked up, then down again. The hum of the refrigerator broke the strained silence.

Ella traced a circle on the table with her finger. "Alton, do you really think there might have been another witness?"

He looked up. "Not another witness. From the evidence I've gathered, it was the murderer."

RECLINING ON HER COUCH, Trudy was just about to drift off to sleep when the doorbell chimed. She checked the time and scowled. "Hold on. Hold on." Her cats settled in the warm spot she left when she answered the door.

Looking through the etched glass, Trudy opened the door just a crack. "You're late."

"Deal with it."

"You should have called," said Trudy.

"Can I come in?"

Trudy chuckled. "*May* I come in?"

"For heaven's sakes."

"Don't swear. It's not becoming…" said Trudy. She opened the door and stood to the side. "I was getting ready for bed."

"This should only take a minute."

Trudy offered a wry smile. "I've only got a minute." She held out her hand.

"It's all there. You can count it."

"I trust you." Trudy started to close the door. "I'll see you in a few days."

"Do you mind if I use the restroom?"

"Fine." Scowling, Trudy pointed toward the hall. "Be quick. I don't want anybody to know you're here. "

AN HOUR LATER, after asking more questions, Alton thanked the women for their time. Ella walked him to the door, then locked it and sat on the couch next to Shelby. Oatmeal jumped up and settled between them as Eleanor eased into the wingback chair.

"That was intense," said Eleanor.

Shelby nodded. "No kidding."

Eleanor sighed. "You don't think he suspects Viv, do you?"

"I don't think so." Ella crossed her legs. "Can either of you see Viv doing anything like that? She can't even kill a spider."

Shelby chuckled. "Yeah, remember the time she found that big wolf spider in the storeroom? She went all search and rescue until she captured it in a bowl. Then she drove out to the hills and released it." Shelby shuddered. "Just thinking about that gigantic thing gives me the creeps. But not Viv. She wouldn't hurt anything."

"I agree," said Ella. "But——"

Oatmeal jumped off the couch and ran to the door, growling. A few moments later, someone knocked.

Oatmeal's barks turned into yips. He danced in front of the door, scratching at it.

"Must be a friend," said Ella as she got up. "Okay, Oatmeal. Just a minute." She looked through the peephole and stepped back. "It's Laura. And Vivian." Ella turned and put her finger to her lips. "Shush. Nothing about what we were discussing."

"Vivian?" asked Eleanor. She and Shelby looked at each other with wide eyes.

Ella opened the door. "Ladies. What brings you over?"

Laura walked in, her lavender blouse billowing behind her. "Oh, Ella. Eleanor. We just heard... I'm so, so sorry..." She embraced each woman, then stepped back. "Viv and I brought some food... Dinners for the next few nights..."

Eleanor blinked. "Thank you."

"I hope you don't mind us dropping by," said Vivian. "We just had to do something." She gave Ella and Eleanor each a quick hug.

"Let's put those in the fridge," said Ella. She ushered the women into the kitchen, then they all came back into the front room. Laura pulled up a chair while Vivian sat on the couch next to Shelby.

"Is there anything we can do, hon?" asked Laura. "Do you need help with any arrangements?"

Eleanor shook her head. "I don't think so."

"We'll know more tomorrow," said Ella. "Meeting with the funeral director at three-thirty... Oh, that reminds me, Viv, can you watch the shop in the afternoon?"

"I'd love to... But there's a button meeting at Trudy's at three." Vivian shifted to look at Shelby. "I was hoping you could join us. But under the circumstances..."

Ella sat forward. "Actually, Shelby should join you."

Shelby glanced at Ella, raising a brow. "I thought you wanted me to go to the doctor."

"Doctor in the morning," said Ella. "Button meeting in the afternoon. Don't you think it might be good to hang out with Vivian…" She nudged her friend.

"What about the shop?" asked Shelby.

"I can handle it," said Laura. "You all have appointments. Paige will be there, plus Kent and Susan. By the way, aren't they just the cutest couple?"

Shelby smiled. "Have they made it official?"

"She seemed to sport an engagement ring this morning, but I didn't ask," said Laura.

Eleanor chuckled. "Well, hopefully they say something soon…"

"I've been gone from the shop for almost a week," said Ella. "I really feel like I need to go in and reconnect with everyone."

"Ella's got a point," said Eleanor. "I'll join you. Might help take my mind off everything."

"Are you sure?" asked Ella.

"After talking to Alton, I feel better," said Eleanor.

Vivian straightened. "How did that go?"

"He just asked a bunch of questions about the alley," said Eleanor. She hesitated, then faced Vivian. "He seemed to think someone else was there."

"Oh, my." Vivian glanced at her phone and cleared her throat. "Look at the time. I totally forgot I needed to be somewhere."

"It's almost eight," said Ella. "Where—?"

"Laura, we really should go," said Vivian, standing.

"That's fine, Viv." Laura stood and turned to Ella and Eleanor. "I'll see you in the morning, then I'll take charge in the afternoon."

After Ella walked them to the door, she came back and sat on the couch. "Did you see how Viv's entire demeanor changed when you mentioned the alley?"

"Yes," said Shelby. "And where does she need to be at this time of night?"

"You know that woman cannot tell a lie," said Eleanor.

"So I suppose you want me to snoop at the button club meeting?" asked Shelby.

"Sleuth, hon. Not snoop," said Ella.

"There's a difference?" asked Shelby.

"Remember what Alton said about Viv? How could no one account for her missing for so long?" asked Ella.

"You don't think Vivian's the killer, do you?" asked Shelby.

"No," said Ella, rubbing her neck. "But I think she knows something."

———

SEVERAL GAME SHOWS LATER, Vickie came in holding a white prescription bag. She slammed the door and plopped down on the couch.

Lilibeth sat up and stared at her sister, bleary-eyed.

"I miss anything?" asked Vickie.

"Somebody won," she said. "Somebody lost. What took you so long?"

"Truck hauling chickens overturned. Frantic fowl everywhere. Panicky farmer asking everyone to help round up the birds."

"Did they catch them all?"

"I think most escaped." Vickie laughed. "It was most comical." Her expression changed when John bounded down the stairs.

"I'm going out," he said. Making his way to the front door, he picked up his keys. "Don't wait up."

Lilibeth's eyes darkened. "Hope she's happy to see you."

John said something under his breath, then opened the front door and left.

Lilibeth looked around. She noticed a picture of her and John on the table and picked it up. Throwing it at the front door, the glass shattered inside the frame. "Don't be surprised if you come back and find all your stuff on the lawn."

"Doubt he heard you," said Vickie.

Lilibeth sat on the edge of the couch and poured herself a third glass of wine. "I don't care."

CHAPTER FORTY-FIVE

The next morning after a quiet breakfast, Ella, Shelby, and Eleanor left the house. Although caught up in their own thoughts, the women stopped when a flock of crows caught their attention. They watched the jet-black birds squabble over a furry varmint in the middle of the cul-de-sac.

"Something's got them all riled up," said Shelby.

"Probably one of those rats I heard last night in the attic," said Eleanor.

Ella rolled her eyes. "Just so they don't come inside the house." As Eleanor continued toward the car, Ella walked Shelby to her jeep. "So after the doctor, you'll come to the shop?"

Shelby nodded. "That's the plan."

Ella hugged her, being careful not to bump her swollen hand. "Call if anything changes."

Shelby got in her jeep and buckled in. "I'm glad you're going in to the shop, El," she said. "Everyone misses you."

"After what Eleanor said last night, I realized I needed to be with friends before we go to the funeral home," said Ella.

"Not looking forward to that appointment." She closed Shelby's door, then headed to her car.

Eleanor buckled in and turned to Ella. "You're fortunate to have such a good friend."

Ella smiled and started the car. "Shelby's very special to me."

"To all of us." Eleanor watched the crows hop to the side of the street while Ella pulled away from the curb. Then she continued to stare at them in her side mirror as the birds went back to their prey. Would she be strong enough to get through the morning? Or the afternoon at the funeral home? What if John showed up? At some point, she'd have to tell him the truth.

⸻

AROUND MID-MORNING, Shelby walked into The Bee's Knees, her hand in a splint, her arm in a shoulder harness. Ella rushed up to her. "Oh, my goodness."

"Just a hairline fracture of the meta… carp-something… um, the bone in my hand," said Shelby. "Can't remember the name of it now."

Eleanor came up beside them and touched Shelby's shoulder. "Are you okay?"

"I need to stay in this thing…" She nodded to the splint. "For at least six weeks. He gave me pain meds and said to take it easy. He wants to x-ray it again in a few weeks."

"Oh, hon," said Ella. "I'm so sorry."

Shelby attempted to shrug off her sweater, then winced. "I need to take my medicine."

"I'll get you some water," said Eleanor, heading to the counter area.

Ella put her arm around Shelby. "What else did he say?"

Shelby leaned her head on Ella's shoulder. "That next time I shouldn't take out my anger on a steering wheel."

Ella turned when a group of older women entered the shop. "I should help them. We can talk later."

Eleanor came back with the water. She helped Shelby to the sitting area and sat with her while she took the pain pill. "If there's anything else I can do…"

"Thanks," said Shelby. "But we should take care of you —" A chime signaled an incoming message. She fumbled with her phone and looked up at Eleanor.

"Need some help?" asked Eleanor.

Shelby handed her the phone. "Yes. I'd like to read this email, but can't…"

"No problem." Eleanor swiped and scrolled, then held the phone up.

After reading it, Shelby sighed. "Thanks. You can close the app now."

"Not that it's any of my business… but is everything okay?" asked Eleanor.

"Just got the email I've been waiting for. Though it doesn't matter anymore."

Eleanor said nothing. She didn't want to pry. After all, she had her own secrets.

Shelby took another sip of water. "Eleanor, when things calm down at the register, would you mind asking Ella to come back here?"

"Not at all," she said, patting Shelby's knee. She left and, after a few minutes, Ella walked up.

"You needed to chat?"

Shelby showed her phone. "Just got the email from Houston."

"About the title of the house?" asked Ella.

"Yeah."

"And...?"

"It's in both our names. So Mac needs my signature to sell it."

"What are you going to do?" asked Ella.

"At first I wasn't going to." Shelby took in a deep breath, then sighed. "But after Mac brought the rose, there's no reason to hold on to it..." She turned to Ella. "I'm going to sign. It's time to let go of the past." She pointed to her throbbing hand. "My anger only caused more pain. Once this signing is over with I'll be done with Mac forever and can finally move forward."

Ella leaned over and gave Shelby a hug. "I'm so sorry for everything you've gone through."

"I'll have to face her at the escrow office. El, I really wish you could be there with me..."

"We'll figure it out," said Ella. She looked up at the clock on the wall. "It's almost lunch—" Her phone signaled an incoming call. "Excuse me for a moment." She stood and answered. "Yes, it's Ella Denning... DeShawn White?... Of course I remember you... today? Eleanor and I are going to the funeral home at three-thirty... Before that? I suppose we could squeeze it... oh, just me... One o'clock?... Could you text me your address? Thank you."

"What was that about?" asked Shelby.

"DeShawn White, Harold's attorney. He needs me to come by today before Eleanor and I go to the funeral home."

"That's kind of sudden," said Shelby.

"He said he has information I'll need when we make the arrangements."

Shelby shifted in her chair. "He wanted you to come without Eleanor?"

Ella nodded. "If I didn't have enough to deal with today..."

———

THE FRONT DOOR of The Bee's Knees swung open and Laura hurried inside. She brought in several large pizza boxes, filling the front of the store with mouth-watering aromas of pepperoni and bell peppers.

Still in the sitting area with Shelby, Eleanor smiled. "Looks like Laura just brought lunch."

Shelby stood, holding her arm.

Laura walked back to Shelby and Eleanor, then placed the boxes on the counter by the coffee pot. "Anyone hungry?"

Eleanor took in a deep breath. "How did you know my one weakness?"

Shelby leaned into Eleanor. "You and me both."

Laura put out plates and napkins, then turned. She looked at Shelby and gasped. "Hon, what happened to you?"

"Just a broken hand," said Shelby. "I'm okay."

Laura rushed over. "Sweetie, you sit. I'll bring it for you. And the same for you, Eleanor."

After Laura brought their food, Ella served herself a slice and joined them.

"Anyone need anything else?" asked Laura.

The women shook their heads and continued eating.

"Good, then I'll go up and mind the store." She rushed off, the tails of her sky-blue billowy blouse following her.

Ella wiped pepperoni grease from her chin. "That woman never ceases to amaze me."

"I didn't think I was hungry," said Eleanor. "But somehow she knew…"

"She always knows," said Shelby.

Ella checked the time. "Eleanor, I need to run a quick errand before we go to the funeral home. Do you mind staying here and helping Shelby?"

Eleanor took a sip of water. "Not at all."

"Thanks," said Ella. "I shouldn't be too long." Getting up, she tossed her paper plate in the trash can and gave Shelby a side hug. "Wish me luck," she whispered.

ELLA LEFT The Bee's Knees and drove north on Pinecone Street, then east on First street, past Papercuts Bookstore, and the Old Town Museum. She passed the pet hospital and Dr. Furst's Veterinary Office then waited at the light to turn left onto South Acorn Street. DeShawn White's office was on the corner, offering real estate services, estate planning, and life insurance. As the town's most-trusted attorney, he'd helped Ella after Doug's death.

When Ella opened the front door of his office, a little bell above it jingled. She entered, took one of the four seats in the modest waiting room, and looked around. Art prints of the Post-Impressionist painters still adorned the walls. She stared up at her favorite, Starry Night, by Van Gogh. The swirling clouds and controlled messiness of its blues and yellows had brought comfort during the chaos in the weeks and months following Doug's death.

The inner door opened and a tall gentleman walked up to Ella. He took her hands in his and spoke in a deep baritone voice. "Ella, so good to see you again."

Ella stood. "And you, too. DeShawn. I hope life has been treating you well."

"Can't complain." He motioned toward his office and they left the waiting room.

Once Ella sat down, DeShawn went around to his side of the desk. "Coffee?"

"Oh, no. Thanks. Just had lunch." Ella fidgeted. "I was a bit surprised at the urgency of our meeting."

DeShawn opened a file folder on his desk, then looked at Ella. His deep brown eyes softened. "I'm very sorry. But I needed to explain a few things before you make the arrangements... Once Harold knew the end was nearing, he had me draw up a living trust."

Ella smiled. "Sounds like Harold."

"Did he mention anything to you about it?"

"No," said Ella. "Why?"

"He made you the successor trustee and executor of his estate."

Ella stiffened. "What does that mean?"

DeShawn pointed to the papers inside the folder. "Harold trusted you to take care of any remaining bills, dispose of his property, including his houses, and disperse monies to his beneficiaries."

"I... I don't know if I can do all of that."

"You won't be alone in this." DeShawn closed the file and folded his hands on his desk. "I'm here to help."

Ella stood and paced around the cramped office. "Why me?"

"Ella, he wanted you to carry out his last wishes."

"Do I have to accept?" She brushed away tears running down her cheeks.

"You may decline, if you choose," said DeShawn.

"If I decline, then who would do it?"

"I'm listed as a fiduciary. So in the event you decline, or cannot fulfill your duties as executor of Harold's estate, the responsibilities would fall to me." DeShawn stood and offered his hand to Ella. "I'm aware of how hard this must be for you, but Harold chose you for a reason."

Ella looked at the attorney. Though his hair showed more salt than pepper since Doug's death, his eyes were still kind and understanding. "When would I need to start?"

DeShawn stepped behind his desk and sat. "I'll need you to sign papers today, then open an account at the bank to write checks—which might be necessary at the funeral home. Then early next week we'll meet to go over Harold's will ..."

Ella eased into her chair and let out a ragged breath. "And you'll help me?"

"Of course."

"Part of me says no," said Ella.

"What does your heart say?" asked DeShawn.

Ella placed her hand over her chest. "It says yes."

VIVIAN PULLED into The Bee's Knee's parking lot a little before two-thirty. She looked at herself in the rearview mirror and applied a fresh coat of lipstick. Blotting her lips with a tissue, she fussed with her hair, then exited her car. As she walked up to the front door, Ella pulled up and parked.

Vivian waved and waited for Ella to approach. "How are you doing?"

"It's so good to get back in the shop," Ella said as they walked inside. "Just a lot going on."

When Shelby saw them come in, she went up to the

women. Soon, Eleanor joined them in front of the register counter.

Shelby leaned into Ella. "How did it go?"

"It was interesting," said Ella. "But don't you and Viv need to get going?"

Shelby gave her a side look. What was going on that she couldn't talk now?

"Viv, is that a new shade of lipstick?" asked Ella.

Vivian's face flushed. "Oh, yes. It is. I spruced myself up a bit for our button club meeting. But enough about my beauty routine… Shelby, your arm… are you okay?"

"Broken bone," said Shelby. "Do you mind driving?"

"Not at all." Vivian turned to Ella. "Don't worry, I'll take care of her."

Ella gave Shelby a hug and whispered. "Hope this meeting is productive… if you know what I mean."

After they left, Ella turned to Eleanor. "Looks like we need to leave soon, too."

Eleanor gripped the counter. "Don't know if I can do this, Ella…"

Ella put her arm around her friend's shoulders. "We can do this together." She turned to Laura, who was standing nearby. "Not sure if we'll be in the mood to come back after our appointment. Did Shelby show you how to lock up and set the alarm?"

Laura held up a piece of paper. "Got it. We'll be fine." She took two sprigs of lavender from her pocket and pressed one into each of Ella's and Eleanor's hands. "For calming and peace." The women thanked her and left.

DRIVING through the older neighborhood to Trudy's house, Vivian tapped her fingers on the steering wheel. She slowed, then turned a corner. "It's just up here a bit…"

"Viv, you okay?" asked Shelby.

Vivian let out a chuckle. "Why do you ask?"

"You just seem nervous," said Shelby.

Another chuckle. "Ah, well… They're supposed to be electing a new club president today, so I'm kinda… you know…"

"So that explains the lipstick and new hairdo?"

Vivian patted the side of her head. "Just hedging my odds… These ladies can be quite competitive."

After they parked in front of a Tudor-style home, the women exited the car and stared. Trudy's home featured two front gables and natural brick wall cladding, along with small leaded-glass windows capped by antique timber. A row of perfectly-shaped round hedges lined the front of the house and delicate ivy tendrils crept above the entryway.

"My goodness," said Shelby. "What a beautiful home." They ascended stone pavers accented by red and white miniature geraniums leading up to the arched front door. Looking down at her jeans and pink sweater, Shelby hesitated. "I feel so underdressed."

Vivian smiled. "You're fine, hon." She knocked on the door and they waited. Nothing. She checked her phone. "I think we're a bit early." She knocked again while Shelby crept over to a window and peered inside.

"It's so beautiful…"

"Do you see Trudy?" asked Vivian.

Shelby adjusted her view. "Looks like she's on the couch, resting."

"That woman loves her afternoon naps," said Vivian. She knocked again, then tried the door. It was unlocked.

"Guess she wants us to walk in. We should wake her before the other women get here."

Vivian and Shelby walked into the house. Viv went over to Trudy while Shelby, caught up in the interior view, stopped and stared. Turning, she admired the work that had gone into making the front room so grand.

A moment later, Vivian gasped. "Oh my goodness."

Shelby reeled around. "What's wrong, Viv?"

Vivian fumbled with her phone. "We need to call nine-one-one."

Shelby stiffened. "Is she… sick?"

"No." Vivian looked up at Shelby, her eyes wide. "She's dead."

CHAPTER FORTY-SIX

Shelby shivered on the cold metal bench outside Trudy's home while Vivian paced the length of the front porch. Multiple sirens in the distance became louder. Soon a police unit, an ambulance, and a fire truck pulled up and parked.

Two paramedics rushed up to the women. "Can you show us where…"

Vivian pointed to the door. "She's on the couch, but I don't think it's going to help…" The male and female paramedics entered the house, followed by two male firefighters.

Andrea Cooper hurried up the stone pavers to the women. "I'm Officer Cooper. Please don't leave. I'll be right back."

Shelby bounced her knee and took several deep breaths. "I can't believe…" She closed her eyes and leaned back.

Vivian sat next to Shelby. "Maybe if we'd gotten here sooner…"

Shelby grasped the hand of her trembling friend. "Viv, what are you talking about?"

"Trudy had heart issues... Said she was at risk for a stroke..." Vivian's shoulders shook as she wept.

Shelby took her phone from her pocket and called Ella. No answer. Remembering she and Eleanor were at the funeral home, she didn't leave a message. After all, what would she say? The meeting's cancelled because Trudy's dead. She stared at the flashing emergency lights reflected in the windows across the street. They seemed to dance in silent rhythm, around and around again. Though Shelby closed her eyes, she saw them in her mind's eye. The same pulsating light patterns the night Agnes was found dead.

Shelby opened her eyes and straightened as another police unit pulled up, followed by a white van. Alton exited the first vehicle and waited for the other driver to join him. Where had she seen the short, stocky police officer carrying the handled case before? Shelby gasped. It was the forensics guy—Officer Williams and his 'tackle box.' Was it only last week someone had killed Agnes? It seemed like forever ago.

She watched and listened. The firefighters exited Trudy's house, followed by the paramedics. They stopped for a moment, chatting with Alton. He spoke into his lapel mic, but Shelby couldn't understand what he said. When Alton and Officer Williams got to the porch, Alton pointed inside the house. "Jason, get started while I talk with the women."

Vivian wiped her eyes with the back of her hand and looked up.

"Did either of you touch or move anything inside?" asked the Sergeant.

"I... I patted her shoulder to wake her up," said Vivian. "You know she had heart issues—"

Alton turned. "Shelby?"

"No," said Shelby. "Once Viv said Trudy was dead, I

had to sit down. You know me and dead bodies."

Alton pulled out his notepad and a pen, but before he could ask another question, Cooper stepped onto the porch. "Sir, they need you inside."

Alton nodded. "Have you questioned the women?"

"Not yet."

"Start questioning them, one at a time, and I'll follow up after the coroner's prelim." Another police unit pulled up and a male officer sprinted up the walk. Alton walked up to him and though he spoke in a hushed tone, Shelby overheard part of the conversation.

"Officer Langley, we have an active crime scene. Set up a perimeter, then canvas the neighborhood," said Alton. "Coroner ETA is five to ten minutes."

Shelby stood when Alton reached the porch. "Wasn't it a heart attack? Or stroke?"

"Neither," said Alton. He walked inside Trudy's home and closed the door.

"VIVIAN, LET'S START WITH YOU." Cooper motioned to an area on the front porch with a wrought-iron table and matching chairs. The officer waited for the weepy woman to sit, then took a seat opposite her. "I'm very sorry about the loss of your friend."

"Thank you," said Vivian, wiping her eyes. She checked her phone. "Before we get started, I should mention... The other button club members will be here any time now."

"Button club?" asked Cooper.

"We planned to gather for our club meeting," said Vivian. "About six of us... it's too late to call and cancel..."

"I'll let Diaz know to watch for them," said Cooper. She

spoke into her lapel mic, then took her notepad and pen from her pocket. "Tell me what happened…"

Vivian tried to explain how she'd found Trudy, though her mind was so frazzled, she forgot several details, even referring to Trudy as Agnes on more than one occasion.

"Tell me about Ms. Denton's button collection," said Cooper.

"She was quite adamant about her rarest finds."

"Please explain," said Cooper.

"Well, one of the other women had inquired about purchasing one… a beautiful Victorian Glass button—"

"And what happened?" asked Cooper.

Vivian shifted and lowered her eyes. "She said, 'Over my dead body'."

———

WAITING on the metal bench outside Trudy's house, Shelby watched Officer Langley stretch yellow crime scene tape across the pristine lawn. A few minutes later, another vehicle pulled up. Doctor Minke exited the driver's side, carrying a leather case. From the passenger side, their next-door neighbor, LaTonya Lewis, got out.

When they reached the front porch, Deputy Sheriff Lewis acknowledged Officer Cooper, then turned. "Shelby? Didn't expect to see you here." She pointed to Shelby's arm. "Are you okay?"

"I'm fine. Trust me, I'd rather we were chatting on our front lawns."

"You and me both," said LaTonya. "Please excuse me." She followed Doctor Minke into the house.

———

COOPER CONTINUED QUESTIONING VIVIAN. "Do you have knowledge of anyone that might have been at odds with Ms. Denton?"

Vivian paled. "Only person I can think of... was Agnes. But she's, you know... dead."

"No one else comes to mind?" asked Cooper.

"Can I get some water?" asked Vivian.

"I only have a couple more questions..." Cooper studied Vivian's face. "Where were you last night about eight o'clock?"

Vivian wiped perspiration from her upper lip. "You don't think that I..."

"I'm just creating a timeline of events to document everyone's whereabouts," said Cooper.

Vivian twisted her hands in her lap. "I was at Shelby and Ella's. Laura and I had taken food to them because of Harold's passing."

"When did you leave?"

"I'm not sure. Maybe eight-thirty."

Cooper made eye contact with Vivian. "And where did you go after that?"

"I... I went home."

"Can anyone verify your whereabouts?"

Vivian shook her head. "I live alone."

SHELBY TOOK ANOTHER PAIN PILL, hoping to soothe her throbbing hand. Her thoughts went to Ella. Balancing her phone on her knee, she swiped the call icon. It went to voice mail. "El, sorry to bother you... call when you can.' She didn't want Ella to worry but soon word would out about Trudy's death. Why had she even agre attend the dumb button meeting? Talking to Vivian now would be next to impossible. Her head ached from thinking.

"Shelby? Are you ready to answer a few questions?" asked Cooper.

"Yes, but I really didn't see anything," said Shelby.

"Let's go over to the table." Cooper waited for Shelby to ease into her chair, then sat. "When was the last time you saw Ms. Denton?"

"A few weeks ago at the vet… Doctor Furst's office," said Shelby.

"And nothing since then?"

Shelby thought for a moment. "She came into the shop to say hi to everyone…"

Cooper added to her notes and waited. "Did she ever talk about her button collection?"

"Yes. At the vet's office." Shelby smiled. "She told me all about it and how it included several rare ones."

Tapping her pen on the notebook, Cooper referred to a previous page. "Did she ever mention anything about selling or trading among the club members?"

"I know little about the meetings. I only attended one… last week."

After making notes, Cooper looked up at Shelby. "Do you have knowledge of anyone that might have been at odds with Ms. Denton?"

Shelby shook her head. "Trudy seemed like a nice lady."

Cooper closed the notebook. "Thank you. You've been most helpful."

"Can we leave now?" asked Shelby.

"Let me check with Sergeant Nolan," said Cooper.

Cooper went inside Trudy's house, then the front door opened again. Alton stepped outside. "You ladies are free to leave. Thank you for your time. I'll let you know if I have further questions." He turned and went back inside.

Vivian grabbed Shelby's good hand. "Let's go before they change their minds."

The women walked across the lawn, carefully ducking under the crime tape. "I can't believe someone murdered Trudy," said Shelby. "You really think it was over her buttons?"

With trembling hands, Vivian opened her purse and took out her car keys. She dropped them not once, but twice.

Shelby put her hand on her friend's shoulder. "You okay?"

Vivian stiffened. "There's something else… Something I never mentioned to anyone… it's tearing me up inside…"

"What are you talking about?" asked Shelby.

Vivian lowered her voice. "Remember how you asked about the alley the night of Agnes' death?"

Shelby nodded. "When you mentioned you went the wrong way?"

"That night, when I was running away from Agnes and the others, there *was* someone else in the alley."

Shelby's eyes widened. "Who was it, Viv?"

Vivian looked back at the house, then lowered her voice again. "Trudy. I almost bumped into her."

Shelby gasped. "Are you sure?"

Vivian nodded. "Very sure."

"Then what happened?"

"I wanted to get out of there. It was dark. There was a flash of lightning. When I turned back, Trudy was just standing there watching something. And you know what? If I was a betting woman, I'd bet my last dollar she saw who stabbed Agnes."

CHAPTER FORTY-SEVEN

As the afternoon sun set behind the Pheasant Valley mountains, Ella and Eleanor left the funeral home. The sky, a brilliant shade of purple, cast a violet tint on everything below. Kit foxes scurried across the parking lot while a gentle breeze rustled through the branches of a nearby pine tree.

While Ella buckled in, Eleanor eased into the passenger seat. "Suppose we should go by the shop and let everyone know about the arrangements?"

"It's almost closing time," said Ella. She took her phone off silent mode. It vibrated, signaling missed calls. "We can wait until tom…" Five? Gladys, Shelby, Gladys, Alton, Shelby. And as many voice mails. She swiped an icon and listened. "Oh, no…"

"What?" asked Eleanor.

"Something terrible has happened." Ella inserted the key into the ignition and turned it. "We need to go home."

ELLA OPENED the front door of her home and hurried inside. "Shelby?" Oatmeal barked and yipped, vying for attention. She dashed into the kitchen, then looked down at the quivering dog and petted him. "Where's Shelby, boy?"

"How can I help?" asked Eleanor.

"Wait here while I check upstairs," said Ella. She climbed the stairs, two at a time, and found Shelby asleep on her bed. Sitting on the edge, she rubbed her friend's shoulder. "Hon…"

Shelby rolled over and opened her eyes. She sat up, cradling her injured hand.

Ella embraced her. "Are you okay?"

Shelby pressed into Ella, comforted by her touch. "It doesn't even seem real…" She pulled back. "We showed up for the meeting… then… so many emergency vehicles and lights and police tape and people, then the tackle box guy and Doctor Minke and LaTonya Lewis and then the questions… More for Viv than me… But…"

"Hon, slow down. Take a breath."

"Ella?" Eleanor's voice came from downstairs. "Did you find her?"

Shelby stiffened. "El, I don't want to talk to anyone else right now."

Ella stood on the landing and nodded to Eleanor. "She's in her bedroom, but needs rest. I hope you understand."

"Of course," said Eleanor. "I'll heat something for dinner. Give her a hug for me."

"Thank you. I'll be down soon." Ella went back into the bedroom and shut the door.

Rubbing Mr. Butterfinger's ears, Shelby motioned for Ella to sit with her. "What a day, huh?"

"Guess we both have a lot to talk about," said Ella.

Shelby nodded. "Between Trudy's murder…"

"Wait. Are they sure?"

"Alton declared the area an active crime scene," said Shelby. "They seemed to think it was related to her button collections."

"How's Viv taking it?"

Shelby reached for her water and took a sip. "El, she told me she saw Trudy in the alley right before Agnes was killed. Which means Trudy might have—"

"Witnessed the murder. Did she tell Alton?"

Shelby shook her head. "Viv doesn't want anyone to know. She's afraid they'll charge her with withholding evidence or something like that." She took another sip. "El, Trudy saw what happened."

"Looks like whoever murdered Agnes just made sure Trudy didn't tell anyone," said Ella.

Scents of baked chicken and savory spices drifted into the bedroom. Ella rubbed her stomach. "I've had nothing since that slice of pizza at the shop. Whatever Eleanor's heating up is calling to me."

Shelby sniffed the air. "No kidding." Mr. Butterfingers stretched and jumped off the bed. He looked back at the women and meowed. "Looks like he's hungry, too," said Shelby. "By the way, El, what happened at the attorney's office?"

"I'm sorry I haven't told you…" She lowered her voice and leaned closer to Shelby. "Harold named me as successor trustee and executor of his estate."

"Wow. How do you feel about that?" asked Shelby.

"Scared… honored… overwhelmed. It's a big responsibility." Ella rubbed her forehead. "I'll do it, of course, though I'm still numb over his death."

Shelby squeezed her friend's hand. "You know I'm here for you, El."

"Thanks. I don't want to overburden you. You've got the title signing and your hand to deal with."

Shelby was silent for a moment, then her eyes widened. "You know, this could help us figure out who killed Agnes."

Ella raised an eyebrow. "I'm not sure I want to know what you're thinking."

"You're going to have access to Harold's personal things, right?"

"I suppose so. Why?"

"Harold and Agnes had been at odds forever," said Shelby. "Maybe we'll be able to find something to show a motive."

"We?" Ella's eyes widened. "You don't think Harold killed Agnes."

"Not at all. But I think Harold, or Eleanor, might have known why she was killed," said Shelby. "Remember the minutes of the button meeting?"

"Too much has happened. Remind me." Ella's gaze shifted to the window. She watched the leaves rustle against the glass.

"The part about the meeting going into executive session. They disqualified Eleanor from running for president of the button club. Then elected Agnes." Shelby stopped to think. "Then I overheard the women at the shop. They said Agnes had some dirt on Eleanor... a secret or something like that... That's all I remember. Sorry, those pain pills make my head woozy."

"I remember now." Ella turned. "I can't do this on my own. You're better at finding those minute things that all add up."

"Is that a roundabout way of asking me to help you?"

Ella smiled. "The funeral home asked me to go by

Harold's tomorrow to pick an outfit for his service. And, since you have such a flair for fashion——"

Shelby pursed her lips. "Well, I suppose you could persuade me to join you. For picking out a suitable, er, suit."

"Oh, wait," said Ella. "Eleanor expressed a desire to help."

"That's even better," said Shelby. "We'll task Eleanor with finding several appropriate outfits while we sleuth."

"You mean snoop," said Ella.

Shelby rolled her eyes. "Call it what you want. My gut tells me several answers we're looking for have to do with Harold or Eleanor. Maybe we'll find something at his house. Or in conversation with Eleanor."

Ella patted Shelby's arm. "Fuzzy head or not, you might be on to something."

She nodded. "While Alton alluded Trudy's murder had something to do with the button club, I think it's something else."

"I'm willing to go with your theory," said Ella. "We just need to be super sensitive right now. Eleanor's hurting. We just can't come out and ask her what happened."

"Maybe not," said Shelby. "But think about it. When Agnes, Harold, Eleanor, and Viv left that night, Agnes was murdered. Viv told me Trudy had witnessed it. Now, Trudy's dead. With Harold gone, the only two left are Eleanor and Viv."

"Are you saying those ladies are in danger?" asked Ella.

"El, I hope I'm wrong. But if not, one of them could be next."

CHAPTER FORTY-EIGHT

E leanor pushed back from the dinner table. "Best baked chicken I've had in ages."

Feeding tiny shreds of meat to Oatmeal, Ella nodded. She collected their plates and took them to the sink.

"I don't mind doing the dishes," said Eleanor. "Keeps my hands and mind busy."

"Are you sure?" asked Ella.

Eleanor filled the sink with soapy water. "You've been so kind to let me stay here. It's the least I can do."

Ella gave her a quick hug, then she and Shelby went into the front room, followed by Oatmeal and Mr. Butterfingers. The pets took their usual spots—Mr. Butterfingers on top of the couch, Oatmeal sitting on Ella's lap.

"It's only seven-thirty, but I'm ready for bed," said Ella, covering a yawn.

"No kidding." Shelby stroked Oatmeal's ears. A moment later, he raised his head and sniffed the air. Then he jumped off the couch and ran to the door, barking.

Ella got up and looked through the peephole. She turned to Shelby. "It's Laura."

Shelby smiled. "Maybe she's bringing more yummy food."

Ella opened the door. "Laura, so good to see you. Please come in."

Laura entered, though she was only carrying a notebook and pen. "So sorry to drop by unannounced, but I'm on deadline."

The women looked at each other.

Eleanor walked into the front room, drying her hands on a cloth dishtowel. "Laura? I thought I heard your voice. Your chicken was wonderful."

Laura blushed. "I'm so glad you enjoyed it." She looked at Shelby. "Hon, do you have a few minutes?"

"I guess… What's this about?"

She stepped closer to Shelby, her flowery blouse billowing behind her. "Can we go to another room and talk?"

Shelby glanced at Ella, then to Laura. "I… guess so." Shelby motioned for their neighbor to follow her into the kitchen. "Will this work?"

"Yes, thank you." Laura pulled out a chair, sat, and opened her notebook.

Shelby stared at the notepad. "Did I hear you say you were on deadline?"

Laura nodded. "For our newspaper, the *Roost*. I hope this doesn't come across the wrong way, but I'm trying to get more information on today's untimely—"

"Are you saying you need a statement about Trudy's death?"

"Yes. I called Vivian, but she won't talk to me."

"She was pretty freaked out," said Shelby.

"I'm really sorry. If you want me to go, I'll understand."

Shelby cradled her injured wrist. "What do you need to know?"

"Anything you can recall about the scene… conversations overheard. You know."

"I know Alton declared it an active crime scene."

Laura jotted some notes. "Anything else. Can you confirm how she died?"

"I'm sorry, I can't. Do you know?" asked Shelby.

Laura caught her eye and nodded. "According to the coroner's preliminary report, it was an apparent strangulation."

"That's terrible," said Shelby.

"I thought you knew." Laura stared at Shelby. "I know you and Ella have a knack for figuring things out. Do you have a theory?"

Shelby stood. "It's been a long day and I'm really wiped out."

"I understand." Laura closed her notebook, then followed Shelby into the front room. "Ella, I'm putting together tomorrow's edition of the *Roost*. Do you know when Harold's memorial service might be?"

Ella nodded. "Next Friday. Two o'clock at the funeral home."

"Thanks." Laura opened her notebook, jotted something, then glanced at the women. "I appreciate your time." She went to the door and opened it. "Have a good evening, ladies."

Ella closed the door after she left, then turned to Shelby. "What was that all about?"

"I guess she was hoping for a scoop about Trudy for tomorrow's paper."

"And did you give her one?" asked Ella.

"No, but she mentioned how Trudy died. I'm really concerned, El."

THE NEXT MORNING, after Ella and Shelby had left for the shop, Eleanor paced through the house. She stopped only to check her phone. Eleven o'clock. Into the kitchen, turn around, to the front room, repeat. She looked up at the clock on the kitchen wall. Eleven fifteen. What was taking her so long?

As Eleanor passed by the couch for the umpteenth time, Mr. Butterfingers stretched out a paw. Oatmeal sprawled across the couch, following her with his eyes. She stopped again, checked her phone, then placed it on the coffee table.

"Where is she?"

Oatmeal raised his head, then lowered it again.

Eleanor went to the window and pulled back the thick curtain. She stared at the street, letting out a deep sigh. Dark clouds hung over the mountains. Tops of pine trees shook and trembled as light breezes developed into full gusts. Wind chimes on the front porch played harsher tones.

Someone coming across the grass caught her eye. Oatmeal jumped off the couch, barking and pawing at the entry. Eleanor rushed to the door, opening it wide.

"Where have you been?"

SHELBY STARED at the clock on the wall of The Bee's Knees. Willing it to strike noon only seemed to make the minutes pass more slowly. She watched as Ella comforted another group of sobbing women, no doubt friends of Trudy's.

"Yes, we're all saddened to hear of her passing," said Ella. She patted the arm of one distraught woman.

"We've known each other for fifty years," said the one with blue-tinted hair. "We'd go to the Corner Café and get pie every Friday."

Another in a green-checked pantsuit nodded and twisted an embroidered hankie. "Trudy was my granddaughter's dance instructor. Hubby and I went to all the performances..." She pulled a tissue from her pocket and wiped her bulbous nose. "I can't believe..."

Ella took time with each one, offering a kind word and a listening ear. "I'm so very sorry for your loss. And yours..." She looked up and noticed Shelby waiting. "Ladies, will you excuse me for just a moment?" The small group parted, then walked out the front door together, sharing more Trudy stories.

"You holding up okay, El?" Shelby reached for her friend's hand.

Ella nodded. "Though it doesn't seem real. I'm still trying to deal with Harold's pass—" The clock chimed twelve deep tones.

"Thank goodness," said Shelby. She looked around. "I'll let Kent and Susan know we're leaving."

The front door opened. Paige strolled in, a red glittery body suit accentuating her shapely hips. She shoved her purse and balled-up coat behind the counter, then turned to Ella. "You look like you've had a rough morning."

Ella smiled. "Trudy had a lot of friends."

"Yeah, been handing out tissues all morning at the Café. Everybody had a story to share..." She wandered away, distracted by her own thoughts. As Kent and Susan came up to the front, Ella and Shelby left the shop and made their way out to Ella's car.

"When's Eleanor meeting us at Harold's?" asked Shelby as she got in.

"She texted. Gladys wanted to stop by for a visit, then take her to lunch. Said to expect her by two o'clock." Ella turned the ignition key. "Figured we could grab something, then get over there and look around before she arrives."

Shelby buckled her seatbelt and nodded. "Hopefully that will give us enough time.

GLADYS SAT on Ella's couch next to Oatmeal. "You should never bring it up. It'll only cause more problems."

Eleanor wiped her eyes and stroked Mr. Butterfingers as he slept on her lap. "I've lived with this lie too long. It's hurt too many people."

"Hon, it won't make a difference. Let it go."

"I can't," said Eleanor. "The nightmares have returned."

"No one knows but me and you," said Gladys. "Why now?"

"Because it's the right thing to do. And it's what he wanted," said Eleanor. She stared out the window and shuddered. "I'm supposed to meet Ella and Shelby at two."

"Please reconsider," said Gladys. "After lunch, I'll drop you off at Harold's."

"I can't wait any longer." Eleanor wiped her eyes. "I'm telling them this afternoon."

As ELLA GOT out of her car at Harold's, she noticed the front door of the neighbor's house open and close. A few minutes later, a balding man in a heavy green overcoat and green rubber boots rushed across his lawn and over to the women. He gave a half wave and pulled out a pen and notebook. "Afternoon ladies, Eduardo Gonzales."

Shelby jumped back. "Hello."

"My apologies for dashing over, but I'm monitoring Mr. Madrigal's residence. I need to know who you are and what business you have here."

Shelby's eyes widened. She looked at the man, then to Ella.

Ella offered her a hand. "Ella Denning." She pointed to her friend. "Shelby Heaton. Nice to meet you, Mr. Gonzales."

Eduardo scribbled their names, then looked up and shook Ella's hand. "You own that crafty store in town, don't you?"

Ella nodded, then proceeded to the front door. "Thanks so much for watching over Harold's home..." Sifting through a set of keys from the attorney, Ella located Harold's and unlocked the heavy wooden door.

"But you didn't tell me your business... or if you're even supposed to be here..."

Ella turned to the neighbor. "I can tell you're very busy. How about we chat later?" She and Shelby stepping inside and closed the door.

"He strike you as odd?" asked Shelby.

Ella laughed. "Seems like a harmless, nosy neighbor."

"Maybe he's sleuthing," said Shelby.

"Like we have room to talk." The scent of lemon cleaning wax hung in the air. Though Ella had just been there a week earlier to retrieve his medicine, she shuddered. "Feels kind of strange to be here without... you know," she said.

Shelby nodded. "I keep waiting for him to come out and greet us."

Ella looked around. Being in such a rush last time; she hadn't noticed how neat and clean everything was. "Harold was meticulous about his housekeeping."

Shelby stood by a floor to ceiling bookcase in the formal living room. She ran her fingers along the spines of a row of books. "Alphabetized by author. Ha, I'm lucky if I even put mine on the shelf, much less in order."

"You should see his spice cabinet," said Ella.

"Seriously?" asked Shelby.

"From Adobo to White Peppercorns, if I recall," said Ella.

"Hopefully, his paperwork will be just as organized," said Shelby.

"No kidding." Ella looked around. "I think his office is this way…" She headed past the kitchen and down the hall.

"Hold on, I can't help myself." Shelby dashed inside the kitchen and opened a cabinet. "Wow, this is awesome. Everything is in order. Lookie. Even the lids are color-coded."

Ella chuckled. "Not only a shrewd businessman, but an amazing chef. Doug and I enjoyed many of his private dinners. Michelin star-worthy meals."

"I'm sorry I missed those." Shelby closed the cabinet and followed Ella down the hall.

"Here," said Ella, opening a set of glass and mahogany French doors. They walked into a long, narrow room. Though it was overcast, the office was naturally lit by floor-to-ceiling window panels. Outside one could see Harold's backyard garden.

Towering bookcases lined the left side of the office, separated by a long cabinet in the middle. Harold's wide mahogany desk sat in the middle of the room, a large computer screen on one side and a single engraved pen and box of tissues on the other. An oversized marble fireplace took up most of the wall in front of the desk, though there was a leather chair and ottoman near the window.

Shelby looked up. "That ceiling. All wood inlay."

"As is the floor," said Ella. "Harold didn't spare any expense, did he?"

"Guess not…" said Shelby, walking over to the window.

Ella pulled out the leather chair from behind the desk. It let out a soft poof as she sat. "Fancy." She tapped her fingers on the desktop, then opened the widest drawer in front of her. Taking out a folder, she laid it on top. "I feel bad going through his things."

Shelby sat on the ottoman. "I'm sure this isn't easy, but remember, he wanted you to be the one to help him."

Ella nodded. She opened the folder and scanned several documents. "Looks like business deals he was involved in." She closed the folder and slipped it back into the drawer. "Now where would he keep his checkbook…?"

Shelby looked around. "Well, there are file cabinets and drawers along both walls. Your guess is as good as mine."

Ella looked up. "If we're going to find anything of interest before Eleanor gets here, I'm going to need your help."

Shelby winced. "I feel like I'm violating his privacy."

"I understand," said Ella. "But the sooner we look, the sooner we can get it over with."

Shelby pointed to the side closest to her. "Guess I'll start over here."

Ella opened another desk drawer and pulled out a folder. After a quick scan, she replaced it and took out the next one. Meanwhile, Shelby dug through each folder she found, skimmed a few lines, then put it away and started over. She pulled on another drawer without success. "These file cabinets are locked."

Ella scrutinized the three drawer file cabinet set in one of the wall units. She tried several keys, with no luck. After another attempt, the drawer opened.

Shelby smiled. "Awesome."

Ella stood in front of the compact unit closest to the window. She opened the top drawer with trembling hands and pulled out a nondescript binder. "I think I found something." Placing the binder on the desk, she opened it. Inside were several leather checkbook cases. Bank statements with canceled checks. Underneath were three business-sized envelopes with familiar names on them.

Shelby came around the desk and stood behind her. "Now what?"

Ella looked up. "We need to go through everything in this cabinet."

A Grandfather clock chimed from another room. "Two o'clock," said Shelby. "Didn't you say Eleanor was supposed to be here soon?"

"Find a box or something. We need to get this stuff out of here before she arrives. Then we can go through it at home…"

Shelby looked around. "If only I'd brought my giant purse."

Ella opened the first checkbook. "Look at this…"

"I thought we were packing it up," said Shelby.

"This entire checkbook has entries made out to 'AgCo'." Ella looked up. "Agricultural Company? Never heard of it, though Harold had quite the portfolio of investments."

Shelby ran her finger along the entries. "Five hundred

dollars. A thousand dollars. Looks like he wrote them a check each week——"

Ella's phone rang. She looked at it, then answered. "Eleanor, is everything okay?... Oh so sorry, we didn't hear the doorbell. One of us will be there in a moment to let you in..." The women looked at each other. "Go let Eleanor in, then follow her to Harold's room and help find his funeral clothes," said Ella. "It will give me time to hide this stuff again."

"Oh great, an accomplice." Shelby rolled her eyes.

As Shelby and Eleanor walked upstairs, Ella shoved everything back into the top drawer. She closed it, but stopped to examine the three envelopes. One made out to her. One to Eleanor. And the last one...

"Ella?" Shelby called from the hallway. "Eleanor needs your opinion."

"Coming..." She locked the file drawer, then rushed to join them in Harold's bedroom.

CHAPTER FORTY-NINE

Leaving Harold's house, Ella pulled her coat closer. She unlocked her car door but before she could get in, Mr. Gonzales appeared in his yard waving at the women.

"Leaving, ladies?"

"Evening, Mr. Gonzales," said Shelby.

He ran across his lawn, down to the sidewalk, then up to Ella. "No, I asked if you were leaving. L-E-A—"

"Yes, we are." Ella got in as the other women buckled in and locked their doors.

Mr. Gonzales rapped his knuckles on Ella's window. He waited for her to roll it down. "Just doing my job as the designated captain of the Block Watch Team…"

Ella smiled. "And such an excellent job you're doing, Mr. Gonzales. I should let you go." She rolled up her window and started the car, then frowned as she looked through the front windshield. "Not liking the look of that sky."

Shelby followed her gaze. "Maybe we should wait to go to the funeral home."

"It's on the way and I'd rather get it done today." Ella

watched the neighbor retreat to his house, then pulled away from the curb.

Eleanor shuddered.

"Everything okay?" asked Ella.

"I just have the strangest feeling about that guy," said Eleanor. "Always watching everything that goes on."

"Have you chatted with him before?" asked Shelby.

Eleanor straightened. "Never really talked to him, but every time I came by Harold's, I'd see him at his window. I always wondered what his real motive was for tracking everyone."

"Maybe he's just lonely," said Shelby.

The women were quiet for a long while. Shelby watched the sky. Ella, the road. And Eleanor sent and received text messages on her phone. By the time they dropped Harold's blue suit at the funeral home, the skies had turned deep purple. Moments later, sheets of rain drenched the road. Blasts of wind pushed against Ella's car, causing them to ping-pong between the yellow line and shoulder of the two-lane roadway.

"You doing okay, El?" asked Shelby.

"If I could just see the road…" she said.

"Thank goodness we're almost home," said Eleanor.

"I need coffee," said Shelby.

Eleanor shivered. "I might need something stronger after this wild ride."

Shelby stared out the side window, jumping each time a gust slammed into their car. Ella's voice remained calm, though her knuckles turned white, gripping the wheel to stay in control. When they pulled into the gravel driveway, Eleanor offered a prayer of thanksgiving.

Rushing up to the porch, Ella unlocked the door. They went in, leaving wet prints on the carpet. Ella shed her coat in the bedroom and changed into a powder blue jogging suit.

Shelby came in and closed the door. "I let Oatmeal out, though I don't think it thrilled him to pee in that rain. The quickest squat and go I've seen in a while…" She grabbed a towel and dried her damp hair. "You notice Eleanor hightail it up the stairs when we got home?"

"No, why?" asked Ella.

"I know it was hard being at Harold's, but she seemed…"

"Agitated?" asked Ella. "Do you think she knows we found that stuff?"

Shelby gathered her hair into a loose ponytail. "Let's hope not."

"HOLD ON GLADYS…" Eleanor placed her phone on the bed and changed out of her wet clothes. She slipped a hand-knitted sweater over her head, then picked up the phone and held it between her chin and shoulder as she pulled on a dry pair of pants. "Couldn't bring myself to tell them… No, I still plan to… Yes, I'm sure. It just wasn't the right time… Wait until after the funeral?… Gladys, this is going to eat me up inside. I appreciate your counsel, but I can't live this lie any longer…"

ELLA SCOOPED several heaping tablespoons of grounds into the coffee maker's filter and turned on the machine. Within a few minutes, scents of French vanilla permeated the kitchen and surrounding rooms.

Shelby sniffed the air and sat at the table. "Ahhh. Just what I need to warm up." She scratched Oatmeal behind the ears and reached out to stroke Mr. Butterfinger's long tail.

After filling two mugs, Ella joined Shelby. "Leftovers for dinner sound good?"

Shelby nodded. "Something simple." She leaned closer to Ella. "Since the shop is closed tomorrow, we should have more than enough time to—"

Eleanor came into the kitchen and paused. "Am I interrupting something?"

"Of course not." Ella got up, filled another mug, and placed it on the table. "Please join us."

Eleanor pulled out a chair, then eased herself slowly into it. "I just wish it was all over…"

"Funerals are hard." Ella patted her arm. "It will be difficult for all of us."

"Still feel like it's all my fault," said Eleanor.

"You didn't know Harold was so sick," said Shelby.

Eleanor turned to her, tears welling in her eyes. "I'm not… it's not… If I'd only…" She reached inside her sleeve for a tissue and blew her nose.

Shelby and Ella looked at each other but said nothing.

Eleanor sipped her coffee, then wiped her nose again. Big tears rolled down her cheeks.

"Hon, is there something you want to talk about?" asked Ella.

She glanced at Ella and opened her mouth, then looked down again.

"Anything you tell us will be in confidence," said Ella.

"Except for Gladys, I'm the only one who knows now." Eleanor shook her head. "It shouldn't make a difference…"

Ella reached for Eleanor's hand. "Does this have to do with Harold?"

Eleanor nodded.

"About his illness?"

Eleanor shook her head.

Ella looked at Shelby and raised an eyebrow.

"His estate?" asked Ella.

Eleanor looked at Ella. "In a way…"

"I know we talked about how you and Harold had cared for each other… Is it something from the past?"

She nodded.

Ella sipped her coffee, then straightened. "You gotta help me out here."

Eleanor looked at the women and blinked back tears. "I was in high school. Harold had already graduated. We were so much in love…" She took in a deep breath and let it out. "In a moment of passion, I… we… um, gave into temptation."

Ella looked at Shelby and waited for Eleanor to continue.

"But that one night turned into a nightmare… My parents… they found out… and threatened to have Harold arrested. Even though I'd consented, I was just a few weeks shy of my eighteenth birthday. Harold was nineteen…"

Ella gasped. "Statutory rape."

Eleanor nodded. "They said if he'd leave town and never come back… they wouldn't file charges. So Harold left. I was alone… And afraid."

"They never pressed charges, did they?" asked Shelby.

Eleanor shook her head. "My mother and Gladys were best friends. She's the one who talked my parents out of filing charges. But…"

"But what?" asked Ella.

"They made me marry Richard soon after... It was a turbulent marriage, but we made it work. John loved his daddy so much. It broke my heart when Richard died and John had to give up veterinary school..." Tears ran down Eleanor's cheeks.

"So now that you've told us why Harold really left, you feel better, right?" asked Ella.

Eleanor shook her head and continued to sob. "My son never knew... And I think that's why our marriage was so hard. I think Richard knew... but he never asked..."

"What are you trying to tell us?" asked Ella.

"I wanted to tell you all afternoon. But I just didn't know how to bring it up. You don't know how hard it's been. Living a lie for over forty years..." Eleanor wiped her eyes, then looked up. "Richard wasn't John's biological father."

CHAPTER FIFTY

Downstairs in her room, Ella propped herself up on an elbow and turned her pillow over to the cooler side. She stared at the alarm clock until it came into focus. Not even midnight. Laying back in bed and closing her eyes, she listened. The white noise machine hummed. Rain pinged the window. Oatmeal snored.

Upstairs, Shelby sat up and rubbed her eyes. Her phone showed just after midnight. *Maybe some milk would help.* She crept down the stairs and went into the kitchen, only to find Ella sitting at the table eating a banana.

"Hope I didn't wake you," said Ella.

"After what Eleanor told us…" said Shelby. "Who could sleep?" She poured herself a small glass of milk and joined Ella.

"I have so many questions," said Ella.

"I wonder if that's why John hated Harold so."

Ella offered Oatmeal the last bite, then she leaned back in her chair. "Eleanor said he didn't know."

"What if he did?" asked Shelby. "How could he not see the resemblance…? Same smile. Same voice, almost."

"You know how most of us deal with the most obvious things?"

"Yeah," said Shelby. "We ignore them and hope they go away." She cradled her broken hand and sighed.

"Do you think Eleanor should tell John before the funeral?"

"I don't know." Shelby sucked in her breath. "I just hope no one gets wind of this. Can you imagine the ramifications…?"

———

ELEANOR POKED at the last of her scrambled eggs. Looking up from her breakfast, she noticed Ella and Shelby watching her. She stood, took her plate to the sink, then stared at the raindrops dripping down the windowpane. Turning, she cleared her throat. "Sorry to have dropped that news on you last night. I couldn't hold it inside any longer."

Ella stood. "The emotional pain you've been in, I can't imagine.

"I wanted to tell you when we were with Harold at that motel," she said. "I'd hoped we could tell you together. But…"

Shelby fed the last of her eggs to Oatmeal and Mr. Butterfingers. "Is there anything we can do?"

"Not now," said Eleanor. "I'm sure you have questions. But if you don't mind, I need to be alone today. To figure out what to do next."

Ella went to Eleanor. "We're here for you when you're ready." She caught her eye. "Hug?"

Eleanor's shoulders relaxed. She accepted Ella's warm embrace, not moving for several moments. Stepping back,

Eleanor smiled. "I didn't realize how much I needed that." Then she turned and went upstairs to the guest room.

Ella leaned closer to Shelby. "Guess that gives us more time to go back to Harold's and delve through our finds from yesterday."

"I feel bad for her. Wrestling with when to confront John…"

"I hope she doesn't go it alone," said Ella. "He has quite the temper."

"After what you told me about the incident at the motel, I agree. Who knows what he'll be capable of when he finds out?"

After washing the breakfast dishes, Ella and Shelby left home. By now, the steady rain and wind had turned into a slow drizzle and a gentle breeze. After a short drive across town, they arrived at Harold's house. Ella watched as the curtains of Mr. Gonzales' house fluttered and his round face appeared in the window. "Our friendly neighbor is on duty."

"Oh man. Let's try to slip inside without… Never mind."

Eduardo was already at Harold's sidewalk as the ladies walked up. He hitched up his droopy britches and followed them to the front door with a notebook and pen in hand. "Morning ladies."

"You're up early, Mr. Gonzales." Ella stopped for a moment and offered her hand. "So glad to see you again. You have a wonderful day." She turned, unlocked the heavy door, and the ladies went inside.

"You're so polite. I don't think he knows how to take it," said Shelby, laughing.

"Figure I'd acknowledge him, then keep going. Better than ignoring him." The women walked down the hall and

312

into the cold office. Ella closed the drapes, then turned to Shelby. "Just in case."

"You mean Gonzales?"

"I don't trust that guy," said Ella.

"You are the successor trustee and have a right to be here."

Ella nodded, unlocked the file cabinet, and extracted several folders. She clutched them to her chest. "Even though I *can* be here, it doesn't mean I *should* be. I think I'm supposed to wait until after I meet with the attorney tomorrow."

"Do you *really* want to wait?" asked Shelby.

Ella raised an eyebrow. "You know perfectly well I don't."

Shelby grinned. "Didn't think so." She eased herself into Harold's plush leather chair next to the fireplace. "He sure lived an elegant life, didn't he?"

"Spared no expense with decorating." Ella placed the checkbooks, bank statements, and personalized envelopes on top of the desk. "He gave generously to many charities. Not to mention he didn't even blink an eye when he loaned Doug and me the startup costs for our coffee shop business." She flipped open a checkbook. Scanning the entries, she pointed to one and showed it to Shelby. "Apparently, he even donated to get our new ice rink up and going."

"Am I reading that right?" Shelby gasped. "Fifty-thousand dollars?"

Ella nodded. She continued through the entries and stopped. "Look at this..." she showed Shelby. "There's an entry for The Bee's Knees but no amount shown..."

Shelby frowned. "I thought he wasn't able to help because of Agnes."

Ella flipped past the entries to the checks and pointed.

"Here's the check—he never made it out or tore it out of the register."

Shelby scanned it. "According to this, he made it out..." She opened her phone to a calendar app. "The night he came over to talk about our expansion."

Ella continued to look at the entries. "All the Ag Company checks are gone." She picked up another register. "This one is from last year. And the other one, the year before..." She scrutinized two of them again.

"Maybe we should look at the bank statements," said Shelby.

Ella thumbed through the folders, pulling out several months' statements. She spread them over the polished desk. "Nothing recent, mostly last year's." She sat on the chair again, leaned back, and closed her eyes.

"The attorney should have more recent bank info for you tomorrow." Shelby picked up a statement. "Looks like all those Ag Company checks were made out to CASH."

Ella opened her eyes and straightened. "What do you mean?"

"El, look at the cancelled checks."

"What about signatures on the back?" asked Ella.

"For Deposit Only." Shelby showed it to Ella. "There *is* an account number."

"Does it match the ones on the checks?"

Shelby raised an eyebrow. "No. And why should it? Harold wouldn't be writing checks to himself, would he?"

"Just wondered."

"Don't we have our business account at Bank One?" said Shelby.

"What are you getting at?" asked Ella.

"I know a few tellers... Maybe..."

"You know that's against the law," said Ella.

"Would you rather go to Alton and ask him to get a search warrant?"

"On what grounds?" asked Ella. "We don't even know whose bank account, or if they've done anything wrong."

"So what do you want to do?" asked Shelby.

Ella looked at her friend. "You're the super sleuth."

"Sounds like you want me to—" Shelby's phone signaled an incoming text. She pulled it out of her jean's pocket, opened the app, then showed it to Ella.

Ella's eyes widened. "Alton wants to meet with you tonight?"

"Follow-up questions regarding Trudy's death," said Shelby. "Mind if he comes by after dinner, about seven?"

"That's fine."

Shelby checked her calendar. "I'm also supposed to sign those escrow papers for Mac this week."

"As if we didn't have enough on our plates."

Shelby straightened when her phone pinged with a new message. "Viv. Apparently Alton is meeting with her tonight, too." She looked up at Ella. "Poor thing. She's freaking out and headed to our house right now."

"Guess the checks and bank statements can wait," said Ella. "I was really hoping to go through these envelopes, though…"

"Which ones?" asked Shelby.

Ella held up the three envelopes. "One for Eleanor. Me. And… guess who?"

Shelby rubbed her forehead. "Oh no."

CHAPTER FIFTY-ONE

John walked into his front room, mumbling.

Lilibeth, wineglass in one hand, was engrossed in a thick book. She looked up. "What's wrong now?"

He peered out the front window and glowered. "Barely dusk and those crazy coyotes are already showing up. Must be more ewes getting ready to lamb."

Vickie sat next to her sister scrolling through a social media app. She looked up. "They *were* loud last night."

"This is all I need," said John. "Lilibeth, you think you can put that wine down long enough to help me deal with this mess?"

His wife finished her glass, then emptied the rest of the bottle. Holding the wineglass up, she smirked. "I'm still thirsty, dear husband."

John rolled his eyes. "Lotta help you are." He stomped over to the coat closet and pulled out his jacket. "If we lose our flocks, it's the end of your Wooley Sisters business."

Vickie whispered something to Lilibeth. They giggled.

"Well, someone's got to go protect our stock." John put

on his jacket and grabbed a shotgun leaning against a wall by the door.

Lilibeth turned her book upside down on the coffee table. "Maybe you could convince little sis here to help you." Her words slurred. She took another sip of wine. "Though I've got no idea why either of us should. I'm sure it's just another excuse to leave again and go to your... girlfriend."

John gripped the shotgun barrel and straightened. "Fine words coming from a binge-drinker."

Lilibeth stood, swayed, then sat again. "Just go protect the flocks. That's all that matters."

John took a step toward his wife, but stopped when Vickie stood.

"How about I keep an eye on him, sis?" Vickie asked.

Lilibeth nodded and went back to reading her book.

John opened a box of shells. Sitting on a footstool by the door, he turned the shotgun over, grabbed a shell from the box, then pushed it into the loading flap with his thumb. Once he heard and felt the click, he repeated the sequence, filling the magazine. John got up, pumped the slide backward and forward, loading the chamber, then glared at Vickie. "I don't need a babysitter."

She slipped her boots on over heavy socks, then grabbed her coat from the closet. "Where's my gun?"

John grabbed a second shotgun from near the door and shoved it at her. "Shells are in the box. You know how to load it."

Vickie sat on the stool and loaded the gun.

John glared down at her. "Just don't go shooting me in the back."

Vickie looked over at her sister and winked. "It wouldn't be on purpose."

Grumbling, John opened the front door and left.

Vickie fastened her coat and turned back to Lilibeth. "Enjoy the quiet." She walked outside into the chilly, moonless night. Spotting John waiting at the end of the gravel driveway, she ran to catch up with him. Breathing hard, her breath floated away with the wind.

John and Vickie walked in silence. Away from the house. Past the fence line. The shrill yipping of coyotes echoed in the distance. They continued toward the bleating ewes.

John held his shotgun in the crook of his arm. After a while, he stopped and turned to his red-haired sister-in-law. "Thanks."

"For what?" asked Vickie.

"You know."

Vickie nodded.

John took Vickie's arm, guiding her behind an outbuilding. He propped his gun against the wooden exterior, then pulled her close. Brushing back her hair, he caressed her freckled cheeks with the back of his fingers, then kissed her for several moments. Stepping back, he smiled. "She doesn't suspect a thing."

CHAPTER FIFTY-TWO

Ella walked into the kitchen dressed in dark jeans and a burgundy cable-knit sweater. She stepped over Mr. Butterfingers, basking on a spot on the floor warmed by sunshine. Looking outside, she smiled. *Blue skies. Finally.* She poured a cup of coffee, filled a plate with eggs and homemade Potatoes O'Brien, and sat next to Shelby. "Thanks for making breakfast."

Shelby nodded. "Pet-friendly potatoes—No onions." She covered a yawn.

"It appears more sleep would have helped." Ella chuckled.

"Most days, I'd agree with you," said Shelby. "But I've got too much on my mind. Last night after Alton left, I couldn't stop thinking about Vivian. I'm frustrated she refused to tell him about seeing Trudy in the alley. I think she's making a big mistake." She ate the last of her potatoes, then finished her coffee. "Plus, with you having to leave the shop mid-morning, I wanted to get an early start so we could prepare for the day."

Ella ate most of her eggs, then started on the potatoes.

"I wonder if Viv knows more than she's saying. She was outside for a while. If I remember, her daughters, Lilibeth and Vickie, were quite concerned."

"It only seemed like an argument between Harold and Agnes, but now... I don't know," said Shelby.

After feeding leftover pieces of egg to Oatmeal, Ella finished her coffee. She took her dishes to the sink, rinsed them, then went back to the table. "Care to share what's on your mind?"

Shelby turned and looked up. "Just snippets of ideas so far. Nothing I can really put into words."

"You know Alton's itching to solve these cases," said Ella. "He's putting pressure on his officers and anyone else who might know something. I'm sure that's why he was here last night."

"Why do I feel he's hoping we come through for him again?" asked Shelby.

"Hon, he trusts us to do our best." Ella smiled. "And right now, that's all we can do."

Under the table, Oatmeal perked up, tail wagging. He rushed to Eleanor as she came into the kitchen.

"Well, good morning, Oatmeal," she said, scratching him behind his ears. "I'm going to miss you when I leave."

Ella turned. "You're leaving us?"

Eleanor poured herself a cup of coffee and leaned against the counter. "Probably after the funeral." She stirred creamer into it and took a sip. "I need to get back to a normal routine. Whatever that means."

"Let us know how we can help," said Ella.

She looked at Ella, tears in her eyes. "Just get me through this week."

Ella pulled up in front of The Bee's Knees and parked. She exited the car, along with Shelby and Eleanor. Once inside the shop, Ella flipped on the lights and adjusted the temperature to compensate for the warmer weather. Shelby went behind the counter and pulled out the clipboard with the volunteer schedule.

"Who's in today?" Ella asked, while putting her things away.

"Besides me and Eleanor, looks like Vickie and Lilibeth this morning…" Shelby turned to the next page. "And Kent and Susan this afternoon." She looked up at Ella. "More than enough help."

"It's almost the end of the month," said Ella. "Everyone over schedules just to make sure they get their hours in."

Shelby placed the clipboard near the register. "Do you think Kent and Susan will announce a date soon?"

Ella smiled. "I suppose when they're ready."

"What time is your appointment with DeShawn?" asked Shelby.

"Not until ten-thirty, but I need to leave early to run a few errands." Ella glanced at the clock and opened the register. "It's almost nine."

"Shall I do the honors?" asked Shelby. "There's a few people standing outside."

Ella handed her the key. "Thanks. Give me a moment to recount the cash in the drawer and verify the beginning balance." After finishing, Ella closed the drawer and looked around. "Where's Eleanor?"

Shelby scanned the shop. "I think she's making coffee."

"Sounds good," said Ella. "Time to open up."

Shelby unlocked the front door and held it while several regular customers came inside. "Good morning, Hazel," said Shelby. "Nice to see you again, Mrs. Buford."

Hazel Price, a short, petite woman with raven-black hair and large cat-eye framed glasses, grinned. "Don't ya just love this spring weather?"

Shelby nodded as several others entered. "My favorite time of the year."

Mona Buford, one of Pheasant Valley's former librarians, nodded. "I noticed my bulbs peeking out of the ground this morning. Soon, my garden will be awash with color."

"I always love driving by your home in the Spring," said Shelby. "Didn't you plant just about every variety of daffodil?" She continued walking and talking with the women as they browsed.

"Not just Daffodils. Also Iris, Hyacinths, and Tulips…"

Shelby turned around as the door opened again. In rushed Lilibeth and Vickie.

"So sorry we're late," said Vickie. "Someone…" she eyed her sister, "… slept in."

Lilibeth gave a sheepish grin. "Just one of those mornings." The sisters signed in, then chatted with Ella.

"Oh, I must catch Lilibeth before we leave," said Hazel. "I've been meaning to thank her for her hubby's handiwork."

Shelby straightened. "He did something for you and Bob?"

Hazel picked up a gingham-lined basket, then looked at Shelby. "He installed a dishwasher 'bout two weeks ago." She walked over to Laura's booth, picked up a lavender candle, and held it to her nose. "Poor Bob was beside himself. He tried to do it, but a hose came loose. Water everywhere. And then to top it off, the power went out."

Mona lifted her glasses and read the label on a sample jar of Laura's lavender-infused hand cream. She opened it, dabbed some on her wrist, then took in the thick, calming scent. "Wasn't that the night of the massive storm? We lost power, too."

Shelby gave Mona a side glance. "Are you referring to that terrible wind and lightning storm?"

Hazel placed three candles inside her basket. "Yes. It was a doozy, wasn't it? Reminded me of the storms we'd get in——" She paused and looked over to where Lilibeth and Ella stood. "Excuse me ladies, I'll be right back."

Shelby observed Hazel, then turned to Mona. "If you need anything, let me know." She followed Hazel and picked up a flyer laying on the counter.

"You okay?" asked Ella. "You look flushed."

Shelby put a finger to her lips and nodded. "Toss me that rag so I can dust… stuff."

Ella raised an eyebrow.

"I'll explain later," said Shelby. She plodded along, wiping the glass surface, stopping just behind Lilibeth and Hazel.

"That hubby of yours sure saved the day, rather, night for us…" said Hazel.

Lilibeth eyed the woman with a raised brow. "John?"

"Oh, my. Yes," said Hazel. "Brought over a generator so we had light. Hooked up the dishwasher. He's a lifesaver."

Lilibeth raised an eyebrow. "He mentioned something about it."

"Wouldn't accept anything for his time. Rushed off afterward." Hazel placed her basket on the carpet. She cleared her throat and opened a small, black pocketbook. She pulled out two bills, folded them, and shoved them into Lilibeth's hand. "You take this and do something nice for you and the hubby. Don't tell him it was from me." She grabbed her basket again, then hurried back to Mona, who was studying a display of hand-carved birds.

Lilibeth shoved the money into her jeans pocket and turned.

Staring at her wide-eyed, Shelby grinned, then held up the rag. "Guess it's as clean as it can be." She handed the rag back to Ella. "So, what else do you need done?"

Ella gave her a look, then turned to the sisters. "Vickie, I'd like you and Lilibeth to help with customers today. Shelby will handle the register while I'm at an appointment…" She glanced around. "Still no sign of Eleanor?"

"I thought she was making coffee," said Shelby.

Ella nodded. "Okay, let's get to work, ladies."

As Shelby walked away, Ella touched her arm. "What was that all about?"

The front door opened and an older couple walked in. Ella smiled and acknowledged them, then turned back.

"We need to talk." Shelby glanced around. "But there are too many customers." She smiled. "I smell hazelnut brewing. You want some?"

Ella breathed in. "Definitely. But make mine in a to-go cup, since I need to leave soon."

A few minutes later, Shelby came back with two steaming coffees. She handed a thick paper cup with a lid to Ella, then went behind the counter with her mug.

Eleanor walked up an aisle toward them, then stopped to check her phone. She looked up. "Gladys just invited me to brunch. Okay, if I leave for a few hours?"

"No problem," said Ella. "We have enough help if you need to go."

Eleanor sent a text, then read an incoming one. "On her way." She got her things, left the shop, and stood outside.

"El, I'm concerned. Every time Eleanor sees Gladys, she's more confused about... you know what?"

"I've noticed it, as well." Ella sipped her coffee. "Though Gladys might try to help, I'm not sure if her counsel is wise. Eleanor is so conflicted." She looked up at the clock. "I should get going. Need to run a few errands before I go see DeShawn." She grabbed her purse and hugged Shelby. "Hope it goes well."

"With the way everything is unfolding, what could go wrong?"

Ella straightened. "I'd rather not think about it."

———

PULLING into the lot behind DeShawn White's office, Ella parked and got out of her car. She stood in the parking lot and looked up at the clear blue sky. Birds twittered and chirped in a nearby tree. A gentle breeze touched her cheek. She raised her coffee cup as in a toast and whispered, "This is for you, Harold. I hope I live up to your expectations."

She took a seat inside the attorney's office and scanned a coffee table for something to read. A variety of gardening and home renovation magazines fanned over a low cherry wood table. She thought about The Bee's Knees renovation project. Their goal had been to complete it by May, but with everything that had happened in the past two weeks... who knew when they would start, much less finish?

DeShawn entered the small waiting room. "Ella, good to see you. Please come in." His deep voice calmed her. It reminded her of her father's who sang baritone in a barbershop quartet. Ella had fond memories of the four men practicing their repertoire in the family's den.

"How are you doing today? asked DeShawn.

"As well as expected."

The attorney motioned to a padded chair across from his desk and then waited for Ella to sit. Several file folders lay on his desk, along with a blue ring binder.

"Fortunately, Harold was very meticulous and organized," said DeShawn.

"That will help a lot," said Ella.

"From the funeral to his living will, he left detailed instructions on how he wanted everything handled." DeShawn turned the binder around and pushed it to Ella. "You'll need this to carry out his requests for the disposal of his monies and property."

Ella looked at DeShawn. "This doesn't seem real." Along the bottom right, she read the gold embossed words of the three attorneys in the building: *Bluhm, Slater & White.*

He reached out and patted her trembling hand. "Let's just take it one page at a time."

She nodded and opened the binder. It started with a letter addressed to Harold. She read it to herself, then looked up. "This was dated less than three weeks ago."

DeShawn nodded. "Harold knew the end was near and wanted me to make sure everything was in order."

Ella continued, then looked up again, her eyes filled with tears. "I don't know if I can deal with all of this today." She flipped through the pages, then noticed tabs numbered 1 through 6 and started reading. "Restatement of Trust in its Entirety? Conveyance of Property to Co-Trustee?" She rubbed her forehead. "DeShawn, my head is already spinning. I don't know what any of this means."

He took her hand again. "A lot is complicated, but necessary, legalese. I'll explain as we go along. What you need to understand right now is Part One, Section 6.02.

The Distribution of Trust Estate, Specific Distributions, and Part Two, Harold's Last Will and Testament."

Ella closed the binder and stood. "I need to... I don't know. Walk around. Breathe fresh air..."

DeShawn went and pulled back a curtain, then opened the window. "Does this help?"

Ella went over and took in a deep breath, and let it out. She closed her eyes, then opened them and nodded.

"Just those two parts today?" she asked.

"Yes. We can go over the rest later. Let's start with Section Two, Harold's will."

Ella sat again. She opened the binder and flipped to the first page of Section Two and started reading out loud. "I, Harold James Madrigal, over the age of eighteen (18) years, residing in the County of Kern, State of California, and being of sound and disposing mind and memory and not acting under fraud, duress, or undue influence of any person whomsoever, do hereby make, publish, and declare this is my Last Will and Testament as follows—"

DeShawn's cell chirped. "Excuse me. I need to take this."

Ella closed her eyes and waited. She opened them as he ended the call.

DeShawn stared at Ella; his brow furrowed. "That was the company that monitors Harold's house. Something triggered the silent alarm. They've dispatched the police."

CHAPTER FIFTY-THREE

Once inside Harold's house, neither intruder bothered turning on a light. Using cell phones for illumination, they tiptoed down the hall. The scent of lemon wax and mahogany enveloped their senses as they entered Harold's office. The first one inside stopped and turned to the other. "Are you sure no one will find out?"

The friend squinted in the dim room. "Why are you so nervous?"

The first one pulled on a file drawer with trembling hands. "Because we're not supposed to be here."

"You and Harold were friends. He gave you a key."

"It's locked," one said, and tried another drawer. "How am I going to get what I came for?"

Walking over to the file cabinet, the friend removed her floppy hat and felt around her hair. "Got it," she said, showing off a bobby pin.

"Do people still use those things?"

"They have several uses." She straightened the pin, pulled off the coated tips with her teeth, then wedged the sharp end into the keyhole. Wiggling it around, she listened, then wiggled it again, and smiled. "I think that did the trick. Try to open it again."

OFFICERS COOPER and Langley pulled up and parked in front of Eduardo Gonzales' home. They ran the plates of the late model car in front of Harold's. After receiving the information they needed, they left their unit and proceeded up the walkway, guns drawn.

Even before the police arrived, Mr. Gonzales had been peering out the window. Making note of the events and times they took place, he continued to watch. When he saw the police unit in front of his house, he donned an oversized sweater, cinching it tight around his waist. Checking his reflection in a mirror near the front door, he licked his fingers and straightened a few hairs atop his head. He opened the door, pen and notebook in hand, then stepped onto the porch. But when Gonzales noticed the officers had drawn their weapons, he backed up, went into his home, and locked the door. Maybe it was best to let the uniforms handle it this time.

Cooper and Langley made their way across the grass and up to Harold's front door. Langley pointed. Cooper acknowledged it was ajar. She communicated using hand movements, then stood back and waited.

Langley pushed the door with the tip of his boot. "Pheasant Valley Police, show yourself."

They waited for a response. None came.

Langley raised his voice and repeated the warning. "Pheasant Valley Police, show yourself. We've got the K-9 unit."

Cooper gasped. She knew Langley had six years'

experience on the streets of Los Angeles, but this was Pheasant Valley. Plus, they didn't even have a K-9 unit.

A moment later, a woman's shaky voice came from down the hall. "It's just Eleanor."

Then another voice. "And Gladys."

Langley let out a long breath. "Come out where we can see you, hands in the air."

"It's only Eleanor and Gladys," said Cooper. "I highly doubt they're carrying."

Langley holstered his gun. "I never take chances. The one and only time I let my guard down, I lost my partner. They need to know we're serious. They've broken the law."

Cooper met the women as they walked down the hallway. "Eleanor, do you have permission to be in Mr. Madrigal's residence?"

Eleanor's eyes widened. "I have a key."

Gladys nodded and lowered her arms. "She has a key."

"Did you have permission to enter?" asked Langley.

"How did you know we were here?" asked Eleanor.

"Silent alarm was tripped," said Cooper. "Why are you here?"

The women looked at each other, waiting for the other to speak. Eleanor cleared her throat. "I, um, was getting something for Harold's funeral… it's—"

"—Hold that thought," said Cooper. "We're going to question each of you, separately."

Eleanor lowered her arms and folded them across her chest. "We've done nothing wrong."

"It's dark in here. Let's go outside in the sunshine and talk." Cooper pointed to the door and waited for the women. She followed closely behind, shadowed by Langley.

ELLA PACED DeShawn's small office. She checked her phone. "I feel helpless."

He nodded. "The police will keep us updated."

"Who would break into Harold's house?" she asked. "Or why?"

"Harold was a man of means. Maybe someone…"

"This town used to be friendly." Ella went over to the window and stared up at the scattered clouds. "We'd leave our doors unlocked. No one ever gave it a second thought."

"Ella, nothing's changed," said DeShawn. "We still live in a town made up of wonderful folks who care about each other."

"Sometimes I wonder."

"Why do you say that?" asked DeShawn.

Ella turned and looked at him. "Two murders. And now someone has the nerve to break into Harold's house… Are any of us safe anymore?"

"How about we don't jump to conclusions and let the police sort it out?"

She picked up her cell phone. "I'm calling Alton."

"If you think it will help…"

Ella scrolled through her contacts, then swiped. She held her phone to her ear and waited. "Alton… sorry to bother you… Do you…" She stared at DeShawn. "Yes, I can come… I'm with Harold's attorney… I'm sure he'll understand…"

DeShawn gave an exaggerated nod.

"… Ten minutes… See you then." She ended the call and placed the phone in her back pocket. "Interesting."

"Are you going to enlighten me or make me guess?"

"I'm sorry," said Ella. "Just processing what he said."

"Which was…?"

"When the officers arrived to investigate, they found

Eleanor and Gladys in the house. Upon further investigation, they discovered someone had tampered with and opened a locked file cabinet in Harold's office."

"Any idea what they might have been after?" asked DeShawn.

Ella thought back to the envelopes she'd discovered a few days earlier. She gripped the attorney's desk. "I'm afraid so."

ELLA LEFT the attorney's office and arrived in Harold's neighborhood within a few minutes. She pulled up behind the unit in front of the Gonzales' house. As she walked past the police car, she noticed someone sitting in the back seat. Before she could figure out who it could be, Eduardo rushed out of his house.

"I noted everything…" he called.

She held up her hand. "Thanks so much, Mr. Gonzales. How about I get back to you after I speak to the authorities?"

He stood a few feet from her, wheezing. "Well, you tell them… if they need a witness… I'm prepared… to give a statement."

Ella reached out and patted his arm. "I appreciate your diligence." She noticed another unit drive up and park across the street. Recognizing Alton, she turned back to Eduardo. "Please excuse me."

"Tell them I'll be home all day…"

As Ella started across the street, she turned and saw Officer Cooper standing with Eleanor on Harold's porch. She glanced around. *Where was Gladys?* Reaching Alton, Ella let out a long sigh. "So what happened?"

Referring to his notes, Alton said, "According to Officer Langley, he and Cooper responded to the silent alarm. They found the door ajar. Upon entering, they called out. Soon after, Eleanor and Gladys showed themselves."

Ella shielded her eyes from the mid-day sun. "What's this about them breaking into a locked file cabinet?"

Alton leaned against his vehicle and rubbed his forehead. "As I mentioned, Langley found evidence of tampering—scratches on the file cabinet. Plus, he found a bobby pin jammed inside the lock."

"Was anything taken?" Ella held her breath and waited.

"I don't know and that's why I wanted you to meet me here," said Alton. "Appreciate it if you'd look and let me know."

Ella nodded. "What will happen to Eleanor and Gladys?"

Alton caught her eye. "Right now, I can arrest them for unlawful entry, which is trespassing. Included in that could be burglary and possibly petty theft."

"Sounds serious, Alton."

"It is," he said. "Worst-case scenario, a felony. Best case, we're looking at a misdemeanor, but even that could result in jail time and a fine."

Ella straightened. "Are you going to arrest them?"

Alton scrutinized her for a moment. "As successor trustee in charge of Harold's estate, you may file charges."

Ella glanced up at the massive oak trees lining the street near Harold's house. A light breeze rustled through the leaves. Bright white billowy clouds meandered across the sky. She refocused and stared at Alton. "I don't want to. And before you say anything, I'd like to make a proposal."

Alton rested his hand on his leather belt. "I'm all ears."

"I'd like to chat with Eleanor."

"You have a way with people," said Alton.

"I'm not excusing her behavior, but she's been through a lot. And…"

Alton's eyes narrowed. "You might know something, right?"

"Do you trust me?

"I'm for anything that leads to the truth." He nodded to the unit in front of Eduardo's house. "While you two talk, I need to deal with that feisty woman."

Ella smiled when she recognized Gladys. "She's very protective of her friends."

"I'll let Cooper know you'll be chatting with Eleanor while I check to see if Gladys has calmed down."

"I don't envy you," said Ella.

Alton rolled his eyes. "Lord help me. If that woman didn't remind me so much of my Nana…" He leaned in and pushed the button on his lapel mic, instructing Cooper of Ella's intentions. "Okay, you're good to go. Good luck."

"And to you, too." Ella walked across the street and up the path to Harold's front porch. Cooper acknowledged Ella and stepped away from Eleanor.

Ella waited for Cooper to leave them alone, then she turned to her friend. "What were you thinking?"

Eleanor wiped her swollen eyes. "I… had to get… it."

"You're talking about that envelope addressed to John, aren't you?"

"You knew about it?" asked Eleanor.

"I found it the other day when Shelby and I were here." She pointed to two decorative wrought-iron chairs next to them. "Let's sit."

Eleanor nodded and eased herself into one chair, then sighed. "I'm sorry."

"Did you find it?"

"The police came just before we opened the file drawer," said Eleanor. "I never had time to search."

"You know if you had taken anything from the house, Alton could have arrested you. He said something about felony charges."

Tears streamed down Eleanor's cheeks. "When John finds out the truth, prison might be the only safe place for me."

Ella took Eleanor's hand. "Do you think he'll try to hurt you?"

She looked up. "My son's entire life has been a lie. The man he thought *was* his father wasn't. The man he hates *is* his father..."

"Do you know what's in that letter?" asked Ella.

Eleanor nodded. "The truth. I know Harold wrote John a letter explaining everything. In case something happened to me... he wanted John to know. Especially why he left me alone and pregnant."

"Hon, he deserves the truth," said Ella.

"They say the truth will set you free," said Eleanor. "But if John disowns me, I'll be alone. I suppose it's a fitting sentence. Imprisoned because of my own foolish mistakes."

Wrapping her arms around Eleanor's trembling shoulders, Ella held her sobbing friend.

CHAPTER FIFTY-FOUR

Ella trudged in the front door of The Bee's Knees just after one o'clock carrying a grease-stained bag and large paper cup from Burgers and More. Sipping from the straw, she gave a half-wave to Shelby, who was ringing up a customer order. Ella continued to the seating area and collapsed into a chair. She sat there, staring at nothing, holding her drink.

A few moments later, Shelby walked up. Pulling another chair over, she sat. "Everything go okay with the attorney, El?"

Ella turned. "I don't even know where to begin." She set the cup on a small end table, balanced the bag on her knee, and took out a carton of fries and a burger. Unwrapping the paper, she took a bite. A tear rolled down her cheek.

"Oh, El." Shelby's warm hand held Ella's arm. "I'm sorry this has been so hard."

Wiping her face, Ella sniffed. "The attorney's stuff was bad enough. But then... I had to deal with Eleanor and Gladys..."

Shelby straightened. "Why would they show up at the attorney's office?"

Ella shook her head. "They didn't. They'd entered Harold's house and tripped the silent alarm. I had to leave DeShawn's and meet Alton…"

Shelby gasped. "Alton got involved?"

Ella took another bite of her burger and nodded. After swallowing, she said, "Cooper and the other officer had them on unlawful entering, burglary…"

"Oh, my goodness. She arrested them?"

"No," said Ella. "I wouldn't press charges. Alton let me talk to Eleanor. We had a long talk about why she and Gladys broke into the file cabinet."

"Wait a minute," said Shelby. "Does this have to do with the letter?"

Ella nodded as she chewed. "Harold wrote something to John, explaining everything. I understand why Eleanor is afraid to tell John, but what I can't figure out is why she's so afraid of him."

Shelby pointed to the fries and Ella offered her the carton. "You know," said Shelby, "I just thought of something. A few weeks ago, right after Agnes' murder, you got that cryptic voice message from Harold." She looked up and closed one eye. "Something about 'the apple doesn't fall…' Do you remember?"

Ella stopped chewing. "I should still have the message. Give me a moment to find it." She put her food on the table and pulled out her phone. Scrolling through the voice mails, she stopped. "Here it is." She swiped play, then put it on speaker. The sounds of babies crying in the background, then Harold's voice. "I need your help—you and Shelby's. The apple doesn't fall far from the tree." The women looked at each other. "I still can't make sense of it," said Ella.

"It refers to traits found in children similar to their parents," said Shelby.

Ella offered Shelby the fries again. "I understand the meaning, but why would Harold say it?"

Shelby pointed in the air with an unusually long fry. "We know John was Harold's son, right?"

"Yes," said Ella.

Shelby bit off the end of the fry. "Maybe Harold was trying to tell us—"

"—Wait," said Ella. "Maybe he was trying to warn us."

"But if John had violent tendencies, wouldn't that mean he inherited them from Harold?" Shelby's eyes narrowed. "El, how much do you really know about Harold's past?"

After Ella rinsed the last of the dinner dishes and loaded them into the dishwasher, she glanced up at the kitchen clock. "Almost seven."

Shelby sat at the table, reading something on her phone. She looked up. "Still no word from Eleanor?"

"No." Ella dried her hands on a hand towel, then sat. "I'm concerned."

"Maybe she's afraid to come home and face you."

"After discussing everything at Harold's, I thought we were good," said Ella.

"You should call, El. Just to make sure she's okay."

Picking up her phone, Ella scrolled through her contacts and swiped. She waited. "Voice mail," she said, holding up a finger. "Hey Eleanor. It's Ella. Just… checking to see if you're doing okay. You missed a splendid dinner…" She looked at Shelby and rolled her eyes. "Anyway, hope to see you soon. Um, bye." She placed the phone on the table and rubbed her temples. "That was awkward. 'Missed a splendid dinner.' Why did I say that?"

Shelby smiled. "You were just being friendly."

"You've been on your phone for a while." Ella leaned closer to Shelby. "What's got your attention?"

Shelby pointed to the screen. "I'm looking through public records to see if I can find anything on Harold or John."

"And...?"

"Well, so far nothing specific on John but a few articles on their fiber farm, including something about a prized ewe having three lambs..."

"Is that unusual?" asked Ella.

"I guess not. One to three is average," said Shelby. "But get this, some ewe in Minnesota birthed eight lambs." She turned the phone to Ella. "Look how cute."

"Oh my, that's a lot of babies." Ella eyed Shelby. "Getting back to the business at hand, anything else useful, aside from the fertile ewe?"

Shelby chuckled. "Yeah. I read something about Harold and an ex-wife. Accidental death, but no charges filed..."

"That was quite a while ago. I vaguely remember an incident at a chamber meeting. Someone provoked Harold. His face turned beet-red. Then he jumped out of his chair and told them to shut up or get out."

"Doesn't sound like Harold," said Shelby.

"I wasn't close enough to hear the entire conversation. It was the only time I'd ever seen him react with such fury."

"Were you concerned for your safety?" asked Shelby.

"Not for mine. The woman finally left, which was a good thing."

Shelby scrolled through her phone, then clicked a link. "I found it."

"Found what?" asked Ella.

"The incident. Listen to this," said Shelby. "'Chamber Meeting Goes to Pot. Shouts erupted at tonight's Chamber of Commerce meeting between Harold Madrigal and long-time city council opponent and current wife, Agnes Cormack.'" She looked at Ella. "Agnes?"

"Keep reading," said Ella.

"'Witnesses report Cormack taunted Madrigal about recently dismissed murder charges of his first wife, Alice Madrigal. Quoting Cormack, 'If it had been up to me, you would have stood trial and paid for your deadly anger. Self-defense, my arse.' Other witnesses declined comment, saying they didn't want to get involved in a domestic dispute. After Madrigal threatened Cormack, she left without further incident.' Wow, can you believe it?"

"When was that?" asked Ella.

Shelby scrutinized the article. "Four, no, almost five years ago."

"I'd almost forgotten it was between Harold and Agnes," said Ella. "So, considering that information, let's get back to Harold's cryptic message about the apple not falling far from the tree. Do you think he was warning us about John's anger issues?"

"Anyone can get angry when provoked," said Shelby. "You said John was explosive when he found you and Eleanor at that motel in Bakersfield."

"Yes, I'm just glad the police were there." Ella shuddered. "I was afraid he'd have come through the door and hurt us."

Oatmeal got up from under the table and rested his head on Ella's leg.

"I'm okay, boy." She reached down and scratched his ear. Soon, the dog settled down and lay at Ella's feet. "You know," said Ella. "You just reminded me of something... Eleanor said John kept insisting she had killed Agnes when knocking her out in the alley. That's why he didn't want her to talk to Alton."

"But it makes no sense," said Shelby. "Eleanor said Agnes was alive when she ran away."

Ella straightened. "If Trudy was in the alley and saw what happened..."

"What are you thinking, El?"

"How do we know Eleanor didn't go back and kill Agnes after everyone left?"

"And if Trudy saw it all, then..." Shelby gasped. "Wait, are you saying that Eleanor killed Agnes, and then Trudy?"

Ella's eyes widened. "I just thought of something terrible."

"What?" asked Shelby.

"Harold said he had left the alley before Agnes' murder. But what if he actually went back, and either stabbed Agnes or helped Eleanor? What if Harold's letter to John details Agnes' murder instead?"

"I think you're jumping to conclusions, El."

"Why else would she risk breaking into that file cabinet?" asked Ella. "The fact that John is Harold's son doesn't seem like enough to risk committing a felony. But if that letter proves her guilty, she'd do anything to destroy it."

Shelby swallowed. "I hate to ask, but where are those letters now?"

"Fortunately, Eleanor and Gladys didn't tamper with that cabinet. So, before I left Harold's, I opened the cabinet and removed them," said Ella. "Then hid them in the bedroom while you were making dinner."

Shelby's eyes flashed. "If Eleanor comes back and finds out you have them, we could be in grave danger."

CHAPTER FIFTY-FIVE

Lilibeth set a half-filled glass of wine on a table in the crafting room. The scent of lanolin, sweet and grassy, hung in the air as she opened a large bag of sheared wool. Rolling a handful into a ball, Lilibeth used a long, barbed needle and stabbed the soft form repeatedly. Weaving the fibers together, a shape formed. She held up the lopsided figure for her sister. "What do you think?"

Vickie laughed. "A new Wooley is being created."

Nodding, Lilibeth focused her efforts and continued. Stab. Pull. Stab. Pull. Again. And again. "I just wish John and the guys could sheer the sheep and alpaca sooner. I hate using all this precious wool for the inner shapes and outer covering."

Across the table, Vickie swirled a wine glass, then drew attention to another bag. "This dryer lint seems to work. In fact, John brought more in last night."

Lilibeth stopped poking and sipped her wine. "You know, I think your theory about him cheating on me is spot on."

Vickie, who'd been taking a drink, coughed until her eyes watered. "What makes you say that?"

Lilibeth pointed to the lint with her sharp needle. "Last couple of weeks, he's been adamant about doing the laundry. I figure there must be some evidence he's trying to get rid of... lipstick on the collar... perfume. I mean, I don't mind him doing some of the chores. But something provoked him into helping. After all these years of marriage... I don't think it was love. At least, being in love with me."

"Sis, if the hubby wants to do the laundry, don't knock it." Vickie held up several layers of colorful lint. "It makes the perfect insides for our Wooley's."

Lilibeth nodded. "True. And using less wool, we make more profit."

Vickie worked a blue-tinted piece of lint into a ball, then wrapped it with a layer of finely brushed alpaca wool. She poked a barbed needle in and out until it became a rigid ball. "I think it's a genius idea. I bet we can make twice as many Wooleys with half the wool."

"Which means double the profits," said Lilibeth.

"I thought John sold a lot of your raw wool," said Vickie.

"He does," said Lilibeth. "In fact, sales direct to consumers keeps our farm going. This year has really been tough on us, financially. He's had to sell most of it just to keep up. Even took out a second mortgage so we could stay afloat."

Vickie raised her wineglass. "Here's to the lint. A win for the farm and our Wooley Sisters business."

AFTER DINNER ELLA went into the front room and sat on the couch. She curled her feet under her and tried reading, but she was too distracted watching the front door, expecting Eleanor to come home. Oatmeal rested his head on her lap, but perked at any sound from outside.

Lounging in the wingback chair, Shelby's legs dangled over the side. She clicked a computer mouse, scrolling and concentrating on her laptop screen.

Ella lay the book on the couch. "What are you looking for?"

Shelby turned. "That quote from Harold, about the apple falling from the tree, got me to wondering."

"Do you ever let your mind just relax?" asked Ella.

Shelby smiled. "Not tonight. I've got one-hundred ideas and need to see if anything works."

"Care to explain?" asked Ella.

"Do you remember anything about Harold's father?" asked Shelby.

"I never met the man," said Ella. "I think he passed years ago. Why do you ask?"

"According to Harold's obituary, his parents were Santiago and Maria…"

"What rabbit hole are you going down now?" asked Ella.

"Like I said that cryptic message of Harold's… So when I searched online for Santiago Madrigal, I got quite a few hits."

Ella shifted on the couch. "What exactly are you looking for?"

"Hold on…" Shelby scrolled, then clicked. She sat up, her eyes wide. "Oh no, listen to this… Madrigal accused of murdering ex-wife Maria in a fit of rage…"

Ella got up and stood near Shelby. "Keep reading."

"… of rage stemming from Maria's infidelity during their forty years of marriage. A year after their divorce, Madrigal allegedly used a key and entered her residence. Then stabbed Maria as she slept. After committing the heinous crime, he called the police, waited for them to arrive, then confessed. As he was being arrested, they quoted him as saying, 'She deserved it. Now I can die in peace.' Madrigal never stood trial for the crime. Two weeks after the murder, he passed away suddenly from a rare form of cancer."

Ella gasped. "The apple doesn't fall far from the tree…"

Shelby set the laptop on the coffee table. "You know, it was about two weeks after someone murdered Agnes that Harold passed away. Which means…"

"That letter Harold wrote to John was his own confession to killing Agnes."

Shelby nodded. "The only way to know for certain is to read John's letter before he does."

"I can't do that," said Ella. "DeShawn said no one was to know what's in the will until after the funeral… Harold's request."

"Are the letters mentioned in Harold's will?" asked Shelby.

"Don't know." Ella sat down on the couch again. "Just as I was about to read it, DeShawn received the call about the silent alarm."

"So, reading the letters wouldn't be a breach of Harold's wishes…?"

Ella raised an eyebrow. "That's assuming he didn't mention them in his will."

"Do they say, 'Do Not Read Until…' on them?" asked Shelby.

"Actually, they just have each person's name."

"Well, there you go," said Shelby. "No harm, no foul."

Ella looked at her partner. "We can't read those letters."

"You could read yours," said Shelby.

Ella let out a long sigh. "You won't let this go tonight, will you?"

Shelby gave a toothy grin. "What do you think?"

"I hate knowing how your mind works."

"I thought you loved my mind," said Shelby.

Ella shook her head. "Whatever."

Shelby got up and plopped on the couch next to Ella. "Think about it. If we read Harold's confession, then we can take the evidence to Alton, it will solve the case. You want to help solve these murders, don't you?"

Ella cleared her throat. "Well, yes. But…"

"But what?" asked Shelby. "If Harold killed Agnes and… Wait a minute."

"What now?" asked Ella.

"Trudy."

"You're not making sense," said Ella.

"Even if Harold's letter is a confession to killing Agnes, that wouldn't solve Trudy's death," said Shelby.

"But maybe it would lead to her killer," said Ella.

"So you're saying we're going to read your letter?" asked Shelby.

Ella stood and pointed a finger at Shelby. "You know this is against my better judgement."

"Of course, El. I know you'd never disregard someone's wishes… Unless that someone was the killer."

"Fine," said Ella.

"Fine."

The women walked through the kitchen, followed by Oatmeal. They proceeded down the short hall to Ella's bedroom. Once inside, Shelby closed, then secured the door.

Ella went over to a locked cedar chest. With trembling hands, she pulled a key from inside a tiny pocket in her jeans. Bending down, she inserted the key into the lock. A moment later, a loud scratching came from behind the bedroom door, causing both women to jump.

Shelby caught her breath. "Mr. Butterfingers." She went to let him in, then closed the door again. He meowed and jumped on the bed. Shelby sat next to him, stroking his ears.

"You scared the stuff out of me, cat," said Ella. She took another deep breath and held the key. She turned it, waiting for a click. After it opened, she lifted the latch, then raised the lid. The pungent scent of cedar surrounded them. Digging deep into the chest, under her grandmother's hand-sewn quilt, past several photo albums, her fingers touched the corner of the large envelope holding the three letters. She looked at Shelby and swallowed, then pulled it out. "You know, once we open one, there's no going back."

"Aren't you going to read them all?" asked Shelby.

"What do you think?" asked Ella.

"Seems appropriate under the circumstances."

"Seems inappropriate to read the ones that don't belong to me," said Ella.

"So start with yours."

Ella pried open the metal clasp, then opened the envelope. She took it over to the bed and sat. Tipping it sideways, they waited for the letters to fall onto the bed. Ella looked at Shelby, then down at the envelopes. The names Ella, Eleanor, and John clearly were marked on one side. The backs were sealed with wax, then stamped with an ornate M. "Nice touch, Harold." She looked at Shelby. "Once we break the seal, there's no denying it."

"It's for the best," said Shelby.

Chewing her lip, Ella picked up her envelope. "I hate doing this."

"I know, El. And if we had any other choice…"

"Maybe we should give them to Alton."

Shelby rolled her eyes. "Do you really want to do that?"

Ella shook her head. She slid her finger under the corner of the wax-sealed edge. "One last chance to——"

"Would you just open it already?"

Ella looked down. In one motion, she broke the wax closure. She paused, then pulled out several pages of legal paper, folded in thirds. She closed her eyes, then whispered, "Forgive me, Harold, but we need to know the truth."

CHAPTER FIFTY-SIX

Vickie finished the last of her wine and set the glass on their workspace. "I've made a half-dozen Wooley people. How's your count?"

Lilibeth glanced up at her sister. "Let's see. Half a bottle of wine, and four, five, six... sheep, two piggies, and a frog. Not bad for a night's work."

"Don't you just love working with our new stuffing?" asked Vickie.

"Easier to manipulate, for sure."

Vickie grabbed a sheet of paper and a pen. "Let's inventory and price these so we can get them into the shop tomorrow."

"You seem in quite a hurry, sis."

"Spring is already here," said Vickie. "No time like the present to move products."

"How about you finish up?" Lilibeth poured herself another glass. "I'm fading fast."

"No problem." Vickie smiled. "Go get your beauty sleep. I'll take care of everything."

ELLA STRAIGHTENED as she smoothed the pages of Harold's letter. "I hope we're making the right choice."

Shelby nodded, but said nothing.

Ella began:

> Dearest Ella,
>
> If you're reading this, well, I guess we both know what happened. You're one of my closest and dearest friends and I wish I'd stuck around long enough for a proper goodbye. Sorry about not telling you about the successor trustee job. I know if I'd have mentioned it before I passed, you would have refused. Passed. An odd thing to say about yourself. Life is too short. And mine was taken way too early. But not much I can do about that now. By the way, tell your partner-in-crime-solving "Hi" for me. I know Shelby's reading this with you, so I might as well acknowledge her.

Ella smiled. "Couldn't pull one over on you, could we?"

> I'm sure you're curious about Agnes' death...

Ella stopped reading and looked at Shelby.

... while nothing else would have given more pleasure, I didn't do it even though I had the chance after Eleanor knocked her out cold. Agnes is unconscious and the knitting needles next to her. I thought about it. Believe me, I did. That woman had been a thorn in my side since the day she learned my secrets. Tequila and confessions seem to go hand in hand, and I spilled the beans big time after we married. She never let me forget any of my transgressions, even to the end. Quite fitting for my thorn in the side, taking it in the side, though not by my hand. To be honest, I didn't know how to do it, plus I was never fond of blood. Not even my own.

Ella looked at Shelby. "Then who did?"
Shelby shrugged as Ella continued.

Bet you're wondering if I know who did...

Ella rolled her eyes. "Good one, Harold."

I do know. Saw it with my own eyes. In that moment, just knowing she could no longer hurt anyone was worth seeing what happened.
By the way, the other two letters won't spell

it out for you. You're going to have to figure that out on your own. But being the practical guy I am... or rather was... I'll give you a few hints. The answers will be in the checkbook and the box. Got that? Maybe not yet, but as my mother (God rest her soul) used to say, "Everything will come out in the wash."

She was a kind woman and loved reading Cervantes's Don Quixote. If you don't know the connection, search for it. I've heard the internet is great for that kind of stuff.

Oh, a few last pearls of wisdom, my dear friend.

1: DO NOT give the other two letters to their intended recipients until after my funeral.

2: The job of successor trustee comes with compensation. It's all stipulated in the will, which by now you may or may not have read. Take the amount I set aside. It should more than cover your shop's expansion with enough left over for your needs and a nice nest egg.

I think that about covers it. Sorry I can't divulge any more. I know how you and Shelby love to solve mysteries and didn't want to rob you of that pleasure.

Hope to see you in the next life.

All my love,
Harold

Ella stared at Shelby and sighed.

Shelby nodded. "It's a lot to process."

"While I appreciate the hints about Agnes' murder," said Ella. "I don't understand what any of it means."

CHAPTER FIFTY-SEVEN

Tuesday morning, just after breakfast, Shelby and Ella left home trying to beat a foreboding spring storm. Trees shuddered as the wind ripped through them, scattering pink and white blossoms across the road like tiny, lost snowflakes.

"Never fails..." Shelby shivered and stopped at the intersection. She pointed out the window. "... and today's the day we sign Mac's escrow paperwork."

"When do you meet them?"

Shelby checked her phone, then sped up. "Ten-thirty. Then I need to head next door to the bank."

Ella raised an eyebrow. "Depositing or withdrawing?"

Shelby turned. "You know I'm going in there to snoop."

"Well, just because you have someone to ask about those checks made out to cash doesn't mean it's right," said Ella. "They're going to tell you to mind your own business."

"I have to try," said Shelby. "You know, if we find out who Harold was writing those checks to, we might have a lot more information to share with Alton. Besides, Harold said one clue was in the checkbook. So I'm following up on that."

"Let's hope your hunch pans out," said Ella. "I had wanted to go back to DeShawn's today, but he was booked solid. Tomorrow we'll finish going over the stipulations in Harold's will."

"I don't envy you there," said Shelby. "Although just the thought of knowing what's in it piques my interest." Waiting at the light, she tapped the steering wheel. "Besides, aren't you curious about Harold's generous compensation?"

"Maybe." Ella surveyed the parking lot of The Bee's Knees as Shelby pulled in. "I don't know. Part of me feels guilty." They got out of the jeep and rushed to the overhang, avoiding big fat raindrops.

"I understand," said Shelby, walking in behind Ella. "You realize he made sure you couldn't pay him back."

"Shrewd move, Harold." Ella stepped behind the counter and pulled out the clipboard with the volunteer sheet. "Looks like Eleanor and Gladys are scheduled today."

"Eleanor never came home last night, did she?" asked Shelby.

Ella shook her head. "Not sure if that was a good thing or not."

"The longer she waits to face you, the worse it might be," said Shelby.

After running her finger over the list of names, Ella placed the clipboard behind the counter again. "Honestly, I just want this week to be over. The will. The funeral. Those last two letters." She looked up at the wall clock and pointed to the door. "Sorry to be griping. Let's refocus and open for the day."

Forcing a smile, Shelby glanced at Ella. "Putting on my cheerful face." By the time Shelby reached the entrance, several ladies had gathered outside. She opened the door and greeted the women. A few unfamiliar faces, followed by Eleanor, Gladys, and Paige. Shelby followed behind them, catching bits of conversation.

Paige held Gladys' arm. "If he'd asked if the strawberries were fresh one more time... I don't know what I would have done..."

Gladys smiled. "Hon, you know we pick our fruit daily."

Eleanor stood back, eyeing Ella. When Ella looked her way, Eleanor smiled, but seemed hesitant to sign in.

Ella walked over to her. "You doing okay?"

Eleanor nodded.

"I was concerned after you didn't come back last night."

"After what happened, I didn't think I'd be welcome," said Eleanor.

Ella reached for her friend's arm. "I'm sorry you felt that way."

Gladys came up to them. "Morning, Ella."

"Good morning, Gladys," said Ella.

"Thanks for not, you know, pressing charges," said Gladys. Eleanor nodded, but stayed silent. "Guess something snapped, and I talked my friend into doing something we should have never done."

Ella stepped further away from the counter and motioned for the women to join her.

Gladys glanced at Eleanor, then back to Ella. "When is the reading of the will?"

"Interesting question," said Ella. "Why do you ask?"

Eleanor stepped closer. "Do you know who needs to be present?"

"Not yet," said Ella. "Again, why do you ask?"

"I have to know..." said Eleanor.

"What do you need to know?" said Ella. "You're not making sense."

"Because…" Eleanor looked at Gladys and swallowed. "Reading that will… will open a can of worms that will tear this town apart."

SHELBY STOOD behind the register ringing up a customer when Vickie and Lilibeth walked into the shop, each carrying an armful of Wooleys. Vickie nodded to Shelby as the women headed down an aisle to their booth. Once Shelby finished bagging the customer's purchases, she motioned for Ella.

"What's up?" asked Ella.

"I want to go see what the sisters brought in," said Shelby. "I just love all their creations."

Ella looked up at the clock. "Don't you need to leave soon?"

Shelby nodded. "Just going to take a moment, then go." Dashing across the carpet, she soon caught up with Vickie and Lilibeth as they stacked their new products on the shelves.

"Oh, how cute are these?" said Shelby.

Vickie smiled and held up a palm-sized pink pig. "You want a closer look?"

Shelby held out her hand as Vickie set the felted animal in it. She turned it over and rubbed the tiny ears. "Your creativity inspires me," said Shelby. "To think this used to be a bunch of random wool…"

Lilibeth smiled. "Wool and a bit more, this time."

"A bit more?" Shelby caught her eye. "What do you mean?"

"Until the lambs and crias are born, John and the guys can't sheer the animals. Until then, we have to improvise," said Lilibeth.

Shelby handed the pig back to her and picked up a chubby blue and white cow. "Improvise?"

Lilibeth leaned close to Shelby. "Dryer lint."

She scrutinized the small barn animal. "Really? Can you do that?"

Vickie placed a set of sheep on a shelf. "When we run low on wool, we normally use cotton batting, but John suggested the colorful lint. It works fine, plus adds a little pizzazz, wouldn't you say?"

"Interesting," said Shelby. "Wonder where he came up with that idea?"

Holding a giggle, Lilibeth whispered in her sister's ear. "Guilty conscience."

Vickie coughed. "Notice the variety of colors…"

Shelby nodded.

"They give a subtle hint of what was washed and dried." Lilibeth pointed to the different Wooleys. "Blue jeans, pink t-shirts, and green sheets. All cotton, so we're still keeping with natural fibers."

Shelby picked through several of the animals. "I just love these. I'll take this one, and that one…" Before she knew it, her hands were full.

"That's half of our new inventory." Lilibeth laughed. "Guess we'll be making more tonight, sis."

Shelby's phone pinged, reminding her of the upcoming appointment. "Time to stop shopping." She nodded to the sisters and headed to the front of the store.

Taking the animals from Shelby, Ella rang up the purchases. "Starting a collection?"

"You might say that."

Ella raised a brow. "You're up to something."

"Moi?"

"You're not ready to tell me, are you?"

"You wouldn't believe me if I did." Shelby placed the wool-felted animals in a cloth bag, smiled, and left the shop. Along with the escrow office and the bank, she had just added one more thing to her to-do list.

CHAPTER FIFTY-EIGHT

S helby drove to the escrow office, her windshield wipers on high. The fat raindrops had turned into a deluge, soaking streets and anyone caught outside. After parking as close to the office as possible, she rushed inside, holding her sweater close with her good hand.

A dark-haired woman in a business suit looked up as she approached. "Good morning. How may I help you?"

Shelby scrutinized her tag. "Hi Estelle, I'm here to sign escrow papers."

"Last name?"

Shelby paused. "Mine or hers?

"Either is fine," said Estelle, her hand resting on a computer mouse.

"Heaton or Jacobs," said Shelby.

Estelle scrolled through the screen, then stopped. "Yes. Give me just a moment." She picked up the phone and buzzed an office. After hanging up, she smiled. "An escrow officer will be with you shortly."

Shelby took a seat and scanned through a pile of magazines. Home improvement, cooking, and travel. About

360

to pick up one with a bathroom renovation, she stopped when the front door opened. Mac walked in, brushed rain off her jacket, then stepped up to the counter.

Shelby held the magazine in front of her face, hoping to avoid the inevitable.

"Shelby?"

She lowered the magazine. "Hi, Mac."

"Didn't know you had gotten here until I saw the sparkly tennis shoes." Mac shrugged off her damp jacket and held it.

Shelby forced a smile. "How are you?"

"I'm good. What happened to your hand?"

Shelby looked down at her cast. "Broken bone, no biggie." *What was keeping that escrow officer?*

A few moments later, a tall, bearded man walked into the waiting area. "Heaton and Jacobs?"

As Shelby stood, Mac walked up to him and shook his hand. "I'm Mackenzie Jacobs."

He glanced at Shelby. "And you must be Ms. Heaton."

Shelby nodded.

"Geoffrey West. Please follow me," he said, leading them down a long hall.

Less than an hour later, Shelby and Mac came back into the waiting room with Mr. West. "Shouldn't be long until everything's complete. You should both expect your checks within a week, give or take a few days."

Mac shook his hand again and Shelby thanked him. She turned to Mac. "I guess this is goodbye."

"I guess so," said Mac, her voice strained. "I'd offer a hug…"

"Thanks for saving the rose," said Shelby. "It means a lot to me."

Mac nodded. She put on her jacket, smiled at Estelle,

then walked out into the rain.

Shelby took in a deep breath and sighed. Waiting by the big picture window until Mac drove away, she ducked outside and hurried over to Bank One in the building next door.

Once inside, she searched for her friend Wendy. Shelby spotted her talking to a customer. Shelby waved. Wendy acknowledged and held up five fingers. Shelby nodded and took a seat. She scoured the table for something to pass the time, but found nothing to read but investment brochures. *Wish I'd brought the bathroom renovation magazine.*

A few minutes later, a thirty-something woman rushed up to Shelby. "Sorry to keep you waiting, hon."

"No problem, Wendy." Shelby stood and gave her a quick hug. "How's it going?"

"You know—life." She checked her phone. "How about we get out of here and talk? There's a great cafe around the corner."

Shelby nodded. "You lead the way."

Hurrying through the rain, Wendy soon pointed to a small Italian bistro, and smiled.

"Best subs in town." After ordering, Wendy picked up their cups. "I'll fill these while you grab a table. This place will get crazy full in a few minutes."

Shelby found a spot near the back, away from the others. She set their order number on the napkin container and wiped off the table.

Wendy came back with two sodas and sat. "Nice to be off my feet for a bit."

An older teen carrying a red tray with a red and white checked paper liner came over to them. "Thirty-nine… Here are your sandwiches, extra napkins, extra pepperoncini."

"Thanks." Wendy took the tray and handed Shelby her order. "Enjoy."

"I'm too nervous to eat." Shelby sipped her soda and eyed Wendy. "Did you find anything out for me?"

Wendy took a big bite and then pointed to her mouth. She nodded.

"Is that your way of telling me to eat?" asked Shelby.

Wendy nodded again.

Shelby rolled her eyes. She nibbled on a piece of salami until her friend swallowed. "Okay, now that you've eaten something... tell me."

"Goodness, girl." Wendy laughed. "Fine, here's all I can divulge."

Eating another piece of salami, Shelby leaned closer to her friend.

"So I asked around if anyone had noticed customers coming in with checks made out to cash, either depositing or cashing them."

Shelby stared, wide-eyed. "And...?"

"Over the last few years we've had one customer who regularly brought them in," said Wendy. "And strangely enough, in the past two weeks, another one did the same thing."

"And...?" asked Shelby.

"I can't tell you names. But if you ask the right questions, I might nod or shake my head."

Shelby breathed out through her nostrils. "Were the checks made out to businesses?"

Wendy shook her head.

Shelby pinched off a piece of French bread and chewed it. "Odd, since the ones we saw were to an agricultural company."

Wendy raised an eyebrow.

"Ah, a clue." Shelby stared at her friend. "Was it a company?"

Wendy shook her head.

"A person?"

Wendy took a bite of her sandwich and nodded.

"Well," said Shelby. "I've got two choices... A man?"

Wendy shook her head.

"A woman?"

Wendy nodded.

"Well, that narrows it down to half of Pheasant Valley." Shelby sighed and looked up at the ceiling. "AgCo... AgCo... a woman?"

Wendy smiled.

"Okay, I must be getting close." Shelby rolled her head to the side, cracking her neck. "AgCo... must be a woman's na—"

Wendy's eyes brightened. "You figured it out, didn't you?"

"And the other woman... Her initials were different, correct?" Shelby bit into her sandwich.

Wendy smiled and nodded. "Congrats, super sleuth. Does this help solve the case?"

Shelby swallowed. "Not completely, but it gets us one step closer." She wrapped up the rest of her sandwich, picked up her drink, and stood. "I hate to run, but I have one more errand. Then I need to go back and tell Ella."

"You owe me," said Wendy.

Shelby leaned in and hugged her friend's shoulder. "Lunch or dinner, my treat. And I promise not to run out."

Wendy laughed. "Love you, girlie."

Shelby smiled. "You, too." She rushed out into the rain and put her food on the seat next to her. She gripped the steering wheel, hopeful this latest information might help solve Agnes' murder.

CHAPTER FIFTY-NINE

The next morning, after Ella finished her morning coffee, she rinsed her cup in the sink. When she turned around both pets were staring at her. She bent down and scratched Oatmeal behind his fluffy ears. "Headed to the shop, boy. You and Mr. Butterfingers be good." She offered him a biscuit and then grabbed a handful of treats for the cat, placing them on the kitchen floor.

Shelby came into the kitchen, wrapping a brightly knitted scarf around her neck. "Ready?"

Ella nodded. "I'll drive us into town since I meet with DeShawn today." The women left the house and walked to Ella's car. LaTonya was in her front yard next to her unit, wearing her deputy sheriff's uniform.

Shelby waved. "Howdy, neighbor."

She grinned, waved back, and walked toward them. "Drive safe. Roads were flooded after last night's storm. Been getting calls all night."

"Thanks for the head's up," said Shelby.

"You both in the shop today?" asked LaTonya.

Ella shook her head. "Meeting with Harold's attorney. But Shelby should be there."

"Again, I'm sorry about your loss," said LaTonya. "Funeral's Friday, correct?"

Shelby nodded. "Will you be attending?"

"I really never had a chance to know the man…but I told Alton I'd support him. So we'll both be there."

"Thank you." Ella smiled. "It means a lot."

"Well, I better not keep you…" She checked her phone. "Need to get to the sheriff's office." She turned and walked to her vehicle.

Ella started the car and backed out of the gravel driveway. After pulling into the street she turned to Shelby. "So have you decided what to do with your windfall?"

"I know Mac wanted me to have twelve thousand from the house sale…" She cradled her casted arm. "But it feels like a bribe."

"Maybe it's a way for her to say she's sorry," said Ella.

Shelby stared out the window. "I'm thinking about donating it."

"It could help get your design business up and running."

Nodding, Shelby said nothing.

"Please know. I'm not trying to push you into any decision," said Ella. "And whatever you decide, I'll support you one hundred percent."

Shelby turned to her friend. "Thanks."

Ella pulled up behind another car, waiting to turn at the light. "Besides, we have more than enough going on right now."

Shelby watched a murder of crows eating something on the side of the road, then sighed. "More than enough is right."

AFTER DROPPING Shelby off at The Bee's Knees, Ella drove to the attorney's office. She got out of the car and stopped to admire a large flowering bush covered with yellow daisies still wet from rain the night before. Bees flitted from flower to flower gathering pollen.

While she watched, a black carpenter bee landed on one flower, its stem bending under the weight of the thumb-sized insect. It went about gathering the yellow bits of pollen, then took off up and over the building.

Ella smiled, noting how though the stem was stressed from the heaviness of the bee, it didn't break. It stayed resilient. Much like everything she'd been experiencing. Though the burden of Harold's trustee request and upcoming funeral weighed heavy on her mind, she was determined to remain strong.

As soon as Ella walked inside, DeShawn greeted her with a warm handshake and an invitation into his personal office. She took a seat, noticing Harold's binder on his desk.

"It's so good to see you, Ella." DeShawn's quiet demeanor calmed her nerves. "Something to drink... Tea? Coffee?"

"No. Thank you," said Ella. "We should probably get started. I'm sure you have things to do."

DeShawn smiled. "I set aside all morning." He opened the binder and turned it toward Ella. "You know about the letters, don't you."

Ella nodded.

"Have you read yours?"

She nodded again.

"While I don't know what's in them, I know Harold

wanted you to read yours right away, while the others would need to wait."

"Yes," said Ella. "I'm aware of that."

"Very well then. Shall we begin?"

"I... I..." Ella's eyes welled up. "How about you read the most important points to me. I'm finding this much harder than I imagined."

DeShawn reached out and patted Ella's hand. "I can do that, if you prefer." He turned the binder around again. Flipping past a few pages, he stopped and read to himself. Then, he looked up at Ella. "In a nutshell, Harold has left his entire estate to you, with a few exceptions."

Ella gasped. "Why would he do that?"

"Let me keep reading... He left everything to you to sell, keep, or give away as you see fit. The only exception, is that Eleanor is provided for... for life."

"Oh my. Does she know about this?"

"I don't think so."

"Did he explain how...? I mean were there stipulations?" asked Ella.

"No. But knowing Harold, he would like you to set aside a trust for her so she will have what she needs – a home and anything else to provide a comfortable life."

Ella nodded.

"He also left a provision of fifty thousand dollars specifically for The Bee's Knees... for the renovation, upkeep, and whatever else was needed."

She covered her mouth with her hand.

"Along with that, Harold made provisions for you to receive two percent of the trust assets."

Ella's eyes widened. "I don't know what that means."

DeShawn smiled. "Harold's estate is valued at just over

ten million dollars. Which means you'll receive two-hundred thousand dollars, annually."

She gasped.

DeShawn came around to the other side of the desk and held Ella's trembling shoulders. He waited patiently knowing no words would take away the hurt she was feeling. DeShawn might have been an attorney, but primarily, he was Ella's friend.

After she calmed down, DeShawn offered her a glass of water. "Thank you," she said. "I... I never expected any of this."

"As you know, Harold was very generous. In the end, he wanted to take care of the people who meant the most to him." DeShawn closed the binder. "There's more, but we can go over it later as it's just the legal stuff that can wait a few days."

"Thank you." Ella wiped her eyes. "Once we get past the funeral, and reading those letters, I think I'll be able to deal with the 'legal stuff'."

"About the funeral... After the service, we'll need to gather at The Bee's Knees with those who Harold requested to be present. That includes Shelby, Eleanor, Vivian, along with her two daughters. And John."

"Of course, since one of the letters is addressed to him," said Ella. "Let's hope everyone is civil."

"Just so you know..." DeShawn's eyes darkened. "I requested Sargent Nolan and Deputy Sheriff Lewis be there... just in case."

"Probably best," said Ella.

"I'll be at the funeral. Afterwards, I'll meet you at the shop with the documents... Did you bring those letters?"

Ella reached inside her sweater and handed DeShawn the two envelopes with Eleanor's and John's names on them.

"I think we're all set for Friday."

"Let's hope so," said Ella.

ON FRIDAY AFTERNOON, Harold's friends gathered in the chapel at the New Pheasant Valley Cemetery for his celebration of life. Sprays of multicolored flowers stood tall on both sides and across the front of the room. Fragrances from the purple and blue hyacinths and delicate sprays of baby's breath mingled with the sweet scents from creamy gardenias and purple alyssums inside the room. In front of the flowers, a long table covered with a lace tablecloth displayed the handcrafted ceramic urn with Harold's cremains. The urn, embellished with metallic swirls of blues and greens, featured a dragonfly in flight. As friends arrived, many left pictures, notes, and other reminders of their dear friend on the table.

Behind the table, a black easel held a large photo of Harold, smiling, standing in his garden with the words, "In Loving Memory" across the top. Under his picture, his name, birthdate, and the date he passed.

Ella and Shelby stood at the entrance, greeting mourners, and offering hugs. Laura, her navy blouse flowing behind her, offered lavender sprigs to those who wanted them.

Paige entered wearing a simple, black calf-length dress, her hot pink nails sparkling in the overhead lights. DeShawn took a seat near the back, nodding to friends and acquaintances. Holding hands, Kent and Susan entered and sat next to DeShawn. Not wanting to talk to anyone, Eleanor had arrived early with Gladys and Ed. They sat in the front row, off to the side. As Eleanor wiped her eyes,

Gladys pulled a well-used tissue from her bra and blew her nose. Vivian walked in and sat next to Gladys. Vickie and Lilibeth settled in the row behind them. A few more friends came in, took sprigs of lavender, and found a seat. Further back, Alton sat between LaTonya and Dr Minke. Alone, in the last row, was Eduardo Gonzales. Dressed in his Sunday best, he wiped his eyes with the corners of a large white handkerchief.

The mortuary chaplain came up to Ella. After she nodded, he went up to the front and stood behind a wooden lectern. "If everyone could take their seats, we can get started."

He waited, then cleared his throat. "On behalf of Ella, thank you for coming..." He looked at his notes and opened a Bible. "Matthew, chapter five, verse four says, 'Blessed are those who mourn, for they shall be comforted'." He closed the Bible and looked out over the people gathered. "For those of us who knew Harold, can we agree he lived a full life? Giving much, expecting little. Lifting others up, yet never boasting about his own accomplishments. He was a man of faith, both in the Lord and in his friends. Though taken way too young, he impacted anyone and everyone who knew him..."

Ella's thoughts drifted to the first time she had met Harold when he was excited to help fund her and Doug's coffee shop. He'd offered business advice and encouragement. She was nervous, as was her husband. But Harold had been gracious, a true gentleman who wanted to help the couple see their dream of owning their own business come true.

"... and in our hour of mourning..."

Through her tears, Eleanor smiled, remembering the young man who had taken her breath away in high school.

And even though they couldn't be together until the end, he had always been kind, making sure she was okay and keeping in touch. She thought back to the laughter, the tears, the last few days when she had been with Harold when he was most vulnerable and needed someone who would just sit and offer comfort.

"… does anyone want to say a few words about our friend, Harold?"

Ella blinked back to the present. She looked at Shelby.

"You should say something," said Shelby.

"Not now," said Ella.

The chaplain waited. Several people took turns sharing their memories of Harold, including Dr. Minke, who broke down in the middle of a sentence. Not able to continue his story, he looked at Ella, then Eleanor, then whispered, "I'm very sorry for your loss. He was a great man."

Ella wiped her eyes and nodded.

The chaplain went up front again. "Thank you, Doctor. Anyone else?"

When no one came forward, he said a final prayer, then invited Ella to the front.

She gripped the lectern and forced a smile as the aromatic scent of gardenia enveloped her.

"Thank you, chaplain. Thank you everyone for coming. We'd love for all of you to stay awhile. There's coffee and our dear friend, Laura brought some delectable desserts." She stepped down and went to help Laura and Shelby with the refreshments.

Shelby hugged Ella then pulled back. "Next up, this evening's meeting."

"The one I'm least looking forward to," said Ella.

CHAPTER SIXTY

After leaving the Celebration of Life, the small group requested in Harold's will gathered at The Bee's Knees. Shelby and Ella arrived first and made coffee. Followed by Eleanor and Gladys, DeShawn entered carrying the leather briefcase. He proceeded to the sitting area, where he poured himself a cup of coffee and took a seat next to a small table.

Eleanor sat next to Gladys, gripping her hand. Vivian came in with her daughters. While they got coffee, she took a seat next to Gladys. Alton arrived with LaTonya, though they kept their distance from the others.

"Are we ready to begin?" asked DeShawn.

"We're waiting for one more—" Ella stopped when the shop door swung open, then closed. As she watched, everyone followed her gaze.

Eleanor gasped.

John glowered at everyone and took a seat next to Lilibeth. "Hope this doesn't last long. I've got farm chores waiting."

Lilibeth stared at him, but said nothing.

Ella turned to DeShawn and nodded. "Everyone is here."

DeShawn opened his briefcase and took out a large envelope. He stood and cleared his throat. "On behalf of Harold, thank you for coming." He opened the envelope, and pulled out a stack of paperwork, along with two letters. "As most of you know, Harold requested this specific group gather after the funeral."

Eleanor blinked back tears.

"What most of you don't know is that he also left letters for three specific people. They will be read tonight."

Vickie and Vivian whispered to each other.

John stood. "I still don't know why I'm here. I'm neither a friend nor family."

"Harold requested you be here, John," said Ella. She looked at Alton, then back at John. "Please... take a seat."

Scowling, John complied, folding his arms across his chest.

DeShawn opened the documents and began again. "In his will, Harold instructed everything in his estate to go to Ella. He left a generous endowment to The Bee's Knees. And for Eleanor, who—"

John jumped to his feet. "Makes sense he'd leave something to Mom. After all, he ruined her life."

Eleanor turned. "John, you have it all wrong."

"Not according to my sources," said John.

"And what sources are those?" asked Eleanor.

Alton came closer and stood behind John's chair. "Please be seated, Mr. Morgan."

John begrudgingly took his seat again.

Alton walked to the front of the room, then turned to DeShawn. "Please continue."

"As I was saying, Harold also made provisions for

Eleanor…" He stared at John, expecting another interruption. John stared at the floor and DeShawn continued. "Harold also left three letters. One addressed to Ella, which she's already read. One to Eleanor…"

Eleanor began sobbing.

"And the last one, to John."

John looked up. "I want nothing from that man."

Ella took in a deep breath and let it out. She removed her letter from her sweater pocket and waited.

DeShawn pulled the other two from the envelope. He handed one to Eleanor and the other to John. "You may read them now."

Eleanor's hands trembled. She turned the envelope over and over. "Do I have to read it out loud?"

"That's up to you," said DeShawn.

She looked at John, then down at her hands. "I'm sorry."

"For what?" asked John.

"For everything." She closed her eyes, said a silent prayer, then opened her envelope. Opening her eyes, Eleanor flushed, noticing the others watching her. She unfolded the letter, read it, and gasped.

"What does it say?" asked Vivian, much louder than she intended.

Lilibeth turned to her mother. "She might not want to tell us."

John straightened. "Better get this over with so I can leave." He opened the envelope, took out the letter, then read. His shoulders slumped.

Eleanor's shoulder's shook. "I'm so sorry, John."

He scowled at her. "For what?"

"For goodness sakes," said Gladys. "Would someone read their letter?"

Eleanor and John stared at each other. They turned their letters around to the others. They were identical, containing seven words with a Bible reference.

Gladys moved closer and squinted. "... and the truth will set you free. John 8:32." She straightened and looked heavenward. "That's it? That's all we get, Harold?"

Ella nodded. "But, in his own way, it's enough." She turned to Eleanor. "Don't you think?"

Eleanor wiped her eyes and nodded. "Yes." She observed her son, knowing whatever she said next would either enrage him or estrange him, or both. She closed her eyes again, praying for the right words. Then she opened them. "John. I need to tell you the truth..."

He stared at her, arms crossed, saying nothing. Lilibeth felt the fury building in her husband. She wanted to run, but knew she had to stay.

"I love you," said Eleanor. "You need to know I'd do nothing to hurt you..." Noticing his boot tapping, she'd have to make her peace quickly. She cleared her throat, then continued. "I was in high school. Harold had graduated... We were in love and... expressed it. When I found out I was pregnant, my parents were furious. I was shy of my 18th birthday, but Harold, he was 19. They gave him a choice. Leave or they'd report him for statutory rape. I told him he had to leave. Finally, he did. I was alone and pregnant. Soon after, I married Richard..."

John's eyes widened. "Wait, a minute...." His fists clenched. "... Are you saying what I think...? That my dad was not my dad?"

Eleanor nodded, tears running down her face.

"You mean all this time..." His face turned crimson. "Harold was my father?"

Eleanor nodded again and whispered. "I'm so sorry."

He clenched his jaw and stared at her, his eyes penetrating her soul. Mumbling something under his breath, he shook his head. "Why didn't you tell me?"

"I wanted to," said Eleanor. "Harold, and I wanted to, so many times. But you had such a hatred for him. I just didn't know how to bring it up."

John pointed a finger at his mother. "I... I don't even know what to say." He got up and paced behind the chairs.

Gladys shifted in her seat.

He stopped and stared at Ella. "Can I leave now?"

Ella shook her head. "We still need to deal with something else."

"What else?" John stomped his foot. "Isn't this enough to fill the *Roost's* gossip column for years to come?"

Alton stepped to the front. "John, I'm sure this isn't easy..."

He stopped and stared at Alton. "And what part are you referring to? That my mother is a liar. That my father wasn't my father. Or the man who took advantage of her was? I don't even know who I am." He glared at Eleanor and pointed. "Or who she is."

Ella leaned close to Shelby. "Well, this didn't go the way I expected."

"And I don't think it's going to get any better," said Shelby.

Alton motioned to John. "What about your letter, John?"

"I'm not hiding anything."

Alton rested his hand on his leather belt. "Remember the night of the big rainstorm? Where were you that night?"

"I was tending the flocks." John looked around at everyone. "Coyotes were out."

"What about helping Hazel's husband install a dishwasher?"

"Yeah, so what about it?" asked John. "I don't need any good Samaritan badge for helping a neighbor."

"After you fixed it, you agreed to haul the box away."

"No crime in that," said John.

Alton pressed on. "You left it in the alley… behind Ella's shop."

"Still, no crime committed."

"When you got there, you must have found Agnes lying there unconscious."

John stared at Alton. "You have no proof of that."

"She'd threatened to dredge up your mother's past and had been blackmailing you for years. Did you even know what information she had?"

Lilibeth gasped.

John placed his hands on his hips. "I don't know what you're talking about."

"Maybe you hadn't planned on killing her, but the opportunity came up. She's out cold. The knitting needles next to her."

"Look, Sargent. I know you want a conviction, but really?" said John.

"The thing is, John. With your veterinary training, you knew exactly how to use the needles correctly. Right between the ribs, directly into the heart."

John's breathing increased. "You can't prove anything."

Alton glanced at Ella. "It's time for you to read your letter… just the parts underlined, if you will."

She nodded and began.

I'm sure you're curious about Agnes' death. Just to let you know, while nothing else would have given more pleasure, I didn't do it. I had the chance after Eleanor knocked her out cold. Agnes is unconscious and the knitting needles next to her. I thought about it, believe me I did... To be honest, I truly didn't know how, plus I was never fond of blood. Not even my own.

Bet you're wondering if I know who did. I do know. Saw it with my own eyes. In that moment, just knowing she could no longer hurt anyone was worth seeing what happened.

By the way, the other two letters won't spell it out for you. You're going to have to figure that one out on your own. But being the practical guy I am... or rather was... I'll give you a few hints. The answers will be in the checkbook and the box. Got that? Maybe not yet, but as my mother (God rest her soul) used to say, "Everything will come out in the wash."

Eleanor stared at Ella, wide-eyed.

"Still proves nothing," said John.

Alton smiled. "True. But fortunately Harold left enough clues for us to figure it out. We already know how the box— the dishwasher box puts you at the scene. The checkbook— well, we know AgCo was Agnes Cormack. Not only was she blackmailing Harold, but she was blackmailing you, too. Your wife confirmed unexplained expenditures from the

Fibre Farm account and a second mortgage. With your veterinary training, you knew anatomy and what it would take to deliver a lethal wound. The only thing confusing was the last quote about the wash. A death like that would produce a lot of blood. I'm sure it got on your hands and your clothes. You needed to wash everything, several times. But we still couldn't prove anything…" Alton turned and looked at Shelby. "… Until we figured out the missing piece."

John followed Alton's gaze and stared at Shelby.

"It seems you had a sudden urge to do the laundry right about the time of Agnes' murder. Not uncommon for a husband to help, but from what your wife said, it was most unusual."

John's face reddened. "I only did it to help with those wooley things…"

"Maybe," said Alton. "But when the gals mentioned they'd started stuffing the wool-felted animals with dryer lint, Shelby had a thought."

Shelby looked at Ella and smiled.

"The day Shelby bought half of their inventory, she brought them to me for analysis," said Alton. "I called in a favor with an expert in Forensic Genetics, specializing in DNA research. She ran tests on the lint inside the wool-felted animals and fast-tracked the results. You want to guess what she found?"

"Enlighten me, Columbo," said John.

"Did you know dryer lint can contain DNA from blood found in clothing?" said Alton. He paused, looking around the room. Everyone leaned forward, waiting for him to keep talking. "And do you know whose DNA we found in your dryer lint?"

Lilibeth suppressed a scream, then turned to her

husband and slapped his face. "It will all come out in the wash. You idiot."

John rubbed the raised mark on his cheek. "Wait a minute, Nolan. Are you saying by helping them stuff those stupid wool animals, I ended up handing over the evidence to convict me?"

Alton nodded. "Not only did you murder Agnes, not knowing why she was blackmailing you, you made it easy for us to gather the missing pieces of the case."

John shook his head. "So if good ol' dad knew I did it, why didn't he just say so?"

Alton stood in front of him. "Knowing Harold, he wanted to give you the opportunity to confess."

"Nothing personal, Sarg. Dad had it all wrong," said John. "My truth wouldn't set me free; it would put me away for years."

"I think he was talking about your conscience," said Alton.

"Spare the Bible lectures, Nolan. I didn't sign up for Sunday School."

"Fair enough," said Alton.

John caught Alton's eye. "So if you knew so much, why didn't you arrest me?"

"A few reasons," said Alton. "One, we needed more to go on that a wayward box and a few suspicions. There is something called probable cause, you know."

John rolled his eyes. "And we're all waiting on pins and needles to hear the other reason."

"Trudy."

John turned. "What about Trudy?"

"Though we *could* tie you to Agnes' death, we couldn't quite with Trudy's."

John clenched his fists again. "That's because I didn't do it."

"No need to raise your voice," said Alton. He briefly glanced at Vivian, then back to John. "We know Trudy was also in the alley the night Agnes was killed. Though you didn't until a few days later when she approached you with a proposition. Pay her and she'd keep quiet. Sounded like a clever idea at first, but then she got greedy and upped her price. You already had a second mortgage on the farm from paying Agnes. Now Trudy was out to ruin you." He stopped talking to look at John, who offered no expression. "So you decided you'd take care of her, too."

"I didn't kill her," said John.

"After her death, my officers canvassed the neighborhood," said Alton. "Several neighbors identified your truck parked at Trudy's frequently. Should have changed your O-rings. The haze of blue gave you away each time. In fact, three eye-witnesses confirmed your truck was parked outside Trudy's house around the time of her murder."

Lilibeth stood. "I can't even stand to be in the same room as you." She stomped away, standing next to LaTonya.

"Fine," said John. "Trudy was also blackmailing me. With nothing to lose, I went to her house to kill her." John's eyes rose to Alton's. "But when I got there, she was already dead."

CHAPTER SIXTY-ONE

The clock on the wall ticked away the minutes. The coffee pot sputtered as drops of moisture hit the hot warming platform. After John admitted going to Trudy's to kill her, Vickie gasped. Gladys clutched her hankie and shook her head.

Alton poured himself another cup of coffee and sat next to Ella. He looked at each person in the room, then focused his attention back on John. "Remember the night you reported your mother kidnapped?"

John looked up and nodded.

"The room she'd been staying in was quite a mess. Staged well to look like an actual kidnapping. But they made a mistake."

Vickie covered her mouth with her hand.

"The person was so proud of themselves, they told someone. Another overheard and told someone else. You know, small towns and small town gossip... So we did some digging. And do you know what we found out?"

Vickie's eyes widened. Her heart rate increased.

John stared at the floor. "No, not really."

Alton turned his attention to Vickie. "We found your fingerprints in the outbuilding where Eleanor had supposedly been kidnapped."

Vickie shook her head. "You don't understand."

Alton placed his cup on the table in front of him. "The night of Trudy's death, you needed to leave the farm to run an errand—to get a prescription filled, correct? But your car needed brakes, so you borrowed John's truck."

"That's not true," said Vickie.

"After Shelby and Vivian found Trudy dead, we talked to the neighbors. Several mentioned seeing the truck and smelling that acrid haze in the afternoon of her death," said Alton. "Then, they said the truck and smell came back a few hours hour later. It was perplexing."

"I've never even been to Trudy's house." Vickie looked at Lilibeth. "Tell Alton I was with you all afternoon and night."

Lilibeth turned away.

"Vickie, we found your fingerprints in Trudy's bathroom," said Alton. "And on the table near her couch. We also found them on the doorknob on the front door. If you'd never been there, how did your fingerprints get there?"

"You're the smart one." Vickie's eyes flashed. "How about you explain why I'd do such a horrid thing?"

Lilibeth stepped closer and pointed at John. "To protect that scum, your lover."

Gladys began fanning herself. "Lord have mercy."

Vickie stared up at her sister. "You knew?"

"You kept teasing John about having a lover," said Lilibeth. "Sometimes the one who accuses is the one who knows the truth. I noticed both of you 'checking the herds' on several occasions. So, I followed you." She clenched her jaw. "You two make me sick."

Eleanor blinked. "My son…"

Vivian wiped her eyes and stared at her daughter. "Thought I raised you to be better than this."

Vickie shrugged. "Guess you thought wrong."

John caught Vickie's eye. "*You* killed Trudy? Why?"

Vickie reached out to John. "Hoping you'd finally leave that drunken wife of yours."

"We agreed I'd never leave her," said John, turning away from her.

Lilibeth glared at John. "You two deserve each other."

Alton rubbed the back of his neck. "John, anything else you want to say before we go?"

John looked at his mother. "Agnes wanted to hurt you, plus she was ruining our business. You couldn't protect yourself against that evil woman, so I acted on yours and our behalf—it was self-defense."

Shelby turned to Ella. "Harold killed his ex in self-defense… That message he left on your phone makes sense now. The apple *really* doesn't fall far from the tree…"

While Eleanor wept, Alton cuffed John and read him his rights. A few feet away, LaTonya did the same with Vickie while Vivian clutched Lilibeth's hand. After Alton nodded to Ella, he took John outside, followed by LaTonya and Vickie.

Ella glanced at Shelby. "So many broken lives."

"If only I'd been truthful with John from the beginning…" said Eleanor.

Gladys took her friend's hand. "You can't take the blame for others' actions."

"I don't know if I'll ever heal," said Eleanor. "I've lost everyone."

"Not everyone," said Lilibeth. She came over and took Eleanor's other hand. "We'll get through this together."

CHAPTER SIXTY-TWO

Kneeling on the grass in front of a flower bed, Shelby patted down the dirt around the newly planted rosebush, then straightened a carved wooden marker bearing the name Charisma. Smiling, she got up, wiped her dirt-caked hands on her jeans, and joined Ella on the front porch.

Ella sipped her coffee and smiled. "I'm glad you planted her rose in the front yard."

Shelby sat in a chair. "I wanted it to be where I could spend some quiet time in reflection."

LaTonya, dressed in a bright purple jogging suit and sparkly purple tennis shoes, walked past their yard. When she saw Ella and Shelby, she stopped and waved. "Mornin' neighbors. Beautiful day for a quick walk around the cul-de-sac. Care to join me?"

Ella waved. "Maybe next time."

Stretching to one side, then the other, she pointed to the women. "I'm gonna hold you to your word."

"You do that." Shelby laughed as LaTonya marched past them and down the street.

"Hard to believe it's been two weeks since Harold's funeral," said Ella.

"I still find it hard to believe John never knew what information Agnes had against him," said Shelby. "He was so protective of his mom, he never even asked."

"No kidding," said Ella. "I'm just glad that's all behind us."

"And so much has happened since then…" said Shelby.

"Kent and Susan finally announced their engagement and December wedding," said Ella.

"Timed it with Winterfest and the opening of the new ice arena," said Shelby. "You hear Officer Langley is quite the hockey player and wants to form a team?"

"Yes," said Ella, grinning. "Don't count on me signing up… I'm so happy Eleanor and Lilibeth have gotten closer. She's selling her house and moving in with her daughter-in-law to help her run the Fibre Farm."

"You were very generous when you offered to pay off Lilibeth's farm mortgages," said Shelby.

"Harold would have wanted me to. It'll give Lilibeth operating capital to keep the farm open for the kids' tours, plus I've heard she and Eleanor have plans to expand their crafty offerings."

"I'm glad something good came out of that whole mess," said Shelby.

Ella sipped her coffee. Looking up at the wind chimes, she listened to the soft, melodious sounds as they swayed in the gentle breeze. "You ever figure out what you were going to do with your escrow money?"

"At first I'd thought about resuming my design business, but my heart wasn't in it." Shelby glanced over to her rose, then back to Ella. "So I called the funeral home and talked to the funeral director…"

"That sweet woman, Sandy…?"

"Yes, she's got the biggest heart for people," said Shelby. "I asked her if they had an Angel Garden—"

"Angel Garden?" asked Ella.

"It's a special place set aside in a cemetery for parents to bury babies who received their wings early—the ones lost through miscarriage."

"And what did she say?"

"Turns out they didn't," said Shelby. "I'm donating my money from Mac's escrow to the New Pheasant Valley Cemetery to set aside an area for grieving parents." She looked back at the rose bush. "Something I wish I would have had for Charisma."

Ella reached out and held Shelby's hand. "That's beautiful, hon. I'm sure it will mean a lot to those parents."

"That's not all…" said Shelby. "She asked me if I'd be interested in starting a grief group, you know, for parents who have lost babies too early. Once I told her I was interested, she called Marcie at the library. They've already set aside a room so we can meet weekly."

"I'm so proud of you."

"You know, El, after The Bee's Knees renovation is complete, maybe the group can meet there… if there's still room on the calendar."

Ella laughed. "Once we announced the renovation was on and Kent gave us an estimated completion date of June first, crafters wanting to teach classes have inundated us."

"Harold would be so proud to see what your idea has sparked," said Shelby.

"I can't take all the credit," said Ella, catching Shelby's eye.

LaTonya walked past them again, back toward her

house, huffing. "Next time, ladies… I'm counting on you to join me."

Ella waved. "I'll put it in my calendar…"

Shelby raised an eyebrow. "Guess you'll need a pair of sparkly tennis shoes."

"I didn't tell you the good news, did I?"

Shelby straightened. "Good news?"

"Remember those sneakers you gave me?"

"You mean the ones you were wearing when you stepped on the knitting needle? And they confiscated one for evidence?" asked Shelby.

Ella smiled. "Yes. When John gave a full confession, Alton returned my shoe."

Shelby winked. "Should I tell LaTonya we'll walk with her tomorrow?"

Ella looked over at the screen door. Oatmeal stood behind it, pawing at the screen. "You know, maybe we should break them in today. I think Oatmeal would love to get out." She stood and looked at Shelby. "You want to join us?"

Shelby stuck out her shoe and wiggled it. "Already wearing my pink sparkles… might as well. By the way, did you hear the story of how Kent proposed to Susan?"

"Must have missed that when I was out of the shop." Ella reached for the door handle and paused. "I'd love to hear about it while we walk." She went into the house and changed into her blue leather sneakers with the glittery stars. After leashing Oatmeal, she rubbed Mr. Butterfingers behind the ears, then gave him treats. Leading her dog out onto the front porch, she closed the screen door. "So tell me about the proposal."

Shelby and Ella made their way across the lawn. "Well, I

had a feeling something was going on when they kept picking the same shifts…"

FREE STORY!

Thank you so much for reading *Crafty Motives*. If you've enjoyed this second book in the series and would like to know the story of how Kent proposed to Susan, you can read that story, *Crafty Proposal*, for free.

To get your exclusive copy of this sweet story and join **The Bee's Knees VIP Reader Group**, click the book cover image or if you are reading the print version go to: https://www.joanraymondwriting.com/crafty-proposal

Crafty Proposal as my way of saying thank you as it's not available anywhere else. When you download the story, you truly are a VIP!

ACKNOWLEDGMENTS

Thank you to everyone who supported and encouraged me while I authored this book.

First, to my husband, David. Thank you for understanding my obsession with crime-related podcasts and crime-fiction courses and never questioning why I needed them. Your love and support means more than you know.

Thanks to my adult children, Michelle, Brian, and Matt who go along with their mother's proclivity to reading and watching mystery shows and not getting upset when I blurt out who I think the killer is before the end.

Heartfelt thanks to my critique partners Donnee and Jenny, who read the first, messy drafts and offered kind criticism and advice to make my writing shine. And to my VIP Readers, Angela, Annis, Jenny, Julie, Natalia, Patsy, Sandy, and Tara, who read the last version and gave helpful feedback. Your comments and suggestions were invaluable.

Sincere thanks to those folks who helped with my specific questions on the technical stuff by offering your expertise and experience. For police procedure, thanks again to B. Adam Richardson of the Writer's Detective Bureau Podcast and Facebook Group for always taking the time to answer my questions without making me feel like I was bothering you. Thanks to the Trauma Fiction Facebook Group for clarifying my death-related questions. And thanks to the Author's Fire/Rescue Facebook Group for the wonderful feedback on my first-responder questions. Any mistakes are my own.

Thanks to my friend and funeral director, Sandy Moffett, who became a real character in my book because of your compassionate heart for families going through grief after a loved one's passing. Your help with multiple scenes means so much.

Thanks to Ana, the delightful woman at the Clerks' Office in Harris County, Texas who even though you knew I was doing research for a book, still answered all of my questions about the document search portal.

Thanks to Cathy Walker of Cathy's Covers for your cover design skills. Once again you created the perfect cover for my continued series.

To my readers, thank you so much for your patience while I took *Crafty Motives* from a hint of an idea to a fully realized story. Your continued support and comments mean so much to me. Because of you, I continue to create my quirky characters and write my stories.

ABOUT THE AUTHOR

Joan's earliest memories of writing go back to the fourth grade. An avid reader of The Happy Hollister's Mystery series, she penned her first two short stories, "The Mystery of the Missing Bread" and "The Snake That Had Legs." Not best-sellers by any means, but her teacher loved them, as did her classmates, which sparked her interest in writing.

Joan lives in Bakersfield, California, with her family and four rescue pets: Two energetic Australian Shepherd mixes (Madison and Jackie), a claustrophobic Maine Coon mix (Molly), and an independent tuxedo cat (Stormie).

Joan welcomes contact from her readers. Find her at aheartforwriting.com where you can sign up for her free course, read her blog, and find her on social media.

facebook.com/joanraymondwriting

instagram.com/aheartforwriting

youtube.com/@aheartforwriting

ALSO BY JOAN RAYMOND

For Adults

Bee's Knees Mystery Series

Crafty Alibis (Book One) 2021

Crafty Motives (Book Two) 2022

Crafty Suspects (Book Three) Coming soon!

Women's Fiction

Guardian of the Gifts 2019

For Children

Metamorphosis Series

Fly on the Wall (Book One) 2020

Spaghetti and Meatball (Book Two) Coming soon!

Made in United States
North Haven, CT
16 March 2023